# A GOLDEN BASIN
# FULL OF SCORPIONS

Also by Con Coughlin

HOSTAGE

# A GOLDEN BASIN
# FULL OF SCORPIONS

### The Quest for
### Modern Jerusalem

## CON COUGHLIN

LITTLE, BROWN AND COMPANY

A *Little, Brown* Book

First published in Great Britain in 1997
by Little, Brown and Company

Copyright © 1997 by Con Coughlin

The moral right of the author has been asserted.

A CIP catalogue record for this book
is available from the British Library.

ISBN: 0 316 91442 8

*Maps by Neil Hyslop*

Typeset by M Rules in Berkeley
Printed and bound in Great Britain
by Clays Ltd, St Ives plc

Little, Brown and Company (UK)
Brettenham House
Lancaster Place
London WC2E 7EN

'As to the saying that Jerusalem is the most illustrious of cities – is she not the one that unites the advantages of This World and those of the Next? . . . Still, Jerusalem has some disadvantages. Thus it is reported, as found in the Torah (or books) of Moses, that "Jerusalem is as a golden basin filled with scorpions."'

MUKADDASI, writing in AD 985, quoted in
*History of Jerusalem Under the Moslems* by Guy le Strange

# CONTENTS

# CHRONOLOGY

*BC*

1850 First mention of Jerusalem in Egyptian execration texts –
known as 'Rushalimum'

1400 Mentioned in Amarna letters as 'Urusalim'

*c.* 996 David captures Jerusalem from Jebusites

954 King Solomon commences construction of First Temple

930 Secession of Kingdom of Israel from Jerusalem rule

722 Conquest of Kingdom of Israel by Assyria

701 King Sennacherib of Assyria besieges Jerusalem

597 Jerusalem falls to King Nebuchadnezzar of Babylon – first
Babylonian deportation

586 Destruction of Solomon's Temple by Babylonians

538 Jews allowed to return to Palestine by Cyrus, King of Persia

332 Alexander the Great seizes Palestine from the Persians

301 Ptolemy I, founder of Ptolemaic dynasty, captures Jerusalem

200 Seleucids take control from Ptolemies

164 Jewish revolt led by Judah the Maccabee

63 Pompey lays siege to Jerusalem and sacks it – 12,000 Jews
massacred

37 Herod lays siege to Jerusalem and overthrows the Hasmonean
dynasty

20 Herod commences work on reconstructing the Second Temple
4 Death of Herod the Great

*AD*
c. 0 Birth of Jesus
6 Rome assumes direct control of Jerusalem
12 Jesus visits Jerusalem and Second Temple
29 Death of John the Baptist
33 Death of Jesus
44 Palestine annexed to Rome by Claudius and ruled by procurators
64 Execution of St Paul in Rome by Nero
70 Capture of Jerusalem by Titus
132 Last Jewish revolt suppressed – Jews banned from Jerusalem
324 Constantine becomes undisputed leader of Roman Empire and permits tolerance of Christians
330 Founding of Constantinople
335 Dedication of the Church of the Resurrection in Jerusalem
451 Council of Chalcedon establishes first Jerusalem Patriarch
569 Birth of Mohammed
614 Persians capture Jerusalem and burn down the Holy Sepulchre
629 Jerusalem recaptured by Byzantium
632 Death of Mohammed
638 Arabs capture Jerusalem
660 Muawiya, founder of the Omayyad dynasty, proclaimed Caliph in Jerusalem
691 Dome of the Rock built by Abdul al-Malik
877 Palestine conquered by Egypt, end of Abbasid domination
969 Fatimids occupy the Holy Land
1009 Church of the Holy Sepulchre destroyed by Fatimid caliph Hakim
1048 Holy Sepulchre rebuilt by Byzantium
1054 Split between Greek and Latin church
1071 Jerusalem occupied by Seljuk Turks
1076 City reverts to control of the Fatimids
1095 Council of Clermont launches crusades

1099  Crusaders capture Jerusalem

1187  Saladin reconquers Jerusalem and readmits Jews

1192  Richard the Lion-Heart fails to recapture Jerusalem

1204  Sack of Constantinople by Crusaders

1219  Francis of Assisi visits Jerusalem

1229  Crusaders temporarily regain control of the city

1244  Jerusalem laid waste by Khwarzimian Turks – falls under control of Mamluks

1260  Jerusalem briefly captured by Mongolian chief Hulagi Khan, then recaptured by Mamluks

1275  Marco Polo visits Jerusalem en route for China

1291  Fall of Acre

1303  Mongols attack Jerusalem

1342  Franciscans made guardians of the Holy Places

1453  Fall of Constantinople

1492  Expulsion of Jews from Spain

1516  Jerusalem occupied by the Ottomans

1535  Francis I of France negotiates the 'Capitulations' with Suleiman the Magnificent

1799  Napoleon campaigns in the Holy Land

1808  Holy Sepulchre destroyed by fire

1831  Mehemet Ali captures Jerusalem from Ottomans

1838  First British consul appointed to Jerusalem

1856  Treaty of Paris concludes the Crimean War

1862  Prince of Wales (Edward VII) visits Jerusalem

1865  Palestine Exploration Fund founded

1869  Suez Canal opened

1876  British purchase of Suez Canal

1878  Congress of Berlin

1882  First Jewish colonists arrive in Jaffa

1887  Jerusalem brought under the Sultan's personal control

1894  Dreyfus trial

1896  Theodore Herzl publishes *Der Judenstaat*

1897  First Zionist Congress held at Basle

1903  Joseph Chamberlain suggests Uganda as Jewish homeland

1916  Arab Revolt launched against Ottoman rule

1917  November 2: The Balfour Declaration

1917  December 8: General Allenby captures Jerusalem

1920 Britain given Class A Mandate to administer Palestine at San Remo – civil administration established in Jerusalem

1920 Arab–Jewish riots in Jerusalem

1921 Sir Herbert Samuel becomes first High Commissioner

1922 Cairo Conference creates Kingdom of Transjordan

1922 Churchill's White Paper on Palestine

1929 Arab–Jewish riots in Jerusalem

1933 Nuremberg Laws passed by Reichstag

1936 Arab Rebellion erupts in Palestine

1937 Peel Commission report recommends partition

1939 Third White Paper on Palestine

1942 Hitler's 'Final Solution' agreed at Wannsee

1944 Irgun declares war on British Mandate

1946 Anglo-American commission on Palestine

1948 British Mandate ends – State of Israel proclaimed – Jerusalem divided

1950 Secret Israeli–Jordanian deal on Jerusalem

1951 King Abdullah of Jordan assassinated in Jerusalem

1967 Jerusalem reunited after Israel's victory in Six-Day War – East Jerusalem annexed

1973 Yom Kippur War

1977 President Anwar Sadat of Egypt visits Jerusalem

1979 Camp David peace treaty between Israel and Egypt

1980 Knesset passes Basic Law confirming Jerusalem as capital of Israel

1991 Madrid Peace Conference opens

1993 Oslo Accords signed in Washington

1994 Yasser Arafat returns to Gaza

1994 Peace treaty signed between Jordan and Israel

1995 Yitzhak Rabin buried in Jerusalem following assassination

1995 Interim agreement signed on returning West Bank and Gaza to Palestinian control

1996 First Palestinian elections – first suicide bomb attacks in Jerusalem

1999 Date agreed in Oslo Accords for conclusion of negotiations on final status of Jerusalem

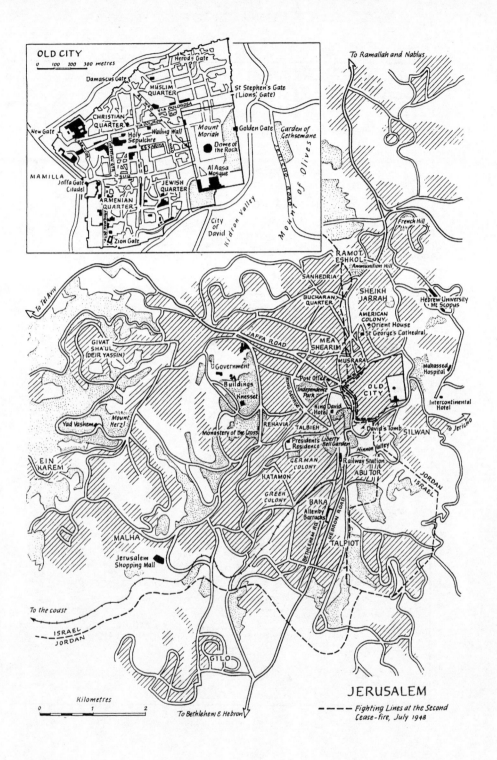

## OLD CITY

0   100   200   300 metres

Damascus Gate
Herod's Gate
MUSLIM QUARTER
St Stephen's Gate (Lions' Gate)
VIA DOLOROSA
CHRISTIAN QUARTER
Holy Sepulchre
New Gate
Wailing Wall
EL-WAD
Mount Moriah
Golden Gate
Garden of Gethsemane
EL SALITA
Dome of the Rock
MAMILLA
Jaffa Gate
Citadel
Al Aqsa Mosque
ARMENIAN QUARTER
JEWISH QUARTER
City of David
Kidron Valley
Mount of Olives
Zion Gate

To Ramallah and Nablus

French Hill

RAMOT ESHKOL
Ammunition Hill
SANHEDRIA
SHEIKH JARRAH
Hebrew University Mt Scopus
BUCHARAN QUARTER
AMERICAN COLONY
Orient House
St George's Cathedral
To Tel Aviv
JAFFA ROAD
MEA SHEARIM
MUSRARA
Makassed Hospital
GIVAT SHA'UL (DEIR YASSIN)
Government Buildings
Post Office
Independence Park
OLD CITY
Intercontinental Hotel
Knesset
KING GEORGE ST
King David Hotel
To Jericho
Yad Vashem
Mount Herzl
REHAVIA
TALBIEH
David's Tomb
SILWAN
Monastery of the Cross
President's Residence
Liberty Bell Garden
Hinnom Valley
EIN KAREM
GERMAN COLONY
Railway Station
JORDAN
ISRAEL
KATAMON
ABU TOR
GREEN COLONY
BAKA
Allenby Barracks
MALHA
Jerusalem Shopping Mall
TALPIOT
HEBRON ROAD
BETHLEHEM RD
To the coast
ISRAEL
JORDAN
GILO
To Bethlehem & Hebron

## JERUSALEM

– – – Fighting Lines at the Second Cease-fire, July 1948

Kilometres
0   1   2

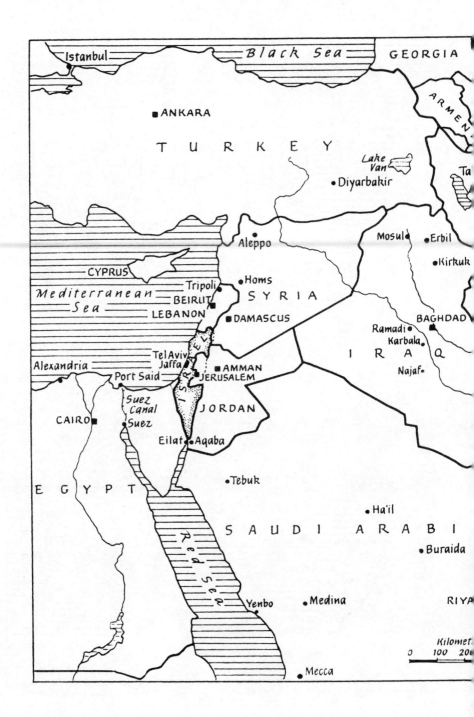

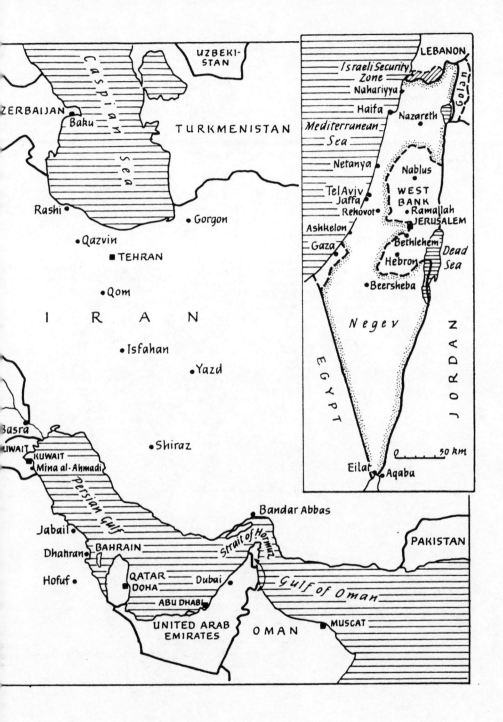

Arab and Jewish populations
by neighbourhood

- [Arab pattern] Arab
- [Jewish pattern] Jewish
- [Mixed pattern] Mixed

0  1  2  3 km

Kafr
Aqab
5 200

Atarot
Ind.
Zone

To Bir-Nabalu

To Ar-Ram

Neve Ya'aqov
35 200

To Hizna

Bet
Hanna
16 900

Pisgat Ze'ev

To Givat Ze'ev

Ramot
38 700

Shuafat
(West)

Shuafat
(East)
28 500

To Ma'ale
Adumim

French
Hill

Isawiya

Ramot
Eshkol
12 000

Mt Scopus

8 700  4 700

Sheikh Jarrah
7 500

American Colony

At-Tur
Mt Olives
19 900

To
Abu Dis

Old City
2 400 Jews
27 000 Non Jews

Silwan
6 400

Ras
Al-Amud
9 600

PRE-1967

WESTERN JERUSALEM

Abu
Tor

Arab
Es Sawahra
8 300

East Talpiot
15 000

Umm
Leisun

Bet Safafa
4 600

Sur Baher
Umm Tuba
7 200

Gilo
30 200

Har
Homa

Planned

To Bethlehem
and Gush Etzion

Sources:

Statistical Yearbook of Jerusalem (1995),
Ha'aretz, 11 August 1993

xvi

# Prologue

# QUEST

*'And the Canaanite was then in the land. And the Lord appeared*
*unto Abram, and said, Unto thy seed will I give this land'*
                                                Genesis 12: 6–7

I thought I knew Jerusalem. After more than a decade of visiting, living and working in the Holy City, I have learnt to appreciate its various personae. I have been tear-gassed by Israeli policemen in their own police station, stoned twice within the space of half an hour by rioting ultra-Orthodox Jews and Palestinians, and had my car petrol-bombed within minutes of checking into a hotel. I have been berated as both a closet Zionist by Palestinians, and as an anti-Semite by Israelis, simply for trying to provide an objective explanation of the city's troubles. Like so many visitors, I have been seduced by the imposing majesty of the stone city, aroused by the dramatic shades of light, and stimulated by the fascinating array or tribes, faiths and opinions that are the city's life-force. But now I must explore another side of life in Jerusalem.

I have come to the infamous Russian Compound, Jerusalem's main police headquarters, to report a theft. The Russian Compound figures prominently in the demonology of modern Jerusalem. Apart from dealing with the city's various criminals, this is the place where Palestinians suspected of terrorist offences are brought for interrogation. Some of them have been tortured, and some of them have died from their injuries. Although I have read about the Compound many times, I have been inside only once previously, to report the fire-bombing of a rented car. It was one of those apocryphal Jerusalem stories. I had just checked into my hotel in East Jerusalem, the Arab side of the city, having driven a newly rented Israeli hire-car from Tel Aviv airport. This was at the height of the *intifada*, the violent Palestinian uprising against Israel's continued occupation of the West Bank, which, as far as Palestinians are concerned, includes East Jerusalem. I had barely completed the check-in formalities when one of the hotel porters appeared in the lobby to inform me that my car had been fire-bombed, and was now ablaze. The attack was conducted so expertly that, by the time I reached the car, it was beyond rescue. At first I was informed that the car had been attacked by young Palestinian nationalists because it bore Israeli number plates. Some days later, however, some acquaintances suggested that the attack had nothing to do with Palestinian nationalism and everything to do with an intense rivalry that had developed between rival car-hire firms. The Israeli hire-car had been set alight to persuade me in future to take my custom to a Palestinian firm. How Jerusalem's myths are broken.

It is late on Saturday afternoon, when most of Jewish Jerusalem is still deep in its sabbath slumber, when I arrive at the Russian Compound to register my loss – a large, blue suitcase filled with books and research papers. Initially I had no great enthusiasm to report the matter to the police; the Russian Compound is not known for its clear-up rate for petty theft. But I am encouraged by friends to go through the formalities, just in case the stolen suitcase, which contains nothing of any value to anyone but me, has been handed in. I am directed to the tourist police, where a sad-eyed, middle-aged Israeli policeman, sporting a luxuriant Mexican moustache, receives me.

I am shown into a small, shabby office. It is furnished with the bare essentials. Apart from the policeman's desk and chair, there is a bookcase filled with a variety of forms which appear to have lain discarded for many years. In a vain attempt to deal with the suffocating heat,

2

the policeman has opened a window, and a faint breeze competes with the air-conditioning to make the room habitable. One of the walls contains a noticeboard covered by a wanted poster for a group of Hamas gunmen. There are about eight young Arab faces on the poster, some with neatly clipped moustaches, some without. None of them looks particularly menacing. Even in their police mug-shots, some of the gunmen have the starry-eyed look of the hopeless idealist. Most of the pictures have a crude cross against them, indicating that the Israeli security forces have successfully eliminated their target. A few days previously, the newspapers reported how an undercover unit had ambushed and killed one of the wanted gunmen in a shoot-out at a village near Jerusalem. After the shooting, the army had forced the dead man's relatives out of their homes. An army bulldozer had then reduced the properties to rubble. In addition, they had uprooted hundreds of olive trees in the surrounding area on the grounds that they provided a refuge for terrorists, even though, in this instance, the 'terrorist' was well and truly dead. Since the shooting, someone must have put another cross through one of the photographs on the wall. It puts my concern about the missing suitcase in a different light.

As I sit waiting to fill in the appropriate forms, I am reminded of an Italian friend who some weeks previously had tried to encourage me to spend a Saturday evening at the Russian Compound. 'If you want to understand the real Jerusalem, you must go to this place,' he insisted. 'Everyone is there. Criminals, terrorists, prostitutes, soldiers, manic depressives. This is what Jerusalem is all about.' Like me, he had gone to the police headquarters to report a petty offence – a car theft – and, while waiting in the queue, had been amazed at the Felliniesque parade of misfits and lost souls he encountered. His favourite story concerned two aristocratic Austrian ladies who had been robbed in Saladin Street, the main Arab shopping area on the city's east side. They had arrived at the police station wearing Chanel suits (Italians notice these details), high heels, their hair immaculately coiffured and with a look of haughty contempt for their surroundings. These elegant Austrian ladies, the type who have the best boxes at Vienna's Staatsoper House for the annual ball, had been held up at knife-point while walking at night through one of the most notorious Jerusalem neighbourhoods. They had both been

relieved of their handbags and jewellery. What was even more astonishing was the list of the handbags' contents they provided to the
police: 10,000 dollars – cash; 14,000 Deutschmarks – cash; 15,000
Swiss francs – cash, and so on. Between them they had the Bank of
Israel in their handbags. Why, I had asked my Italian friend, were
they carrying so much cash? Saladin Street is hardly the place for
Austrian aristocrats to shop. 'Because they are anti-Semites,' he
explained. 'They have some church property here, so when they come
they bring lots of cash so they don't have to deal with Jews. They stay
on the Arab side of town and pay everything in cash.'

The contents of my suitcase, by comparison, are nowhere near as
interesting and, as the policeman dutifully records the details –
books, papers, files, notebooks, maps, photographs – it seems the
Russian Compound is as good a place as any to explore the city's
many different layers.

In my efforts to understand the city I have visited libraries and universities, interviewed politicians, diplomats, activists, academics,
researchers and journalists. After years of neglect, the issue of
Jerusalem – who owns it, who claims to own it, who should own it –
is back on the agenda, mainly the result of the Oslo peace process.
The future of Jerusalem is one of the most complicated, and probably
intractable, issues of the modern age. Facts, figures, maps, plans and
boundaries are all very well, but they do not build a city's character.
The countless number of treaties, United Nations resolutions, laws,
claims and counter-claims is not what makes the Holy City so special.
Jerusalem is unique because of what it means to so many people
from so many different backgrounds of such varying religious, political and social persuasions. Places like the Russian Compound are
just as likely to provide important clues to the quest for modern
Jerusalem as any number of dusty archives.

After completing the formalities at the police station, I drive with
some friends to David's Village, the scene of the crime. Even if the
police are unable to help, it seems worth making one last effort to
retrieve the stolen papers. David's Village is a relatively new development in the area known as Mamilla. When I first lived in Jerusalem in
the mid-1980s, Mamilla was derelict. During the 1948 war, the first of
many between Arab and Israeli, Mamilla, which had been an Arab
commercial area, found itself in the front line, and suffered heavy

damage. After the disengagement agreement, the area was left to rot in no-man's-land. When, during the 1967 Six-Day War, the Israelis conquered the Arab east side and reunited the city, Mamilla came under Israeli jurisdiction, but for years the city authorities were unable to decide what to do with it. At one point it was a popular venue for American film producers who wanted to make Ramboesque films about Beirut and the Lebanese civil war, but didn't want to risk having their crew kidnapped by Islamic fanatics by filming in Lebanon. I recall one film where a dramatic US Marine operation to rescue some hostages in Beirut rather lacked conviction when, as they made their getaway, the Ottoman ramparts of Jerusalem's Old City were clearly visible in the background (the terrorist actors also spoke in Israeli-accented Arabic). After twenty-five years' prevarication, Mamilla's fate was decided in the early 1990s when an internationally renowned architect was allowed to develop it into exclusive condominiums that afford the best views of the city for those who can afford to pay. Most have been bought by wealthy Jews who live abroad, who seek to assuage their guilt about not living in Israel by forking out a million dollars plus on apartments that most Israelis can only dream of owning.

The theft occurred while my car was outside a friend's apartment, and, as I look around the neighbourhood, I consider various possibilities as to where the missing suitcase could be. The Old City, which 'David's Villagers' have paid a fortune to look at, is one possibility. It is impossible to accuse anyone of anything in Jerusalem without running the risk of accusations of racism, but my suspicions about the Old City are based purely on practical considerations, such as the fact that it is the nearest populated area, even if it is an Arab neighbourhood.

From previous Jerusalem experiences, I have learnt that one must always expect the unexpected. The night my car was stoned twice within half an hour is a good example. Like the car fire-bombing, it happened during the *intifada*. It was late on a Friday night, and I was driving home from my office in the city centre. Although most of the building was used as offices, there was an Israeli cinema located in the basement. At the time – this was in the late 1980s – all social entertainment was banned in Jerusalem during the Jewish sabbath by rabbinical decree, which included showing movies. But a group of rebellious, secular Israelis had decided to flaunt the religious laws by opening the basement cinema on Friday nights. And, to ensure they caused the religious authorities maximum offence, they were showing soft-porn movies such as *Emmanuelle Goes to Bangkok* and *Swedish Nurses on the Job*. It was not long before this act of defiance attracted the attention of the city's influencial ultra-Orthodox Jewish community, who started demonstrating outside the cinema on Friday nights, stoning anyone seen coming in or out of the cinema for breaking the sabbath observance. On the night in question I left the office, unaware of the controversy. As I got into the car, it came under a deluge of stones and rocks thrown by enraged Jewish protesters. I did not bother to find out what offence I had caused, and sped away to safety. I then drove to East Jerusalem, where I was to dine with friends. The car, however, had Israeli licence plates, and as I negotiated the darkened streets in search of an address, the car again came under a hail of stones. This time they were thrown by Palestinian youths protesting at the presence of a car with Israeli plates driving through *their* side of the city.

For all the concentrated efforts of successive Israeli governments to change the demographic balance, the population of the Old City remains predominantly Arab – most of them Muslims, with a sprinkling of Christians. It would take only a few minutes for someone to drive over to David's Village, rob a car, and return with the booty, rather like a medieval raiding party. But I am quickly disabused of this notion by my lunch host, who has joined in the hunt. However much the Arabs might fancy the idea of 'revenge' attacks on Jewish neighbourhoods, it is out of the question. The Israeli police know enough about Arab criminals to track them down. 'They'd be lynched if they tried anything like that in this neighbourhood,' my host explains. 'The Israelis are not going to build multimillion-dollar apartments and let the Arabs vandalise them.'

So could the theft have been carried out by Jews? The robbery took place in the middle of Shabbat, the Jewish sabbath, when most Jews in Jerusalem, religious or not, take their rest day very seriously. But I have heard of cases, especially during the Palestinian *intifada*, when Jewish criminals deliberately targeted geographically ambiguous areas – like Mamilla – hoping the police would attribute Arab nationalist motives to their crime. Then there is the Russian mafia. Since the great influx of Russian Jewish immigrants from the collapsing Soviet Union in the early 1990s, the Hebrew press has been filled with gory tales of how the country is being taken over by Russian hoods. Anyone who gets in their way is likely to have their head severed, put in a box and shipped to Moscow as a warning to others. What these desperadoes could want with a suitcase filled with paper is beyond me, but I am encouraged by friends not to discount the Russian connection. Nor should I rule out the Romanian construction workers who have been shipped in to work on the nearby building site for the Hilton hotel. Finally, I am advised to give careful consideration to the kind of people I have been associating with; there is always the possibility that I have aroused the interest of some suspicious agent of a foreign intelligence service by asking the wrong questions in the wrong place at the wrong time.

I need help, clearly, to navigate the labyrinthine complexity of Jerusalem's criminal underworld. I consult Mounir, an old Palestinian acquaintance who owns the gift shop at the American Colony Hotel, a former pasha's residence that has been turned into one of the better hotels in the Middle East. Apart from selling oriental trinkets to tourists, there are few people in Jerusalem Mounir doesn't know, especially among the city's seedier characters. A tall man for a Palestinian, he has the loping gait of a basketball player, albeit one who has irredeemably entered middle age. I first appreciated Mounir's resourcefulness a few years previously over the car fire-bombing affair. Because it happened during the *intifada*, the Israeli government was obliged to pick up the bill for the damage, so long as I could persuade the police to sign the appropriate forms. Mounir offered to accompany me, and I was astonished at the welcome we received when we entered the Russian Compound. There are not many Palestinians who volunteer to enter Jerusalem's equivalent, by reputation rather than size, of the Black Lubyanka. But it was clear Mounir was as much at home there as he was in his shop. High-ranking police officers waved cheerily at him, and with his help we were able to complete the formalities in record time. Mounir pointed to a room where, he said, as a youth he had been taken by the Israelis and beaten. But it did not seem to bother him. Mounir is a man with connections.

When I arrive at his shop, he is dressed in a colourful Caribbean-

style shirt and silk trousers, and is preparing for an important meeting. Yasser Arafat, the Palestinian leader, has been in touch and wants
him to go to Gaza 'to discuss some business'. I know from past experience that trying to get a meeting with Arafat is not easy. Even before
his return to international legitimacy with his election as head of the
Palestinian Authority in January 1996, Arafat is arguably the world's
most elusive interview. Journalists have been known to spend weeks
hanging around one of the PLO leader's lairs on the off-chance of getting a few minutes of his attention. Not Mounir. When I suggest he
might have a frustrating trip ahead of him, Mounir is insistent. He has
a fixed time for the meeting, and at the appointed hour the meeting
will take place. 'No waiting. In, out. Business, business,' he says.
'That's how you do it. He wants to see me, he sees me. Otherwise I
come home.' He is sympathetic when I tell him about my predicament, and offers to help. He wants to know all the details – place,
time, contents. He then makes a few calls on his mobile phone,
speaking quietly in Arabic. When he finishes, he gives me a reassuring pat. 'If it is Arabs, we will get it back soon. Don't worry, I have a
good feeling about this.'

My next call is to an Israeli journalist who has been helpful to me
in the past. Hillel Cohen is the kind of reporter who, if he had worked
in Manhattan in a different age, would always be wearing a trilby hat,
even in his shirtsleeves, with a cigarette permanently fixed in his
mouth. But, as he is Israeli, he wears a T-shirt, jeans and sandals. I
have come to respect Hillel, a short, wiry man in his mid-twenties
with closely-cropped hair and round, gold-rimmed glasses. He is
well-connected to Jerusalem's many different worlds. Once, when we
met while watching a group of extremist Israeli settlers parading
through the Muslim quarter of the Old City, I overheard one of the
settlers remark: 'That's Hillel. He's the devil. He comes from an ultra-
Orthodox family, but now all he does is write lies about us.' Another
time I expressed an interest in meeting some Palestinian collaborators, not exactly the easiest people to find in Jerusalem, and within
minutes I was sitting with two of the Palestinians' most notorious
traitors, all thanks to Hillel. He also has good contacts with the Israeli
security forces, and so I call him to relate my tale of woe. He is less
encouraging than Mounir. 'You have to remember,' says Hillel, 'there
are hundreds of criminals in this city.'

As a final gesture I place a number of advertisements in the local press offering a reward for the stolen suitcase:

Generous reward offered for return of author's vital documents in a dark blue suitcase stolen from Eliayu Shama'a St between 2.30–4.30 P.M. No questions asked. Telephone . . .

Friends also help me to get a similar message broadcast on Kol Israel, Jerusalem's main radio station, and 'Good Morning Palestine', the flagship of the newly formed Palestine Broadcasting Service. The Israeli announcer even phones me back to say he knows some criminals, and will ask around. Twenty-four hours later, when I am about to give up the suitcase as a lost cause, I receive a message. Someone has responded to the mention on Palestinian radio. I'm told that I should go to a local park, Hadek al-Jaras, and ask for a man called 'Adeeb'. This man, I am informed, will 'have what I'm looking for'.

After making inquiries I learn that Hadek al-Jaras is in fact Liberty Bell Park, a large recreational area in central Jerusalem, close to David's Village. It is named after a large iron bell given to Jerusalem by the citizens of Pennsylvania. I set off in search of Adeeb. I have no idea what this man looks like, except that he is an Arab, and so, as I walk through the park, I ask several groups of Arab youths if they know a man called Adeeb. I receive some strange looks, and in one case a group of young Arabs erupts in fits of giggles, but I think no more of it. Finally I stop a young Israeli who, with his stocky build and short-cropped hair, looks like a security guard. I enquire if he knows anyone called Adeeb.

'Is he gay?' the Israeli responds. 'If he's gay I might know him. I'm gay. How about you?'

It is only now that I realise why I have received so many strange looks in the park. One middle-aged Palestinian literally ran away from me when I asked him what I thought was a fairly innocuous question. Hadek al-Jaras, it transpires, is Jerusalem's main gay pick-up point. I inform the Israeli of the nature of my inquiry and, although he looks a little disappointed, he offers to help. He says he has a Palestinian boyfriend who knows most of the Arabs in the park.

We find his boyfriend, a slim, broody-looking youth of about seventeen, sitting beneath an olive tree. The youth is unshaven and wearing an American baseball cap back to front. He is smoking a hand-rolled cigarette that smells of marijuana. He does not appear pleased to see either of us. The Israeli puts his arm around his shoulders and kisses his ear. The Arab responds with a vague smile. 'By the way,' the Israeli says, addressing me, 'my name is Muki.' With his heavily accented pronunciation, it sounds like 'mucky'.

'Does your boyfriend know this Adeeb?' I ask.

He whispers something in the youth's ear in Arabic, and the youth laughs.

'I'm sorry,' says Muki. 'No, he doesn't. It's an unusual name. We'll ask around. Sit down here, and we'll soon find out.'

I sit down on the bench beneath the olive tree with Muki and his spaced-out Palestinian boyfriend. A brass plaque on the other side of the path informs us that this area of the park is dedicated to Yonatan 'Yoni' Netanyahu, the Israeli paratroop officer who led the operation to rescue a group of Israelis hijacked in Entebbe, Uganda, in July 1976. Netanyahu was killed in the raid, a fact which many Israelis believe helped to shape the uncompromising, anti-Arab policies of his politician brother Benjamin, the Israeli Prime Minister. It is difficult to imagine that either of the Netanyahu brothers would approve of the unusual Arab–Israeli intercourse being conducted beneath the olive tree.

Every time an Arab passes us, the boyfriend (I am not told his name) stops them and asks if they know anyone called Adeeb. None of them knows anything about Adeeb, although some of them appear to be interested in getting to know us. Throughout this ordeal, Muki provides a running commentary.

'Look at that one,' he says on one occasion, pointing to a slender Arab teenage youth. 'Isn't he beautiful? He knows I'm in love with him, but I can't afford him. It's too much to bear.'

'How much does he want?' I enquire.

'Only one hundred dollars,' he replies. 'I can afford it. But the point is that if I have him once, I'll want to have him a hundred times. And I can't afford that much money. I've told him I'll give him twenty dollars, but he just laughs at me because he knows how much torment I'm suffering.'

While we sit waiting for Adeeb to materialise, Muki seeks to entertain me with a story about how he was picked up by an immigration officer at London's Heathrow airport. Drawing his conclusions from that lone encounter, he seems to be under the impression that everyone in London is gay. He has had a similar experience with a New York taxi-driver – 'we did it in the back of his cab', he boasts – and has drawn similar conclusions about American taxi-drivers. All the time Muki is talking, his Palestinian boyfriend is looking at his dirty fingernails, saying nothing. Too many 'cigarettes'.

After I have spent fifteen minutes sitting with this peculiar couple, I grow restless. We have now spoken to most of the Arab men walking around the park, and none of them knows anything about 'Adeeb' or a dark blue suitcase. It is time to leave. As I part company with Muki and his boyfriend, I have the sinking feeling of someone who has been on the receiving end of an elaborate practical joke. I can certainly understand the warped appeal of persuading an unsuspecting foreigner to visit Jerusalem's main gay hang-out, offering a 'reward' to an unknown man. There is even the possibility that the caller has been watching my painful peregrination through Liberty Bell Park, enjoying a good laugh at my expense.

That is the last I hear of the suitcase. No one else responds to the adverts, and nothing is handed in to the police. I have always wondered what became of my suitcase and its contents. I ponder how the thieves reacted when they finally got somewhere they could open the loot. Having lugged around something that weighed over 100lb, they must have thought they were on to a winner: gold bars? Antiques? Electronics? To find it full of nothing but paper must have been profoundly disappointing. I suppose there is always the chance that one of them took it to the Jerusalem equivalent of the lost-and-found department at Baker Street station, where it now languishes with an exotic collection of discarded objects, such as artificial limbs, glass eyes and dentures. But I have wasted more than enough energy looking for that wretched suitcase. I must attend to a far more important Jerusalem quest.

# 1

# ROCK

*'Let us go and serve other gods'*
Deuteronomy 13: 6

Imagine. The Jebusite Liberation Front storms the Temple Mount, takes a group of hapless pilgrims hostage and unfurls a banner from the roof of the Dome of the Rock – 'Jebusites for Jerusalem'. Whatites? Jebusites? Who *are* these people? The security forces and camera crews scramble into action with equal zeal to deal with the latest international incident to afflict the Holy City. Could these Jebusites be some bizarre offshoot of the Palestinian liberation movement? A fanatical Jewish group that wants to evict all the other religions and make the city an exclusively Jewish domain? Or are they some weird bunch of American millennialists seeking international salvation through their own destruction? Producers at CNN's Atlanta headquarters lose no time digging out a galaxy of experts on Middle East terrorism to expound a variety of theories that, by the very nature of the medium, immediately assume the status of established fact. The Jebusites, ventures one sage, are part of a radical Islamic group, financed by Tehran's mad mullahs, which is committed to the destruction of the West. This is just one of many wild claims that are advanced, only to be laid to rest when an anonymous caller telephones a Western news agency in downtown Jerusalem with a statement listing the demands of the self-styled JLF.

'In the name of Shalem, the one and only true God of this Holy City, we demand an immediate end to 3,000 years of Jewish, Christian and Muslim occupation,' reads the statement. 'We demand the right to resume the pagan practices that were our custom prior to the invasion of the Hebrew terrorist David 3,000 years ago. We issue this demand in the name of Shalem, our most noble Baal after whom this Holy City is named.'

So there we are. As if Jerusalem did not have enough to contend with: Jews, Muslims and Christians; the perennial Arab–Israeli dispute. Now a new movement appears, insisting that all other claims to the Holy City are utterly irrelevant because, in the final analysis, Jerusalem belongs to the Jebusites.

All this might appear rather far-fetched. The Jebusites, after all, disappeared virtually without trace some 3,000 years ago. Look up the reference books, visit the museums, consult the experts. The answer is the same. Nobody knows. Or rather, nobody knows for certain. There are even some experts – archaeologists in the main – who question whether the Jebusites ever really existed. And if they did exist, whether they inhabited Jerusalem or somewhere else, like nearby Ramallah. These same experts question the existence of the Hebrew warrior king David. For them Jesus is a mythological figure invented purely to make the teachings of the Old Testament available to a wider, non-Jewish, audience. If we were to take them seriously, there would be nothing left. And so for argument's sake, we must assume that the Jebusites *did* exist. And that they were the ones responsible for the creation of 'Jerusalem'. At least that's what it says in the Bible.

Long before David launched a daring commando raid to capture the seemingly impregnable fortress of Zion, the Jebusites' stronghold, the city now known as Jerusalem had been inhabited by a succession of Canaanite tribes. One of the first known references to the city is in the Armana letters, an archive of diplomatic correspondence dating from about the fourteenth century BC between the Egyptian pharaohs and petty Canaanite rulers, where the city is referred to as 'Urusalim'. By the time the ancient Hebrews closed in on central Judea towards the end of the second millennium BC, the city that was soon to become their capital had been occupied by the Jebusites for about two hundred years, the last in a succession of Canaanite tribes to do so. The origin of the Jebusites is unknown, although the prophet Ezekiel provides a clue when he writes, referring to Jerusalem's creation, that 'the Amorite was thy father, and thy mother was a Hittite' (Ezekiel 16: 3). The Amorites were an ancient tribe that occupied the mountainous, inland regions of Canaan (the modern West Bank), while the Hittites, who conquered the land in around 1500 BC, came from the Anatolian plain, in what is now Turkey. The Jebusites probably took control of Jerusalem in about 1200 BC, taking advantage of the vacuum caused by the collapse of the Hittite empire at about that time. Although they controlled the city for some two hundred years preceding David's conquest, all that physically remains of their presence today is part of a wall uncovered by the British archaeologist Kathleen Kenyon when she was excavating the City of David. Today the local Arab residents use it as a garbage dump.

The Canaanite tribes were pagan, and worshipped a variety of baals, or gods. It was not enough for the different Canaanite tribes simply to have their own gods. Every field, vineyard, well and spring had its own baal (or baalah, if it was a god of the female persuasion) as its divine guardian. No wonder the Lord God Most High took such strong exception to this preponderance of Canaanite baals when he had his Mount Sinai get-together with Moses. It was to deal with this competition that Moses was given the first commandment: 'Thou shalt have no other gods before me.' Moses was told to tell his fellow Hebrews that worship of false idols was strictly off-limits, a stricture Moses' followers fully took to heart as they set about defeating the various Canaanite tribes and claiming their inheritance. As each tribe was defeated during the Hebrew conquest of Canaan, so the baals fell like nine-pins, their temples destroyed, their images desecrated.

The Jebusites, who were one of the more obscure Canaanite tribes, called their god Shalem and practised the same pagan rituals as the other Canaanite tribes. They built a temple for their god which was known by the cult name 'Jeru-Shalem', which translates as 'the

14

foundation of the God Shalem'. And that, as Kipling might have said, is how Jerusalem got its name.

As gods go, Shalem, his fellow baals and baalahs, were very demanding of their followers. If the nomadic Hebrews thought they had their work cut out dragging their commandments around the wilderness, these pagan deities operated on an entirely different plane. Unlike the Supreme Being that rules the destinies of the Judaic, Christian and Muslim faiths, the baals had other, more exotic, requirements than merely exalting the faithful to be good and holy. Animal sacrifice was encouraged on the baals' altar – Jews were to practise a similar ritual in their Temple – which was regarded as the god's table. On special occasions the worshippers were allowed to eat the sacred meat of animal sacrifice in order to enter communion with their god, a pagan precursor of the Christian sacrament. But making their temples resemble a crazed slaughter-house was the least of the baals' demands.

The Canaanites, like many primitive peoples, were preoccupied with fertility rituals. While the crops and animals were awarded their individual protectors, human sexual relations were strictly controlled by the goddess Astarte. Such was the devotion she inspired that men and women were happy to offer themselves as prostitutes in her honour in the confines of her temples. The passing of the seasons, especially the harvest, was celebrated with Bacchanalian relish. There was wild dancing to loud music, and wine was freely imbibed, which frequently led to the inhabitants ripping off their clothes and partic-ipating in orgies. Sometimes they got so carried away that they cut their bodies with swords and lances until blood gushed forth. The darker side of these festivities was the natives' susceptibility to sorcery and magic, which often resulted in the sacrifice of children by mak-ing them walk through a blazing bonfire. The stiff-necked Israelites were not impressed. Laden with the moral baggage of the Ten Commandments, they took an exceedingly dim view of these frolics, and were particularly sickened by the Canaanite talent for human sacrifice – 'for even their sons and their daughters do they burn in the fire of the gods'. The triumphant progress of the ancient Hebrews through the Land of Canaan was inspired as much by their desire to claim their divine inheritance as to erase all trace of the abominable baals.

They did a good job. Ask any of the modern residents of Jerusalem – Jew, Arab, Christian, heathen – about Shalem, and you will draw a blank. 'What's Shalem? Who is Shalem?' The same goes for the Jebusites. The vast majority of Jerusalemites don't know, and they don't care. And why should they? Three thousand years is an awfully long time, and after so many centuries of siege, conquest, occupation and liberation by Assyrians, Persians, Romans, Franks, Saracens, Mamluks, Turks and Britons (even the Mongol hordes made a brief, but devastating, appearance in AD 1260), they have more than enough to occupy their thoughts. Nor is there anything in the city to remind us of this lost tribe. There is no Baal Hilton, no Jebusite Street, no Shalem Plaza. The Jebusites have been well and truly erased from the city's collective consciousness. And yet, in an obscure way, the Jebusites matter.

As Jerusalem enters a new millennium, the city is as turbulent and divided as at any time in its eventful past. Apart from its status as a spiritual home for Jews, Christians and Muslims, the Holy City is the victim of an acrimonious struggle between two of the twentieth century's more stubborn political creeds – Zionism and Palestinian nationalism. Tensions between the two have already spilled over into two ugly wars – in 1948 and 1967 – which have served only to exacerbate tensions between Arabs and Jews, particularly those who inhabit the city. The protagonists keep attempting to settle their differences through peaceful negotiation and finding a means of co-existing in a spirit of mutual tolerance and understanding. But where do they start? The Israelis, for whom the conquest of Jerusalem during the 1967 Six-Day War is considered to be Zionism's crowning glory, trace their claim to sovereignty on David's conquest of the city. The Palestinians, who have lived in a mood of sullen resentment since 1967, counter that, if the Israelis want to play it that way, as descendants of the original occupants of Jerusalem they have the stronger claim. In this modern age, this might all seem rather perverse. It's rather like the Celts conquering London and claiming the English – with their mixed blood of Angles, Saxons, Jutes and Danes – are illegal usurpers. Welcome to the Middle East, where history and tradition weigh heavily upon the hearts and minds of men. At any rate, given the conflicting claims of the various protagonists, the fate of the wretched Jebusites might seem worthy of further investigation.

Having scoured libraries and museums in search of clues – and mainly drawn a blank – it seemed appropriate to seek out the archaeologists. If anyone had information on this long-lost deity and tribe, they were the ones to ask. There can be no other place on earth that has a higher density of archaeologists than Jerusalem. It is said that if you raise a stone in the Holy City it will reveal a story. In my experience, it is more likely to expose an archaeologist. They have been crawling around terranean and subterranean Jerusalem with their trowels and spades since the great European explosion of interest in all matters archaeological in the mid-nineteenth century prompted yet another invasion of the Holy City. On this occasion they came not to plunder its present, but its past.

The British, in particular, led the way, taking advantage of their improved diplomatic status in Jerusalem in the aftermath of the Crimean War to unearth secrets that had lain buried for centuries. Rivalry between Russia and the other major European powers – most notably France – for control of the Holy Places is generally given as one of the main causes of the war. Certainly after the war's end the British and French lost no time in extending and consolidating their influence in the Holy Land, and sponsoring religious, educational and academic institutions was an effective means of achieving these aims. Foremost among these inveterate explorers was one Captain Charles Warren who, in October 1867, and accompanied by his faithful companion, Sergeant Henry Birtles, discovered the underground tunnel (known today as Warren's Shaft) through which David's commandos are now believed to have launched their surprise attack on the Jebusites.[1] The British were in fierce competition with French and American archaeologists who, in time, established their own institutes. As if this were not a sufficient concentration of archaeologists in one place, the whole movement was given fresh impetus following Israel's success in the Six-Day War. Led by Moshe Dayan, the victorious Israeli defence minister, a number of generals swapped their guns for spades and embarked on a form of what can only be

1 Warren later went on to delineate the border between Canada and the US before becoming a police chief inspector at Scotland Yard. He is also the Inspector Warren who appears in Sir Arthur Conan Doyle's 'Sherlock Holmes' detective stories.

described as militant archaeology, to prove that Jerusalem indisputably belonged to them.

With so much expertise at hand, surely someone could shed some light on these wretched Jebusites? I was warned off the Israeli Antiquities Authority, which occupies the splendid Rockefeller Museum. Built in the 1920s on one of Jerusalem's prime locations – the outside terrace affords a stunning view of the Mount of Olives – the Rockefeller complex is a compelling example of the lavish expenditure that was showered on archaeology by foreign benefactors in the 1920s. Built to a design which could have been lifted straight from the pages of *1,001 Arabian Nights*, with beautifully crafted cloisters and well-appointed fountains, the Rockefeller endowment bankrupted itself with the purchase of the Dead Sea Scrolls in the 1950s. With unfortunate timing, the museum, which was then located in the Jordanian-occupied eastern sector of the city, was nationalised by the Jordanian authorities in early 1967. This set a precedent for the Israelis when they captured East Jerusalem during the Six-Day War, and the museum became the headquarters for their burgeoning band of archaeologists.

Despite the enormous resources the Israelis have spent on archaeology, however, doubts have been expressed about their impartiality.[2] There was the famous case, soon after the 1967 war, when Israeli archaeologists began a massive excavation to find remains associated with the Jewish Temples of King Solomon and Herod the Great. Ignoring United Nations censorship, the Israelis demolished a Palestinian girls' school and Jews of all ages were invited to 'dig for their past'. Unfortunately, when they eventually uncovered some remains, they turned out to be a previously unknown and magnificent Islamic Omayyad palace, dating from the eighth century AD. A plan to reconstruct the palace was later blocked on the grounds that the structure was 'offensive to Jewish sensibilities'. There have been many more, less well-publicised cases, where Israeli archaeologists have uncovered Canaanite remains which were either ignored or destroyed on the grounds that they were of no interest to the Jewish state. The Israelis did not seem the right people to ask about the Jebusites.

2 See Keith W. Whitelam, *The Invention of Ancient Israel: The Silencing of Palestinian History* (London: Routledge & Kegan Paul, 1996).

At the British School of Archaeology, one of the few relics of the British Mandate still functioning in Jerusalem, my inquiries prompted a few raised eyebrows. The British School, which has seen better days, resembles a small but run-down Oxford college. Founded at the start of the British Mandate in Palestine in 1922, the British School reached its apogee in the 1960s when Kathleen Kenyon was conducting her exhaustive excavations of the City of David. Since then the combination of the Israeli conquest of East Jerusalem and spending cutbacks by successive British governments have reduced it to a state of genteel indigence. Although the staff take great exception to any suggestion that the school is a last outpost of empire ('We are the vanguard of modern archaeological scholarship,' I was haughtily informed by the director), they certainly give the opposite impression. Meals are served with clockwork precision by the locally-hired Arab staff, morning coffee is served on the dot of 11 A.M. with *The Times* – a little pocket of Jerusalem that is forever England. Even though the Israelis have controlled Jerusalem and its environs for three decades, the school's officials still regard them as creatures from another planet who will, in time, disappear if they simply ignore them.

As Miss Kenyon was one of the few archaeologists in recent times to have paid any attention to Canaanite Jerusalem – her finds during the City of David excavations are the only known evidence of Jebusite occupation – the British School seemed the logical place to seek enlightenment. I was not to be indulged. Although the staff were perfectly hospitable, and showed me around an impressive library, they responded to my inquiries about the Jebusites as they might a difficult *Times* crossword clue.

'The Jebusites. Ah. Yes. Fascinating bunch,' replied a senior member of staff. 'Rather a strange crew. Did they ever exist? Now there's a question.'

I was to meet with similar disappointment at the École Biblique Archéologique, which is run by Dominican priests, many of whom are expert archaeologists. The École dates from the late nineteenth century and, like so many European institutions established in Jerusalem during that period, occupies a substantial tract of prime land in the heart of the city, just a few hundred metres north of Damascus Gate. The brothers own so much land – much of which has not been used for years – that the city council proposed using it to build a new road to ease the serious traffic congestion that regularly afflicts the area around Damascus Gate. The proposal was only abandoned when the brothers produced a plan of their own to build a new multimillion-dollar library on the vacant plot.

Father Jerome Murphy O'Connor OP is one of the more distinguished residents of the École, having made his way to Jerusalem from Cork some thirty years ago to devote his abundance of energy to the study of the archaeology and history of the Holy Land. A tall, well-preserved man who boasts a thick white beard, Father Jerry, as he is more familiarly known, is, apart from his many other duties, regarded as a figure-head for the city's ex-patriate community, most of whom are diplomats, aid workers and journalists. Every Sunday, except during the oppressive heat of summer, Father Jerry organises walking trips to sites of particular archaeological interest, often taking his jolly band of followers to the remoter corners of the country. Father Jerry will stride ahead, discerning the contours of an ancient Roman road where everyone else can see only desert, dissecting in detail the remains of a Herodian palace while speculating on how many concubines the Jewish king would have been able to squeeze into an ante-chamber. He is invariably accompanied by Mrs Valentine Vester, a sprightly octogenarian who owns the American Colony Hotel and is also a long-standing resident of the city. Like Jerry, Val is full of energy and mischief; while others in the party struggle to keep up with Jerry's vigorous pace, Val is nearly always at his side, a bundle of curiosity, like an inquisitive schoolgirl on her first outing. To most outsiders they might appear like a courting couple, such is their fond regard for each other. And even though Jerry has been ordained for more than three decades, and Val was happily married for an even longer period, there always seems to be a hint of flirtation in the air when the two of them are together.

Father Jerry is recognised as one of the foremost authorities on the archaeology of the Holy Land, even though he protests that his real interest lies in the life of St Paul, about whom he has written extensively and authoritatively.[3] Nor is Jerry afraid of speaking his mind.

3 *Paul: A Critical Life* by Jerome Murphy O'Connor (Oxford: OUP, 1996) is his most recent publication on the subject.

During one of my first encounters with him he explained, in all seriousness, how the Via Dolorosa, the path Jesus is said to have taken to Calvary, was the wrong way round.

'The Via Dolorosa as currently constituted has absolutely nothing to do with the route taken by Jesus,' he insisted. 'The Via Dolorosa as it stands today is the creation of unscrupulous monks in the Middle Ages who wanted to rip off unsuspecting pilgrims by insisting that their monasteries and churches were located close to the site of Christ's final suffering. In fact, Jesus approached Calvary from a completely different direction.'

Which all rather undermines the activities of the hundreds of thousands of Christian pilgrims who each year faithfully follow what they believe to be the authentic Via Dolorosa. It was Jerry also who pointed out how the entrance to the Holy Sepulchre originally had two doors – one entrance and one exit. One of them, however, was bricked up following Saladin's conquest of the city in AD 1187. This was so that pilgrims could not avoid paying tolls to the Muslim family which had been given this considerable and lucrative privilege by the conquering Kurdish commander.

If anyone knew about the Jebusites, I was confident Father Jerry, with his extensive knowledge and challenging opinions, could help. But for once even a man of Father Jerry's formidable knowledge was stumped. 'The problem with the Jebusites is that there are no records,' he explained. 'We know so little about them. But it is something that ought to be corrected. There hasn't been enough work done on the Jebusites.'

My last call was to the Albright Institute – another lavish American institution dating from the 1920s, named after the famous American archaeologist William Foxwell Albright. The Albright is housed in a large, airy red-roofed villa in Saladin Street in East Jerusalem. Although the front garden is overgrown, and the Institute's general aspect is one of decline, the Albright remains one of Jerusalem's best-funded archaeological research centres. And it was here that I came nearest to finding someone with any interest in my unusual quest, an American woman who had devoted the past twenty years of her life to an exhaustive study of Canaanite culture. Her excitement was equal to mine when we were first introduced. It was not often she met a layman who expressed an interest in such an uncelebrated aspect of ancient history. And after months of scouring the city for any hint or trace, I had finally found someone who shared a similar passion. Unfortunately, although she knew a great deal about the Canaanites, her knowledge about the Jebusites was sketchy. Furthermore, after spending so much time in close proximity with her beloved Canaanites, she had become overly defensive, as academics often do, about her pet subject. She became quite indignant, for example, when I enquired about the custom of child sacrifice.

'Oh no,' she protested. 'They wouldn't do anything like that. Not the Canaanites. This is just black propaganda put out by the Hebrews to darken their name. There is no evidence to support it. It's nothing but malicious gossip.'

So much for the detective work. The trail went cold almost where I'd started. In spite of the formidable amount of work and research that has been conducted into all aspects of Jerusalem's history, it seems there are hardly any leads that can shed much light about Jerusalem's founding fathers and the god that gave the city its name. And so, of necessity, the files on Shalem, the lost god of Jerusalem, and the missing Jebusites, must remain open pending further investigation. Which suggests that the Jebusites have had a raw deal. Compared with today's Jewish, Christian and Muslim leaders, who all take themselves so seriously, at the very least the dear old Jebusites, with their wild orgies and drunken revelries, had a different perspective on life. How refreshing it would be if they were still around. Forget Easter, Passover and Ramadan. Shalem's annual harvest festival would certainly enliven the Jerusalem calendar. While the British and Germans could bloat themselves in the beer tent, the Italians and French could strip off their clothes and proclaim themselves instant converts. One can't help feeling that Jerusalem is a duller place without her Jebusites.

By contrast it is almost impossible to move in the Holy City without coming across some reference to David, the Jebusites' triumphant vanquisher. On King David Street you can check into the King David Hotel where, for those who can afford it, you can book a room with a panoramic view of David's Citadel (which is actually a Mamluk mosque). Alternatively, just a five-minute walk from the hotel is King David's Village where (apart from having your car broken into) a modest two-room apartment – with 'unique views of the old city' – can be purchased by those prepared or able to part with a small fortune. This is not to be confused with the City of David, located on the southern flank of the Old City, which provides a more accurate picture of the modest nature of the Jerusalem David made his capital.

By the time David defeated the Jebusites and conquered Jerusalem he was already well established as the leader of the quarrelsome Israelites. Although the descendants of Abraham had successfully installed themselves in the promised land, the transition from a nomadic to a settled people was not without its difficulties, and the various tribes often found themselves at loggerheads, if not in open conflict. With so many other ethnic groups vying with the Israelites for control of Canaan, it was essential they set their house in order, which they achieved when the elders of Israel came to David at Hebron and anointed him king over all Israel. David resolved to find a new capital that would be acceptable to all the Israelite tribes and help him to forge a united kingdom to ensure he did not suffer the constant bickering that had driven so many of his predecessors to distraction. Hebron, David's base for the seven years following the death of Saul, was located in the southern part of Judah. Gibeah, which had been Saul's capital, lay in the heart of the hardy Benjamite tribesmen's territory, and its adoption as the capital would have been bitterly resented by the men of Judah. David needed to find a capital which was not in territory occupied by any of the tribes, and Jerusalem, which had long been a thorn in the flesh of Israel, separating the House of Joseph and Benjamin from Judah and the southern tribes, offered a solution to David's predicament.

Jerusalem enjoyed the reputation of being impregnable. David, the new king, could not risk the damage a notorious military disaster might inflict on his reputation. So he entrusted the operation to capture Jerusalem to Joab, a valued commander, who had spent much time pondering how such an operation might be achieved. It was David's good fortune that the Jebusites, despite being a warlike people, had grown so used to the idea of their invincibility that they had neglected the city's fortifications and their military training. David would have preferred to secure the fortress, or Zion, by peaceful negotiation. But his efforts were rudely rebuffed when the cocky Jebusites impolitely told David where he might deposit his offer.

Even as David threatened to attack, the Jebusites mocked him, boasting that, even if they manned the ramparts with the blind and the lame, any Israelite assault was surely doomed to failure. The Jebusites were to rue their taunts.

Joab devised a clever plan to send a group of commandos through Warren's Shaft, the water tunnel to the south of the city, while the main body of the attack centred on the north, where the city's defences were at their weakest. The defenders were therefore forced to concentrate their efforts on repelling the main assault, enabling the commando unit to surprise them from the rear. The Jebusites were thrown into confusion and quickly capitulated, a decision which meant they were spared the customary mass executions that accompanied military triumphs in biblical times. David, who selfishly claimed all the credit for Joab's victory, treated the Jebusites leniently and allowed them to live on amicable terms with their conquerors, although their pagan religious practices were no longer to be tolerated. The baals were banned, Shalem banished and, as the victorious Hebrews set about establishing their own god cult, the Jebusites gradually faded into the mists of time, to disappear virtually without trace.

In the wider context of the Israelite conquest of Canaan, the capture of Jerusalem did not seem anything exceptional. Compared with the other Israelite strongholds like Gibeah, Jerusalem was an unlikely candidate for a capital city. A low-lying crop of rock, David's Jerusalem was dwarfed by the surrounding hills, a fact which can today easily be observed simply by visiting neighbouring Mount Scopus, the Mount of Olives or the terrace of the King David Hotel. Its undoubted attraction for David was that, having vanquished the Jebusites, he could claim it for his own without fear that one of his Israelite rivals might lodge a counter-claim. Being an astute politician, David acted quickly to consolidate his good fortune. The newly conquered territory became the City of David, an act which both distanced the conquerors from Jerusalem's pagan connotations and left none of the Israelites in any doubt about who was in charge.

What was to make Jerusalem so special, however, was David's decision to establish the Ark of the Covenant, the symbol of the contract Moses had struck with the Lord God Most High on Mount Sinai, in his new capital – an early example of, perhaps, the union between church and state. The Ark, the portable shrine-throne that had accompanied the Israelites throughout their wanderings between Egypt and Canaan, represented the physical embodiment of God's compact with the Israelites. It was the one symbol that united the Twelve Tribes. The Ark was established in Jerusalem in exactly the kind of tent that had sheltered it in the desert wilderness. By bringing it to Jerusalem David sought to persuade the fractious Israelites that his kingship bore genuine legitimacy. In future if they wanted to pray before the Ark, they would have to visit *his* capital and give *him* a little respect. And so long as the Jews remembered Jerusalem, so long would they remember the name of David.

Apart from bringing the Ark to Jerusalem, David also built an altar so that his followers could fulfil their religious obligations. Building the altar was not exactly David's idea; it was constructed to save the Jews from a vicious pestilence the Lord had sent against the Israelites to punish David. In one of the more improbable tales related in the book of Samuel, Jehovah killed 70,000 Jews with a plague after He had ordered David to conduct a census of the Israelite population, and David willingly obliged (II Samuel 24: 1–10). This might seem rather perverse, as David was only obeying orders. But relations between the Jewish king and his Divine Guardian were always a matter of some complexity.

Although David was highly successful in achieving the Lord's work in military terms, making himself the most successful leader of the Jews, he was not so successful at obeying the Lord's moral commandments. One of the more infamous episodes concerning David's cupidity relates to his courtship, and conquest, of Bathsheba, the wife of Uriah, one of his Hittite bodyguards, and an officer of some merit. (As the Hittites were the 'mothers' of the Jebusites, it is even possible that Bathsheba was related to the Jebusite race David had recently vanquished.) David fell madly in love with Bathsheba after he caught sight of her, one spring night, bathing herself, at the end of her menstrual cycle, on the rooftop of her house which adjoined the royal palace in Jerusalem. David was immediately infatuated by her, and asked his comrades about her domestic arrangements. He learnt that Uriah was a devoted soldier more concerned with fulfilling the desires of his king than his wife. David had Bathsheba, who was alone, roused from her bed and brought to him in the royal bedchamber, where the couple soon fell into a loving embrace. But when, a few months later,

Bathsheba told David she was pregnant with his child, the Israelite leader devised a plan to do away with her husband to conceal the scandal. He ordered Uriah to launch a suicidal frontal assault on Rabbah, a northern city held by the rebellious Ammonites. Uriah was happy to oblige, and duly died when his assault was repelled by the overwhelming superiority of the Ammonite forces, leaving Bathsheba free to join David in nuptial bliss.

As so often happened when David did wrong, he was soon overwhelmed by remorse. 'I have sinned against the Lord,' David conceded, when confronted with his appalling crime by Nathan, then Jerusalem's resident prophet. Nathan, who communicated regularly with the Lord, accepted David's penitence as genuine, and informed him, 'The Lord also hath put away thy sin; thou shalt not die.'[4] But the situation did not look so promising when, a few years later, the Lord sent the plague because David had carried out His request to conduct a national census. It was only when the angel of the Lord 'stretched out his hand toward Jerusalem, to destroy it' that the Lord changed his mind, at the moment when the angel was by the threshing-floor of Arauna the Jebusite (II Samuel 24: 16). Instead David was told to buy the threshing-floor from the Jebusites and to erect an altar on the site to offer sacrifices to the Lord. This is about the last that is heard of the Jebusites and, according to the description provided in the Second Book of Samuel, the Israelites appeared to have enjoyed cordial relations with their former enemies after David's conquest. In all probability, the Jebusites were, in time, absorbed into the Israelite people. Certainly when David approached Arauna, the Jebusite leader welcomed him with the greeting: 'Wherefore is my lord the king come to his servant?', bowing himself before the king with his face to the ground. When David explained his purpose, Arauna offered to hand over the threshing-floor for free. But David insisted on buying the land, explaining that he could not offer sacrifices to the Lord on land that cost him nothing. So Arauna agreed to sell the threshing-floor to David for fifty shekels (measures) of silver. And there David built an altar unto the Lord, and offered a sacrifice of peace, in return for which the Lord stayed the plague from Israel.

\*

4 David and Bathsheba: II Samuel 11–12.

David's purchase of the threshing-floor was an act of extreme significance for Jerusalem's development, and one that today lies at the heart of the modern dispute over Jerusalem's future. In pagan times, and particularly in Canaanite culture, a threshing-floor was considered a holy place. In a culture where gods were appointed to guard every field and vineyard, the site whence the fruits of the harvest were brought was a place where the majesty of the gods was made manifest. If the gods were pleased, the crop would be abundant; if not, the populace could be stricken by famine. The threshing-floor purchased by David from Arauna the Jebusite was a broad expanse of rock on an exposed hill, a few hundred metres to the north of the royal palace. The fact that the Jebusites were still occupying a site so close to the Israelites' new seat of government indicates the pacific nature of relations between the two peoples. According to Jewish tradition, it is said that Arauna was actually buried in a cave located beneath the threshing-floor. The Midrash records that Jews returning from exile in Babylon found Arauna's skull located beneath the rock. Certainly it would have been a great honour for a pagan king to be interned so close to an epicentre of holiness.

Whether the threshing-floor was regarded as a holy place by Jews at the time David purchased it, or whether it became so afterwards, is unclear. This is, after all, an area of history where the details are extremely vague, to say the least. According to more modern Jewish tradition, however, the rock upon which David built his first altar, the holy of holies, and the place where Solomon was later to build the first Jewish Temple, is replete with both religious and historical significance. If Jerusalem is the heart of the universe, this rock is the foundation stone. In the third century AD, the sages of Israel, writing some 1,300 years after David's conquest, explained that 'The land of Israel is the middle of the earth. Jerusalem is the middle of the land of Israel. The Temple is the middle of Jerusalem. The holy of holies is the middle of the Temple. The holy ark is the middle of the holy of holies. And the Stone of Foundation is in front of the holy of holies.'[5] It is, perhaps, as a result of this interpretation that medieval maps portray Jerusalem as *Umbilicus Mundi*, the navel of the world. Jewish

5 Quoted in Zev Vilnay, *Legends of Jerusalem* (Philadelphia, PA: The Jewish Publication Society, 1973).

tradition also attributes a central role in the world's creation to this barren rock, claiming it is a surviving remnant from the Garden of Eden. It was also here that, after David built his altar, the Ark of the Covenant, God's personal covenant with mankind, was placed. The Zohar, the principal work of the Jewish cabalists, claims that groups of angels and cherubim hover over the Foundation Stone, and that from there all the world is blessed. Nor is it only Jews who afford this pagan granary with extraordinary significance. Christians and Muslims, as well as Jews, claim this rock is Mount Moriah, the location where Abraham was ordered to sacrifice his son Isaac (Muslims believe he was ordered to kill Ishmael, his bastard son).

The construction of an altar on an ancient pagan holy place confirmed Jerusalem's destiny as a religious capital. Had David simply been content to make Jerusalem his military headquarters, the city would in all probability have suffered the same fate as many another Canaanite or Israelite encampment (even at the height of David's power, the City of David covered less than one acre). It would have been conquered by a later generation of invaders and consigned to oblivion. But by confirming the city with an aura of sanctity, David ensured his capital occupied a special place in the heart of the Jewish people. The Torah, the Jewish book of Mosaic law that comprises the first five chapters of the Old Testament which relates to the period prior to David's conquest, refers to Jerusalem only as Shalem, its original (pagan) godly occupant. After David's conquest the city became a central mantra for the Jewish faith. 'If I forget thee, O Jerusalem: let my right hand forget her cunning,' is perhaps the most famous Jewish lament, together with 'next year in Jerusalem', the dream nurtured by countless generations of Diaspora Jews. Even today, religious Jews include Jerusalem in their daily prayers, while a Jewish bride is required to break a glass at her wedding to commemorate the loss of the Temple which later adorned David's makeshift shrine. Thanks to David, Jerusalem became the most important place on earth for world Jewry. His inspirational leadership transformed a run-of-the-mill Canaanite city-state into a national capital and centre of religious pilgrimage, a city which became the centre of an empire spreading from the Nile to the Euphrates.

It is a point that modern-day Israelis of a more nationalistic hue cannot help but raise at every conceivable opportunity. No matter that all this happened some 3,000 years ago. No matter that Jerusalem was only the undisputed capital of the ancient Israelites for some seventy years and that, over the last three millennia, the city has been conquered and occupied more than twenty times by peoples from as far afield as Mongolia and England. The military prowess achieved by David is used shamelessly by Israeli nationalists to justify their claim that Jerusalem is the eternal and indivisible capital of the State of Israel. Attend any official Israeli function in Jerusalem – the Israel festival, the Jerusalem film festival, even the Jerusalem book fair – and some gauche politician will get up and make a speech lauding David, thereby seeking to draw a direct parallel between past and present success of the Jewish people in conquering and occupying the ancient city. A good example of this anachronistic jingoism occurred towards the end of 1995, when Ehud Olmert, the fervently nationalist mayor of Jerusalem, launched a festival to celebrate what he and his supporters claimed was the 3,000th anniversary of David's conquest of the Holy City.

Mr Olmert, who ended the septuagenarian Teddy Kollek's 28-year reign as mayor in 1993, enjoys a reputation for being a ruthless career politician. Born in Haifa in 1945, he first came to Jerusalem as a student in the late 1960s to study law at the Hebrew University on Mount Scopus. Since his election as mayor, Olmert appears to have cultivated the impression that he regards Jerusalem as his personal political fiefdom, the perfect platform from which to launch himself on to the larger stage of Israeli politics. The sensitivities of the eclectic religious and racial groups that comprise modern Jerusalem do not figure highly on his list of priorities. If he causes them offence, that is not his concern. His primary concern, as he made clear during his election campaign for mayor, is to prevent Jerusalem becoming part of a Palestinian state. His political opponents also suspect that Olmert is using Jerusalem as a platform to launch his campaign for even higher office, namely that of the Prime Minister, less than one mile away in the city's complex of government offices. Olmert previously served for four years as a Cabinet minister and key adviser to Yitzhak Shamir, whose Likud government during the late 1980s and early 1990s was the most uncompromising in Israel's history. That experience has fashioned Olmert's approach to the administration of Jerusalem. A staunch opponent of the Oslo peace accords, Olmert

saw it as his personal mission to ensure that there would be no political compromise over the future status of Jerusalem. His reaction to
the accords was to encourage Jews to settle in Arab East Jerusalem
and to frustrate any attempt by the Palestinians to establish any form
of official representation in the city. It was hardly surprising, therefore, that the Mayor of Jerusalem should seize upon the idea of an
Israeli-sponsored festival in honour of David and use it as a potent
demonstration of Israel's hegemony over the city. In the glossy
brochure produced in the autumn of 1995 to launch sixteen months
of festivities for 'Jerusalem 3000', Olmert wrote of 'Jerusalem, the
eternal, united capital of the sovereign State of Israel and the Jewish
Nation'. This was hardly the language of the negotiating table.

An impressive cast of international *glitterati* was assembled. Franco
Zeffirelli, the film director, agreed to mount a *son et lumière*: Daniel
Barenboim was booked to conduct *Fidelio* under the Old City walls;
Zubin Mehta was to lead the Israel Philharmonic in a gala concert
dedicated to David. Sir Tim Rice offered to write a musical on King
David to be brought over from Broadway for a special performance in
the Holy City. Talk about hitting on a raw nerve. If Olmert was
unaware of the deep passions the whole issue of Jerusalem could
arouse – both at home and abroad – his proposed homage to David
left him in no doubt. The first salvo of criticism was fired off by the
city's ultra-Orthodox Jewish community, erstwhile allies who had
helped to secure Olmert's election as Mayor. They protested loudly at
the profanity of the Hollywood-style glitz, and that most of the per-
formers were non-Jews. The Palestinians weighed in next with Faisal
Husseini, the *de facto* head of the city's Arabs, denouncing the festival.
'These celebrations are the celebrations of occupying Jerusalem,' he
proclaimed. Even though the Palestinians constitute a minority of the
city's population, they exert considerable international clout. Thus
once Husseini had spoken, it was not long before Olmert found himself having to contend with an international boycott of his festival.
Most European nations, the Vatican and the US all opted to give
Olmert's extravaganza a wide berth.

The final ignominy came when it was pointed out that, in his des-
peration to make political capital from the Davidian anniversary,
Olmert had got his dates mixed up. In archaeology dates can be
something of a moveable feast, but for argument's sake most experts

agree that 996 BC is the most likely date for David's conquest of the Jebusites. The organisers, who cannot have paid much attention to their maths lessons at school, calculated that 1996 would therefore be the 3000th anniversary, forgetting that the pre-Christ dates are counted backwards while the AD calendar advances forwards. If David conquered Jerusalem in 996 BC, then the 3000th anniversary would be AD 2004. There was an element of divine justice in this embarrassing discovery, for it is said one of main considerations that prompted Olmert to hold the festival in the first place was to preempt any planned celebrations of the 900th anniversary of the Crusaders' capture of Jerusalem (1099) and anticipated arrival of some three million Christians to celebrate the millennium.

Unfortunately for Olmert, the blunder was only pointed out long after the guest acts had been booked and several million dollars spent on the arrangements and pre-festival publicity. The organisers attempted to extricate themselves by finding an expert to proclaim that the 996 date was wrong and that the correct date for David's conquest was 1004 BC, but no one was buying it. The organisers had fouled up in a big way, and a festival that began with high hopes became a subject for international ridicule. Mr Olmert is not the first politician to discover that, when it comes to Jerusalem, it is impossible to escape the burden of the Holy City's history.

# 2

# SHRINES

*'Except the Lord build the house, They labour in vain that build it'*

Psalms 127: 1

If David – warrior, poet, lover and leader – gave Jerusalem its soul, Solomon, his son, nourished the body. Solomon's reign was, in essence, peaceful, and under his wise but firm government, Jerusalem prospered as it had never done before. The residue of the Canaanites were reduced to serfdom, the country divided into twelve administrative provinces and an efficient tax service was implemented to fund the king's ambitious construction programme. Solomon's finances were also helped by the great wealth – gold, silver and works of art – that David had accumulated during many wars. This enabled Solomon to fund a lavish lifestyle which included impressive buildings, such as the royal palace, and an extensive harem. This was also the first time in Jerusalem's history that the city was opened to the wider world, so much so that even the Queen of Sheba felt obliged to pay Solomon a visit, during which she gave and received expensive gifts. But for all these accomplishments, Solomon is remembered primarily for building the Temple.

Solomon's Temple was a reflection both of his wealth and Jerusalem's new-found position as a prosperous regional centre. The idea for the Temple was originally conceived by David, who wanted a splendid edifice to cover the altar which he wanted 'to be made exceedingly great to win fame and glory throughout all the lands'. He set about acquiring the raw materials, including the famous cedar wood from Lebanon. But David died before work could begin in earnest, and it was left to Solomon to execute the plan. For religious Jews, this was probably just as well. Although David was an accomplished soldier and politician, he had many failings in his personal life. To call him a double-crossing womaniser would be the least of the criticisms. Certainly he was not a fit person to construct a sacred monument for the Jews, and the Jews felt it was God's will that the undertaking should be left to Solomon.

Compared with the massive structure that was to be built by Herod nearly 1,000 years later, Solomon's Temple was a relatively modest affair. The population of Jerusalem at this time was, after all, no more than 8,000. The Temple was built with the aid of both material and craftsmen supplied by the more advanced cultures of Sidon and Tyre in Phoenicia. It was a rectangular building of large squared stones and cedar beams. It consisted of two apartments, separated by a wall with a connecting door of olive wood. At the centre of the complex was the inner sanctuary, the Holy of Holies, containing the Ark which was surmounted by two cherubim made of olive wood plated with gold. The internal walls were made of cedar, richly adorned with carvings, while the floor was made of cypress wood. Apart from being a place of worship, the Temple, together with the palace and the various other buildings commissioned by Solomon, was the culmination of the campaign launched by Moses to conquer Canaan and make it the national home of the Jewish people.

For all the efforts of David and Solomon to make Jerusalem the capital of a strong, united Jewish state, however, their dream fell apart within months of Solomon's death in 933 BC. Solomon may have been devoted to the service of God, but he also enjoyed the good life. It was not just *raison d'état* that led him to acquire an exotic collection of wives which included Egyptian princesses, women of the Moabites, Ammonites, Edomites, Sidonians and Hittites (there may even have been the odd Jebusite among them). Solomon's concept of

Jerusalem as an international trading city resulted in various temples being built for the worship of other gods, a development that provoked a strong reaction from conservative religious Jews, especially as there was evidence that some of the less strong-willed were back-sliding to the baal-cults. It is even possible that Shalem made a come-back but, unfortunately, there is no record.

Money was the root of the problem. The heavy tax burden levied to pay for Solomon's grandiose projects was much resented by some of the Israelite tribes, especially in the north where they found it hard to understand how they benefited. In the last years of Solomon's life this discontent resulted in an assassination attempt which was thwarted by the prophet Ahijah. This did not prevent dissent resurfacing in more virulent form upon Solomon's death, when the northerners insisted they were not prepared to continue paying the same level of taxes to Solomon's successor, his son Rehoboam. When Rehoboam threatened to resort to force to make them comply, the northerners responded by stoning to death Adoniram, the chief tax collector. They then formally announced their secession and established the Kingdom of Israel, with Shechem as its capital. Jerusalem became the capital of the rump state, the Kingdom of Judah. David's dream of making Jerusalem an eternal capital of a united Israelite nation had lasted less than seventy years.

While Jerusalem remained the capital of the smaller Judaean monarchy, it was now over-shadowed materially by its more powerful, dissident sister-state, Israel. Attempts by the Judaeans to reunite the kingdoms met with little success, while the Kingdom of Israel itself was beset by tribal rivalries which culminated in a spate of political assassinations. The northern kingdom also saw many of its citizens abandon the Jewish faith and succumb to local pagan cults. In 722 BC the folly of the northerners in rejecting David's vision of a united kingdom was confirmed when it fell to the Assyrians.

The Assyrian success sent shock waves through Jerusalem, and when King Sennacherib of Assyria finally marched on Jerusalem in 701 BC, the immediate response of the Judaean king, Hezekiah, was to hand over all the treasures from the Temple, as his predecessors had done when challenged by both the Egyptians and the northern Israelites. Although some form of tribute was exacted, Sennacherib was not satisfied, and resolved to force Jerusalem's submission. On this occasion the city was saved, according to the Bible, not by the valour of its defenders, but by the intervention of the angel of the Lord who 'went out and struck down 185,000 men in the Assyrian camp, and the following morning they were all dead corpses. So King Sennacherib of Assyria broke camp, and retreated.' Sennacherib's account is somewhat different, and claims that after shutting up the Jewish king 'like a caged bird within Jerusalem', he made his way back to Nineveh with a massive amount of booty, which included gold, silver, ivory inlaid couches, ivory armchairs, elephant hides, concubines and Hezekiah's state orchestra. A suitable comparison today might be if, in the event of Saddam Hussein of Iraq conquering Jerusalem, his only demand were to have the Israeli State Philharmonic Orchestra play for him in Baghdad.

The Assyrian siege should have alerted the Jews of Jerusalem to the weakness of their position. But this narrow escape from the devastation of conquest appears to have made little impression upon the citizens who, far from mending their ways, appeared set on a course of self-destruction. During the reign of Hezekiah's son, Menasseh, the strict Judaic code was cast aside and temples to pagan gods once more began to appear, with altars erected for the baals. By the time Josiah came to the throne in 640 BC, the pagan cult had even spread within the confines of the Temple itself. And judging by the lengths Josiah had to undertake to cleanse the city of its paganism, the citizens had succumbed to many of the old Jebusite practices which had so outraged the ancient Israelites. When, for example, Josiah cleared the Temple of all the baals' artefacts, he was also obliged to demolish the cubicles of the male prostitutes.

Josiah's clean-up campaign made little overall impact, for by the time the Babylonians, who had usurped the Assyrians as the up-and-coming Semitic power, arrived at the walls of Jerusalem in 597 BC, Jehoaichin, the eighteen-year-old king, was still doing 'what was displeasing to the Lord'. Jehoaichin was in no condition for a fight, so he surrendered to King Nebuchadnezzar of Babylon, along with his mother and his courtiers, commanders and officers. By surrendering, Jehoaichin avoided wholesale slaughter of the citizens. But it did not stop the Babylonians stripping anything of value from both the Temple and the royal palace. Then, in accordance with Babylonian custom, Nebuchadnezzar carried off the most useful members of the

Jerusalem community, together with the booty, for resettlement in Babylonia. The remnants of the decimated Israelites were placed under the tutelage of Babylon. Internal wrangles over whether Jerusalem should enter into an open alliance with Egypt meant the remaining Jews paid insufficient attention to their obligations, and in 586 BC Nebuchadnezzar paid a return visit. This time the Israelites put up a token resistance, and were roundly defeated for their trouble. On this occasion Nebuchadnezzar was not so magnanimous. The leader of the Israelite revolt, Zedekiah, was captured and blinded. The Babylonians then set about the systematic destruction of every building of import, including the Temple and the royal palace. When they had finished, Solomon's proud city had been reduced to a pile of ashes. What was left of the population was carried off to exile where, by the rivers of Babylon, they had ample time to reflect on the error of their ways.

The exile did not last long. Following the capture of Babylon, the Persian King Cyrus gave the Jews permission to return to Jerusalem, and in 538 BC a caravan of 42,360 Jews and 7,337 slaves left Babylonia. The Jews, like all exiles, were now imbued with an idealised notion of Zion which had been fashioned by the prophet Ezekiel, who nurtured the vision of a new Temple in a Utopian Jerusalem. In fact the returnees soon found the harsh realities of life were far removed from the dreams of prophets, and when work did commence, seventeen years later, on a new Temple, it was nowhere near as grand as Solomon's structure, and reflected the straitened circumstances of the populace. The Jews had to wait another five hundred years before their Temple could be restored to its true majesty.

The influence of the Greeks and then the Romans on the Holy Land effectively began with the conquests of Alexander the Great. Tyre and Gaza were conquered in 332 BC but, although Jewish historians like Josephus would like us to believe otherwise, the great Hellenic commander, like Napoleon 2,000 years later, never found the time to visit to Jerusalem. His legacy was, however, felt in the Holy City for, after his death, the disruption of his empire caused by the wars between his generals led to a renewal of the age-old dispute for possession of Palestine. For the next hundred years Jerusalem was caught up in a succession of wars between the Egyptians and the new Seleucid empire. Invariably Jerusalem was claimed as a prize trophy by the victor, who took Jewish captives and deported them. Such was the high regard with which the city was held that it was included in the dowry of Ptolemy V when he married Cleopatra.

The effect of the new Greek civilisation was especially felt in Jerusalem where the City of David was turned into a Greek gymnasium, a development that produced some unusual sights in the city centre. The youth from the best families, for example, adopted the pose of Greek athletes and indulged in sports such as wrestling. They did this while completely nude except for broad-brimmed hats, adorned with figures of Mercury, that rested jauntily upon their heads. By 168 BC the Temple had been given over as a sanctuary to Jupiter the Olympian, and a statue of the god, to the outrage of the few remaining religious Jews, was placed upon the altar. Heathen sacrifices were offered and the Temple was filled with riots and debauchery; within the sacred precincts men dallied with harlots and pig's blood was poured on the altar.

Hellenism, clearly, had gone too far, and the Jews responded by launching a revolt led by Judah the Maccabee (the Hammerer). Gathering together a body of resolute warriors from among the scattered Jews, he attempted to expunge all traces of Hellenism from the city. The Syrian authorities dispatched troops to quell the uprising, but Judah proved more than a match for them, despite his limited resources. He surprised the enemy with night attacks and routed the Syrian troops, capturing most of their weapons. By the time the Syrians sent reinforcements, Judah and his followers were better equipped, and with 3,000 stout-hearted warriors Judah was able to put a Syrian force of 40,000 to flight. When the Syrians made their third and final attempt to suppress the revolt, it met with a similar fate. Judah was able to march to Jerusalem, where he found the Temple desolate, the altar profaned, the priests' chambers demolished and shrubs growing in the courts as in a forest. Judah and his followers did the best they could to repair the Temple, which was rededicated three years later.

The Hellenic experience nonetheless left deep divisions within the Jewish community, with the Pharisees, who regarded themselves as the main protectors of the Jewish faith, coming into conflict with the

Sadducees, who thought a little Greek culture could do no harm. The tensions between the two camps resulted in a series of bloody skirmishes. During a feast in the Temple, for example, Alexander Jannai, the pro-Sadducee Jewish king, was accused of pouring water on the floor instead of on the altar, as was the Pharisees' custom. The congregation then pelted the king with lemons, who responded by ordering his mercenaries against them. Six thousand people were slaughtered. The rift between the Sadducees and Pharisees then degenerated into civil war. After a series of engagements, Alexander emerged victorious and determined to teach the Pharisees a lesson they would never forget. The ringleaders were seized by Alexander and brought to Jerusalem where, while feasting with the ladies of his harem, the king had eight hundred of them crucified. As a final gesture, while the crucified men were still alive, Alexander brought their wives and children before them and slit their throats.

The Jewish civil war was not finally resolved until the arrival of the Roman general Pompey in the region. Pompey was on one of Rome's perennial campaigns to keep at bay the troublesome Parthians, who originated in what is now north-west Iran, when his attention was drawn to events in Palestine. Rival claimants to the Judaean throne sought his support. Although at first Pompey tried to keep his distance, he was inexorably drawn into the dispute to the point where he had no alternative other than to march on Jerusalem. His arrival prompted yet another round of bickering between the Jews as to whether or not the city should be delivered to the Romans. The followers of Aristobulus, one of the rival claimants, decided to fight it out and barricaded themselves in the Temple. But the Jews had no answer to the Roman siege engines. Josephus, the Jewish chronicler, relates that: 'There was slaughter everywhere. For some of the Jews were slain by the Romans and others by their fellows; and there were some who hurled themselves down precipices, and setting fire to their houses, burned within them, for they could not bear to accept their fate.' In all some 12,000 Jews died and Aristobulus was taken back to Rome in chains as a prize trophy for Pompey's triumph. Judaea was put under the control of the new Roman province of Syria.

The rise to power of Herod the Great can be attributed to the Roman civil wars which erupted soon after Pompey's conquest of Jerusalem, and put an end to the Jewish conflict. Herod proved a deft reader of the vicissitudes of Roman and Levantine politics, even if he had the knack of supporting the losing side. When the fortunes of Anthony, his original patron, went down in the waters off Actium, the agile Herod was able to transfer his allegiance to Octavian, the victor, and to embrace Rome's new master as warmly as he had once held his rival. Octavian, perhaps unconvinced at Herod's professions of loyalty, nevertheless regarded him as the right man to govern a difficult border territory. Herod had already made a favourable impression on his Roman overlords early on in his career when he had executed, without trial, a group of rebellious soldiers while governor of Galilee. Herod was summoned to account for his actions before a tribunal in Jerusalem. The 25-year-old Herod arrived at the tribunal in full battle-dress, giving the clear impression he would dispatch the judges if they did not accede to his wishes. The charges were quietly dropped. Herod's uncompromising style made a favourable impression on the Romans, who admired his ruthlessness and ability to command respect.

Herod rendered valuable assistance unto the new Caesar by providing Octavian's army with supplies, and was rewarded with Gaza and Jericho. A portion of Cleopatra's Celtic bodyguard was also handed over. By maintaining a close working relationship with Augustus, as the elevated Octavian was now known, Herod was able to acquire unlimited freedom in his own domain, and was soon able to extend the borders of the Land of Israel to what they had been under David nearly 1,000 years previously. Under Herod the Jewish province enjoyed its most prosperous period since Solomon. And like Solomon, once the resources were made available, Herod set about initiating a massive building programme, which included extensive renovation of the Temple.

If Herod's masterpiece were still standing today, it would be considered one of the wonders of the world. Josephus, who provides one of the most detailed descriptions of the Temple, describes it as 'a snowy mountain glittering in the sun'. The only remnants are the great slabs of stone that formed the foundations. Archaeologists today marvel at the feats of engineering, ingenuity and human endeavour that enabled Herod to construct this monstrous edifice. The foundation stones, which have been overtaken by centuries of construction, can be seen from a tunnel that adjoins the western wall of Herod's building. More than any of his other structures, Herod's Temple was designed to dominate the city, a monument both to the muscularity and indomitability of the Jewish spirit. The old sanctuary was doubled in size so that the Jerusalem Temple not only far outstripped Herod's other building projects, such as the Antonia fortress (named after Anthony, Herod's original patron), but every known temple in the Graeco-Roman world. It was the largest religious structure in the ancient world, a testament to Herod's confidence in his own authority when Rome's influence throughout the Mediterranean was at its apogee. Every available architectural design was used to adorn the Temple – porticoes, columns, cloisters, massive stone walls. No expense was spared on the project, which was begun in 20 BC and was not completed till long after Herod was dead, in about AD 60. Even the rabbis, who did not approve of Herod's close fraternisation with the pagan Romans, were forced to admit that 'he who has not seen the sanctuary has not seen a magnificent building'. The Temple, more than any of Herod's many other impressive architectural achievements, was the crowning glory of this remarkable, if bloodthirsty, tyrant.

It was while this massive construction work was taking place that a Jewish boy from Nazareth called Jesus first made his mark on the Temple authorities, when his parents took him to Jerusalem for the annual Passover festival. At this time Jews were obliged to make a pilgrimage to Jerusalem three times a year to visit the Temple, at Passover, Shavu'ot and Succoth. When Jesus' parents started on the journey back home at the end of their visit, they discovered their son was missing. After searching for him all over the city, they found him in the Temple, sitting with the Jewish teachers. When his parents attempted to reprimand him, Jesus replied: 'How is it that ye sought me? wist ye not that I must be in my Father's house?' (Luke 2: 49). The activities of Jesus in the Temple once he reached adulthood were not only difficult for his parents to fathom, but also for the Sadducees, who were already overwhelmed with the responsibility of administering the Temple, placating the Romans and keeping the rival Jewish factions at bay. Whenever Jesus went anywhere near the Temple he seemed determined to outrage the administrative authorities. On one occasion, for example, after he attacked the money-changers, he boasted: 'Destroy this temple, and in three days I will raise it up' (John 2: 19). Even in the last week of his life, Jesus appeared to have nothing but contempt for Herod's architectural extravaganza. When the disciples sought to show Jesus the new buildings of the Temple, he flew into a rage. 'See ye not all these things? verily I say unto you, There shall not be left here one stone upon another, that shall not be cast down' (Matthew 24: 2). Jesus' rage over Herod's aggrandisement at the Holy City's expense might also be explained as an expression of frustration at his failure to be accepted into the city during his ministry. Hence the lament: 'O Jerusalem, Jerusalem, which killeth the prophets, and stoneth them that are sent unto her! how often would I have gathered thy children together, even as a hen gathereth her chickens under wings, and ye would not!' (Matthew 23: 37).

It was, perhaps, hardly surprising that the Jewish authorities should take umbrage at these and other statements. It had taken them nearly 1,000 years to restore the Temple to its Solomonic glory, and here was this son of a Nazarene carpenter threatening to knock it down. It was inevitable that Jesus' activities would attract the attention of the authorities. In the run-up to the Passover festivities of AD 30, Jesus was arrested. Jesus had earlier been proclaimed King of the Jewish people in Galilee, an act alone which was sufficient to alarm Pontius Pilate, the Roman governor, whose preoccupation was watching for signs of incipient revolt. Jesus Barrabas, a local Jewish terrorist, had recently been taken into custody for committing murder during an attempted uprising, and the Romans were in no mood to indulge someone like Jesus of Nazareth, whom they regarded as nurturing dangerous political ambitions. When a mundane placeman like Pontius Pilate asks: 'Art thou King of the Jews?' and receives the reply 'My Kingdom is not of this world', he can hardly be expected to comprehend what is going on. Jesus provided Pilate with an opportunity to make an example of a Jewish fanatic, especially one who had upset so many of his fellow Jews. And so, after being cruelly tortured by the Roman garrison, Jesus, the self-proclaimed King of the Jews, was crucified.

The life, preaching and crucifixion of Jesus was not regarded as an extraordinary event, in the years immediately following his death, within the Jewish community or the wider Roman empire. The Jews had a long legacy of killing prophets and kings whom they took against, while the crucifixion of the leader of an obscure Jewish sect, together with two criminals, was nothing out of the ordinary for the Roman legionnaires. When a group of patriots rebelled against Roman rule following Herod's death, for example, 2,000 of them were crucified in one day. But the brutal attempts of the Romans to keep the querulous Jews in their place were not effective. Within a few years of the death of Jesus, fanatical Jews, who called themselves Zealots, were laying the groundwork for an organised revolt against Roman rule, which they portrayed as the war of 'the Sons of Light against the Sons of Darkness'. Tensions between the two communities, the Jews and their Roman overlords, were not exactly helped by the maniacal Roman emperor Caligula, who suggested placing a statue of himself in the Temple. As the Jews became more rebellious, the Romans tried to nip the revolt in the bud, on one occasion beheading one of the Jewish leaders and parading his head around Jerusalem. But the Roman administrators proved incapable of crushing the sedition, and by AD 66 a full-scale revolt had erupted.

At first the Zealots met with some success. They managed to capture and kill the main Roman garrison. The followers of Jesus, who were known by Romans and Jews alike as Nazarenes, were not interested in the Zealots' war of national liberation, and decamped across the River Jordan to the safety of Pella. Many of the more religious Jews, sensing that the revolt could only end in disaster, also made their excuses and left. One of them, Rabban Yohanan ben Zakkai, was smuggled out in a coffin. The moment of truth came in AD 70 when the Romans were finally in a position to suppress the revolt, which was entrusted to Titus, the son of the newly elected emperor Vespasian. After offering stiff resistance, the Jews were finally overwhelmed and massacred. In the mêlée, the Temple was accidentally set on fire. At first Titus tried to persuade his troops to put down the flames, but they were too caught up in the frenzy of battle to take any notice. By the time Jerusalem had been subdued and the majority of the Jewish population slaughtered, Herod's fine building, like Solomon's before it, had been reduced to ashes. It is said that when the Romans laid waste Jerusalem, splinters from the Temple entered the hearts of every Jew.

\*

The Roman subjugation of Jerusalem was a watershed in the city's history. For 1,000 years since David made the city his capital, Jerusalem had been a predominantly Jewish city. The city's Jewish character was now abruptly terminated, especially after the last Jewish revolt was brutally suppressed in AD 135. The reprisals exacted by the victorious Romans following the defeat of the charismatic leader, Simon Bar Kochba, resulted in all Jews being banned from setting foot in the city. The city was given a new name, Aelia Capitolina, and even the fledgling Christian community was purged of its Judaeo-Christian elements. By the end of the second century Jerusalem was little more than a functional Roman frontier town. Between AD 70 and 135, when the last revolt was put down, the Romans slaughtered thousands of Jews, and carried off thousands more in bondage. Six thousand Jews, for example, were taken to Corinth to build new canals.

Jerusalem had to wait another two hundred years before its fortunes revived. The conversion of the Roman province of Palestine to Christianity was the work of Constantine, the Byzantine emperor. Until then Christ's disciples had to overcome considerable obstacles to establish the new faith. For the first one hundred years, the Christians' communion rites led their contemporaries to suspect them of cannibalism, while the habit of addressing each other as brother and sister aroused suspicions of incest. And because, in those early days of the faith, most Christians firmly believed the Messiah would return at any moment, they tended to take an exceedingly condescending view of the world, gloating over its wicked ways and their own impending salvation. They were regarded as both hating the human race and being hated by the human race. It was only with the passage of time, and the growing realisation that it might take a while before the Messiah reappeared, that they began to make alternative arrangements. Initially they confined their conversion efforts to the Jews, but when they showed little interest, the Christians broadened their horizons. Indeed, in retrospect their decision to proselytise among gentiles was fairly revolutionary. Judaism was traditionally far more self-contained and, immediately after the death of Jesus, the early Christian leaders sought to imitate Judaic values. But St Paul and some of the other disciples resolved that Christianity needed a wider audience if it was going to succeed, and the easy access Christians had to the cosmopolitan empire of Rome greatly facilitated its success. Even so they had to overcome the substantial reservations of decent Roman citizens such as Cornelius Tacitus, the historian, who regarded Christianity as just one more contemptible superstition, evidence of the sad capacity of human beings to believe in strange things.

Throughout the early development of Christianity, Jerusalem figures prominently. It was also, despite the derogatory comments Jesus makes during his lifetime, the first headquarters of the new Church. Just before the Ascension Jesus tells the apostles: 'Ye shall be my witnesses in Jerusalem, and in all Judaea and Samaria, and unto the uttermost part of the earth' (Acts 1: 8). Although the city later became significant to Christians because of its associations with the death and resurrection, for the apostles, most of whom were Jewish, Jerusalem was held in the highest esteem both because of its Old Testament tradition and their belief in God's presence in the Temple. The dramatic revelation of the Holy Spirit takes place when the apostles are gathered at a house in Jerusalem for the Jewish feast of Shavu'ot, or Pentecost. St Peter performs his own miracles in the city and also manages to convert 3,000 to the new faith in a single day, no mean feat when the city's population at the time was estimated at no more than 60,000. The apostles believed their best chance for propagating the new faith was to preach in Jerusalem, and the first major clash between Christ's disciples and the Sadducees arises after people from the surrounding villages, hearing of the disciples' miraculous powers, bring their sick to the city to be cured. Peter and John are imprisoned and released on condition that they do not 'speak at all nor teach in the name of Jesus'.[1] When the apostles continue to ignore the warnings of the Jews, the Temple authorities have St Stephen stoned to death outside the city gates. This is followed by a great persecution against the church, and the majority of the new converts are scattered throughout Judaea and Samaria. But the apostles remain in Jerusalem, which they emphatically regarded as their headquarters.

This is also how St Paul, the most effective and widely travelled of the early Christian propagandists, viewed the city. Having trained as a rabbi in Jerusalem, Saul, as he was known before his Damascene

---

1 Acts 4: 18.

conversion, applauds Stephen's execution outside the city walls. Indeed, at the time of his journey to Damascus, he has obtained authorisation from the Jewish authorities in Jerusalem to round up any Christians he might find there and bring them back to the Holy City for punishment. During his travels through Asia Minor after his conversion, St Paul constantly berates the Jews in Jerusalem for denying the teachings of Jesus 'because they know him not'.[2] As with Jesus, it appears Paul is resentful that he has not been recognised by the Jerusalem establishment. But whenever Paul and the other disciples encounter doctrinal difficulties, they make their way to Jerusalem for consultations with 'the apostles and elders'.[3] Thus when a group of Judaean men question whether uncircumcised men can be saved, Paul and Barnabas 'go up to Jerusalem' to have the matter resolved. And after each of his excursions around the Mediterranean, Paul insists that he must return to the Holy City. After his trip to Macedonia 'he was hastening, if it were possible for him, to be at Jerusalem, the day of Pentecost'.[4] Even when his followers warn him against returning, Paul is adamant: 'For I am ready not to be bound only, but also to die at Jerusalem for the name of the Lord Jesus.'[5] Paul returns to Jerusalem, where he provokes a riot when he arrives at the Temple. Eventually he is escorted out of the city by a phalanx of seventy Roman cavalrymen and two hundred spearmen.

While Jerusalem is regarded as the 'Mother Church' by the early Christians, it is another three hundred years before its position is officially confirmed, with the adoption of Christianity as the official religion of the Byzantine Empire. At the time of the Emperor Constantine's conversion to Christianity, the area of Christ's crucifixion and burial in Jerusalem was covered with a temple dedicated to the Greek goddess Aphrodite. Constantine ordered a team of workers to remove the temple, including its foundations. In the course of their labours they uncovered Christ's tomb. 'At once the work was carried out,' the historian Eusebius relates, 'and, as layer after layer of subsoil came into view, the venerable and most holy memorial of the

2 Acts 13: 27.
3 Acts 1: 2.
4 Acts 20: 16.
5 Acts 21: 13.

Saviour's resurrection, beyond all our hopes, came into view.'[6] On hearing of their discovery Constantine gave orders that 'a house of prayer worthy of God' should be built on the site. The Church of the Anastasis (Resurrection), the prototype of the Church of the Holy Sepulchre, was the result. Started in AD 326 and dedicated in 335, the church became the focal point of Christian Jerusalem, a development which Eusebius regarded as God's vengeance against the Jews for their crime of 'the murder of the Lord'. The fortunes of the Jews by this time had reached a parlous state. Persecuted by the Christians at every available opportunity, their numbers continued to dwindle to the extent that when Gamaliel VI, the last Jewish patriarch, died in 425, the headship of Jewish affairs passed from the mother country to other locations, most notably Babylon where a flourishing Jewish community had survived from the days of exile. The origins of the Diaspora were well and truly established.

The development of Christian Jerusalem continued to gather pace. Apart from a brief scare in the middle of the fourth century when the emperor Julian made an abortive attempt to restore the Temple, Byzantine Jerusalem was a splendid city, materially as well as religiously. This pleasant state of affairs lasted for nearly three hundred years, one of the most prolonged periods of peace the city has ever enjoyed. But the city's tranquil repose was crudely shattered in AD 614 when the Persians, who 1,000 years previously had conquered the city and taken most of the Jewish population into captivity, returned to visit their destructive powers on the Christian inhabitants. The arrival of the Persian army at the gates of Jerusalem afforded the long-suffering Jewish population a rare opportunity to avenge the wrongdoings visited upon them. There had been a slight relaxation on the prohibition of the Jews from the city. They were allowed to enter once a year and permitted to mourn the destruction of their Temple by the only remaining part of the structure, the western wall. The Jews would lament and rend their clothes, and the place became known as the Wailing Wall. Now the Jews were offered the opportunity to avenge themselves for the persecution they had suffered at the hands of the Christians.

The Persians were anxious to discover the weak points in Jeru-

6 Eusebius, *Life of Constantine* (3: 28).

salem's defences, and the Jews were able to provide valuable intelligence. Then, having aided the Persian conquest of the city, the Jews actively participated in the orgy of violence which swept the city for three days. Most of the Christian inhabitants were massacred and most of the churches were burnt, including Constantine's Church of the Holy Sepulchre. Zachariah, the Patriarch, was taken off in chains to Persia, together with the 'true Cross', which was said to be the structure upon which Jesus had been crucified. For the next three years, Jewish rule was restored to Jerusalem, but a change of heart on the part of the Persian Shah resulted in the Christians being allowed to return to Jerusalem, and the Jews were again reduced to their pitiful state. Following the defeat of the Persians by a reorganised Byzantine army in 622, the Byzantine emperor Heraklios marched in triumph into Jerusalem in 629 and restored what was left of the 'true Cross' to the rebuilt Holy Sepulchre. The return of Byzantine rule to Jerusalem was short-lived. When, just nine years later, the warriors of the newly proclaimed faith of Islam appeared at the gates of Jerusalem, the memory of the atrocities committed by the Persians was still too fresh for the Christian citizens to offer much resistance. Sophronios, the Patriarch, agreed to surrender. In 638 the Caliph Omar came in person to negotiate the capitulation, and having taken the city, issued the following proclamation: 'In the name of God, the Compassionate, the Merciful. This is a writing of Omar al-Khattab to the inhabitants of the Holy House. You are guaranteed your life, your goods, and your churches, which will be neither occupied nor destroyed, as long as you do not initiate anything blameworthy.' For once, Jerusalem was taken without bloodshed.

The Caliph Omar was a trusty lieutenant of the Prophet Mohammed during the struggle to establish the new Islamic faith in the Hejaz, in what is now modern Saudi Arabia. Omar's first encounter with Mohammed was not auspicious. After Omar's uncle had been beaten up for insulting the Prophet, Omar vowed to avenge the insult to his family's honour by personally taking Mohammed's life. The Prophet had made many enemies in his native Mecca, and the ruling Koreish tribe are said to have promised Omar 100 camels and 1,000 ounces of gold if he successfully completed his mission. But while on his way to the house where the Prophet was in hiding, Omar encountered some relatives who were recent converts to Islam. Omar was persuaded to overcome his intense hostility to Mohammed, and to read the Koran. The fiery warrior was immediately converted to the faith and, when he finally found Mohammed, rather than take his life, he asked for his blessing.

Mohammed ibn Abdullah, who was himself a member of the powerful Koreish tribe, was aged about forty when, during the month of Ramadan in AD 610, the angel Gabriel appeared before him while he was meditating in a cave on a bleak and forbidding mountain called Hira, a few miles outside Mecca. The angel ordered him to recite some of the divine verses of the Koran, an event which was to result in Mohammed's proclamation as the Prophet of Islam. At first Mohammed was confused about what had occurred in the cave. But his devoted wife Khadijah, convinced that something very special was happening in their lives, asked one of her Christian relatives, a saintly priest called Waraqah, to explain the significance of the angel's visitation. It was thus a Christian who first helped Mohammed to understand that God had chosen him for a special purpose, to be the messenger of Islam.

It was during a later visitation by the angel Gabriel that Mohammed embarked upon his famous night journey to heaven, the *miraj*, by way of Jerusalem. The city would have been well-known to Mohammed, who was by nature a devout man, as a holy place, even before the Koran was revealed to him. The city was referred to by Arabs as *Beit al Mukaddas*, 'The Holy House', or the abbreviation *Al Quds*, 'The Holy', which is what Arabs call the city today. In the early days of Islam, the Prophet himself turned towards Jerusalem when he prayed. It was only after he fell out with the local Jewish tribes of Arabia, who refused to convert to Islam,[7] that he ordered his followers to pray towards the Kabah at Mecca. But the legend of Mohammed's fantastic journey through the seven heavens ensured that the Holy City occupied a special place in the teaching and tradition of Islam.

The journey began one night – according to custom, the darkest and most awfully silent that had ever been known[8] – when Moham-

7 One of the Jewish objections was their refusal to eat camel meat, which they deemed non-kosher.

8 Washington Irving, *The Life of Mohammed* (Ipswich, MA: Ipswich Press, reprinted 1989).

med had returned to Mecca. Mohammed was awoken by the angel Gabriel who brought with him a white steed called Al Borak, or 'lightning'. Borak was no ordinary beast. It had a human face, but the cheeks of a horse. It had eagle's wings all glittering with rays of light, and its whole form was resplendent with gems and precious stones. Mohammed mounted Borak which then, soaring above the mountains of Mecca, flew him to Jerusalem. When they arrived, Mohammed dismounted and tied Borak to the wall of the Temple. Mohammed then entered the Temple where he found Abraham, Moses and Isa (Jesus) and many more of the prophets. He prayed with them awhile, until a ladder of light came down from heaven. Mohammed, with the help of the angel Gabriel, ascended the ladder with the rapidity of lightning. He then passed through the seven heavens until he came within the presence of Allah. The Deity gave Mohammed many doctrines that are contained in the Koran, and gave orders that true believers pray fifty times a day. After consulting with Moses, Mohammed returned to His presence and asked for the number to be reduced. The Deity adjusted the number to ten. But when Mohammed reported back to Moses on this major concession, the Jewish patriarch was unimpressed. In what must be a seminal example of Jewish–Islamic collaboration, Moses warned the new Prophet that not even the children of Israel could be persuaded to observe so many prayers. Mohammed was encouraged to make a final plea and succeeded in getting the number brought down to five, which is what devout Muslims are now obliged to observe as the *salat*, the second pillar of Islam. Thereupon Mohammed descended to the Temple of Jerusalem by the ladder of light and, finding Borak where he had tied it, returned to Mecca.

Mohammed's night flight to heaven is related as a vision rather than an actual event. The only reference to the journey in the Koran is elliptical in the extreme: 'Glory be to Him who made His servant go by night from the Sacred Temple [Mecca] to the farther Temple [Jerusalem] whose surroundings We have blessed, that We might show him some of Our signs.'[9] The Temple, of course, had been

9 Koran, Sura 17: 1. The Koran refers to Jerusalem as *al-Aqsa*, the furthest point. The fact that Jerusalem is not specifically mentioned in the Koran is used by Zionist propagandists to play down the city's importance for Muslims.

demolished some five hundred years previously. But these few lines were sufficient to ensure that Mohammed's night journey had a profound effect on Jerusalem's development. For, after Mecca and Medina, Jerusalem became the third holiest city in Islam.

With Mohammed's death in 632, Omar became the first Caliph and determined to continue the Prophet's campaign to spread the new faith. Unlike Mohammed, who could only dream of Jerusalem, Omar not only visited the city, he conquered it. Nor was Omar in any doubt about the city's religious significance. One of his first acts was to ask the patriarch Sophronios for a tour of the holy places. Sophronios naturally took him to see the Church of the Holy Sepulchre, which had only just been refurbished after the Persian invasion. According to tradition, the patriarch invited the conqueror to say his midday prayers in the church, but Omar declined, saying that if he did, other Muslim worshippers would use the church, and it would be lost to Christianity. As Muslims were taught to respect other faiths, Omar insisted on praying elsewhere. He walked out of the church, and threw a stone. He then went to the spot where the stone landed, and undertook his devotions.

After inspecting the Holy Sepulchre, Omar was keen to find other, less Christo-centric sites. To him the church was impressive, but it served as a memorial to another and, by comparison with the Prophet, less important religious figure. The Jews, who themselves had little regard for the Christians after centuries of persecution, led Omar to the ruins of the Temple, and the site that, 1,600 years previously, David had purchased from Arauna the Jebusite. The Jews had recently enjoyed a three-year spell in charge of the city, and may even have attempted to rebuild the Temple before the Byzantines re-established their hegemony. They would certainly have known the location of their former Temples.

By the time Omar entered the city, little remained of Herod's masterpiece. The site was used as a garbage dump, an indication of how relations between the Christian and Jewish communities had deteriorated. It is said that Omar verified the site when he stopped a Christian woman who had travelled from Bethlehem to dump her rubbish in Jerusalem. When he asked her why she had travelled so far, she replied sarcastically: 'Because it is a holy thing to do.' Omar gave orders for the site to be cleared and for a mosque to be constructed.

The original mosque was a modest affair, made of wooden beams placed over the broken columns of the southern portico by the southern wall, close to Herod's Temple. In those early days of Islam it was imperative that new converts were not seduced by the competing faiths of Judaism and Christianity, and Omar was particularly concerned that the opulence of the Holy Sepulchre might tempt the weak-willed to adopt Christianity. It was not until a few years later, in AD 691, that Abdul al-Malik, one of Omar's successors, was able to build the magnificent edifice of the Dome of the Rock, which is now known as the Mosque of Omar. This broad expanse of rock, which today is protected by the huge golden dome that dominates Jerusalem's sky-line, was once the threshing-floor of Arauna the Jebusite, the place where David built his altar, and Solomon his temple. Such was the importance of this place for Mohammed and the first followers of Islam that they used the rock in Jerusalem as their *qibla*, the direction they faced for prayer.[10] As if this otherwise barren patch of land was not already imbued with an abundance of sanctity, after the Muslim conquest it became identified as the place from whence the Prophet ascended to heaven.

As with Jews, Islamic tradition is replete with legends about the rock's origins. According to one interpretation, 'The Rock of the Temple is of the stones of the Garden of Eden. At resurrection day, the Kabah stone, which is in holy Mecca, will go to the Foundation Stone in holy Jerusalem, bringing with it the inhabitants of Mecca, and it shall be joined to the Foundation Stone. When the Foundation Stone shall see the Kabah Stone approaching, it shall cry out: "Peace be to the guest."'[11] Muslims also believe that a mark on one section of the rock is the imprint of the Prophet's heel made when he made his heavenly ascent, which is today covered with a small turret. This is known as Kadam al-Sharif, the Heel of the Noble One.

Between AD 705–715, the Omayyad caliphs radically improved the

10 Mohammed changed the *qibla* towards the Kabah at Mecca, the holy stone (originally thought to be a meteorite) which was the main focus of pagan worship prior to the advent of Islam.
11 Vilnay, p. 19.

primitive mosque built by Omar, constructing the massive stone structure which they called *al-Aqsa*, 'the furthest', after the Koranic reference to Jerusalem in the story of the Prophet's night journey. The whole complex, which basically covered the site of the old Herodian Temple, was called the Haram al-Sharif, the 'Noble Sanctuary'. The Haram has survived intact and is today undoubtedly one of the jewels of Jerusalem's architecture. With its vast esplanade and solemn air of tranquillity, the complex serves as a genuine sanctuary from the frantic bustle that occupies so much of the modern city. As its dimensions are roughly equivalent to those of Herod's Temple, it provides more than a hint of the city's former, Judaic glory. Unfortunately, it also helps to illustrate why the centuries-old religious conflict over Jerusalem is both so complex and intractable. While the area is known as the Haram to Muslims, it is still referred to as the Temple Mount by Jews, in recognition of the fact that the Haram covers Herod's Temple and the holy rock. The Haram encapsulates 1,700 years of the city's multi-faceted religious development and experience. It is the location of three Jewish Temples, the place where Jesus and the apostles overcame intense hostility to establish Christianity on the ruins of the Jewish nation, and where Islam consolidated its emergence from the desert wastes of Arabia.

By standing on top of the Haram's west cloisters it is possible to look down directly on Jews praying on the Wailing Wall below. This is the epicentre of the modern Arab–Israeli conflict, the battle between Arab and Jew for Jerusalem. A short distance away, no more than a few hundred metres, the plain, grey dome of the Holy Sepulchre peers over the ramshackle rooftops of Arab dwellings, festooned with washing lines, television aerials and satellite dishes. All thanks to the vagaries of history, Jews, Christians and Muslims are obliged to live and worship within the confines of a small, cramped city. It is an experience none of them has relished.

# 3

# SKIRMISHES

*'Shall there be evil in a city, and the Lord hath not done it?'*
Amos 3: 6

Ballot boxes. Not the world's most exciting objects, but they fairly reflect the modern power struggle for control of Jerusalem. Those who sought to press their claim to the city in ancient times simply parked their siege engines beyond the ramparts and hammered the inhabitants into submission. Israelis and Palestinians have often shown a strong inclination to act in similar fashion, albeit using more up-to-date technology. Nowadays, however, the dictates of modern diplomacy recommend that the use of force is consigned to the history books. In this post-Cold War world, all the emphasis is on achieving political goals by peaceful means. Ideally this should be accomplished through peaceful negotiations conducted by elected representatives. For those representatives to be elected it is generally deemed to be helpful if they are nominated by free and fair elections. So when the Palestinian electorate of Jerusalem – a mere 30,000 souls – was invited, in January 1996, to vote for the first government in their long struggle for independence, it seemed only logical that they should do so through the ballot box. And that's what caused all the trouble.

After numerous false dawns, the Israeli–Palestinian peace process finally saw light on the White House lawn in the autumn of 1993 when Yitzhak Rabin and Yasser Arafat conducted their historic handshake before an admiring President Clinton and thousands of international dignitaries. At the ceremony the Israeli Prime Minister and Palestine Liberation Organisation leader set the seal on the Oslo Accords, the culmination of months of secret negotiations hosted by the Norwegian government. The accords laid out an elaborate timetable for building a comprehensive peace between Arabs and Jews, the cornerstone of which was the construction of a viable programme of political co-existence and mutual respect for Israelis and Palestinians. The accords stipulated that, once substantial progress had been made on crucial areas such as granting Palestinian Arabs self-rule, the two sides should sit down and discuss Jerusalem's future, whether it should remain the indivisible capital of Israel, or become part of the new Palestinian political entity. If all went according to plan, the final status negotiations, as they were called, would begin by 1996 at the latest – after Palestinian elections had been held and Israeli troops withdrawn from major Arab population centres – and Jerusalem's future resolved by 1999, just in time for the next millennium.

But before the ink had even had a chance to dry on the treaty the pundits were predicting that the issue of Jerusalem's future status would ensure the whole endeavour was still-born. The ceremony itself was used by both sides as an opportunity for them to post their pickets for this latest battle for control of the Holy City. As Rabin and Arafat walked on to the White House lawn for the signing ceremony, the thoughts of both the veteran army commander and the seasoned freedom fighter were firmly focused on their most treasured prize. For nearly thirty years the two men had waged a relentless war against each other and, for all the talk of reconciliation and ending bloodshed, neither man was disposed to make the slightest concession with regard to the city they both considered to be their undisputed capital. In his address, Rabin staked out his position with the assurance of a commander determined to allow his foe no quarter. 'We have come from Jerusalem, the ancient and eternal capital of the Jewish people,' he pronounced. Arafat was not to be out-manoeuvred at such an early stage in the joust. If there was to be lasting peace in the Middle East, he declared, 'all the issues of Jerusalem' must first be resolved, and that meant making Jerusalem the capital of a future Palestinian state.

Just over two years later, when preparations were being made for the Palestinians to elect their own government, the same conflict of interest that had been aired on the White House lawn came to bear on the prosaic matter of which type of ballot box Palestinian residents of Jerusalem could use. What might at first appear a perfectly straight-forward issue was in fact heavily overburdened with an excess of political baggage. After Israel's success in the 1967 Six-Day War, one of its first acts had been to reward itself by annexing the eastern sector of the city, including the Old City with its numerous holy shrines, captured from the Jordanian army. This meant the 150,000 or so Palestinian residents of the city's Arab sector in effect becoming Israeli citizens, a development which most of them regarded as a gross insult and which has been a source of inter-communal vio-lence ever since. The opportunity to participate in their own elections was received as a welcome and long-overdue opportunity by Jeru-salem's Arab residents to show they were no longer beholden to their Israeli masters.

The Palestinian electoral organisers, furthermore, most of whom were PLO veterans, were under considerable pressure to ensure fair play from the scores of international observers present to witness the occasion. While the PLO henchmen had been charged with secur-ing Arafat a convincing victory, they were still obliged to observe the niceties of democratic electoral protocol, even if most of those par-ticipating had already been 'persuaded' about which way they would vote. The effectiveness of Arafat's tactics was revealed to me when I went to interview the only other 'presidential' candidate, an elderly grandmother called Sameeha Khalil, a social worker who boasted no previous political experience. When I went to visit her at Ramallah, the Palestinian town ten miles north of Jerusalem, I learnt a great deal about Mrs Khalil's feeling for snow, but little about her political agenda. My visit happened to coincide with a freak snowstorm, and my 'audience' was interrupted when Mrs Khalil's secretary burst in.

'Sameeha, Sameeha, it's snowing,' she exclaimed. At this point Mrs

Khalil interrupted the ten-minute monologue she had been giving me about why she admired Yasser Arafat to observe the phenomenon first-hand.

'Isn't it beautiful? How refreshing!' she marvelled. Later, after all the votes were counted, Mrs Khalil won just over 10 per cent of the vote.

But back to the ballot boxes. The very mention of the words in the context of Jerusalem was sufficient to send Israel's political classes into paroxyms of trepidation. To allow Palestinians the use of the traditional ballot box (square shape, with a slot on top for voting papers) in Jerusalem was, they claimed, tantamount to surrendering their claim to the city as its eternal, indivisible capital. The Israelis were not concerned about how the Palestinians voted in the rest of the West Bank and Gaza: that had effectively become a Palestinian state-in-waiting ever since the signing of the Washington peace treaty. But Jerusalem was a different proposition. From the day the peace accords were signed the Israeli authorities had implemented a variety of security measures designed to amputate Jerusalem from the rest of the West Bank, a crucial and historic part of the city's natural economic and social constituency. One of the first measures undertaken by the Rabin government to increase its grip over the Holy City was to set up army roadblocks around the city outskirts. Tough restrictions were imposed on the number of Palestinians who could enter. The measures created great hardship for many Palestinian families who found they were suddenly unable to pay simple visits to relatives. Many others lost their jobs.

One of the more extreme cases of suffering caused by the restrictions concerned a young, pregnant Bedouin woman who was turned away at an Israeli checkpoint as she was making her way to a hospital in Jerusalem to give birth. In a state of panic, the woman walked for miles across the surrounding hills in her determination to get to the hospital, but when she arrived she was exhausted, and the baby was still-born.

As the Palestinian elections approached, the restrictions became even harsher as the Israelis sought to keep all political activity in the city to the barest minimum. Had the Israelis had their way, or so it appeared, none of the Palestinians living in Jerusalem would have voted at all. Votes, after all, mean political rights, and political rights, in the context of nationhood, mean sovereignty. Simply to allow Palestinians the use of ballot boxes would undermine the Israeli claims to the city.

So they attempted to work out a compromise. Jerusalem's Palestinian occupants were, according to the Israelis, expatriate Arabs, Palestinians living in a foreign country – i.e. Israel. Instead of ballot boxes they should use post boxes as, technically, they were participating in a postal ballot. The Palestinian Electoral Commission was not impressed. If that were the case, it countered, why were the candidates contesting half a dozen Jerusalem seats? The two sides, under pressure from international observers, were persuaded to put their heads together and thrash out a solution, which was duly reached. Jerusalem's Palestinian electorate would use neither a ballot box nor a post box. Instead the electoral authorities would provide specially adapted boxes where the slot for the ballot papers would be placed at a 45-degree angle at the top. Voters would not be allowed to place their voting slips in the boxes themselves. Instead they would hand their paper to an observer who would complete the task on their behalf.

These strange little receptacles, and the convoluted voting rituals, were just one of many anomalies that occurred when voting finally took place on a bright, chill Saturday morning in late January. Some of the more notable curiosities were the collection of do-gooders assembled from around the world who presented themselves at the various polling booths as international observers. Most had little if any idea about the intricacies of the Palestinian electoral process and were not much help to those aged Palestinians for whom the whole concept of democracy was alien.

Pride of place in this gallery of misfits was reserved for Jimmy Carter, the former American president. Carter likes to regard the Camp David peace treaty between Israel and Egypt as the great foreign policy achievement of his presidency (as opposed to his sycophantic support for the Shah of Iran, which was his most disastrous). If they live long enough, former American presidents have an uncanny knack of attempting to re-write history in their favour (Nixon and Watergate, Reagan and Iran-contra), and Carter is no exception. Dressed in a garish blue observer's jacket and sporting the statutory Carter baseball cap, the former peanut-farmer president was keen to create the impression that the right of Palestinians to vote for their own government had been won for them by none other than J. Carter. Nothing could be further from the truth. In his haste to extract the optimum political credit from the Camp David process in the late 1970s, Carter had effectively sold out the Palestinians. The Camp David Accords did, admittedly, include some appendices which set out some vague provisions for elections, but not for Palestinian self-rule. Gaza was to be under Egyptian control, and the West Bank was to remain part of Jordan. Palestinian self-determination was not part of Carter's agenda when he was America's president. All this appeared to have escaped Carter's memory as he busied himself hither and thither making sure the electoral procedures were properly observed. When I ran into him outside the main Post Office in Saladin Street, Carter was busy berating an Israeli policeman whom he accused of filming Palestinians as they entered the building to vote. The policeman denied the accusation, and the whole scene appeared deeply unedifying with a former American president attempting to bully a humble police officer about voting procedures.

An altogether more interesting experience was to discover that Lord Allenby, the grandson of the First World War liberator of Jerusalem, was also acting as an observer.

'He's up on the Mount of Olives,' I was told when I enquired after his whereabouts.

The scion of the great general was standing not far from the spot where his grandfather had masterminded the capture of the Holy City from the Ottoman Turks in 1917. This Lord Allenby, a ruddy-faced Berkshire farmer and regular attender at the House of Lords, was helping old Palestinian ladies to fill in their voting forms. What, I enquired, had prompted him to proffer his services?

'This is the conclusion of business left over from the British Mandate in Palestine,' he explained. 'At last the Palestinians are getting the chance to run their own affairs that they deserve.' I felt like pointing out that his grandfather was never that well-disposed to allowing the Palestinians self-rule. Immediately after capturing Jerusalem General Allenby proclaimed martial law, which continued even after he returned home at the war's end. But his descendant, like Carter, seemed more interested in haranguing local Israeli official-dom.

The efforts of these exotic worthies were academic: Arafat's henchmen had the election sown up months before the first vote had even been cast. Arafat's triumphant return to his Palestinian homeland in the summer of 1994 after thirty years on the run – the first acid test of the Oslo Accords – had been swiftly followed by cohorts of PLO veterans swarming into Gaza and the West Bank intent on establishing the PLO's hegemony throughout the 'liberated' area. The PLO – and especially Arafat's Fatah party – had never been well-disposed to democratic principles. The Palestine National Council, the organisation's ruling body, was used simply to rubber-stamp Arafat's decisions – on the rare occasions, that is, that he deigned to make them public. Arafat was determined to run the Palestinian Authority, the body set up to administer the self-rule areas of the West Bank and Gaza, in similar vein, and appointed his most trusted apparatchiks for this purpose.

Responsibility for the Jerusalem area and its Arab population was in the hands of Jibril Ragoub, a middle-aged former PLO fighter who revelled in the title 'Preventive Security Chief'. Ragoub spent fifteen years in an Israeli jail for past terrorist misdemeanours and is known as Arafat's 'Saddam Hussein', more for his uncompromising treatment of opponents than his thick moustache and robust frame. Shortly after Arafat's return he installed himself in Jericho, the 'moon-city' of ancient times which, together with Gaza, was one of the two administrative centres for the Palestinian self-rule enclaves. Within weeks of his arrival Ragoub had made a reputation for himself among the local Palestinian community as someone to be taken seriously. Such was the efficiency of his police force in administering summary justice to anyone who upset Arafat or broke the law that he quickly acquired the status of Palestine's bogey-man. Palestinians accused of minor offences such as traffic violations were required to attend Ragoub's office in Jericho to pay fines. Those who failed to turn up could expect a visit at dead of night from Ragoub's police officers, who would forcibly remove the offender. Those guilty of more serious crimes, such as car theft or collaborating with the Israelis, were seized by self-styled punishment squads and given a sound beating.

Similar treatment was meted out to Arafat's political opponents well before the election campaign had begun in earnest. Palestinian activists who had for years lived in dread of a midnight visit from the

Israeli security forces now found themselves being harassed by Ragoub's henchmen. Journalists were a particular favourite, especially those who were in any way critical of Arafat's leadership style. The Jerusalem offices of the respected Arabic daily newspaper *An Nahar* (Today) were closed temporarily for being too critical of Arafat. When publication resumed the editors took the warning to heart and ensured each day's front page contained a picture of Chairman Arafat's beaming visage. A Palestinian businessman who returned from twelve years' exile in Lebanon to start his own, politically independent magazine *Al Ummar* (The Nation), received a visit from forty of Ragoub's 'security officials' after just one issue, which happened to be highly critical of Arafat. On the first visit they severely damaged the presses. When the magazine persisted with its anti-Arafat line, they made a return call. This time they ransacked the newspaper offices, confiscating all remaining copies of the magazine before setting the building alight. The magazine ceased publication. The editor of another Jerusalem newspaper, *Al Quds,* found himself locked up in one of Ragoub's jails simply for failing to give a Christmas message from the Greek Orthodox patriarch to Arafat sufficient prominence. In the message the patriarch, who was intent on making a good impression, had made a flattering reference comparing Arafat to the Caliph Omar, Jerusalem's first Muslim ruler. In his defence the editor argued that he had carried the message on page eight because the front page already contained three pictures of Arafat. The explanation was summarily rejected, and the editor was given five days in jail for this serious error of judgement.

One of Ragoub's more intriguing interventions in the city's affairs at this turbulent time concerned the activities of a Palestinian businessman who had been given a considerable sum of money by Arafat to set up a new Palestinian radio station. The businessman booked into room 39 at the American Colony Hotel, one of the more prestigious establishments in East Jerusalem, where he announced, through a series of advertisements in the local press, that he would like to interview young female candidates, with the appropriate qualifications, who sought a career in broadcasting. Whether his hotel room contained the proverbial casting couch is not known, and what precisely occurred during the 'interviews' was never explained. What is known is that allegations of sexual impropriety were made against him by the daughter of a well-connected Palestinian family who answered the advertisement and went for an interview. Her father complained to Ragoub, who despatched a group of his finest 'security officials' to investigate.

The first the businessman knew he was in trouble was when he answered a knock at his hotel-room door. The hotel staff had seen Ragoub's men enter the premises and had remonstrated with them not to violate the property. Their appeals were to no avail. The security officials went straight to the businessman's room where, it is said, despite being mid-afternoon, they found him sitting in his underwear, with the curtains drawn, surrounded by empty whisky bottles. Without bothering themselves with formalities, the 'security officials' simply seized the man and then made use of one of the hotel carpets to bind him, like an overweight pancake. The struggling bundle was then carried outside, placed in the boot of a waiting Mercedes and driven to Jericho, where Ragoub was waiting for the businessman both to answer the charges of wrong-doing and to account for the substantial sums that had been spent on room-service entertainment. By all accounts the businessman endured an unpleasant few days in one of Ragoub's interrogation rooms until, by a stroke of good luck, the story of Ragoub's carpet raiders appeared in the Israeli press. This prompted Israeli politicians to question why PLO heavies were being allowed to conduct their strong-arm tactics in the Israeli capital. Ragoub now found himself under pressure to account for his actions and, given that the businessman had been on official Arafat business, the PLO leadership was anxious that the truth was not revealed. So the businessman was ordered to go to a pavement café in the centre of Jericho and sit there for the day. The Israeli press was informed of his whereabouts and descended on the town to interview him. When asked what he was doing in Jericho, the businessman merely replied that he was 'having a rest' at the invitation of Mr Ragoub. And there he remained for several days, chastened and, perhaps, a little wiser.

Thanks to the efforts of Ragoub and the rest of the PLO leadership, few were surprised when the Palestinian election results were finally announced. Arafat averaged more than 85 per cent of the vote and Arafat's candidates occupied a comfortable majority of the seats in the new Palestinian Legislative Council, the fledgling state's first democratically elected representative institution. In Jerusalem, the tactics were particularly effective; the PLO won a thumping 88.8 per cent of the vote. If Arafat's henchmen could congratulate themselves on a job well done, ordinary Palestinians felt they had been cheated of their long-held desire for democratic self-rule. While the elections laid the foundations for self-government, the democratic part of the equation did not square. There was widespread electoral misconduct, to put it mildly, to ensure Arafat's success and, with his PLO cronies calling all the shots, the prospects for the future seem decidedly inauspicious. One of the more perverse aspects of Arafat's victory was that it persuaded many Palestinian residents in Jerusalem to apply for Israeli passports. During twenty-nine years of Israeli occupation, most Jerusalem Arabs had resolutely declined Israel's standing invitation to accept citizenship (which was offered after Israel's *de facto* annexation of Arab East Jerusalem in 1967). The election campaign, and the manner in which Arafat conducted himself, persuaded them otherwise. They had taken a long, hard look at the brave new world of Palestinian statehood, and had found it wanting.

Yasser Arafat's stealth-like infiltration of Jerusalem's political landscape exacerbated considerably the highly sensitive nature of relations between the city's Jewish and Arab communities. Even at the best of times the city is a political and religious tinderbox. It is not sufficient that Jerusalem, home of the three great monotheistic faiths, should boast three Patriarchs, two Chief Rabbis and two Grand Muftis, and the centuries of inter-doctrinal discord that they represent. The city is also the subject of a decades-old dispute, by turns violent and always contentious, between Israelis and Palestinians who both claim it as their capital.

The inhabitants of this tormented place, no larger than the average provincial city, conduct their lives with an intensity that is unrivalled anywhere else in the world. There is a hardly a soul who does not have strong views on either the city's religious or political destiny. Everyone considers they are right and expects everyone else to share their view. There is no debate, for no one cares to countenance an opposing argument. It is hardly surprising that most Israelis and Palestinians prefer to keep their distance from the city. For all their constant proclamations that Jerusalem is the 'eternal, indivisible capital of Israel', most Israeli politicians choose to live in Tel Aviv, that hedonistic playground, a healthy one-hour's drive away from Jerusalem's hot-house passions.[1] Ordinary, secular Israelis regard Jerusalemites as being beyond the pale of normal, civilised behaviour. They refer to them as 'the hill people', like West Virginian hill-billies, only with attitude.

The burden of Jerusalem's interminable and various conflicts can have a direct bearing on the most mundane, everyday functions in the most unexpected, and often bizarre, ways. On a personal level I first experienced the city's many fault-lines shortly after taking up residence in the city in the mid-1980s. I had moved to Jerusalem after many years in Beirut – another city where religious harmony is in short supply – and wanted to throw a party. After consulting friends I drew up a guest-list that fairly reflected Jerusalem's ethnological divide. Caterers were arranged, drinks purchased and everything was set fair for a pleasant evening. It was only after the guests arrived that it dawned on me that the whole enterprise had been grossly over-optimistic. Before I had the chance to make the customary introductions, the Palestinians had congregated at one end of the room and the Israelis at the other. The only intercourse between the two groups took the form of fixing each other with forced smiles while muttering derogatory comments that were sufficiently audible to the opposing camp without being overtly offensive to the host. The battleground could not have been more clearly drawn. Nor would either side brook any compromise when I made a vain effort to break the ice by playing some dance music.

A similar predicament presented itself when it came to finding an apartment. To reside on the city's Arab side provokes accusations of anti-Semitism from the Israelis; living on the Israeli side attracts charges of pro-Zionist sympathies from the Arabs. For someone who subscribes to neither persuasion and is simply looking for somewhere to live, the whole city is the wrong side of the tracks. And where else on earth do estate agents pack a pistol in their waist belt when they go out with prospective clients, which is what happened when I went to see an apartment in an exclusively Jewish suburb of the city. Yoav, the agent, was a short, lean man in his mid-twenties who had just

1 A survey published by the Israeli newspaper *Ma'ariv* in November 1996 revealed that the majority of Israelis favoured Tel Aviv as their capital, as opposed to Jerusalem.

finished a tour of duty with the Israeli army in southern Lebanon. Why, I asked, did he need to carry a gun while showing me round an apartment?

'Arabs,' he replied.

'But there are no Arabs here. This is a Jewish neighbourhood.'

'You never know.' Yoav was a man of few words.

'Have you ever had to shoot an Arab?'

'No. But I'm always ready.'

In the end I settled for an apartment which seemed to satisfy these considerations. Situated in George Adam Smith Street, so named after the nineteenth-century Scottish archaeologist, the apartment was Arab-owned but located in a predominantly Jewish neighbourhood. When Israelis asked where I lived, I could tell them French Hill, a modern Jewish suburb built on land captured in 1967. Sheikh Jarrah was what I told Palestinians, an Arab neighbourhood named after one of the Caliph Omar's generals. The fact the apartment was the best available at an affordable rent was of little consequence.

The Oslo Accords certainly appeared to intensify the fierce passions engendered by every aspect of life in the Holy City. But any hope that these tensions could be kept at a manageable level were dashed with the election, within weeks of the Washington ceremony, of Ehud Olmert as Jerusalem's new mayor. In late 1993 Teddy Kollek was nearing the end of his third decade at City Hall. Although a committed Zionist, Kollek was a great advocate of peaceful coexistence between Jews and Arabs, even if the lion's share of municipal funds during his term of office had been directed almost exclusively towards Jewish projects to the detriment of Arab neighbourhoods, which might explain why most of East Jerusalem today looks as if it has been stuck in a 1950s timewarp. But even Kollek's normally congenial composure was sorely stretched on the day of the Washington festivities when, to celebrate the final realisation of decades of struggle for political recognition, crowds of young Palestinians thronged the streets of Jerusalem unfurling the distinctive black, white, red and green of the Palestinian national colours.[2]

2 The Palestinian flag was in fact designed by Sir Mark Sykes of Sykes–Picot fame for King Hussein of the Hejaz during the Arab revolt in the First World War. Its colours were meant to symbolise the past glory of Muslim Arab empires.

For years it had been an offence for any Palestinian to display the flag and during the seven-year Palestinian uprising, or *intifada*, many Palestinians had been shot dead by the Israeli army for doing just that. But this was a day for rejoicing, and, for those of us who had witnessed the brutality of the *intifada* years first-hand, it was surprising to see young Palestinians placing red carnations in the soldiers' gun-barrels while all the time chanting '*Biladi, biladi*' ('My country, my country'). Over on the other side of the city Kollek was not amused. 'The Palestinians' demand for the establishment of two capitals within the framework of a united Jerusalem cannot be accepted,' he fulminated. 'There has never been a Palestinian capital here and, in their prayers, they [the Palestinians] have always faced Mecca.' So far as Kollek was concerned, Jerusalem was the undisputed capital of Israel and so it would remain.

That was to be Kollek's last official pronouncement on the matter. Two months later the venerable Kollek's paternalistic, if politically loaded, tenure drew to an abrupt end with Olmert's election as his successor. Olmert's victory derived from his ability to appeal to the tens of thousands of Jews of Sephardic origin who had settled in the new satellite settlements around the city and the Jewish religious orthodox vote. Israel's Sephardic community is naturally inclined towards voting for the right-wing nationalist Likud party, while Jerusalem's large ultra-Orthodox community votes for whoever agrees to its demands for a more orthodox religious administration of the city. The combination of these forces resulted in the election of a mayor with a mandate to be both more uncompromising and more conservative in his running of the city. At the very moment when peace and goodwill were supposed to be breaking out all over the Middle East, Jerusalem's administration was seized by ideological bigots.

Despots like Olmert and Ragoub somehow deserve each other. Both are masters at using any methods at their disposal for political manipulation. Olmert is not a man to do things by halves. Now that he was in control of a powerful administrative machine,[3] Olmert was determined to manage it for his own political ends. So when Ragoub

3 The Jerusalem Municipal Council has wide-ranging powers which date back to the British Mandate, when the idea was first mooted of making Jerusalem a self-sufficient, international city, immune from the tawdry world of politics.

started to make his presence felt in the city, just a few months after Olmert's election, to build Arafat's power-base, he encountered an adversary who was more than his equal. If Ragoub was expert at clandestine intimidation, then Olmert was a master at deploying every technical device – planning laws, building regulations, law and order restrictions – to counter the threat.[4] The tragedy for Jerusalem was that, while the rest of the world was under the impression that the city's future rested in the hands of Yitzhak Rabin and Yasser Arafat, in reality the battle for day-to-day control of the city was being fought between people like Olmert and Ragoub.

Olmert's first opportunity to play to an international gallery came in the summer of 1994, when Arafat made his triumphant return to Gaza and the West Bank. As soon as Arafat set foot on Palestinian soil the Israeli right – and even some on the Israeli left – claimed that it was only a matter of days before Arafat would install himself in Jerusalem. The official Israeli position was that Arafat, a Muslim, could travel to the Holy City to pray, but not for anything else. This position was, of course, totally untenable for Arafat. To accept such conditions would be to accept Israel's claim to sovereignty over the city. If Arafat were to do that he would be politically, if not physically, a dead man. Olmert chose to ignore this rather salient point and opted to stir up a climate of political and religious hysteria in the city. All it took to provoke Olmert into action was a throwaway remark made by Arafat when he addressed a large crowd of his followers in Gaza. 'Jerusalem, Jerusalem, Jerusalem,' intoned the PLO leader before tens of thousands of cheering Palestinians. And referring to all the kinsfolk who had been killed in the violent conflict to win independence from Israel he said: 'We will pray for the martyrs in Jerusalem, which is the first site for Muslims.'

The mayor could not resist the temptation of making political capital out of Arafat's posturing.

'We will bring one million people to Jerusalem,' to line the walls of the Old City to keep Arafat out, announced the mayor. Olmert's statement was followed by a parade of thousands of religious and

4 Apart from being charged with misappropriating Likud funds while serving as party treasurer in the 1980s, in 1996 Olmert was asked to pay £900,000 by Uzi Sivan, the auditor for Jerusalem City Council, for breaking city regulations.

right-wing Israelis through the centre of Jerusalem demanding that Arafat not be allowed to enter, while flying pickets of religious Jews were dispatched to all the main intersections to bar the PLO leader's passage. Barricades of burning tyres were set up by Jewish extremists on the Jericho road. In a more ominous development, a group of Jewish extremists calling themselves Herev David, the sword of David, claimed responsibility for the murder of a Palestinian in Jerusalem whose body was found with a single shot to the head. The group said the murder had been carried out as a 'welcome present' to Arafat.

Olmert's uncompromising political style was in evidence again a few months later, when President Clinton made a high-profile visit to Jerusalem in October 1994 as a gesture of solidarity to the peace process. Clinton had just attended the signing ceremony for the latest development in the peace process – a peace treaty between Israel and Jordan. On his way home Clinton's aides arranged for him to make a whistle-stop tour of the Holy City, his first since being elected president. This in itself was an ambitious undertaking, for previous White House incumbents tried to avoid entering such a politically charged minefield. Israel's annexation of the city had, after all, never received international recognition. Buoyed by the peace process's apparent success, Clinton decided to press on regardless. Plans were made for Clinton and Hillary, his wife, to make a private visit to the city's three main holy places – the Church of the Holy Sepulchre, the Dome of the Rock and the Wailing Wall. Everything was in place until Olmert decided to get involved. He insisted that, as the city's elected representative, it was his duty to escort the American president on the tour, even if his claim to represent East Jerusalem, which includes the Old City, remains an issue of international dispute. An unholy diplomatic row erupted. Faisal Husseini, the PLO's chief representative in Jerusalem, said Olmert had no right to escort the president on occupied territory, and warned Clinton that the Jerusalem issue was a potential 'black hole' which could swallow up and destroy the peace process. Olmert countered by claiming: 'One thing must be clear. We are sovereign in all of Jerusalem. There is no part of Jerusalem that we, and I as Mayor, will agree is outside our authority.'

Clinton took one look at the nest of vipers he had unwittingly disturbed and thought better of his Jerusalem walkabout. His aides made admirable behind-the-scenes efforts to retrieve the situation, and various diplomatic soundings were taken to see if an alternative guide could be found. One of the candidates approached was a prominent figure among the city's Christian community and, in view of his deep dislike of Israelis, it was probably just as well he was not entrusted with the president's care. This cleric, for example, is in the habit of telling friends his personal definition of anti-Semitism. 'Anti-Semitism,' he confides, 'is hating Jews more than is absolutely necessary.' One can only imagine the impression he might have made if the President of the United States had been left alone in his company for half an hour.

It quickly transpired, however, that the whole undertaking was infeasible, mainly because various Palestinian families possessed the all-important keys to the various shrines, and they were not prepared to open them up without the PLO's permission, which the PLO was not prepared to grant.

The same evening I bumped into a middle-aged Palestinian called Nusseibeh, a member of one of Jerusalem's most celebrated Muslim families. The Nusseibehs have been in possession of the keys to the Holy Sepulchre since they were granted the privilege by Saladin, the Kurdish warrior, after he conquered Jerusalem in 1187. This Palestinian was the family member responsible for opening and closing the church each day, and he was now slumped over the bar having consumed most of the contents of a bottle of Johnny Walker Black Label whisky. An old, large brass key, the size of a man's hand, was lying on the bar next to the bottle – the very key to the shrine which covers the place of Christ's crucifixion and resurrection.

'See this key,' he informed me. 'This is the most important key in Christendom. Clinton wanted it but he can't have it. Even the President of the United States can't tell us Nusseibehs what to do.'

At a dinner held for Warren Christopher, Clinton's Secretary of State, later that evening at the British consulate, the discussion naturally focused on the day's events. In the course of the conversation one of the guests compared modern Jerusalem to a description of the city provided by Mukaddasi, the tenth-century Arab chronicler. 'Jerusalem,' the Arab traveller had written, 'is as a golden basin filled with scorpions.' Mr Christopher said nothing, but smiled wryly.

*

Orient House is another favourite Olmert bugbear. A rambling, Ottoman-style building in East Jerusalem, Orient House has become the PLO's unofficial headquarters in Jerusalem. Built at the turn of the century by the Husseini family, the building had originally been used as a hotel. Kaiser Wilhelm II was one of the hotel's more distinguished guests when he made his famous pre-war trip to the city. The property had then been used for a variety of purposes, including a private residence for the Husseini clan, until, in the 1980s, Faisal Husseini, the predominant PLO figure in Jerusalem, turned it into a quasi-political institution called the Arab Studies Centre. During the *intifada* Orient House was regularly raided by the Israelis, and many of its staff – including Faisal himself – were jailed for PLO membership. It was only after the peace process began in earnest with the opening of the Madrid summit in late 1991 that Orient House became recognised as a quasi-legitimate political establishment. The right-wing Shamir government complained bitterly about the development of Palestinian political institutions in Jerusalem, but there was little they could do with so much international pressure being brought to bear to ensure the peace process's success. And so long as Teddy Kollek was mayor, the attitude of the city authorities was benign, if not uncritical. The situation, however, changed dramatically with Olmert's election.

Whenever I've been inside Orient House to visit various Palestinian officials, I've always been struck by how unlike a hotbed of political insurrection it appears. The corridors are filled with well-dressed, middle-class Palestinian ladies parading up and down with cups of coffee and piles of paper, smiling coyly at the visitors. Most of the officials are educated, articulate Palestinians, some of whom have studied at the Hebrew University on Mount Scopus with their Israeli counterparts. The interior of the building itself is rather run-down, with old chairs and tables and a decidedly pre-Mandate electrical system.

There was one occasion, when I was trying to arrange a meeting with Faisal on the telephone, when his secretary suddenly broke off our conversation.

'Come quick, come quick. The Jews are attacking us. It's terrible. Come quick.' She hung up.

Fearing the worst, I hurried over to East Jerusalem half-expecting, from the hysteria that had gripped the lady's voice, to find Orient

House ablaze and the pavement outside strewn with the corpses of butchered Palestinians. Instead I encountered the peculiar spectacle of a group of Israeli politicians, officials and various hangers-on conducting an ad hoc Knesset committee meeting in the middle of the street. They were sitting around a large, plastic garden table. A collection of bright yellow parasols protected them from the midday sun and, from a distance, they looked as though they were enjoying an alfresco picnic.

The meeting was chaired by Rehovam Ze'evi, the founder and leader of the Moledet (birthright) party which wants the entire Arab population of the West Bank transferred to other Arab countries ('They have twenty-one countries, we have only one' is one of the party's popular campaign slogans). There were a couple of deputy mayors from the City Council and the organisers were expecting – any minute now, they told me – the arrival of Benjamin 'Bibi' Netanyahu, who was then the opposition leader of the Likud party and one of Olmert's closest political allies. The mayor himself was unable to attend the meeting, but had given this strange example of political exhibitionism his personal blessing. The purpose of the gathering was to demonstrate that the whole of Jerusalem was Israeli property and to show the Palestinians trying to work inside Orient House that they had no legitimate political claim to the city. Some of the hangers-on were chanting 'You don't belong here, go to your Arab cousins' at the building's occupants, and some of the more excitable Israelis, *kippa*-wearing settlers, fired shots in the air. The Border Police, a paramilitary unit, who had been asked to keep a watchful eye on the proceedings, kept their distance. I could not help thinking that if Arab demonstrators started firing guns in the air, they would be shot dead on the spot.

It was all part of a highly publicised and highly politicised Olmert campaign to get Orient House closed. But despite his numerous threats to invoke various planning violations to justify the termination of the PLO's activities in Jerusalem, Olmert's efforts, which he pursued relentlessly throughout the summer of 1995, were ultimately frustrated by Yitzhak Rabin, the Prime Minister, who forcibly pointed out that he, and not a mere city mayor, would decide what the PLO could and could not do within the city precincts.

\*

The whole Israeli political climate, and the delicate dynamics of the peace process, suffered a dramatic and traumatic change when Rabin was murdered in November, gunned down by a fellow Jew who fired three dum-dum bullets into the Prime Minister's back at point-blank range. Rabin was murdered in Tel Aviv, where he lived, but the climate of hatred and fanaticism that politicians like Olmert had fuelled in Jerusalem, where Rabin worked, as part of their campaign against the peace process was blamed for the Prime Minister's murder. Rabin's widow, Leah, said as much when she accused Netanyahu and his associates – which included Olmert – of responsibility for her husband's death. 'There definitely was incitement which was strongly absorbed and found itself a murderer, who did this because he felt he had the support of a broad public with an extremist approach,' was her bitter analysis.

Yigal Amir, the assassin, belonged to the lunatic fringe of Jewish fanatics who believed the peace process was a sin against God. He was associated with other extremist groups, like Eyal, which carried out terror attacks against Arabs – often with impunity – and others which planned to destroy the Dome of the Rock and replace it with the Third Temple. The tragedy of Rabin's murder for those Israelis with a deep attachment to Jerusalem was that few had done more than the murdered Prime Minister to secure the city for the Jews. In 1948, during the battle for Jerusalem, the young Rabin had been the commander charged with trying to keep the supply route life-line open to the besieged city. As Israel's commander-in-chief in 1967, he personally supervised the city's conquest. If ever a man was devoted to the cause of Jewish Jerusalem, his name was Yitzhak Rabin. By comparison the macho claims of Olmert and his ilk appeared distinctly pallid.

Rabin's funeral at the military cemetery on Mount Herzl attracted legions of international dignitaries. Their presence in Jerusalem bore testimony to the enormous strides that had already been taken on the path to peace. King Hussein made his first appearance in the city after making peace with Israel, a city where he had seen his great-grandfather, King Abdullah, murdered by a Palestinian nationalist in 1951. President Hosni Mubarak of Egypt made the first visit by an Egyptian leader since Anwar Sadat who, after embarking on his own historic visit to Jerusalem in 1978, was murdered by Islamic fanatics for making peace with Israel. There were other, less familiar faces, taking their seats next to the shrine of Theodor Herzl, the founder of Zionism: the Moroccan Prime Minister, emissaries from Qatar and Oman. The political complexion of the modern Middle East was clearly undergoing a radical transformation.

Only one Arab dignitary was conspicuous by his absence. Yasser Arafat spent the day watching the funeral on television at his office in Gaza. Two years after the glitz of the White House lawn fanfare, Arafat, rather sulkily, claimed he did not feel welcome, and so stayed away. At least that was the official excuse. 'He did not receive an official invitation,' explained one his aides. 'He is not just any old leader. We did not even receive an indication from the Israelis that he would be welcome.' The truth of the matter was that Arafat did not want his first visit to Jerusalem to be dictated by events in Israel, no matter how tragic. Such was the strength of emotions the city aroused in the PLO leader and his followers that Arafat could not even bring himself to honour with his physical presence the memory of his partner in peace. The day that Yasser Arafat went to Jerusalem would be a day of triumph, a day when the city was proclaimed the capital of an independent Palestinian state, *his* Jerusalem. Until then, he was prepared to bide his time, no matter how many inducements were set before him.

The general election that followed Rabin's murder, in May 1996, was essentially a contest over which of the candidates the Israeli electorate wanted to continue the peace process. Yitzhak Rabin, with his distinguished army record, had been elected in 1992 with a clear mandate to negotiate peace by an Israeli electorate that had not enjoyed the experience of being targeted by Saddam Hussein's Scud missiles during the Gulf War. Israelis trusted Rabin. He was a fighter, and he would avoid anything that jeopardised their security. After the experience of the Holocaust and the long struggle to establish their own state, security is a national obsession for all Israelis. The new Prime Minister would need to reassure his public that their future was safe in his hands. In the immediate aftermath of the assassination, Shimon Peres, Rabin's long-time rival for the Labour leadership, with whom he had shared the Nobel Peace Prize in 1994, was the clear favourite. Apart from enjoying the Rabin sympathy vote, Peres was widely regarded as the driving force behind the peace process. If the voters had any reservations about Peres, it was that he could give the impression of being a hopeless romantic who might give too much away to the Palestinians in pursuit of his dream of lasting peace in the Middle East. Had Peres called an election immediately after Rabin's assassination, he would in all probability have won a resounding victory. But he hesitated. Peres was aware he suffered a credibility problem with the Israeli public – he had failed to win a clear mandate on four previous occasions – and he wanted time to continue making progress on the peace process to persuade the Israeli electorate that they could trust him.

Peres's hopes of success, however, were shattered in late February and early March 1996 when two devastating explosions in central Jerusalem made the security-conscious Israeli public question openly the wisdom of pursuing a dialogue of peace. At about 7 A.M. on Sunday 25 February, a Palestinian suicide bomber boarded a number 18 bus on the outskirts of the Old City. Sunday is the beginning of the working week for Israelis, and the bus was full of ordinary workers – Jews and Arabs, even some Romanian construction labourers – making their way to their jobs in the city centre. As the bus reached the end of Jaffa Street, Jerusalem's main shopping thoroughfare, the suicide bomber detonated a powerful device that he was carrying in a duffel-bag on his back. The bomb destroyed the bus, killing and maiming the forty or so passengers on board. A week later, at the same time, at almost the same spot, another suicide bomber blew himself up on another number 18 bus. In total forty-five people were killed in the Jerusalem bus bombings (a third attack took place in Tel Aviv), hundreds more were wounded and Israeli confidence in the peace process shattered.

Messages and gestures of support flowed in, but Peres found it impossible to persuade Israelis that his peace policy was not directly responsible for the attacks. Peres did not help his case by claiming that right-wing activists within Israel's security forces had encouraged Palestinian extremists to commit the attacks to undermine confidence in the Labour government and ensure victory for Likud. Netanyahu furiously denounced the allegation, for which Peres had no evidence, and the Prime Minister's standing with the Israeli public fell further, especially as Peres was ultimately forced to withdraw the comment.

To bolster Peres, President Clinton hastily arranged an anti-terrorism summit at the Egyptian resort of Sharm el-Sheikh. Rudolph Giuliani, the mayor of New York, arrived on a solidarity visit and took a highly publicised ride on a number 18 bus through central Jerusalem. But their efforts were in vain. Peres was regarded as having committed the unforgivable sin of compromising Israel's security for his own political ambition. During the election campaign the worldly-wise Peres was unable to counter the taunts of Netanyahu, his rival, who accused him of making Israeli children too terrified to take the bus to school.

The peace process was the main election issue, and Jerusalem inevitably became a major focus of attention for both candidates. To win over the floating voters, both Peres and Netanyahu made strong declarations in support of maintaining Jerusalem's status as the undivided capital of Israel. In the city itself supporters of the rival candidates covered their cars in stickers with slogans such as 'Jerusalem is united under Peres' and 'Jerusalem is only safe with Netanyahu'. The Peres campaign, however, was slightly hindered by claims – never substantiated – that, in the course of the Oslo negotiations, the Labour leader had made a secret pact with Yasser Arafat on Jerusalem's future. The agreement was said to be contained in a private letter Peres had written to Arafat in which he had made certain commitments regarding Palestinian claims to Jerusalem. Peres himself roundly denied that any such agreement existed, and in his public pronouncements he was unequivocal in stating that he had no intention of surrendering Israeli sovereignty over any part of the city. Even so, one of Peres's final acts as Prime Minister before the elections was to participate in the official opening of the final status negotiations with the Palestinians, under which, according to the terms of the Oslo Accords, the Jerusalem issue would be resolved by 1999.

As with the Palestinian poll, voting for the Israeli elections in Jerusalem in May 1996 was a tense affair. Security was tight in anticipation of further suicide attacks; soldiers were deployed on the streets while police helicopters patrolled overhead. It was not, perhaps, the best atmosphere in which to secure a mandate for peace, and was probably the most likely explanation for Netanyahu's narrow election victory (he won by just 30,000 votes). Netanyahu's success followed a similar pattern to Olmert's victory in the Jerusalem elections three years previously – appealing to a powerful combination of the hard right and the ultra-Orthodox religious establishment. In Mea Shearim, the city's staunchly religious neighbourhood, long queues of religious Jews formed to vote for Netanyahu. 'I don't know much about politics,' said one young Yeshiva student. 'I am doing what the rabbis have instructed, and the rabbis have instructed me to vote almost exclusively for Netanyahu.' Less than half a mile away, in Sheikh Jarrah, the indications at the Arab polling station were that Peres was going to have a bad day. Apart from securing the centrist and secular Israeli vote, Peres's victory depended on persuading Arabs with Israeli citizenship to vote for his Labour party. In Jerusalem there were about 5,000 Arabs entitled to vote, but on the instructions of Faisal Husseini, who regarded Palestinian participation in the election as legitimising Israeli claims over Jerusalem, nearly all of them boycotted the process.[5]

The result was greeted with joy by those opposed to the peace process and with despair by those who had hoped to build a better life. 'Half the Israeli public is now going around with a feeling that redemption is at hand: the other half believes that it is trapped in a hell on earth,' commented the conservative Israeli daily newspaper *Ma'ariv*. No one was more delighted with Netanyahu's victory than Ehud Olmert, who proclaimed, in a surfeit of enthusiasm, that 'the state of Israel has been saved'. Labour supporters were bitter, and claimed the result was in effect a victory for Yigal Amir who, by murdering Rabin, had succeeded in his plan to wreck the peace process. There were shameful scenes outside the home of Rabin's widow, Leah, after she had said, in a throwaway remark, that she felt like leaving the country because of the defeat suffered by her late husband's Labour party. A group of Netanyahu's supporters demonstrated outside her house urging her to leave while a collection box, marked 'contributions for Leah's journey', was passed around.

Within days of Netanyahu's victory the outline of the Jerusalem battleground had undergone a serious revision. On the day that the Likud leader was officially proclaimed the victor, Yasser Arafat

5 This trend was reflected nationwide. An estimated 100,000 Israeli Arabs did not vote in protest against Peres's offensive in southern Lebanon, Operation Grapes of Wrath, earlier that spring. Their abstention cost Peres the election.

declared that the Palestinian people were nearing the point when they would declare an independent state with Jerusalem as its capital. Netanyahu was quick to respond. 'Jerusalem shall never be divided and will remain united under Israel's sovereignty,' he said. As for the agreements signed between Rabin and Arafat on the White House lawn, Netanyahu declared: 'I will not respect any agreement regarding Jerusalem.' After three years of skirmishing between Israelis and Palestinians over their beloved Jerusalem, little appeared to have been achieved but the shedding of more blood.

# 4

# PROMISES

*'Whereby are given unto us exceeding great and precious promises'*

II Peter 1: 4

The origins of the contemporary Arab–Israeli conflict for the Holy City are to be found in the international havoc wrought by the First World War and the city's capture by Britain. Shortly before Christmas 1917, General Sir Edmund Allenby became the first Christian commander to occupy the Holy City since the Crusades. As he led his victorious troops into Jerusalem he was more than aware of the heavy responsibility he was undertaking. A few years previously, in 1897, Kaiser Wilhelm II of Germany had caused enormous offence to the local Muslim population during a visit to Jerusalem by having Jaffa Gate widened, one of the main thoroughfares, so that his considerable bulk could be fitted into the Old City on horseback. By contrast, Allenby dismounted and entered the city bareheaded and on foot, a gesture of humility before the city's overwhelming religious and historical prowess. In his pocket Allenby carried a proclamation establishing martial law, the wording of which had been formulated by the Foreign Office. In view of later events, the statement, which he read from the steps of David's Citadel, contains a certain pathos. 'We have come, not as conquerors, but as deliverers. It is our intention to open a new era of brotherhood and peace in the Holy Land.'

Britain's support for the Arab revolt against the Ottoman Empire, immortalised by the adventures of T. E. Lawrence, had raised concerns at the Colonial Office that, if successful, Britain might cause deep offence among the British Empire's Muslim subjects, particularly those in India. The Caliphate, the supreme body that represented the interests of Muslims worldwide, still resided in Istanbul, and defeat of Turkey might have been interpreted to imply the defeat of Islam. The authorities in London were more concerned with the stability of the Indian empire than the liberation of 'the most famous city in the world', as David Lloyd George, the British Prime Minister, boasted that Christmas. To ensure Muslim sensibilities were not offended, General Allenby not only dismounted but sought to reassure the Muslim population that administration of the city by a Christian power would not affect their religious observance.

There was, however, a fatal flaw in this act of conciliation. Shortly before Allenby's capture of Jerusalem, Lord Balfour, the British Foreign Secretary, issued a declaration on 2 November in which the British government formally endorsed 'the establishment in Palestine of a national home for the Jewish people'. The declaration was partly a response to the sustained lobbying of the recently formed Zionist movement which, in seeking a solution to the constant persecution of East European Jewry, articulated the notion of creating an independent nation for the Jewish people. But Balfour's statement was not solely an exercise in altruism. The great imperialist saw an opportunity, in the post-war world, to secure Palestine for Britain and thereby enhance the protection of the all-important Suez Canal, Britain's gateway to the Indian empire. What Lord Balfour and his Foreign Office advisers overlooked when drafting this statement was that they had already given a similar undertaking, only the previous year, to the Arab leaders as part of the deal by which they promised to support Britain in its war against the Ottoman Empire. In a letter written by Sir Henry MacMahon, the British official responsible for negotiating with Sharif Hussein, the guardian of Mecca and then the region's most influential Arab leader, the British government said it was 'prepared to recognise and support the independence of the Arabs'. The

Arabs took this to mean that if the Arab revolt were successful in freeing their land from Ottoman rule, they would gain independence. As Palestine was part of the territory occupied by the Ottomans, they assumed that, if freed, it would be included in the booty, together with Jerusalem.

One of Britain's more significant contributions to Jerusalem was to turn it into the capital of the new administrative province of Palestine, the first time the city had enjoyed this status since the Crusaders established the Kingdom of Jerusalem in the twelfth century. After Saladin reconquered the city in AD 1187, Jerusalem was regarded by its Muslim rulers as a religious rather than a political centre, and for the four hundred years that the city was under Ottoman rule, it was reduced to the status of a provincial town, part of the Ottoman *vilayet*, or province, of Syria, with Damascus as the regional capital. Jerusalem became a neglected backwater of the Ottoman Empire. The American writer Mark Twain, who visited the city in the mid-nineteenth century, when it had a population of 14,000, found it in a woeful state. He was impressed by the exotic collection of Muslims, Jews, Greeks, Latins, Armenians, Syrians, Copts, Abyssinians, Greek Catholics and Protestants, but in *The Innocents Abroad*, his account of an exotic Mediterranean excursion, he recorded his distaste for the Ottoman administration of the city. 'Rags, wretchedness, poverty and dirt, those signs and symbols that indicate the presence of Muslim rule more surely than the crescent flag itself, abound,' he wrote. 'Lepers, cripples, the blind and the idiotic assail you on every hand . . . Jerusalem is mournful, dreary and lifeless. I would not desire to live here.'

The British decision to make Jerusalem its administrative centre was the by-product of its desire to control the area known, under the terms of the League of Nations mandate conferred on Britain in 1922, as Palestine. Until the British government decided it would be useful to have military spheres of influence on both sides of the Suez Canal, as opposed to just one in Egypt, Palestine was more an idea than a place; like ancient Canaan, somewhere vaguely related to the Holy Land. Britain's geographical illiteracy was revealed in the course of MacMahon's correspondence with Sharif Hussein when British officialdom's vagueness about Palestine's precise whereabouts came to light. Britain's pledge to recognise Arab independence included the proviso that the area west of Damascus would be excluded from the commitment, an area which Sir Henry thought was Palestine but today constitutes much of modern Lebanon. Palestine's borders became more clearly defined during the protracted negotiations at Versailles at the Great War's end, where the victorious powers assumed responsibility for dissecting the corpse of the Ottoman Empire. The Versailles negotiations were characterised by intense rivalry between Britain and France over the post-war settlement, a rivalry that was reflected most acutely in the Middle East. Britain had already set out its intentions regarding the Holy Land and, to achieve this objective, agreed that France should be compensated with a mandate to govern Syria, thereby establishing a new balance of power in the region.

The British Mandate, for all the problems it would later encounter, began in an atmosphere of high hopes and much optimism. Sir Ronald Storrs, the former Indian civil servant and aesthete who was appointed Britain's first Governor of Jerusalem, enjoyed his three-year tenure (1920–22) so much that he later recorded in his memoirs: 'After Jerusalem, there is no promotion.' Under his benign supervision Jerusalem made a swift recovery from the ravages of the war years which had decimated the population. Institutions and services befitting its newly acquired role as a capital city were developed, and the city underwent a period of expansion with the construction of large, modern residential neighbourhoods, started before the war, outside the Ottoman ramparts of the Old City.[1] The presence of the British government bodies in Jerusalem also increased the stature of the main Jewish and Arab representatives, lobbyists keen to win the ear of the British authorities and persuade them to honour the various pledges that had been made during the war years.

From the outset the Zionists were the most active political group in Jerusalem. They had already fought a number of wounding political skirmishes among themselves merely to establish the principle that, if a national home for the Jews were created, it should be in Palestine, the land of their forefathers. When Theodore Herzl, a Viennese Jew, published *Der Judenstaat* (The Jew-State) in 1896 and helped launch

---

1 Storrs insisted that all new buildings have stone cladding, a measure which has greatly enhanced the city's charm.

the Zionist movement, the early activists were unclear about where the new Jewish state should be located. For some Zion, like Palestine, was rather a vague concept, more an object of spiritual inspiration than territorial substance. The British, in particular, had attempted to accommodate Jewish aspirations to have a nation of their own, and suggested a variety of locations, including Uganda. As late as 1938, when the Nazis' treatment of German Jews prompted renewed attempts to find a Jewish homeland at the Evian conference, Rhodesia was offered as a possibility. The early Zionist pioneers seriously explored some of these options, but the proposals came to nothing when presented to the Zionist Congress. The attitude of the opponents was best summed up by Dr Chaim Weizmann, a distinguished chemistry professor at Manchester University who would become Israel's first president. He denounced the Uganda proposal with the damning rejoinder: 'It is not Jerusalem and it never will be.' It was mainly through Dr Weizmann's diligence that the Zionists were able to obtain a commitment from the British government to establish a Jewish homeland in Palestine. Once the British Mandate was established, the Zionists determined to press home their advantage, even though they soon found that the British officials sent to administer the Mandate were not so enthusiastic about the 'Jewish National Home' project as some of their masters. The cultured Sir Ronald was fond of quoting Dryden's couplet as being equally applicable to the Zionists: 'God's pampered people whom, debauched with ease, no King could govern and no God could please.'

The Balfour Declaration was received like a bolt from the blue by the Arabs. They had been under the firm impression that, as a reward for assisting Captain T. E. Lawrence and his comrades to drive the Turks out of Arabia, they would be granted independence in the liberated lands. The Great Powers' cynical manipulation of the former Ottoman territories was bad enough, but the promise to import an alien people to establish a new 'national home' meant that the Ottoman occupiers were about to be replaced by a new breed of settlers. The creation of so many new Arab countries from the remnants of the Ottoman Empire aroused feelings of betrayal among the Arab population of the new British mandatory region of Palestine. Many of them had fought with the British against the Turks but, whereas other Arab combatants had been rewarded with their own governments in

Transjordan, Iraq and, until the French intervened, Syria, the Palestinian Arabs were being invited to participate in quasi-governmental power-sharing arrangements with Jewish immigrants from Europe. Believing that their honour had been impugned, the Arabs categorically refused to co-operate with the British authorities, even though it would undoubtedly have been in their interests to do so. So far as the Arab leaders were concerned, the British Mandate was illegal, a complete betrayal of the agreement that had been negotiated between Sharif Hussein and Sir Henry MacMahon. When, in 1922, the British attempted to set up a Legislative Council in Jerusalem, with a clear Arab working majority, to advise the Mandate authorities, the Arabs refused to participate. The British proposed that the Council be composed of nine Muslim Arabs, three Christian Arabs, three Jewish and eleven British officials. As most British officials were more strongly anti-Zionist than Sir Ronald Storrs, the Arabs, had they taken the opportunity, would have been well placed to curb the Zionists' political agenda. But the Arabs' stubbornness got the better of them, and a golden opportunity went begging.

Neither camp gave much thought to Jerusalem. The city was a British seat of government and, as there was no immediate prospect of Britain relinquishing its role in Palestine, the Jews and Arabs concerned themselves with broader objectives. At the start of the British Mandate the population of Palestine was about 700,000, of whom 65,000 were Jews. In Jerusalem the total population amounted to just 63,000, of whom just over half were Jews. Most of the Jerusalem Jews, however, were religious, not nationalist Jews, who had come to the Holy City to dedicate their lives to mourning the loss of the Temple. Most of these ultra-Orthodox Jews, as they became known, had little interest in Zionism, while a minority actively opposed it. But the main problem of Palestine for the Zionists was that it was inhabited with Arabs, and how to deal with the indigenous population without causing them undue offence occupied a great deal of Zionist thought. At first the Jews hoped to settle in the country without violating the legitimate interests of the Arabs – 'not a hair of their heads shall be touched', Dr Weizmann pledged. They achieved this by buying as much land as possible and building Jewish settlements. While the first settlers dreamed of creating a Jewish majority in Palestine, in reality it was a struggle for survival. For all the efforts of Zionist propaganda, few European Jews, at this juncture, were prepared to swap their bourgeois European comforts for the malaria-infested coastal plain of Palestine.

The main tactic of the Arabs, meanwhile, was to oppose the Zionists at every turn and promote their own nationalist goals. The Arab Awakening, as it became known, had, like Zionism, emerged in the closing years of the nineteenth century. The movement was based in Damascus which, as the administrative centre of Syria (which included modern Syria, Lebanon, Jordan, Israel and the occupied territories), was the main focus of Arab intellectual life. Once it became clear that Britain was to administer Palestine, a number of leading Palestinians, including Haj Amin al-Husseini, the figurehead of one of Jerusalem's foremost families, travelled to Damascus to lobby on behalf of the Palestinian cause with King Faisal, the son of Sharif Hussein of the Hejaz who briefly ruled Syria in the immediate aftermath of the 1914–18 war. These Palestinian Arab leaders were not pressing for an independent Palestine with Jerusalem as its capital, but for Palestine to be reunited with Syria with Damascus as its capital, as it had been in Ottoman times. Even after the French deposed Faisal in 1922 and established their own mandate, Palestinian Arab nationalists continued to argue for the termination of all the mandates and for the establishment of a reunited Syria.[2] There was no suggestion at this stage, not even by the powerful Jerusalemite Arab families, that Jerusalem should become the capital of an independent Palestinian state.

The dilemma that faced the Palestinian Arabs was that they knew better what they did *not* want than what they did want. Everything they did appeared to be a negative reaction to Zionism rather than the active pursuit of their own agenda. The Arabs were quite convinced they did not want Zionist immigration or for their country to be administered by British imperialists. But they were less articulate about what they sought as an alternative. This attitude, which characterised Arab policy for much of the mandate period, put the Palestinians very much at a disadvantage compared with the Zionists, who were clear and determined in their own minds about what they

2 Even today this is the bedrock political philosophy of Syria's President Hafez al-Assad.

wanted and how they could achieve it. The different approach of Arabs and Jews was highlighted when Lord Plumer, the British High Commissioner, attended a Jewish sports meeting in Tel Aviv in 1925. At the end of the meeting the band played 'God Save the King', during which Lord Plumer and his party stood to attention. Before they had a chance to sit down the band immediately continued with the *Hatikvah*, the Zionist anthem (now the Israeli national anthem). Lord Plumer, who did not know what was being played, continued to stand to attention. The next day the Arab papers were full of wrathful comment, condemning what they considered Lord Plumer's homage to Zionism. An Arab delegation called on Lord Plumer in Jerusalem to demand an apology. The High Commissioner received them with grave courtesy, but protested that he would have been failing in his duties as a guest towards his host had he sat down. To cool tempers he offered to come to an Arab sports meeting and, if they played their anthem, he would show it similar respect. 'By the way,' asked Lord Plumer, 'have you got a national anthem?' In some embarrassment, the Arab notables answered that they had not. 'In that case,' said Lord Plumer, 'I think you had better get one as soon as possible.'

It was at about this time that Lord Balfour, while making his one and only visit to Palestine, experienced the polarising attitude of Arabs and Jews. In his maiden speech in the House of Lords in 1922, Lord Balfour had described his Declaration as an 'experiment' and an 'adventure'. When he arrived in Jerusalem in 1925, aged seventy-seven, to attend the opening ceremony for the Hebrew University on Mount Scopus, he was able to assess first-hand how his venture was progressing. Not surprisingly, he was received throughout his visit by Jewish colonists with an enthusiasm which amazed him. The Palestinian Arabs, on the other hand, greeted him with a display of public mourning.

The simmering tensions between Jews and Arabs came to a head in 1928 following a dispute typical of Jerusalem about the erection of a screen to separate men and women praying at the Wailing Wall. At this time the area where the Jews were permitted to pray was little more than a narrow stretch of pavement. On the eve of Yom Kippur, the Jews' Day of Atonement, a Jewish official set up a screen in front of the Wall in preparation for the following day's prayers. Since Ottoman times, the Muslims had resisted any attempt by the Jews to extend their rights at the Wall in order to prevent it becoming a Jewish possession. The demands for the screen to be removed were led by Haj Amin al-Husseini, Faisal Husseini's great-uncle and the Palestinian leader who is credited with the radicalisation of Palestinian political thought during the inter-war years. Al-Husseini had been appointed, somewhat perversely, Grand Mufti of Jerusalem by the British in 1921 at the age of twenty-six, in the hope that he could be persuaded to co-operate with the British administration. Young Haj Amin came from a family which had controlled important political and religious posts in Jerusalem for centuries. An able and determined man, he had no difficulty reconciling his political duties with his deep religious faith. Arab nationalism was one thing, but al-Husseini believed the way to dislodge the Jews from Palestine was to call for *Jihad*, or holy war. The emergence of al-Husseini, moreover, was responsible for a fundamental change in the way Arabs viewed Jews. Previously it had been possible for an Arab to be anti-Zionist without being an anti-Semite. Al-Husseini took care to erase the distinction. For him the enemy was the Jewish people.

Responding to al-Husseini's demands, the British authorities ordered the screen to be removed. When the Jews prevaricated, British policemen were sent to take away the offending structure and were attacked by umbrella-wielding Jewish ladies for their trouble. Unfortunately, this British intervention encouraged Muslim Palestinians in the belief that Britain had finally seen the error of its ways, and would in future side with them. The Muslim authorities now launched a systematic campaign of provocation against the Jews hoping that any reaction on their part would further sour Jewish relations with British officials. The Mufti proposed to turn the narrow area in front of the Wailing Wall into a major thoroughfare – a fact the British reluctantly accepted was within his rights to do – to cause maximum disruption to Jewish devotions. He also encouraged Muslim worshippers to observe certain Islamic feasts by banging drums and cymbals as loudly as possible by the Wailing Wall, thereby driving the Jews to distraction. As a final gesture, a forged picture depicting the Dome of the Rock with the Jewish Star of David flying from its golden roof was widely circulated among the impressionable Muslim community, a successful propaganda ploy claiming the Jews were planning to seize all the Muslim holy shrines and make them their own.

It did not take long for the Jews to react. A protest demonstration was organised in August 1928 by Vladimir Jabotinsky, a young Jewish extremist who believed that Jewish colonisation should not be confined to Palestine, but should be extended to the other side of the River Jordan in the new kingdom of Transjordan. After marching to the government offices in Jerusalem, Jabotinsky and his followers then proceeded to the Wailing Wall where they held an anti-Arab demonstration, made loud demands for ownership of the Wall and took an oath to defend it at all costs. The Muslims were outraged and when, the next day, a Jewish boy kicked a football into an Arab garden, it was, for the Arabs, tantamount to a declaration of war. In the ensuing brawl, the boy was stabbed to death. Now it was the turn of the Jews to be outraged, and the boy's funeral was turned into a political demonstration. The Arabs, however, were in no mood to be intimidated. The following Friday, when great numbers of Palestinian Muslims traditionally came to Jerusalem from the surrounding countryside to attend the weekly prayer service, the British police noticed many of them were carrying clubs, knives and even firearms. The police, few in number, were unable to intervene, and a menacing crowd gathered at the Haram al-Sharif, the vast sanctuary which houses both the Dome of the Rock and the al-Aqsa mosque, the site of the prophet Mohammed's night journey to heaven. After hearing Haj Amin al-Husseini deliver the sermon, the crowd spilled out into the narrow streets of the Old City and attacked every Jew they could find, murdering several. Within days the violence had spread throughout the country and the British authorities, who had scaled down the military presence in Palestine in the mistaken belief that no serious threat was posed to public order, were unable to provide assistance. Before reinforcements could be drafted from Egypt, the Arabs had committed some particularly gruesome atrocities, the worst occurring at Hebron where twenty-three Jews who had taken shelter at an inn were slaughtered by Arabs, who then proceeded to dismember their bodies with axes and knives in an upstairs room.[3]

One of those who played a minor role in the 'disturbances', as

3 The Hebron massacre is one of the reasons Israeli extremists remain determined to maintain a presence in the city, even after it was handed over to Palestinian control in January 1997.

British officials euphemistically termed them, was a three-year-old Jewish boy called Rehovam Ze'evi, who today leads Israel's hard-right Moledet party. Ze'evi's parents were Zionists who lived in Mea Shearim, by tradition an ultra-Orthodox neighbourhood of Jerusalem. Because his father was away on business, young Ze'evi's mother asked the local commander of the Palmah, the Jewish underground army, for help in protecting the community if the Arabs attacked. A lone Jewish volunteer, dressed as a Bedouin, was duly dispatched. A few days later an angry Arab mob descended on the neighbourhood chanting 'Slaughter the Jews' and 'Palestine is our land and the Jews are dogs'. The Jewish guard was at first able to keep the Arabs at bay by dexterous use of a sling-shot. But after a while he tired and the Arabs looked as though they were about to overwhelm him. Just as all seemed lost the volunteer succeeded in dispersing the crowd by firing a pistol in the air. While the heroic actions of the Jewish defender may have prevented a massacre, it attracted the wrath of British officials. Possession of a firearm carried an immediate life prison sentence, and when British soldiers began a house-to-house search in Mea Shearim for the pistol, Ze'evi's mother came to the volunteer's aid. As the British soldiers arrived at her house, she placed the pistol under young Rehovam's pillow. Then, when a soldier entered the bedroom, she pinched the child's face, making him cry out. Believing himself to be the cause of the child's distress, the disconcerted British soldier retired from the room, and the volunteer's freedom was preserved. In later life the young Rehovam was to become not only a senior officer in the Israeli army, but a leading right-wing, anti-Arab Israeli politician. Today 'Gandhi', as Ze'evi is known (because of his lack of hair, not his pacifist tendencies), represents an Israeli political party whose primary agenda is the expulsion of the entire Arab population from Israel and the West Bank. One can only guess as to how his childhood experiences shaped these views.

The spiral of violence that began with a mundane argument over the positioning of a screen was to be a watershed in relations between Arabs and Jews. After the massacres, the moderate line taken by Dr Weizmann towards the Arabs, which had been the mainstream Zionist position, was now shunted to the sidelines, and the more hard-line figures like Jabotinsky, who until 1929 were regarded as the wild men on the fringe, took centre stage. The Arabs also became more uncompromising, especially under the leadership of Haj Amin al-Husseini who, from the late 1920s, emerged increasingly as the main Arab figurehead.

The British administrators in Jerusalem rued the day they ever set foot in Palestine, and especially regretted the grandiose promises that had been made during the war to both Arabs and Jews. A rare insight into the impossible position the British had steered themselves into with their various, ill-conceived commitments to both Arab and Jew is revealed in a confidential dispatch sent by J. R. Chancellor, the High Commissioner, to the Colonial Office in London in January 1930 entitled 'Future Policy in Palestine'.[4] The British Civil Service, the report divulges, clearly felt themselves hard done by. They had, after all, 'given the country a railway system, good roads, agricultural and veterinary services, an efficient public health service, modern postal and telephone facilities, and opportunites for employment on public works. A system of public education in which instruction is given in the vernacular tongue has been created. Local government, elective in character, has been developed. The British officials generally have established relations of mutual confidence with the inhabitants of the country with whom they work.' And yet the people who inhabited this Utopia of imperial munificence were at daggers drawn. The reason for this, Chancellor concluded, was that the Arab peoples, 'who have never forgotten their pride of race and empire', were deeply suspicious of the British authorities' every act because of Balfour's commitment to build a Jewish national home. The best way to improve relations with the Arabs, and thereby facilitate Britain's administration of Palestine, would, the High Commissioner recommended, be 'to withdraw from the Jews the specially privileged position (as compared with the Arab inhabitants of the country) which has been given them under the Mandate . . . and to grant the people of Palestine a measure of self-government'.

Chancellor's report was just one of many fact-finding missions and commissions that were instigated during this period to find a *modus vivendi* that would be suitable to all. But all these worthy investigations could conclude was that the obligations and commitments

4 The author is grateful to Alexander Chancellor, grandson of J. R. Chancellor, for lending him an original copy of the report.

undertaken by and on behalf of the British government were irreconcilable. Winston Churchill's 1922 White Paper had been a clumsy
attempt to obfuscate the precise nature of the promises given during
the war years. The White Paper of 1930, the British government's
response to the disturbances of 1929 – which no doubt drew heavily
on Chancellor's recommendations – further alienated the Zionists
because it appeared to go out of its way to reassure the Arabs. One of
the few conclusions British officials reached in the aftermath of the
1929 riots was that, in order not to exacerbate Arab sensibilities, the
level of Jewish immigration should be restricted on the grounds that
high levels of Jewish immigration created high levels of unemploy-
ment among the Arabs. The Jews saw no reason why they should be
punished for what they regarded as Arab wrong-doing and, as a consequence, relations between the Jewish community and the British
administration were severely strained. From this point on, the British
in Palestine had few friends and many enemies. They could build all
the roads and sewers they liked, but they could never satisfy the
political aspirations of the Jews and Arabs of Palestine.

The decisive event which finally destroyed any chance the British
might have had of maintaining the peace in Palestine, but over which
they had no control, was the rise to power in Germany of Adolf
Hitler. Until Field Marshal von Hindenburg reluctantly and against
his better judgement appointed Hitler Chancellor of the Reich, Jewish
immigration to Palestine had dropped to a paltry 4,000 people each
year, which hardly compensated for those Jews who did not like the
earthy hardship of Zionist life and chose to emigrate. After Hitler
came to power, there was a dramatic increase in Jewish immigration;
30,327 in 1933 rising to 61,854 by 1935, nearly all of them from
Europe. The persecution of European Jewry, validated by the Nuremberg Laws, provided Zionism with a moral imperative against which
it was impossible for anyone other than the most virulent anti-Semite
to argue. It was now essential for the Jews to have their own state, and
Palestine was the perfect answer to Hitler. The boost the Nazis gave
to Zionist immigration ultimately resulted in the creation of the State
of Israel. But the arrival of boatloads of Jews at Jaffa and Haifa har-
bours only served to confirm Arab suspicions that the Zionists were
intent on taking their country. In 1933 the Arab leadership initiated

a series of anti-British riots and demonstrations in Jerusalem and elsewhere to protest at the level of Jewish immigration, while in Tel Aviv, the centre of the Zionist community, Zionists staged anti-British riots to demand the relaxation of immigration restrictions. By 1936 Arab resentment of Jewish immigration was uncontainable, and the Arab Rebellion was launched by the Arab Higher Committee in Jerusalem with a six-month general strike, called by the Mufti, which was to end only when the British government agreed to restrict Jewish immigration.

The violence of the Arab Rebellion, which lasted, off and on, until the outbreak of the Second World War, highlighted how relations between Arabs and Jews had reached the point of no return. While the main thrust of the Arab campaign was against the British authorities, marauding Arab gangs also carried out a succession of gruesome attacks against Jewish civilians. The Jews' initial policy was to observe *Havlagah* – a Jewish form of pacifist resistance with no armed operations by the Jews against the Arabs. This attempt to win the moral high ground won the Zionists many friends abroad, but was not popular with the settlers and members of the Haganah, the underground Jewish defence force, which bore the brunt of Arab attacks. The policy was adopted both out of idealism and a desire to obtain the goodwill of the British, but in the face of repeated Arab provocation it was eventually abandoned in favour of armed resistance. In Jerusalem the British felt obliged to enforce a *de facto* division of the Old City into its four quarters – Armenian, Christian, Muslim and Jewish – as a means of containing the Arab Rebellion. Barriers and checkpoints were set up throughout the Old City, and restrictions imposed on the movement of Arabs and Jews outside their own quarters. At one point during the rebellion the Arabs attempted to seize control of the entire Old City with the intention of making it a 'no-go' area. The British authorities were anxious to re-establish law and order, but were constrained by fears that any attempt to recapture the city might involve damage to the holy shrines, thereby arousing international criticism. Eventually a plan was devised to retake the Old City using detachments of the Coldstream Guards and the Royal Northumberland Fusiliers, supported by the Black Watch. The soldiers must have looked a peculiar sight for, apart from normal battledress, they were required to wear white plimsolls in order not to slip on the stone streets. The mission was accomplished in a matter of hours, and British rule was restored to the Holy City.

The deterioration in relations between Jews and Arabs forced the British government to initiate a further review of its Palestine policy. At the end of 1936 another Royal Commission, this time under the stewardship of Lord Peel, a grandson of Sir Robert Peel, the Prime Minister, was sent to Palestine. The idea of partitioning the warring communities had first been aired in 1933 when the British Colonial Office had encouraged the production of a partition plan which envisaged the 'cantonisation' of Palestine. A northern canton would have been Jewish, a southern canton Arab, while Jerusalem, Bethlehem and Nazareth, the three Christian holy cities, would have been given some form of international administration. This plan, which was proposed by Ahmed Khalidi of the Government Arab School in Jerusalem, was succeeded by several others with a variety of different boundaries. In all of them Jerusalem was regarded as a special entity which required its own administration, not to be sullied by political unpleasantness. It was even suggested that Jerusalem be given an economic hinterland to make it self-sufficient, partly agricultural, but also stretching down to the Dead Sea with its potash deposits. Some of these ideas were taken up by Lord Peel and his fellow commissioners when they reported back to London the following year. Their suggestion was to establish a small Jewish state, a larger Arab one, while Jerusalem, together with Jaffa, would be a British mandated territory with a special administration of its own.

In trying to resolve the 'Palestine Question', the planners worked on the assumption that Jerusalem was a special case, and so they sought to detach the Holy City from the overall framework of their proposals. They respected Jerusalem for its religious, not political, clout. Just because it was the capital of the British Mandate did not mean to say it should retain this status once the Mandate had been dissolved. Apart from a brief period when, under David and Solomon nearly 3,000 years previously, Jerusalem had been the capital of a united Israelite nation, and the 100-year Crusader interlude, the city was in essence a provincial backwater whose significance derived from its sanctity. If there were to be any attempt to resolve the Palestine issue, most officials were agreed that, for the sake of preserving the city's unique character, Jerusalem would have its own settlement.

The very presence of Britain's administrative centre in Jerusalem, however, meant that it was increasingly taking on the appearance of a political capital. The Jewish community established institutions in Jerusalem which provided an organisational basis for a measure of self-rule and, in the long term, self-government. The Chief Rabbinate, the Jewish Agency, the Jewish National Fund and a variety of other Zionist organisations opened offices in the city. The *Palestine Post*, later to become the *Jerusalem Post*, began publishing in Jerusalem in 1931 while construction of the King David Hotel, the city's first five-star establishment, and the imposing YMCA, nurtured the city's pretensions of acquiring capital status. The Arabs had no real need to bother developing institutions in Jerusalem because they already had a sufficiency. Even before Haj Amin al-Husseini brought his Machiavellian skills to bear, the office of the Grand Mufti was a position of enormous influence, controlling the destiny of the entire Muslim community in Palestine and beyond. Haj Amin's influence was further consolidated by his election to the head of the Supreme Muslim Council, which made him the king of Palestinian patronage, presiding over all Islamic property, the religious courts and the appointment of ordinary muftis around the country. In addition the office of mayor was held by Palestinian Arabs, usually a member of the Nashashibi or Khalidi families, who were the Husseinis' deadly rivals in Jerusalem.

The various proposals to resolve the Palestine Question received, as was to be expected, a mixed press from the Arabs and Jews but, for the time being, the future of Jerusalem was the least of their worries. Although they had many reservations, the Zionists were generally enthusiastic about the partition proposals because they fulfilled the Zionist dream of creating their own homeland. When, during the hearings of the Peel Commission in Jerusalem, one of the commissioners told Dr Weizmann that the partition of Palestine, with an Independent Jewish State 'as independent as Belgium', would be the best way to end the Mandate, the ageing professor was overcome with emotion. He took a young aide for a walk on Mount Scopus where he confided that the long toil of his life was at last about to be crowned with success. If the price of full nationhood was to have Jerusalem, with its Jewish, Christian and Muslim holy places administered by an independent, but friendly, power, then the Zionists were prepared to pay it. The Arabs under Haj Amin's leadership, meanwhile, were so determined to crush the concept of an independent Zionist state in its infancy that they rejected the partition model out of hand, even though some Palestinian leaders believed it contained some virtues. Haj Amin still clung to the slogan 'Palestinian independence within the framework of Arab Unity', articulated at a meeting of the General Islamic Congress in Jerusalem in 1931. When he appeared before Lord Peel's commissioners he told them bluntly he would prefer to have corrupt Ottoman rule restored to Jerusalem rather than tolerate the continuation of British dominion. To ensure he got his way, Haj Amin engineered a vicious campaign to silence his Arab critics, particularly the Nashashibi family which had developed close links with Zionist leaders and was more inclined to compromise. Thanks to Haj Amin, some 6,000 Arabs died at the hands of their fellow countrymen as the rebellion against British rule and Zionist settlement degenerated into an ugly inter-Arab civil war.

The British Mandate was, in essence, a nursery in which two societies competed in the race for self-government, and the Jews were to win by a considerable distance. The fundamental difference between the Jewish and Arab camps in Palestine was that one was preparing for statehood, while the other was going through the motions. Many of the Zionist institutions established in Jerusalem, such as the Jewish Agency, were easily converted into government departments once the Jewish state became reality. The Arabs, for all their posturing, had only a vague concept of statehood. Arab power was concentrated in the hands of a few family élites which, in turn, sponsored their own political parties. Their agenda was more concerned with consolidating their own position rather than helping to build a state. As the pre-eminent family in Jerusalem, the Husseinis were as guilty of this as any of their rivals so that, under their leadership, the supremacy of the Husseini clan in Jerusalem always superseded the wider interest of Palestinian nationalist ambition.

The outbreak of the Second World War dictated that further discussion on the future of Palestine, much to the relief of the authorities, had to be suspended. Britain's White Paper of 1939, which determined British policy in Palestine during the war years, was a classic product of the appeasement vogue which had taken root in the British government. Nearly all Lord Peel's recommendations were ignored on the grounds that, with the advent of hostilities with

Germany and the Axis powers, the Jews would have no choice as to which side they supported. Britain wanted to keep the Arabs happy, so all mention of an independent Jewish state was dropped. There was a vague commitment to create an 'independent Palestinian state' within ten years, but in view of the recent events in Palestine, no one took this seriously. Despite the deep sense of betrayal with which Jews throughout the world received the White Paper, the Zionist movement nevertheless decided to lend its support to the Allied war effort. Out of a Jewish population in Palestine of 500,000, about 28,000 Jews volunteered for active service with the British. Among them was a charismatic young officer called Moshe Dayan, who was later to play a key role in shaping the destiny of modern Jerusalem. Dayan's first encounter with the British was to be thrown into Acre jail on gun-running charges. Upon his release in 1941 he more than compensated for his indiscretion by throwing himself whole-heartedly into the British war effort, losing an eye when he was shot through his field glasses while fighting the Vichy French in southern Lebanon.

The activities of Haj Amin during the war years, by contrast, were so hostile to the Allies that, after 1945, they seriously considered putting him on trial for his life for war crimes. The Mufti had been forced to flee Jerusalem, climbing down the wall of the Haram al-Sharif to escape his British pursuers, after Lewis Andrews, a British official, was murdered by Arab gunmen. From his new domicile in Lebanon, Haj Amin continued to direct the Arab Rebellion, in particular against his Arab rivals. The appeasing balm of the 1939 White Paper did little to improve his temper. After the outbreak of the war, he turned up in Baghdad where he was suspected, in 1941, of encouraging Rashid Ali's rising in favour of the then triumphant Axis powers. Rashid Ali's revolt was suppressed by the Allies, and Haj Amin fled to Germany where he received a warm welcome from the Jew-hating Nazis. Haj Amin's activities in Germany have been immortalised by the Israelis at the Yad Vashem Holocaust memorial in Jerusalem. Set among the harrowing documentation of Hitler's 'final solution' is a picture of a smiling Haj Amin shaking hands with Heinrich Himmler and inspecting a Bosnian Muslim SS unit in Yugoslavia. Haj Amin spent the war making propaganda broadcasts on German radio urging Arabs and Muslims to slaughter Jews and, on the twenty-sixth anniversary of the Balfour Declaration in November

1943, received a message of solidarity from Himmler to the effect: 'The National Socialist Party has inscribed on its flag "the extermination of world Jewry". Our party sympathises with the fight of the Arabs against the foreign Jew. Today, on the anniversary of the Balfour Declaration, I send my greetings and wishes for success in your fight.'

It is ironic that Haj Amin's pathological anti-Semitism should be enshrined at Yad Vashem, for the horrific persecution of European Jewry in the Nazi Holocaust banished for ever any reservations the international community may have entertained about the wisdom of allowing the Jewish people to have their own state in Palestine. In the immediate aftermath of the war, as the horrendous scale of the Holocaust became known, the British authorities were placed in the invidious position of condemning Nazi atrocities while obstructing efforts to help the victims. If the rest of the world felt it had a moral obligation to help the Jewish survivors, the British government believed it had a moral obligation to maintain the *status quo* in Palestine, and that meant restricting Jewish immigration to pre-war levels when there were hundreds of thousands of homeless and destitute Jews stranded in Europe. Relations between the British and Zionists Jews, who had shared the VE day celebrations in Jerusalem with equal enthusiasm, quickly deteriorated, and whatever domestic British support remained for retaining the Mandate quickly evaporated once British officials and soldiers became the targets of Zionist terrorists. By the end of the war, keeping the peace in Palestine required a garrison of 80,000 British troops which the financially stretched Treasury could ill-afford. The bombing of the King David Hotel, which the British used as offices, in 1946 by a Jewish terrorist group led by Menachem Begin, the future Israeli Prime Minister, killed 91 people (28 British, 41 Arabs, 17 Jews); it was the last straw. British involvement in Palestine had always been regarded as a sideshow compared with India, the jewel in the imperial crown. Once the Attlee government had taken its historic decision to grant India independence, obviating the need to protect the Suez Canal, the gateway to India, there was no longer any reason for the British to remain in Palestine.

In February 1947 the British government decided to wash its hands of Palestine and refer the Mandate back to the United Nations, the successor to the League of Nations which had initially granted it.

The United Nations came up with a new partition plan, which drew heavily on the exhaustive work carried out by the Peel Commission ten years previously. The UN plan proposed the partition of Palestine into Jewish and Arab states, with Jerusalem being made 'neutral' territory. The Zionists were prepared to accept the plan while the Arabs, as had become their custom, would have nothing to do with it. Zionist leaders, in their usual pragmatic fashion, even debated different cities as potential capitals of the new Jewish state. David Ben-Gurion, who had replaced Weizmann as leader of the Palestinian Jews, suggested Beersheva in the Negev desert, while the young Golda Meir suggested somewhere in northern Palestine, the site of the ancient state of Israel. No one liked the idea of giving up their claim to the Holy City, but with the storm clouds of war gathering around them, both sides had more important matters to consider.

The last few months of the British Mandate were not a proud episode in the annals of Britain's imperial adventures. The British priority was to get their 'boys' home in one piece. Most of the British troops withdrew to heavily fortified compounds to await their orders for embarkation home. In Jerusalem the strength of the fortifications around the main government buildings in the city centre were wryly called 'Bevingrad' after Ernest Bevin, the Labour Foreign Secretary, who was derided by the Jews in Palestine as an anti-Semite. The British view was that both the Arabs and Jews were spoiling for a fight, and it was none of their business to get caught in the middle. Little was done to curb the activities of the Haganah, the underground Jewish army, as it stockpiled weapons. Nor did the British feel obliged to intervene when Arab irregulars began to swarm into Palestine in readiness for the coming war against the Jews. Indeed, rather than impeding their advance, the British handed the Arabs some of their best military positions.

The British Mandate in Palestine officially ended at nine o'clock on the morning of 14 May 1948, when Sir Alan Cunningham, the last British High Commissioner, took his leave of Palestine aboard a Royal Navy launch from Haifa harbour. The British 'experiment' and 'adventure' which Lord Balfour had initiated thirty-one years previously was about to end in disaster. The lowering, for the last time, of the Union Jack from Government House, the imposing building overlooking Jerusalem, was taken as the signal for battle to commence.

# 5

# BATTLE

*'The Lord gave, and the Lord hath taken away'*
Job 1: 21

Most of the old Arab houses have been demolished and the local residents are using the minaret as somewhere to fasten their television aerials, but the elderly Arab man has no difficulty remembering the haunts of his childhood. The two of us stop to pause by a semi-derelict stone house, overlooked in the frantic scramble to layer the hillside with concrete housing blocks. The house has a forlorn appearance. The terraced garden is overgrown and the lone pomegranate tree looks weary from years of neglect. 'See that little window,' my companion remarks, pointing to one side of the house. 'I must have climbed through it a hundred times. The house used to belong to my cousins and I would go there to play. Now they are all living abroad. As you can see, the house has not been lived in for many years.' It is several decades since the old man has lived in the Palestinian village of Malha. Then it was a typical Arab village set on a hilltop, a sentinel guarding Jerusalem's western approaches. All that remains are a cluster of stone houses which protrude like an ageing carbuncle among the new sprawling Israeli housing estates. In the adjoining valley, where the villagers tended the terraced olive groves, a new temple, in the shape of the Jerusalem shopping mall – 'the biggest in the Middle East' – has arisen. Unlike the city's many other places of worship, this one, teeming with its burger bars and shops, is dedicated to Mammon.

Like hundreds of Arab villages, Malha's fate was determined by the headlong plunge of Arabs and Jews into open warfare in the spring of 1948. During the opening skirmishes the villagers attempted to negotiate their own non-aggression pact with Jewish Agency officials in Jerusalem. The villagers even ejected a group of Palestinian irregulars who had decided Malha would make a useful base from which to attack Jews. But, as hostilities in Palestine intensified, it soon became clear there would be no place for neutrality. Britain's precipitate departure meant the future of Palestine would be decided by feat of arms. Peace-loving Arab villagers, like peace-loving Jewish settlers, were given little alternative but to arm themselves. Once the women and children were moved to safety, the Palestinian menfolk of Malha raised money to buy rifles and ammunition by selling their valuables. For two weeks three hundred fighters from the village fought Jews living in nearby settlements. Then, their ammunition spent, the men evacuated the village and took refuge behind the front lines of the regular Arab armies. They were never to return.

Ahmed Ibrahim Rashid was thirteen years old when the clouds of war first cast their shadow over Malha. Prior to the commencement of hostilities, relations between the Arab villagers and the nearby Jewish settlers were affable. The Jews would buy milk and produce from the Arabs and the Arabs would buy consumer goods from the Jews. Every day Jewish and Arab schoolchildren would travel on the same bus. These delicate seeds of co-existence were violently uprooted by war. In the case of Ahmed's family, they became refugees. After the hostilities ended Malha found itself on the Jewish side of the disengagement line, and the newly established State of Israel constructed a steel fence to prevent the villagers returning. Ahmed's family squatted in various empty houses, most of them the homes of Jewish evacuees, until, in 1966, the family was finally rehoused in a refugee camp on the city's outskirts, where they have lived ever since.

It takes just fifteen minutes for the two of us, driving on the network of highways that dissect the modern city, to travel from Ahmed's modest, two-room concrete dwelling in Shuafat refugee camp to Malha. To do so we have traversed generations of conflict between Arab and Jew. After 1948 the Israelis renamed the village Manhat, but somehow the old name has stubbornly survived. Modern Malha is known as an up-and-coming fashionable neighbourhood, popular with artists and Israeli trend-setters for whom ownership of an Arab-style house is the epitome of chic. We have been in the village only a few minutes when a middle-aged Israeli, dressed in an ill-fitting soccer strip, appears from one of the narrow alleyways to ask us our business. Ahmed, who walks with the aid of a walking stick, has entered the courtyard of the old mosque to see if he can go inside. The door is firmly bolted, but by peering through the iron grille he can determine the contours of the empty prayer room, which is covered with a thick layer of dust. Although the mosque itself is unoccupied, the surrounding Arab houses have been tastefully renovated as Israeli dwellings including, according to Ahmed, the house which was used by the original Arab inhabitants to wash the dead before burial.

'What are you doing here? The mosque is closed,' demands the Israeli. Ahmed explains he was born in the village and wants to see the condition of the mosque.

'The mosque is closed and that is the best thing for it,' the Israeli replies. 'We were told some Arabs were going to come here to pray, but it will stay closed. Israelis live here now, not Arabs. We don't want any trouble here.'

Another Israeli, an older man with untidy white hair and a neat moustache, joins us. His name is Eliahu and he is altogether more friendly. He greets Ahmed in Arabic and is not in any way agitated by the presence of the elderly Palestinian. He says he comes from Iraq where his family owned a big farm with hundreds of orange trees. Then, in 1951, the Israeli government did a deal with the Iraqis and all the Jews were forced to leave.

'We lost everything we had,' says Eliahu. 'I never wanted to leave, nor did the rest of the family. But we were forced to come to Israel. I came here with my watch, my wedding ring and the clothes I was wearing. When we arrived we had to live in tents in the most primitive conditions. After we complained about our treatment we were sent to this village.'

When Eliahu and his family moved into Malha, the houses were in a semi-derelict state. All the furnishings and fittings had been plundered by other new immigrants. The Iraqi Jew used blankets to cover the doorways and windows. Later, when he had saved some money, he renovated the house and made it a proper home.

'But you see,' he says to Ahmed, 'we are both losers. You have lost your house and I lost my farm. What can I do? I landed here and I will die here.'

The two men part company, leaving Ahmed to explore the remains of the village in peace. On the outskirts of the village, building contractors are putting the finishing touches to a new housing estate which has been built upon the old Muslim cemetery. 'If someone got out of his grave and saw what they had done to the village he would get straight back into his coffin,' Ahmed remarks with bitterness. 'It is better to die than to see this happen.' The housing estate is soon to be filled with new Russian and Ethiopian immigrants, ignorant of the past. 'Here I am, a resident of Jerusalem, and I cannot even live on my own land,' he says. 'You have to be a Russian or American Jew to live here now. Is that justice?'

The war of 1948 created modern Jerusalem. For the first time in its turbulent history, Jerusalem became a divided city with its own 'Berlin Wall' of barbed wire and machine-gun posts. The physical division of the city had an even deeper impact on the Jewish and Arab communities. The notion that peaceful co-existence was possible between Arabs and Jews was utterly destroyed. Throughout the city the abandoned houses, most of them still filled with possessions left behind in the hasty flight of the residents, bore testimony to the conflict's terrible human tragedy. Homeless families, clutching their few ragged belongings, were a familiar symbol of post-war Europe in the 1940s. It came as a profound shock for Jerusalem's well-to-do middle-class residents, both Arab and Jew, to come through the Second World War relatively unscathed and find that their comfortable existence in the Holy City was not sacrosanct. The war created deep personal and political antagonisms between the Jewish and Arab inhabitants which, in the more extreme cases, turned to blind hatred.

The deep wounds caused by the political, social and ethnic division of the city have never healed and most Jerusalemites believe they never will.

This was not the fate that was anticipated for the city when, in November 1947, the United Nations voted for the partition of Palestine. The one principle upon which the international community was united when it came to discuss the future of Palestine was to ensure the safety and security of the Holy City. Whatever became of the rest of the country, they intended that Jerusalem should be robed in a variety of international guarantees that would save her from the ravages of conflict which seemed certain to break out elsewhere. The terms of the UN partition plan proposed that Jerusalem should become a neutral city, administered by an international peace-keeping force. However, the UN partition plan, which was drawn up by a group of eleven 'neutral' delegates, did not carry a unanimous recommendation. Three of the delegates regarded the whole idea of partition as unworkable, and recommended instead the transformation of the Mandate into an independent federal government of Jewish and Arab cantons, with Jerusalem as its capital. But the diplomats at the newly constituted United Nations in New York opted for the majority view. Although they had many reservations, the Zionists accepted the partition plan because it fulfilled their ultimate goal of creating an independent Jewish state. Arab leaders, on the other hand, were opposed to it. Within days of the UN vote for partition on 29 November 1947, it became clear that the Palestine Question was not going to be resolved peacefully. The Jews were determined to have their own state, and the Arabs were determined to oppose it. The six months before the British finally withdrew thus became a phoney war, a time when both sides made detailed preparations for the war they not only expected but, in many cases, actively sought.

From the Israeli perspective, the 1948 battle for Jerusalem is remembered for epitomising the suffering and sacrifice the Jewish people endured in their struggle to create their own state. The annual Jerusalem Day celebrations are given the same importance as Independence Day in the Israeli national calendar. The day usually starts with memorial services held at Mount Herzl and Ammunition Hill, two of the city's most important war memorials for Israel's war dead. The speeches, made by Israel's political élite, inevitably refer to the city as the 'eternal, indivisible' capital of the state of Israel, laying special emphasis on their desire that the city shall never again suffer the fate that resulted from the 1948 war, a conflict generally known as the first Arab–Israeli war, but by the Israelis as the War of Independence. After the serious formalities are completed, the day is then filled with various events designed to emphasise the Israelis' affection for their capital city. There are fun runs, street carnivals, concerts, all of which stress the theme that Jerusalem belongs to Israel. Few Palestinians, if any, are to be found at these occasions. The Palestinians do not celebrate Jerusalem Day because the city is no longer theirs. They had their chance to seize control of the city in 1948, but they failed. Instead, after months of bitter fighting, the city was divided, a state of affairs which only hardens the Israelis' resolve never to allow any recurrence of what many of them hold to be the greatest shame against the nation's name.

Looking at the modern city today, it is hard to imagine that just over fifty years ago, Jerusalem was a truly cosmopolitan city where Arabs and Jews, for the most part, lived side by side in some degree of peace and harmony. While it would be naïve to claim there were no tensions between the respective communities, the city was nowhere near as polarised as it is now. Before the war of 1948, there was no East Jerusalem and West Jerusalem, rigidly defined Jewish and Arab areas. There was just Jerusalem. It was an administrative centre, the city had developed a considerable academic reputation and, of course, it was an important focus of religious study and devotion. In spite of all the political difficulties, which occasionally spilled over into violence, the presence of so many foreigners – diplomats, soldiers, doctors, civil servants, churchmen, businessmen and even foreign correspondents – made Jerusalem's social life both exotic and stimulating, the kind of place an Olivia Manning character might seek out for a romantic tryst. If the countryside was awash with terrorism and banditry, the disturbance most likely to be heard in the airy salons of Jerusalem's middle classes was the clatter of silverware on the china dinner service. Encouraged by the significant public building programmes initiated by the British, the 1930s bore witness to the construction of a number of elegant, spacious villas which, even now, provide the city with some of its finest architectural specimens. Wealthy Arab areas like Katamon backed on to Jewish Rehavia, and the two communities intermingled amiably. Words like 'division' and 'separation' were not a part of the everyday vocabulary. Even during the hardships of the Second World War, these were the popular haunts of civilised society. As the Arabs owned more property in the city, the better properties tended to be Arab-owned. Jewish families often rented apartments from Arab landlords, a state of affairs that is almost impossible to conceive in today's city. Even as the prospect of armed conflict loomed, few in Jerusalem thought they would be directly affected. Every attempt to resolve the Palestine Question had contained specific provisions for the city's protection and city-dwellers on both sides of the political divide thought they had little to fear.

Jerusalem's rude awakening came within days of the UN partition vote. While the Jewish population received news of the vote with jubilation, driving through the city streets with their car horns blaring, acclaiming the creation of the first Jewish state for 2,000 years, the Arabs responded three days later by storming through the Jewish commercial district, looting and burning shops and attacking Jews. Within weeks the division of the city was under way. On both sides, the terror tactics of the extremists engendered an atmosphere of fear and ethnic hatred. The Arabs, under the prompting of Haj Amin al-Husseini, the Mufti of Jerusalem, carried out a series of spectacular bombings of Jewish targets in central Jerusalem. In swift succession the *Palestine Post*, located to the west of the city centre, was blown up in early February 1948; the main Ben Yehudah shopping district, in the heart of the city, was bombed in late February; and the Jewish Agency, the headquarters of the fledgling Zionist government in King George Street, attacked in March. Of these, the worst atrocity was the Ben Yehudah bombing which, with 54 dead and over 100 wounded, was the biggest terrorist attack the city had seen since Menachem Begin's bombing of the King David Hotel two years previously. The collapse of government authority which preceeded Britain's withdrawal from Palestine was just the moment Begin's Irgun terrorists had been waiting for, and they more than compensated for the Jewish victims of Arab attacks by carrying out scores of indiscriminate assaults and bombings against Arab civilians.

These tit-for-tat terrorist exchanges created a *de facto* division of the city into communities of Jews and Arabs. Yacir Plessner, for example, remembers how, when he was thirteen years old, his parents announced they were moving from the comfortable apartment they rented in the Arab neighbourhood of Katamon to a nearby Jewish neighbourhood.

'We had this very nice apartment which we rented from an Arab family,' he recalls. 'This family were as much our friends as our land-lords. But my parents were told that it was no longer safe to live in an Arab area and that we should move.'

Plessner's German father, Martin, had moved to Palestine in 1933 because, despite being a distinguished university professor, he was unemployed because of Adolf Hitler's Nuremberg Laws. Ironically, Martin Plessner belonged to a fringe Jewish group called Brit Shalom – covenant of peace – which was opposed to the creation of a Jewish state. Plessner senior believed there was no need for an Israeli nation, and that any attempt to create it would lead to unnecessary conflict with the Arabs. He saw no reason why Arabs and Jews should not live together in one state. Consequently he opposed the UN partition plan and Ben-Gurion, the Zionist leader. But in the uncompromising political climate that was consuming Jerusalem, there was little room for the liberal convictions of the city's educated middle classes, be they Jewish or Arab. The Plessner family moved to a Jewish neigh-bourhood where they remained for the duration of the war.

Plessner's other abiding memory of the city's decline to open hos-tilities was a clandestine visit he made to his parents' old Katamon apartment a few weeks after they moved (which they accomplished by bribing two British police officers). By now the situation had dete-riorated to the extent that Iraqi snipers had installed themselves in the area and were shooting at Jewish neighbourhoods. Plessner, how-ever, like most young teenagers, was oblivious to danger and made his way to the Arab house in which his parents had rented an apart-ment. When he got there he found the door to the Arab family's quarters open and dinner laid out on the table. But there was no sign of the Arab family. 'They had just disappeared, taking the few pos-sessions with them they could carry,' he remembers. 'They must have decided the situation was too dangerous and gone somewhere more safe.' It is perhaps worth mentioning that, despite enduring the ordeal of the siege of Jerusalem, Yacir Plessner, who later became a senior executive at the Bank of Israel, would never contemplate living in the modern city. He lives in a comfortable suburb on the outskirts of Tel

Aviv. 'I could never live in Jerusalem now,' he says. 'It is far too intense. That is no way to live a life.'

It was clear that the fate of Palestine would be resolved by force of arms and the Arab forces, under Haj Amin's command, made Jerusalem their primary target, mainly because the city was easier to attack than Jaffa or Haifa, which were located deep within the heart of Zionist settlements. Jerusalem, with its 100,000 Jews, was also highly vulnerable. The main supply route was the road from Tel Aviv which wound through the Judaean hills. Once the road left the low-lying Jewish settlements, it ran through hostile Arab territory, easy prey for Haj Amin's guerrillas. Within days of the UN vote, a series of Arab attacks on food convoys from Tel Aviv to Jerusalem brought supplies to the city to a standstill. Haj Amin's tactics, aided by Glubb Pasha, the British commander of the Arab Legion, were to lay siege to Jerusalem. Glubb Pasha, in fact, was given specific instructions by King Abdullah of Transjordan to make Jerusalem his priority. Their tactics were highly successful, and for two months in the spring of 1948, Jerusalem was like modern-day Sarajevo, the population forced to subsist on anything they could find – grass, roots – while all the time being subjected to constant bombardment.

The failure of the Zionist forces to afford Jerusalem proper protection during the 1948 war remains a source of great contention among Israelis. The young Yitzhak Rabin – he was twenty-six years old – was the commander in charge of the Harel brigade which was given responsibility for both the defence of Jerusalem and keeping open the main road between Jerusalem and Tel Aviv. According to his close friends, the suffering he witnessed on the Jerusalem road was 'the most decisive experience of his life'.[1] The Jewish forces were fully occupied tackling the various Arab armies – Syrian, Egyptian, Jordanian – together with the bands of irregulars who came to fight from as far afield as Yemen and Iraq once the British finally withdrew. But because the Jewish leadership had not expected Haj Amin and Glubb Pasha to concentrate their forces on Jerusalem, they made inadequate provision for its defence. As a result Rabin was so short of men that he had to send a platoon of sixteen-year-old

1 David Horowitz (ed.), *Yitzhak Rabin: Soldier of Peace* (London: Peter Halban, 1996).

scouts into action to fight off Arab attempts to close the road. On a personal level, the experience made Rabin deeply suspicious of politicians interfering in military decisions. Politically, it made him determined to do everything in his power to ensure that the Jewish residents of Jerusalem should never again suffer the same fate, a consideration that was paramount in his thoughts when he signed the Oslo Accords with Yasser Arafat on the White House lawn forty-five years later.

More than the failure to protect Jerusalem, however, and the appalling suffering the city's Jewish residents endured during the siege, the aftermath of the 1948 war is remembered by Israelis for the city's division, the loss of the Old City and with it access to the Wailing Wall, the holiest shrine in Judaism. Looking back, one of the more remarkable aspects of the battle for the Old City was that the Jewish defenders managed to hold out for so long. At the outset of hostilities there were about 2,000 Orthodox Jews living among 30,000 Arabs. The Jews were mostly unwordly souls, whose lives were devoted to prayer and study. There were those among them who said they wanted to live for God, not to die for a Jewish state. If God wanted to deliver the Jews from the Arabs, He would do it in His own way. This attitude was intensely irritating for the 100 or so Jewish fighters, many of them teenagers, who were charged with the enormous responsibility of defending the Jewish community. From early February the Old City's Jewish Quarter was effectively cut off from the New City – that which lies beyond the Ottoman ramparts – after the British evacuated their position at Zion Gate and allowed it to fall into Arab hands. After the battle began in earnest on 15 May 1948, the beleaguered Jewish fighters were forced to adopt similar tactics to those used in the Warsaw ghetto battles of 1943, hopping across the rooftops firing at the Arabs to prevent them swarming into the streets. But the odds were against them, and once the Arabs started dynamiting Jewish houses it was clear the plight of the Jews was hopeless. It is a credit to them that they managed to hold out for two weeks, but on 29 May the commanders reluctantly agreed to surrender, fearing that if they continued to hold out they would expose the 2,000 civilians to the risk of a massacre at the hands of the Arabs.

That there was no massacre was mainly due to the presence of

Abdullah Tel, the Jordanian commander responsible for the Old City.[2] The Arab mob had been so stirred up by the intensity of the fighting that it was more than capable of committing the type of atrocities committed against the Jews of Hebron during the 1928 disturbances. Tensions had also developed between the Jordanian and Palestinian Arabs: the Palestinians teased the Jordanians for being stupid Bedouins, while the Jordanians in turn regarded the Palestinians as traitors who sold their land to Jews. To ensure there was no repeat of 1928, the Jordanian soldiers of the Arab Legion agreed to guarantee the free passage of all Jewish civilians to West Jerusalem under the terms of surrender agreed with the Zionist commanders. Tel insisted, however, on detaining the Jewish fighters. The Arab Legion, at Tel's command, were as good as their word and none of the Jewish civilians was harmed, even though they had to fire warning shots in the air to keep the local Arabs at bay. Some of the wounded Jews were carried to safety by the Arab Legionnaires. According to Shaul Tuval, the young Israeli commander who negotiated the ceasefire with Tel, the Jordanian officer was amazed at the paltry number of Jewish fighters who were taken prisoners of war. When they had all been counted, he discovered just thirty-five young Jews had managed to hold hundreds of Arab fighters at bay. 'My God,' Tel exclaimed. 'If I'd known you had so few fighters, I could have defeated you with sticks, not guns.'[3]

The dignity and respect which the Jordanian officers and soldiers afforded the defeated Jews made a deep impression on the leaders of the new Israeli state, and was one of the few positive developments of the whole sorry episode. Altogether some three hundred Jews were taken to Jordan as prisoners of war, where they were given privileges not normally granted to former enemies. The Jewish prisoners were effectively allowed to run their own camps during their nine-month incarceration. According to Tuval, who was one of the camp commanders, the Jordanian guards were given express orders by King Abdullah 'not to touch the Jews'. When the time came for the Jewish

2 Tel was later implicated in the successful plot to assassinate King Abdullah in Jerusalem in 1951. Tel was opposed to the secret dialogue Abdullah was conducting with Golda Meir.
3 Interview with Shaul Tuval in Jerusalem, June 1995.

prisoners to be returned to Israel, relations had become so cordial that the inmates and guards exchanged gifts.[4] Thus was forged a measure of respect between the Israelis and Jordanians that remains an important dynamic in the modern politics of the Middle East.

The Palestinian Arabs were not completely deprived of their craving for vengeance. As the Jews were gradually beaten into submission the local Arab militias set about eradicating all traces of the Jewish presence in the Old City. The Hurva synagogue, the principal temple of the Ashkenazim and regarded by Jews as a monument of great beauty, was the most notable casualty. The Hurva is said by Jews to have made a similar contribution to the beauty of the Jerusalem skyline as the Dome of the Rock and the Holy Sepulchre. Thanks to the Arab commandos, its graceful eighteenth-century parabola was reduced to rubble. In addition a further twenty-seven synagogues were destroyed while Jewish homes and shops were looted. War correspondents who had covered the horrors of the Second World War compared the scenes of devastation in the Old City to those they had witnessed at Stalingrad and Berlin, albeit on a much reduced scale.

The loss of the Old City and the Wailing Wall left a deep scar on the Jewish psyche. Through all the centuries that Jews had been scattered across the continents, Jerusalem, and its holy shrine, were constantly in their thoughts. The city occupied a central place in the Jewish daily prayer ritual, and the main ambition for any Jew of a holy disposition was to visit the Wailing Wall to be within the presence of Jehovah. In their efforts to establish a new Jewish nation, the Zionists had allowed the most important Jewish treasure to fall into the hands of their Arab foes. This failure became and remains a source of bitter recrimination over whether this calamity could have been avoided. Tuval, one of the survivors of the battle for the Old City, continues to insist the defeat was unnecessary and that the surrender of the Jewish Quarter 'is a shame not just on the name of Israel but for the whole Jewish world'. It also taught the Zionists an important lesson: never again would they trust anyone else to protect the Holy City. Through all the years that various international bodies had proposed mechanisms and guarantees for Jerusalem's protection, at the crucial moment the city had been abandoned to its fate. The

4 Ibid.

founders of the new State of Israel made a collective vow to make the protection of Jerusalem a central priority.

If Jerusalem's Jewish residents bore the brunt of the suffering during the 1948 war, the Palestinians have endured the lion's share of misery and anguish ever since. One of the main consequences of the hostilities was the creation of what today is called the 'Palestinian refugee problem'. Once the Zionists had accepted the partition plan, their main problem concerned the presence of so many Arabs in their 'sector'.[5] If they were to succeed with their dream of creating a Jewish homeland, they needed somehow to reduce the Arab population. Demographic transfers – another term for ethnic cleansing – had become a popular method for eradicating troublesome racial disputes. Britain had assisted with the mass transfer of Greeks from northern Thessalonika at the end of the First World War. Many of the East European Jews who were the founding fathers of Zionism had personally experienced Stalin's enormous population transfers in the 1930s, which had reshaped the demographic composition of the Soviet Union. Certainly, as the conflict developed in Palestine, the Zionists had few qualms about encouraging the indigenous Arab population to leave.

How much the Palestinians were pushed, and to what extent they went of their own accord, remains an issue of enormous complexity and contention. The truth probably lies somewhere in between. There were, undoubtedly, occasions when Palestinians were forced to flee at gunpoint, one of the more infamous examples being the expulsion of some 50,000 Arabs from the twin towns of Lydda (today's Lod) and Ramleh, south-east of Tel Aviv. In his memoirs Rabin controversially refuted the long-held Israeli view that the residents had gone quietly of their own accord. The residents of Lod were forced to evacuate the town at gunpoint and march fifteen miles to positions held by the Arab Legion. The elderly, pregnant women, young children – none were spared, even though it was a hot summer's day.

5 Two studies by the Israeli historian Benny Morris examine this controversial issue in exhaustive detail: *The Birth of the Palestinian Refugee Problem* (Cambridge: CUP, 1987) and *1948 and After* (Oxford: OUP, 1990). Though written from an Israeli perspective, they contain one of the most detailed examinations of the facts yet undertaken.

Palestinian writers have claimed that many elderly people and small children died through lack of water. The residents of nearby Ramleh saw what happened and, when the Jews arrived at their town, agreed to go voluntarily. A similar pattern occurred in other parts of Palestine, with the result that, when hostilities ceased, there were hundreds of thousands of homeless Palestinians.

It was a similar story in Jerusalem. Some of the more well-to-do, and less politically committed, Palestinian families, did, it is true, decamp for more serene destinations. Dr Hussain Khalidi, a leading member of the Arab Higher Committee (AHC) which represented the Palestinians' political interests, complained as early as January 1948 that most of the committee members had already abandoned the cause. 'Everyone is leaving me. Six are in Cairo, two are in Damascus – I won't be able to hold on much longer . . . Jerusalem is lost.'[6] The faint-hearted, however, were generally in the minority. The majority of Jerusalem's Arab population who were made refugees during the war left their homes as a result either of intimidation or brute force. The evacuation of Katamon, for example, followed the bombing of the Semiramis Hotel which Jewish commanders believed, mistakenly, was being used as a headquarters for Arab irregulars. Even though the British were still responsible for the city's security, they did nothing to prevent the exodus of Arab families from their homes. Few of these families thought they were leaving for good. In most cases they believed that their flight was a temporary measure, a prudent move to ensure their safety as the security situation in the city deteriorated drastically. They intended to return to their homes once the conflict had been resolved, hopefully in their favour. But even at this early stage the Zionists had other plans. As early as February 1948 Ben-Gurion was expressing his satisfaction that 'in many Arab districts in the West – one sees not one Arab. I do not assume that this will change.'[7] Ben-Gurion acted quickly to ensure his assumptions were correct by ordering his military commanders to re-settle Jews in the abandoned and conquered Arab districts. By the time the battle for Jerusalem proper began in the spring, West Jerusalem was entirely Jewish. The division of the city had been

6 Quoted in Morris, *The Birth of the Palestinian Refugee Problem*, p. 51.
7 Ibid., p. 52.

accomplished as the British were still preoccupied with packing their bags. And it was while the British mandatory authorities were making the final travel arrangements that Jewish fanatics committed their worst atrocity of the war, an atrocity which, for the Palestinians, has come to symbolise the violence with which they were evicted from their homes.

Unlike Malha which, with its shopping mall and cinema complex, is an important feature of modern Jerusalem, the Arab village of Deir Yassin has disappeared – at least so far as the city's road signs are concerned. The village, located on a ridge on the western approaches to the city, was once home to about 1,000 Arabs. That was until, one fateful day on 9 April 1948, Menachem Begin's Irgun launched a surprise attack on the village. Until the Irgun attack, the village elders had managed to keep their little sanctuary relatively neutral from the all-consuming fray of conflict. The villagers had persuaded the various bands of Arab fighters not to seek sanctuary in their midst, and the Zionists had responded by leaving it in peace. But Begin's Irgun had other ideas. Keen for his organisation to win an important propaganda coup, he agreed to link up with another notorious Jewish terror group – the Stern gang – and launch an attack against Deir Yassin to capture it for the Jews. The Irgun and Stern fighters who took part in the attack were more accustomed to throwing bombs at Arab buses than conducting difficult military exercises, a fact which may explain why, after they had captured the village following a two-hour gun-battle, they conducted a wholesale massacre of the survivors. In all 284 villagers – from new-born babies to women in their eighties – were slaughtered. Although the massacre was roundly condemned by Jewish leaders, it was seized upon by the Arabs as a graphic example of the tactics employed by the Zionists to drive innocent families from their homes.

Out of curiosity I ask a Palestinian acquaintance to take me to Deir Yassin to see what remains of the village that is now enshrined in Palestinian mythology. Samir al-Junali, a short, stocky, engaging man in his late thirties, is a veteran PLO activist. Twice jailed by the Israelis – once for being a member of the PLO, then a banned organisation – Samir these days divides his time between running his own jewellery business in the Old City and supervising the sports curricula of local Palestinian schools.

'I fought for my rights when I had none,' he explains philosophically. 'But now we have peace and I want to believe in the future.'

A Jerusalemite, he has only recently discovered, while on a visit to neighbouring Jordan, that his paternal grandfather owned a large house in Deir Yassin. His grandfather was a stone-mason and had been working on a restoration project at the Dome of the Rock, and so had been absent during the massacre. The family had subsequently become refugees in the Old City, where Samir was born. The loss of the family home had been so traumatic that Samir was raised knowing little of his family past. It was only when he reached adulthood that he learned that his family came from Deir Yassin, and his subsequent inquiries turned up the fact that the family house was still standing.

'We'll take your car,' he insists when I suggest we try to find his house. 'I'll feel more comfortable. I don't think they like Arabs driving around that area.'

For guidance we have an old sepia photograph of the house, a handsome-looking stone building, which Samir found in a Jordanian account of the Deir Yassin massacre. The only other clue we have is that, according to the book, the house is being used as a dormitory for Israeli doctors who work at a local hospital. We drive across the city for about twenty minutes in the general direction of the village without knowing its specific whereabouts. As we reach the outskirts, Samir motions me to stop.

'Let's ask this man directions,' says Samir. 'He should know where to go.'

'How do you know that?' I ask.

'Because he's an Arab.'

'Really?'

'Well, he's not a Jew, is he?'

I find it difficult to tell the difference. But Samir is right, and after exchanging a few pleasantries, the Arab tells us to follow the signs for Givat Shaul, an Israeli industrial zone located at the start of the main Jerusalem–Tel Aviv motorway. We drive on for another mile until we reach an ugly collection of factories. To my eye the buildings look like any other industrial park, charmless utility blocks of no particular interest. But Samir has seen something.

'Look at that,' he remarks. 'See there, in the middle of that building.

112

That's the remains of an old Arab house.' As I study the outline of the building, I can see what he means. The lower part of the building, which appears to be a warehouse, has clearly been built in the traditional Arab style. But the original structure has been subsumed by a number of ugly, haphazard additions which virtually erase its noble profile. We stop the car to take a closer look at our surroundings. We find that several Arab buildings have been assimilated in similar fashion.

'This is it. This is Deir Yassin,' says Samir.

Apart from the vague outline of the old Arab buildings, there is little to suggest this has once been an exclusively Arab dwelling-place. We come across two Arab houses that have been turned into a school. The old garden is filled with swings and sandpits, and the young children are playing with abandon, oblivious to the tragic past concealed in the earth beneath them. There is little else to suggest the land's ancestry. All the new development confirms we are in a modern, working-class Israeli suburb. The village land has been covered with roads and buildings, and the old stone quarry is now the main municipal works depot. As we drive around we attract the interest of various Israelis who are surprised to see an Arab with a foreign chauffeur.

'They keep looking at me as though I'm a suicide bomber or something,' Samir remarks.

Although he is starting to feel uncomfortable, Samir insists that we continue with our mission. On the outskirts of the neighbourhood we come across a large Jewish cemetery that has been carved out of the confiscated land. 'They massacre our villagers so that they can bury their dead,' says Samir. 'What sense does that make?'

We stop by a group of men who are sitting under a tree preparing a gravestone. An Israeli supervisor is smoking a cigarette while his two Arab employees are chiselling a Hebrew memorial into the thick stone slab. Samir has not noticed the Israeli when he asks me to stop, and looks uneasy as he asks the Arab workers for directions to the local hospital.

'Which hospital?' asks the Arab craftsman.

'The one in Deir Yassin,' Samir replies.

The Israeli frowns. 'There's no Deir Yassin here. This is Givat Shaul,' he says.

Samir persists. 'Is there a hospital near here, or some kind of health centre?'

One of the Arabs offers to show us the way to save Samir further embarrassment from the Israeli manager and, after a short drive, we find ourselves at the gate of a hospital complex.

'I think this is what you're looking for,' he says.

The sign is in Hebrew, which neither of us can read and, rather than try to explain what we want to the guard, we decide to stride purposefully in. If challenged, we agree to say we are going to visit a patient. Once inside, Samir notices an Arab cleaner collecting some laundry. He winks at me and goes over to the Arab, and the two men speak briefly in a conspiratorial hush. When he returns, Samir is excited.

'The house is up here. Follow me.'

We walk up the hospital's main thoroughfare and, as we become accustomed to our surroundings, we are both struck by the same breathtaking realisation.

'Do you know where we are? This is the main street of Deir Yassin,' Samir exclaims.

On each side of the hospital road stand the unmistakable outlines of Arab houses. Each house has a sign on it, denoting the various medical departments. Some of the smaller buildings remain boarded up – untouched since the infamous events of 1948. As we walk along we see that the whole lay-out of the original village has been pre-served intact, almost like an Arab heritage museum. Little alleyways, with arched coverings, meander off the main street. Wooden covers lie across the old wells. Bold, arched doorways protect secluded courtyards. The mystery and majesty of the simple, parochial Arab architectural style is here in abundance.

At the top of the thoroughfare a large, imposing house confronts us. Samir fumbles for a minute in his Jordanian book until he finds the picture he is seeking. He holds up the book, looks at the picture and then back to the building.

'This is it. This is our family home,' says Samir. Apart from its design, the building no longer looks like an Arab home. A large Israeli flag is draped across one of the walls. As if for emphasis, just a few yards away another Israeli flag hangs limply from a flagpole. A sign written in Hebrew, Arabic and English confirms that the building is now a dormitory for the medical staff. On closer inspection it also reveals something even more astonishing than what we have already witnessed.

As we have walked through the hospital grounds we have both noticed some rather odd-looking people – men and women – hovering in the shadows. They do not look like ordinary patients because they are wearing everyday clothes. Some of the men wear kippas on their heads and, while we have become used to people staring at us during our perambulation through the Israeli development zone, some of the stares we attract from the hospital patients are distinctly unnerving. The sight of a PLO activist accompanying a British visitor on a tour of the hospital complex might appear unusual, but some of the patients respond to our presence by dribbling down their fronts and, in one case, banging himself enthusiastically on the head with his hand. Everything is now revealed. The former Arab village of Deir Yassin has been transformed, the sign informs us, into the Givat Shaul Psychiatric Hospital.

Samir is visibly upset and cannot help but state the obvious.

'This is madness,' he says. 'I thought I wanted to see our house, but now that I see what they have done to our village, I wish I'd never come. It is the worst possible nightmare. Your family is thrown out of their village and then, when they return, it has been taken over by the insane. Let's get out of here before I go crazy myself.'

Before we take our leave of this Dante-esque scene, Samir bends down to pick some wild weeds growing at the side of one of the buildings. 'These are the kind of flowers that would have grown here when my family lived in the house,' he says. 'I'll take some of them with me to keep. To remind me of the land we lost.'

# 6

# SPOILS

*'Go to, let us build us a city, and a tower'*
Genesis 11: 4

There must be an Israeli election taking place.

—How do you know?

Because I can't sleep.

—Why's that?

Because it's 2 A.M. and the City Council is digging a big hole outside my apartment. There's a big mechanical digger going BANG, BANG, BANG at the road. It's been going on for hours. They say they'll stop at dawn, when the traffic starts up. It's driving me MAD.

—What's it got to do with an election?

Plenty. I'm living in East Jerusalem, okay? Everyone knows no one from City Hall ever shows their face here. You don't believe me? Just look at the place. It's a museum piece. No one's touched the roads here in years (1967 to be exact). Or anything else, for that matter (please, let's not talk about the sewage). All of a sudden, without warning, they've decided to start a road-improvement scheme. In the middle of the night. On a road hardly anyone uses.

116

—I still don't get it.

Nor did I till I went up to the guy in charge and asked him what the hell he was doing waking everyone up with his infernal machines. I wasn't the only one there. Lots of other people were complaining too. Lots of Arabs with little pot bellies poking through their pyjamas (too much houmous). We were all livid. We got the Arab working the machine to stop the BANG, BANG, BANG while we shouted at the Israeli foreman.

—What did he say?

He said he had his orders.

—From whom?

City Hall. The Mayor's Office. Mr Olmert, to be precise. Not only did he have his orders, he also had a police permit! A police permit to dig up a road! Why? Because the bureaucrats at City Hall thought they'd provoke a riot if they started digging up a road in the middle of the night. So they've made sure the road diggers have got two policemen to protect them, just in case.

—Why go to all this trouble?

Because there's an election going on. At least that's what the local Arabs tell me. Olmert's one of these Israeli politicians who thinks he can do whatever he likes whenever he likes, and to hell with those – like the thousands of Arabs living on his doorstep – who dare object.

—But why dig up a road in the middle of the night?

Because it's in East Jerusalem – *Arab* East Jerusalem – and Olmert wants to prove he's got as much electoral testosterone as anyone else in Israel. Now there's a Middle East peace process going on, everyone in Israel is getting totally hysterical about Jerusalem – all Jerusalem, their eternal, indivisible, conquered, liberated, it's-ours-whatever-you-say-and-you-can't-have-it-back-yah-boo-sucks Jerusalem.

—So he decides to dig up a road in the middle of the night to show who's boss?

Precisely. As mayor, he's in charge of the whole city, including all the Arab parts the Israelis annexed in 1967. Normally the Israeli officials who run the council have little to do with the Arab areas. When they do, it's only to deny them planning permission or to take their land. But with an election looming, Olmert thought he'd impress the Israeli voters by digging up an Arab road.

—Smart work.

Dirty work, more like.

—How much longer is this going on?

A few more days. The election's next week. Olmert will have made his point by then. And won a few more votes.

—And what are you going to do in the meantime?

Pray that Olmert loses.

Jerusalem has changed a great deal since the bitter days of 1948. The modern city, both in terms of its size and demographic composition, is largely unrecognisable from its pre-war form. The best view of the modern city is not from the Mount of Olives but from the Tomb of Samuel, located high on a ridge to the north-west. During the 1948 war Glubb Pasha's Arab Legionnaires used the ridge to shell the city. In the 1967 Six-Day War, when the Israelis forcibly reunited the city, Yitzhak Rabin, the Israeli Chief of Staff, made the recapture of the ridge and its mosque one of his top priorities. The interior of the mosque itself says a great deal about the city's political, religious and ideological transformation. The mosque is virtually deserted. The last time I visited it the only inhabitants were some feral cats that were basking in the comfort of the prayer mats. I was told Muslim prayer services still took place on Fridays. For the most part the mosque is now a Yeshiva, a Jewish study centre. Samuel may be acclaimed as a prophet by both Jews and Muslims, but one of his first acts was, after all, to help the Israelites smite the troublesome Philistines,[1] so it is hardly surprising the Jews should have the upper hand. The mosque is just one example. Look at Jerusalem from this historic vantage point and, for as far as the eye can see, the city has been entombed in a massive concrete sarcophagus. Gone are the gentle hills and mysterious valleys that provided sustenance for the city's wounded spirit, the quiet places for contemplation and reflection that nourished the soul. They have been replaced by ugly, Kafka-esque housing developments and traffic-choked inner-city road networks that dominate the landscape. The traditional, cherished view of Jerusalem – spires, domes and terraces – has all but been obliterated by Israel's frantic effort to consolidate its conquest of the city. To look at Jerusalem today is to

1 The Arabic for Palestinian is 'Filesteen', from 'Philistine'.

view the ruthless triumph of Zionism over the spiritual capital of the world.

The first important step towards Jerusalem's conurban metamorphosis came soon after a final ceasefire had been agreed in 1948, when the leaders of the new state of Israel decided to make Jerusalem their capital. To listen to Israel's present-day political élite, it would appear the decision was a foregone conclusion. In fact, while most Israelis wanted Jerusalem as their capital for historical and emotional reasons, the decision was not straightforward in the immediate aftermath of the war. Apart from being divided, the city was accessible only by means of a narrow corridor linking it to the main centres of Jewish population on the coastal plain, and supply convoys were still susceptible to attack long after the ceasefire was implemented. In addition, there were various foreign proposals still being discussed for the internationalisation of the city. Among the more controversial plans advanced was that of Count Folke Bernadotte, the first of many United Nations mediators to visit the city, who suggested it be placed under Arab control. Although Bernadotte changed his mind after realising his proposal was unworkable, on 17 September 1948, as he was being driven to Rehavia, the Swedish aristocrat was murdered by members of Yitzhak Shamir's Stern gang.

In 1949 the United Nations Palestine Conciliation Commission produced its plan for Jerusalem under which it would become a separate entity under United Nations control. Some very senior Israelis at the heart of the decision-making process were very tempted by the UN proposal. They regarded Jerusalem as a liability, and thought it could be traded to secure a better deal for the rest of Israel, so long as the city's Jewish population was protected by international guarantees. All this is now conveniently overlooked by Israeli politicians, most of whom recoil in horror at even the remotest suggestion that the entire city may not be the sole, legitimate property of the Jewish people. As with so much else that has happened to the city over the past fifty years, the facts have been tailored to fit the politicians' cloth.

Teddy Kollek, who worked as a political adviser to David Ben-Gurion immediately after the war, recalls a sharp debate within Israel's fledgling leadership over where to locate the capital. 'Jerusalem was a miserable little place. It had been devastated by war and it was divided,' explains Kollek. Now well into his eighties, he pontificates on the foibles of his successors at City Hall from his office at the Jerusalem Foundation, an organisation situated off the Bethlehem Road which many Israelis regard as his 'council chamber-in-exile'. As a former confidante of Ben-Gurion and one of the few survivors of that remarkable Zionist epoch, Kollek's views still carry considerable weight. As someone who has devoted most of his adult working life to the city's development, he has the advantage of knowing what he's talking about.

'I remember Golda Meir suggested somewhere in the north like Haifa because it was in the centre of the country, whereas Jerusalem was a frontier town, with all that meant. Others spoke about Tel Aviv, where a lot of our official offices were located, while Ben-Gurion himself was quite keen on Beersheva.' Beersheva, a new town in the Negev desert, was a cause close to Ben-Gurion's heart. To make Israel a thriving, prosperous state, he believed Zionists should make the desert bloom. Eventually the politicians opted for Jerusalem, not because it was the ideal location, but because of its extraordinary significance for the Jewish people.

One of the first acts undertaken by the newly formed state of Israel was the removal of all immigration controls imposed by Britain. This opened the floodgates for hundreds of thousands of Jews from all over the world to settle in the first Jewish state for 2,000 years. The vast majority were, of course, the survivors of Hitler's holocaust – Germans, Romanians, Hungarians, Czechs and Poles. There were large numbers of Jews from the Soviet Union, victims of the massive tide of human misery created by the fluctuating military fortunes at the Russian front. Then there were immigrants from more exotic locations, North Africa and the Middle East, oriental Jews who either actively sought to join the exciting adventure taking place on the eastern shores of the Mediterranean or who were forced to do so by Arab governments seeking to avenge their defeat in the 1948 war. While Israel eagerly collected together these disparate strands of the Diaspora, the influx of so many people from such a variety of backgrounds created enormous problems. The new citizens of Israel spoke a multitude of tongues, enjoyed widely differing social customs and, in short, had little in common except their Jewish heritage. What the state dearly needed was an emblem, a talisman to which all these different Jewish cultures might rally. The founding fathers realised the need to bind the state together, to forge a sense of nationhood and national identity. These considerations greatly influenced David Ben-Gurion's decision to make Jerusalem the new capital.

'Pray for the peace of Jerusalem.'

'If I forget thee Oh Jerusalem.'

'Next year in Jerusalem.'

To be a Jew is to worship Jerusalem. The Zionist leadership might not have been the most regular synagogue attendees, but they had no doubts about the city's significance for world Jewry. The Israeli government, following the precedent set by King David nearly 3,000 years previously, sought to unite the members of their new nation by making Jerusalem the capital. The decision in favour of West Jerusalem, that portion of the city under Israel's control at the end of the 1948 war, had the wholehearted support of Israeli public opinion which, after the experience of 1948, no longer had any faith in promises of international protection. While Jerusalem was regarded as an integral part of the new Israeli state, for most Israelis this claim only applied to that section of the city – what Israelis called the New City – under Jewish control. Few Israelis were interested in governing Arab East Jerusalem. People like Menachem Begin, the fiery heir to Vladimir Jabotinsky's Revisionist tradition, would no doubt have argued in favour of Israel's occupation of the whole city as part of the quest to occupy *Eretz Israel*, but they occupied the extreme fringe of the Israeli political spectrum, and enjoyed little support.

Modern Israeli politicians behave as though there was never any doubt that Jerusalem would become the state's political capital. With their mantra-like references to Jerusalem being the 'eternal capital of the Jewish people', they often blur the distinction between Zionism and Judaism to score a political point at the Palestinians' expense. This is especially ironic as most Israeli politicians prefer to live in Tel Aviv, and conduct much of their work there. Even most Israelis who live outside the city have only a vague idea about the geography of their capital. Asking an Israeli taxi driver at Tel Aviv's Ben-Gurion airport to be taken to a Jerusalem address is like asking for a ride to the moon. But it is people like them who support the politicians, and they can never resist the opportunity to make pseudo-religious, nationalistic statements. Unfortunately, Jewish history is not particularly helpful for their cause. Jerusalem was the political capital, under David and Solomon, of a united Jewish state for approximately seventy years. Its paramountcy ended because of the tribal rivalries of the ancient Hebrews. Even the ill-fated Crusader Kingdom of Jerusalem in the eleventh century, which survived for eighty-eight years, had a longer life-span. After the division of the Israelite nation in 993 BC the city continued to be the administrative centre of a rump Jewish state for another two hundred years. It was a Jewish capital, but not *the* Jewish capital. (Shechem became the capital of the ancient Kingdom of Israel in the north.) After the destruction of both the Kingdoms of Israel and Judah, Jerusalem reappeared in Roman times as a Jewish administrative centre, mainly thanks to Herod's flattery of Augustus. But when it tried to assert its independence, it was mercilessly crushed. In essence David's dream of making Jerusalem the capital of the Israelite nation was short-lived, and for most of the past 3,000 years the city has known a variety of masters, none of whom has chosen to make her their capital.

The politicians, both Labour and Likud, would be on far stronger ground if they kept their musings on Jerusalem to a more modern context. Yes, Jerusalem is undoubtedly important, crucial even, for the Jewish people. It is not only the holiest city in Judaism, it is the *only* city in Judaism, the only place on earth where Jews believe the spirit of the Lord Jehovah is present. Even for Jews who are not religious, the concept of Jerusalem is a vital part of their cultural heritage. But the politicians will insist on playing with their history books. Take some of the utterances of Likud leader Benjamin Netanyahu during the 1996 general election campaign. 'Jerusalem has been the capital of the Jewish people for the last 3,000 years. It is going to remain that way, undivided, united, with freedom of access to all faiths. In terms of sovereignty, it will remain the capital of Israel, the capital of the Jewish people.' Netanyahu is worth quoting because he won. Not that the view of his opponent, Shimon Peres, was much different. 'There is one thing on which we all stand united: Jerusalem will always be the united capital of Israel. We only have one Jerusalem, and we will not allow anyone to divide the city. We are the only people for whom Jerusalem has not only been in our prayers, but our capital. The city has never been the capital of another people.'

Back in 1948, the new Israeli government was not quite so forth-right in its view of Jerusalem. Ben-Gurion and the other Zionist leaders felt humiliated that the war had resulted in the city's division, particularly as it meant religious Jews were denied access to the Wailing Wall. It appeared that the Zionists had succeeded in creating a state for the Jewish people in which Jews were not allowed to pray at their holiest shrine. The division of the city between 1948 and 1967 was arguably more traumatic for the Israelis than the Arabs, which is one of the reasons why today's Israeli leadership is so insistent about stressing its claim to the whole city. Ben-Gurion devoted much energy to rectifying this state of affairs, and entered into secret negotiations with King Abdullah of Transjordan. During the period between 1948 and 1951, the Israelis and Jordanians had a lengthy, and constructive, dialogue. Ben-Gurion tried to persuade Abdullah to grant Israel sovereignty over the Jewish Quarter of the Old City and access to the Wailing Wall in return for extending Jordan's control over Arab areas of the city under Israeli control. Certainly both countries were more interested in cutting their own deal on Jerusalem rather than leaving the city's fate to some amorphous international supervision. The negotiations came to nothing, and religious Jews were excluded from praying at the Wall until the Six-Day War. Had Abdullah survived, it seems likely that the two sides would have worked out an arrangement to their mutual advantage. Neither Abdullah nor Ben-Gurion paid much heed to the requirements of Palestinian Arab leaders, who were hardly consulted.

The modern insistence of Israeli leaders that Jerusalem is the eternal capital of the Jewish people – a claim, moreover, based on events that happened 3,000 years ago – often antagonises all those with an interest in the city, particularly Christians and Muslims, and can attract unnecessary feelings of ill-will. If followed to its logical conclusion, of course, this assertion would mean Jerusalem is the capital for a Jew living in New York, London, or Paris, which begs the question: since when did a person's religious beliefs qualify them for dual nationality? Do Catholics claim citizenship of the Vatican? Do all Muslims qualify for Saudi Arabian nationality? Surely it would make more sense if Israel simply stated that Jerusalem was its capital because it was an important and historic Jewish population centre, was home to a seminal Judaic shrine, and had been won through force of arms after a lengthy and, in terms of human suffering, costly war. Given the political and geographical changes that have taken place in mainland Europe over the past century, few would argue with that. There is an important distinction between a site that is revered as a place of worship and a city that has been adopted as a seat of government.

The annual Ammunition Hill memorial service is one of many occasions in the official Israeli calendar when this awkward interlinking of Judaism and Zionism manifests itself. The ceremony, which takes place on Jerusalem Day, is held ostensibly to commemorate the Israeli soldiers killed in the 1967 war. Ammunition Hill, which is now located in the bustling Israeli suburb of Ramat Eshkol (named after the Israeli Prime Minister of the time), was the site of the toughest and ultimately decisive battle for total control of the city. The original Jordanian trenches, where some two dozen young Israelis met their deaths, have been preserved intact amid tastefully landscaped gardens. The service I attended had been adapted for Mayor Olmert's Jerusalem 3000 celebrations, with simultaneous translations in English, French and Spanish. The main purpose of the ceremony, so far as I could ascertain, was to encourage the audience of predominantly Latin American Jewish fundraisers to even greater exertions on behalf of the Jewish National Fund. A sophisticated sound and light system had been set up for the evening, and the various guest speakers – an Israeli general, the mayor, veterans of both the 1948 and 1967 wars – made speeches that contained a host of biblical references, from King David to the flight of the children of Israel from Egypt, which inevitably ended with statements such as 'Jerusalem was always the capital of the Jewish people' (loud applause) and 'Jerusalem is the indivisible capital of Israel, and will always remain so' (sustained cheers).

Throughout the ceremony squads of young, and heavily-armed, Israeli paratroopers patrolled the perimeter, guarding against the possibility of a terrorist attack, tangible proof that the various claims being made from the podium did not merit universal approval. Elsewhere in the city thousands of Israeli schoolchildren spent the day on a 'mass hike' through the city. For organisational purposes the children were divided into small groups of forty, and each group had two adult assistants armed with automatic rifles to protect them from attack as they traversed the Arab-populated areas of Israel's 'united and indivisible' city.

One of the major accomplishments of Zionism has been to inspire the Palestinian Arabs to pursue their own nationalist goals. But if the Israeli claims to the city have their flaws, those of the Palestinians are even harder to substantiate. They may claim that from the seventh century, the time of Omar's conquest, Jerusalem has been an Arab city run by a Palestinian mayor, but it has never been an Arab capital. During the pre-Crusader Muslim period Ramleh, not Jerusalem, was the regional Arab metropolis. After the Crusaders were expelled by Saladin in AD 1187, the city fell under the auspices of more important regional centres such as Damascus, Cairo and Istanbul. This was very much in keeping with the Islamic tradition whereby it is regarded as profane to site an ungodly government capital in a holy place. The capital of Saudi Arabia is Riyadh, a city specially built for the purpose, not Mecca or Medina. Even when Sharif Hussein of the Hejaz (King Hussein of Jordan's great-grandfather) enjoyed the title 'Custodian of the Holy Places' at the turn of the century, he made Jeddah his administrative centre. Similarly in Iraq and Iran, holy places such as, respectively, Najaf and Qom, are untainted by the worldly claims of political intrigue.

The refusal of Arab Muslims to make Jerusalem their capital could be said to enhance, rather than diminish, their regard for the city. Israelis are fond of playing down the city's significance for Muslims, pointing out that it comes only third in importance after Mecca and Medina, whereas Jerusalem is first and foremost a holy city for Jews. This rather derogatory attitude, which does the Israelis little credit, is a serious misjudgement of the importance of Jerusalem for Muslims. If the twin cities of Mecca and Medina, the sites of the Prophet's birth and ministry, have equal status in the thoughts of Muslims, Jerusalem comes a close second. Apart from containing many important holy Islamic shrines – of which the Haram al-Sharif complex is the most important – Muslims, as do Jews and Christians, believe Jerusalem will be the scene of the great ingathering at the Last Judgement. *Al-Quds*, The Holy, is regarded as an essential part of the *Haj*, the pilgrimage all devout Muslims are required to undertake as one of the five pillars of Islam. In the early days of Islam the faithful

even developed the habit of circumambulating the sacred rock at the
Haram (the rock originally purchased by King David from Arauna the
Jebusite), much the same as pilgrims parade around the Kabah at
Mecca, although this practice has long-since stopped. Today *al-Quds*
is the traditional starting point for the *Haj*. Any Muslim who commences the *Haj* in Jerusalem is forgiven all their sins, and a prayer
said at al-Aqsa mosque is worth five hundred times more than one
said at any other mosque.[2] Muslims who are unable to originate their
*Haj* from Jerusalem are nevertheless encouraged to visit the city.
Those who do so are known as *Taqdees*, 'more holy', which comes
from the Arabic word *Qaddasa*, which literally means 'to make holy',
but is understood more generally by Palestinians as 'to be Jerusa-
lemised'.

Before 1967, hundreds of thousands of Muslims from all over the
Middle East would complete the *Haj* in this manner. Since Israel
took control of the city, political considerations have meant that very
few are now allowed to enter. While the Israelis may claim to have
good reason to impose such tough restrictions, denying devout
Muslims access to Jerusalem should make them more careful in their
public pronouncements about the importance of the shrines to Islam.
By seeking to diminish the importance of Jerusalem for Arabs, as
Israeli politicians often do, Israel not only succeeds in causing outrage among Palestinian Muslims, it also runs the risk of committing
a grave insult against the entire international Islamic community – all
one billion of them.

The flaws in the Palestinian arguments, however, appear the
moment Yasser Arafat and his PLO leadership claim Jerusalem as the
capital of an independent Arab state. If Israeli politicians are guilty of
obscuring the distinction between Zionism and Judaism, the
Palestinians find it equally difficult to distinguish between Islam and
Arab nationalism. To pray in Jerusalem is a special privilege; to
govern the city is another matter entirely.

The genesis of the PLO's claim to Jerusalem as the undisputed
capital of an independent Palestine is a surprisingly recent development. As with the Israelis, Palestinian politicians scoff at any
suggestion that their claim to the city is less than valid, and even

2 From an interview with Ekrima Sabri, Grand Mufti of Jerusalem, April 1995.

claim descent from the ancient Jebusites to support their case. But throughout the 1920s and 1930s Palestinian Arabs never articulated the notion that the city should become the capital of an independent, Arab-governed Palestine. Nor did this position change substantially in the aftermath of the 1948 war. The war was fought more to prevent the establishment of a Jewish state than with any clear-cut objective in mind of what would become of 'liberated' Palestine if victory were secured.

Soon after the war Jerusalem and the West Bank, those areas of Palestine still under Arab control, were unilaterally annexed by the Hashemite dynasty in Jordan. Having lost control of Mecca and Medina after Sharif Hussein's expulsion from the Hejaz by the Sauds, the Hashemites were keen to lay claim to Jerusalem to justify their ancient title of Custodians of the Holy Places. King Abdullah of Jordan, son of Sharif Hussein of the Hejaz and the founder of the modern Jordanian state (formerly Transjordan), ordered Glubb Pasha to concentrate his guns on Jerusalem during 1948 with this specific purpose in mind, with the result that the eastern sector of the city, together with all the major Islamic shrines, came under his protection after the war. Having established a foothold in Jerusalem, King Abdullah had no desire to relinquish it. Abdullah was particularly flattered by Count Bernadotte's plan which placed Jerusalem directly under his suzerainty. When it became clear the Israelis were going to declare Jerusalem their capital, he followed suit by annexing the territory under his control to Jordan.

The swift assertion of Jordan's claim to Jerusalem was not received with widespread enthusiasm by the city's Palestinian community. There were those who privately rejoiced that the move effectively isolated Haj Amin al-Husseini, who was now in exile in Egypt. But the Palestinian Arabs sought some form of independence from Jordan and appointed their own mayor, the staunchly nationalist Arif al-Arif, to run East Jerusalem. Tensions between Palestinians and Jordanians were ever-present during the nineteen years Jordan was responsible for administering the city's remaining Arab neighbourhoods, the most notable example being the murder of King Abdullah in 1951 when he travelled to Jerusalem to pray at the al-Aqsa mosque. The sinister hand of Haj Amin was suspected of orchestrating the assassination plot, which ensured that the deposed Mufti spent the remainder of his days in exile until his death in Beirut in 1975. In 1953 King Hussein of Jordan – who succeeded Abdullah because of his father's ill-health – made East Jerusalem 'the alternative' capital of Jordan, although the Jordanians did little to put this into practice. Palaces, government departments, universities, hospitals – all the infrastructure of a capital city – were concentrated in Amman, not Jerusalem. The Hashemites preferred to honour the Islamic custom that a holy city should not be a centre of government, while at the same time securing their own future in the new Jordanian kingdom.

The failure of the Jordanians to make sufficient investment in Jerusalem was a constant source of complaint among Palestinians, who accused Amman of deliberate discrimination and turning the city into a village. The dissent reached boiling point in 1963 when Palestinians demonstrated against King Hussein, and called for the establishment of a Jordanian republic made up of Jordanian and Palestinian citizens. The brutal response of the Jordanian army – eleven demonstrators were shot dead in Jerusalem – prompted local Palestinian leaders to respond in a way which would have a lasting and dramatic impact on the political destiny of the Palestinian people.

The first meeting of the Palestine National Council (PNC), a summit of all the leading Palestinian leaders and families, was convened in May 1964 at Jerusalem's Seven Arches Hotel,[3] one of the few prestigious developments constructed in Jerusalem during the Hashemites' reign. From this vantage point on the Mount of Olives, with its spectacular view of the Dome of the Rock, the initial conference was opened by King Hussein himself in an attempt to heal the bloody rift between Palestinians and Jordanians that had preceded the meeting. But the driving force behind the series of meetings that continued throughout May and June 1964 was Arif al-Arif, the former mayor. At the end of the sessions the PNC issued its Covenant, setting out a set of principles and demands. One of the more noteworthy of the thirty-three articles was the twenty-sixth, which authorised the Palestine Liberation Organisation to perform the role of liberating Palestine. But nowhere in the document was any mention made of Jerusalem.

3 It is now the Intercontinental Hotel.

The Covenant referred in detail to Palestine being 'the homeland of the Arab Palestinian people'. Like many of the Palestinian political initiatives that had preceded it, the Covenant was more concerned with the destruction of the 'Zionist occupation' of Palestine than the construction of an independent Palestinian state with Jerusalem as its capital. Some Palestinian apologists claim that no mention was made of Jerusalem at this time out of deference to the Jordanians who were still in control of the city. The fact that the initial meeting of the PNC was held in Jerusalem, where the golden Dome of Mohammed's shrine formed an impressive backdrop to the delegates' deliberations, should be taken as sufficient proof of the Palestinians' intentions.

The Palestinians publicly articulated their desire for Jerusalem to be the future capital of a Palestinian state only after the Israelis drove the Jordanians from the capital in the 1967 Six-Day War. With the Hashemites out of the way, Yasser Arafat, the new leader of the Palestine Liberation Organisation, was free to claim that, in future, Jerusalem would be the capital of an independent Palestinian state. But the claim only acquired substance in the aftermath of Israel's 1967 victory. It was the first time an Arab leader had ever regarded the Holy City as a potential capital. Officially, Jerusalem was first claimed as the capital of a future Palestinian state at the PNC meeting in Cairo in 1974, when it was one of ten new principles agreed by the conference delegates.

The politicisation of Jerusalem, then, is a recent phenomenon, and one that has had a dramatic impact on the city. Perhaps the greatest transformation has been in terms of the city's size. In 1948 there were 100,000 Jews living in the city out of a population of 165,000; by 1995 the number had risen to 500,000 out of 650,000. If the Jordanians ignored the city out of deference for its sanctity and the Hashemite desire to establish a new dynasty on the east bank of the River Jordan, the Israelis were unencumbered by any such constraints and seized their opportunity with relish. The primary requirement for a developing city is land, and the Israelis found they had it in abundance with all the deserted properties that had fallen into their hands following the flight of the Arabs from their homes during 1948. The war had been conducted with such bitterness that few Israelis had much compassion for their former Arab neighbours. Most of them took the view that if the Arabs had won, they would not have shown any leniency towards the Jews. An estimated 60,000 Jerusalem Arabs were either evicted or fled their homes during the war. But it was not just the waves of new Israeli immigrants who coveted the abandoned Palestinian properties.

The Israeli architects who have constructed modern Jerusalem – what the Palestinians call the 'Judaization' of the Holy City – have accomplished their task with such aplomb that the expropriation of the old Arab areas is almost seamless. Traces of old Arab villages can be found on the city outskirts in places such as Deir Yassin, Malha and Ein Karem, on the western approaches. But when one looks at buildings such as the Knesset (the Israeli parliament), it is hard to imagine that this impressive structure is built on land that was once the Arab village of Lifta. Indeed, most of the modern government complex in West Jerusalem is constructed on land seized from Arab families after 1948. Apart from the Knesset, the Prime Minister's offices, the ministries of Foreign Affairs and the Interior are all built on what was once Lifta. Other parts of the old village have been used to build modern hotels such as the Sonesta and Holiday Inn. On one occasion, when I had arrived early for a meeting at the Prime Minister's office, I went for a stroll on some wasteland nearby and was surprised to discover I was walking on the rubble, long-covered with weeds and grass, of derelict Arab dwellings.

The pattern is repeated throughout West Jerusalem. The Ministry of Trade and Industry, in Agron Street, is located in a building which was the city's first Palestinian theatre and remains an outstanding example of 1930s Arab architecture. Independence Park is built on part of the former Muslim Mamilla cemetery, while the residence of the Israeli president occupies a large area of the previous Palestinian quarter of Talbieh. In Katamon, the old Arab bourgeois neighbourhood, the airy villas are still standing, but now are either occupied by well-to-do professional Israelis or have been converted into flats. Even Yad Vashem, the Israeli shrine to the Nazi persecution of Jews in Europe which is located on the outskirts of Jerusalem, is built on the terraced land of dispossessed Palestinians from Ein Karem. According to Ibrahim Matar, of the Centre for Policy Analysis on Palestine, who has researched the amount of land taken from the Palestinians by the Israelis after 1948, Yad Vashem 'testifies to the fact that the Palestinians are in fact the last victims of Hitler, as they had to pay with their villages, lands and country for the establishment of the Jewish state'.

The task of taking Arab property and using it as a base to construct the new capital of Israel has been accomplished with ruthless efficiency by a series of laws passed soon after the creation of the Israeli state. All Palestinian property that had been abandoned during the war was seized under the Absentee Property Regulations of 1948. The property was handed over to the Custodian of Absentee Property who was in charge of administering it, but, initially, was not allowed to sell it or lease it for a period exceeding five years. The next step came in 1950 when Israel effectively confiscated the property through the Absentee Property Law, which re-affirmed the right of the Custodian to administer it but provided for the sale of the property, as its official value, to a Development Authority established by the Knesset. In modern parlance, when one looks at events in the former Yugoslav republics, the demographic transformation that took place in Jerusalem after 1948 can best be described as ethnic cleansing. The situation then, of course, was far more complex and the Israelis, surrounded by numerous Arab regimes and peoples who sought their destruction, felt they had no alternative other than to expunge their Arab neighbours. The manner in which the Arabs lost their homes and properties in 1948, however, remains by far their greatest grievance.

The abiding image of Israel's conquest of East Jerusalem and the holy shrines of the Old City is of young paratroopers praying at the Wailing Wall. It sums up Israel's extraordinary military success when, within the space of just six days in June 1967, her armed forces not just defeated, but annihilated the combined armies of Egypt, Syria and Jordan. Apart from bringing the division of Jerusalem to an end, the war left Israel in control of the West Bank of the River Jordan, captured from Jordan, and the Gaza Strip, from Egypt. The conquest of these territories, and the subjugation of some 700,000 Palestinians, added a completely new dimension to the Arab–Israeli conflict. But the capture of Jerusalem was greeted with a mixture of relief and jubilation by the Israelis. Within hours of the conquest of the Old City, Shlomo Goren, the chief rabbi of the Israel Defence Force, was leading a procession of jubilant soldiers and Jews to the Wailing Wall while all the time blowing on a shofar.

The celebrations were all the more poignant because, at the commencement of hostilities, the Israelis had not expected to fight for Jerusalem. In the build-up to the war King Hussein had indicated he did not want to get involved in Gamal Abdel Nasser's Pan-Arab crusade, and the Israelis had sent various messages to Amman reassuring the Hashemite monarch that they had no hostile intent towards Jordan. Having stayed out of the initial exchanges, Jordan only entered the war after the Egyptians, desperate to open a new front to distract the Israeli onslaught against their positions, misled Hussein into thinking Israel was on the brink of defeat. Hussein, the perennial opportunist, who was anxious not to be excluded from any post-war settlement, gave the order for his armed forces to mobilise. Within hours his tanks and fighter-jets had been reduced to twisted heaps of burning metal scattered across the Judaean desert. The decision cost the Jordanian monarch dear. Not only was nearly one third of his kingdom seized by the enemy, but his reckless gamble lost Jordan control of Jerusalem, the sole remaining Islamic jewel in the Hashemite crown.

Israel may not have expected the war to result in the capture of East Jerusalem, but once the entire city had been conquered, Israeli leaders wasted no time making sure the city remained firmly under their control. Although the future of the city was supposed to be decided by the politicians, in effect it was a collection of Israeli generals, past and present, who resolved the city's fate. Moshe Dayan, as defence minister, was directly responsible for the city's administration in the immediate aftermath of the war. In his determination to reunite the city he ordered the immediate dismantling of the barriers that divided the city, brushing aside protests from people like Teddy Kollek, now mayor of the whole city, who warned the move could provoke an orgy of violence between Arab fanatics and Jewish hotheads. During this period Dayan relied heavily on the advice of Yitzhak Rabin, the victorious Chief of Staff, who could enjoy the personal satisfaction of avenging the defeat of 1948, and Rehovam Ze'evi, the extreme right-wing general who had been the commander in charge of central operations – i.e. Israel's pre-war border with the Jordanian West Bank.

Rehovam Ze'evi, the Moledet leader whose party today campaigns for the transfer of all Arabs out of Israeli-controlled territory, was the man entrusted by Dayan to draw up Jerusalem's modern boundaries. From what I've heard about him, I half-expect to meet some rabid fanatic when I visit his office at the Knesset. One of the irascible Ze'evi's more notorious recent exploits was when, in March 1997, he called Martin Indyk, the American Ambassador to Israel, a 'Jewboy' and a 'son of a bitch' at a memorial ceremony for Yitzhak Rabin. Ze'evi was still upset at the level of support Indyk, an American Jew, had apparently lent Shimon Peres during his unsuccessful 1996 election campaign. Indyk was reported to have responded to the insult by saying: 'The last time somebody called me a "Jewboy" was when I was fifteen, and then he got a punch in the face.'

Ze'evi, who is well into his seventies, replied: 'Well, try me. Let's see you. You are a Jewboy.'

'You are a disgrace to your people,' said Indyk, seeking a more diplomatic resolution to the ugly confrontation.

'You are a son of a bitch,' countered Ze'evi.

The exchange caused what is euphemistically called a 'diplomatic incident'. 'We expect that all members of the Israeli Knesset, including the individual in question, will treat our ambassador with dignity,' said an outraged State Department official. Ze'evi was obliged to apologise, the apology was accepted by the ambassador and the episode closed.

I am greeted by a polite and courteous man. Ze'evi has a lean frame which, with his shock of white hair, is punctuated by a pair of sharp, steel-framed glasses. He opens the conversation by stressing that, despite fighting for the removal of the British Mandate in the 1930s and 1940s, he has a warm regard for Britain and the British. He emphasises the point that he is a fifth-generation Jerusalemite and that, contrary to his reputation, he does not hate Arabs.

'It's a lie put about by my opponents that I don't like Arabs,' he explains. 'I have many Arab friends – far more than many so-called left-wing Israelis who would like to give our country back to them. But having been raised with the Arabs, I know that it is impossible for us to live together. Israel does not want the Arabs. We are a small country. The Arabs have twenty-one countries, so they can go and live there. All the Arab countries together are five hundred times the size of Israel. They have plenty of space. They do not need to live here.'

Once into his stride, it is hard to steer Ze'evi from his favourite subject. But I have not come to hear him justify his xenophobia. I want him to explain the role he played in helping Moshe Dayan design the boundaries of modern Jerusalem. Because Rabin was pre-occupied with so many other military problems that arose after the Six-Day War, Dayan asked Ze'evi, an officer with considerable experience of the West Bank area, to draw a new boundary for Jerusalem. The aim was to enable the Knesset to pass an annexation law which would both consolidate the reunification of the city and reward Israel's stunning war victory. It has become part of Palestinian folklore that Ze'evi's initial draft had the city's municipal boundaries taking in half the West Bank – from Ramallah in the north, to Jericho in the east and Hebron in the south. Could this be true?

'My initial proposal was rather over-ambitious, I admit,' Ze'evi says. 'I felt strongly that, given the strength of international opposition to Israel's claim to the city, the Knesset would only be able to pass one annexation law. So I thought it would be a good idea to take in as much land as possible. But Dayan would not agree. He told me not to be in a hurry, that we could take more land later.' Ze'evi was sent back to the drawing board and, at the third attempt, drafted a boundary that was finally acceptable to the Knesset, a boundary which survives to this day. Towards the end of our meeting I ask Ze'evi if Rabin, who was, after all, the Israeli Chief of Staff, was consulted at any point.

'Don't be silly,' he says. 'What did Jerusalem mean to him? Rabin was never religious.'

The formal annexation of East Jerusalem on 22 June 1967 by the Knesset was the signal for another frantic round of development to be undertaken by the Israeli government to consolidate its hold on the city. The flurry of construction activity, which has created the modern city, is mainly an extension of the policies initiated in West Jerusalem after 1948. The first of the new developments, as the Israelis prefer to describe them, or settlements, as they are referred to by the Palestinians and most foreign governments, began with Ramat Eshkol, which was constructed around Ammunition Hill, one of the toughest military targets of the Six-Day War. The first new Jewish residents moved into their apartments in 1969. Since then some 30 new neighbourhoods have sprung up throughout and around the city, enveloping it in strategically located barricades of concrete.

One of the more significant features of new suburbs such as French Hill, Gilo and Ramot, which have provided accommodation for some 200,000 Israelis, is that they are exclusively Jewish. Not one Arab family has been housed in these new developments constructed in the city since 1967, even though Israeli politicians – Teddy Kollek, in particular – have always stressed that their objective was to encourage peaceful co-existence between the two communities. The reality is that Israel's occupation of the city, which has been roundly condemned by various United Nations resolutions, has amounted to a sustained campaign of discrimination against the indigenous Arab population in favour of extending Israeli hegemony over the city, a dominance that was confirmed in 1980 when Menachem Begin's right-wing Likud government reaffirmed Israel's annexation of the city by passing a 'Basic Law' that declared Jerusalem to be 'the eternal, undivided capital of Israel'.

It is the prerogative of the conqueror to savour the fruits of victory. During Jerusalem's long history of conquest and re-conquest, the victors have generally been unable to resist leaving their imprint. Some, like the gauche Crusaders, who fixed a cross from the top of the Dome of the Rock following their victory in 1099, were insensitive to the city's myriad dimensions. Others, like the Mamluks, captured the spiritual and aesthetic essence of the place. But of all the peoples who have occupied the Holy City, none – with the possible exception of Herod 2,000 years ago – has been more systematic and enthusiastic than the modern Israelis in fashioning Jerusalem in their own image.

Since 1967 virtually every Israeli government department – housing, interior, trade and industry, religious affairs, justice, even the foreign ministry – has had its hand in the Jerusalem pie, channelling funds and promoting legislation to strengthen the fortifications of Israel's prized conquest. Roads, housing and industrial developments have transformed the modern city. The old Green Line, which marked the division of Jerusalem between Jordan and Israel, is now a six-lane highway linking the city centre to the new Jewish suburbs on the northern outskirts. In 1967 Palestinians owned 90 per cent of the land in East Jerusalem; by 1995 they had only 13.5 per cent to live on and develop. As a consequence of these land seizures, a further 50,000 Palestinian Arabs have been made homeless. Restrictions on

Palestinian construction projects, imposed by an Israeli ministerial committee in 1973, have been successful in limiting the Palestinian population of the city to 26 per cent of its total. Any Arab house built without the proper authority is liable to demolition; it is inconceivable that a Jewish property could suffer a similar fate. During 1995, thanks to Olmert, more Arab houses were demolished in Jerusalem than during the entire seven-year Palestinian *intifada*. By using his considerable powers in this manner, Olmert sought to undermine the Labour government's peace process and make the Arab residents of the city aware, as if they needed any reminding, of who was boss. Even though there are many Israelis who do not subscribe to Olmert's tactics, there are very few who are actually opposed to Israel's annexation of large areas of the city. Even Peace Now activists, who have been among the more effective in rallying anti-Establishment support, have few objections about Israel's use of confiscated Arab land in Jerusalem. One peace activist I met, who was a vehement campaigner against Israeli settlements in the West Bank, was rather non-plussed when I asked whether he felt the same about the new Jewish neighbourhoods of Jerusalem that were built on Arab land. 'That's not really an issue,' he replied. 'These neighbourhoods are part of the city's territorial integrity.'

The number of Palestinians living in Jerusalem in 1996 – 150,000 – has not changed since 1967, despite the higher Arab birth rate, while the Jewish population has soared to 500,000, a five-fold increase since 1948. Of these, 170,000 Jews live in East Jerusalem, while the Palestinians who have lost their homes have been encouraged to live beyond the municipal boundaries in suburbs like Beit Hanina and towns such as Ramallah. In addition to the activities of the various government departments, the city authorities have ensured that a multitude of planning and development regulations have worked in favour of building a substantial, and comfortable, Jewish majority, much of it in East Jerusalem. Buildings in Jewish neighbourhoods, for example, can be eight storeys high, while Palestinians can only build two storeys. For every 2,200 new apartments built for Jews, there are just 230 for Arabs. Since 1967 the municipal authorities have built just one housing project for local Arabs, the Nusseibeh project, in which several hundred homes were erected in the north of the city.

Otherwise Arab residents have been left to fend for themselves. The initiation of the Oslo peace talks prompted the Israelis to introduce even tougher measures to curb the growth of the Palestinian population, thereby seeking to consolidate Jewish supremacy in the city before the negotiations on its future had even commenced. Arab residents of Jerusalem living abroad had their residency cards withdrawn, and Interior Ministry officials took it upon themselves to define new city boundaries which only applied to Arab residents, which meant that teenagers living in Arab suburbs, such as al-Ram and Abu Dis, were refused identification cards on reaching the qualification age of sixteen. New-born babies were disqualified from registry on their parents cards. The overall effect of these and all the other discriminatory measures the Israelis have applied against the city's Arab residents has been to stamp the indelible imprint of the Jewish nation upon the entire city.

Teddy Kollek, who presided over Jerusalem's modern transmogrification, now admits, in retrospect, that more could and should have been done for the city's Arab residents. 'Our attitude was that if you have a minority you have to make them feel they are getting a good deal,' he says by way of explanation. 'The Arabs have justified complaints, but what we did for them was quite good.' The Palestinians, it must be said, have not helped matters by consistently refusing to co-operate with the Israeli authorities. Sometimes it seems as though the Palestinians actually relish the fact that Saladin Street and the other commercial centres in East Jerusalem are completely run-down, to act as a permanent symbol of protest against the Israeli occupiers, their attempt to emulate the IRA's dirty protest in the 1980s. If the Palestinians' attitude has been unhelpful, a city council which claims to represent the interests of all the city's inhabitants clearly has a responsibility to be just and fair. In his defence, Kollek cites various 'headline-seeking' projects undertaken for the Palestinians, such as a medical centre in Sheikh Jarrah and an impressive library. The city council introduced garbage collection to Arab villages on the outskirts of the city and even persuaded the telephone company to install public pay phones on the streets. But this represents only a tiny fraction of the Israelis' investment in Jewish Jerusalem.

A different perspective on how the city authorities have handled the Palestinians for the past three decades is provided by Amir

Chessin, who acted for many years as Kollek's Arab affairs trouble-shooter at City Hall. 'Teddy was a great politician, but a lousy manager,' he says. 'When things fouled up I was called in to sort them out.' Kollek's biggest 'foul-up', or so many of his supporters believe, was losing the 1993 election and allowing Olmert to take control of the city. Chessin is certainly one of the supporters who thinks this; he was sacked by Olmert for being too close to the Arabs, which is surprising given that Chessin himself is hardly an idealist when it comes to Arab–Israeli relations.

'Our policy was always to give the Arabs something to keep them happy, but not to overdo it. We saw no point on wasting too much money on them when we knew that they hated our guts. So we went for "headline-grabbing" projects which made us look good but cost us nothing. It would have been a lot easier for us to run the city without any Arabs, but we made the effort to include them because we hoped they could be persuaded to participate. But, basically, we failed. We had some Arabs working at City Hall, but they refused to accept any responsibility or take decisions. And so the city was only united superficially and artificially. In reality it was divided. But at least we made the effort. After Olmert took over the city, the attitude became: "The Arabs can stay here, but they can go to hell."'

Despite the enormous satisfaction Israel has derived from building its new Jerusalem, the Israeli policies of the past fifty years have not won many plaudits from the international community, which continues to maintain an almost universal diplomatic boycott of the city. The international displeasure over Israel's treatment of the sensitive Jerusalem issue goes back to the foundation of the state. When Israel's Foreign Ministry moved its offices from Tel Aviv to Jerusalem in 1953, for example, at least six countries – the US, Britain, France, Italy, Turkey and Australia – all condemned the move and insisted that the UN plan be revived for Jerusalem to have some form of international status. After Israel's conquest of the entire city in 1967, this demand was quietly dropped, although the United Nations Security Council unanimously adopted Resolution 478 of 1980 in response to the Begin government's 'Basic Law' annexing East Jerusalem, which was declared to be a violation of international law. This remains the position of the vast majority of foreign governments – including all the Western powers – which continue to maintain their missions in

Tel Aviv on the grounds that, at the very least, a negotiated settlement must first be reached with the Palestinians on the city's future.[4]

This curious state of affairs – unique in the diplomatic world – means that foreign diplomats are obliged to observe a variety of recondite protocols whenever they visit the city. Visiting dignitaries, for example, are advised not to use Jerusalem airport because, technically, it is occupied territory. The justification of the British Foreign Office, in its quaint, post-colonial way, for having its embassy on the Tel Aviv seafront is based on an official government statement issued in April 1950, the last time the subject was raised in Parliament. According to the statement, Her Majesty's Government recognises that Israel exercises *de facto* authority in West Jerusalem. More recently the Foreign Office has updated its position to the effect that the British government, along with its European Union partners, insists that no unilateral attempts to change the status of Jerusalem are valid, and that formal recognition of Israel's claim to Jerusalem will continue to be withheld until an overall agreement is reached between the parties concerned. Thus while the main hub of British diplomatic activity takes place in Tel Aviv, the mission of Her Majesty's Consul-General, located in a smart, but well-fortified, complex in Jerusalem's Sheikh Jarrah neighbourhood, is regarded as the physical expression of the British position by virtue of the fact that the Consul-General is not accredited to any government.

The insistence of all the world's leading powers of treating Israel's capital city as though it were a leper colony not surprisingly provokes, on occasion, an angry response from Israel's political élite. In 1996, when American President Bill Clinton made a stop-over visit to Israel after attending an anti-terrorism summit in Cairo (convened to display international solidarity for the Peres government after the Jerusalem and Tel Aviv suicide bomb attacks), Clinton's aides caused a serious diplomatic row by arranging for the president to meet Israeli officials at the American embassy in Tel Aviv. Ezer Weizman, the Israeli president, threatened to boycott the visit on the grounds that the American president was insulting the Israeli nation by refusing to travel to Jerusalem. But it is not just the Israelis who are sensitive to the city's extraordinary diplomatic predicament. A similar controversy

4 In 1997 only Costa Rica, El Salvador and Bolivia had embassies in Jerusalem.

arose with Palestinian leaders in 1995 when an American Congress dominated by right-wing Republicans called on the Clinton administration to relocate the American embassy from Tel Aviv to Jerusalem.[5] There were vehement protests from the Palestinians, who threatened that, if such a move were made, the whole future of the peace process would be jeopardised. The Palestinians were similarly irked when, in November 1995, Malcolm Rifkind, the then British Foreign Secretary, who came to Jerusalem to attend Yitzhak Rabin's funeral, declined an invitation to meet Palestinian leaders at Orient House out of respect for the memory of the dead Israeli Prime Minister.

If the Israelis have good reason to applaud their astonishing success in making Jerusalem their capital, the Palestinians have by no means given up the fight. After decades of failing to interrupt the Zionists' triumphant creation of infrastructural 'facts on the ground' throughout the city, the first tangible sign of effective Palestinian resistance appeared after the signing of the Oslo Accords. For years Palestinian attempts to highlight their plight had fallen on sympathetic, but ineffectual, ears. The situation began to change with the Rabin government's announcement, in the spring of 1995, that it was seizing 133 acres of Arab land on a hill called Abu Ghneim in the southern outskirts of the city to build 6,500 new Jewish homes for a settlement called Har Homa. The land had originally been expropriated by Teddy Kollek in 1967, who had planted it with a forest of pine trees to prevent any development on the site until the city authorities decided how they wanted to develop it. Arafat was able to foment such a storm of protest that the Israelis, for the first time since 1967, were forced to back down and put the plans on hold. The climbdown was condemned as 'a disgrace to the State of Israel' by the right-wing opposition. A year later, at a Paris conference on Jerusalem, a member of the Palestinian delegation suggested that the PLO might drop its objection to the development if the Israelis allowed Arabs, as well as

5 In 1995 the American government was reported to have purchased a plot of land on the Bethlehem Road, the site of the old Allenby Barracks, for its new embassy. Britain is also thought to have acquired a site nearby, in the hope that the Oslo-inspired peace process would resolve the Jerusalem dispute.

Jews, to benefit from the new housing. 'If we are planning a future of mutual co-operation and co-existence, then it is logical for Jews and Arabs to live together,' said the delegate. His suggestion was emphatically rejected by the Israeli representatives.

The Israelis finally got their way in the spring of 1997 when twelve members of the government's ministerial panel on Jerusalem, headed by Prime Minister Benjamin Netanyahu, gave the go-ahead for construction to begin. The decision was taken just weeks before Israeli and Palestinian negotiators were due to start talks on the final phase of the Oslo peace schedule, the final status negotiations, during which the two sides were to attempt to reach a final settlement on Jerusalem's future. Although Netanyahu was sympathetic to the Har Homa plan, he was encouraged to make the decision by extreme right-wing members of his coalition government who were angry that West Bank land occupied since the 1967 war was being returned to Palestinian control as part of the peace process. Mayor Olmert, supposedly one of Netanyahu's close political allies, expressed the feelings of many right-wing Israeli politicians when he thundered: 'If there is no Har Homa, there is no Bibi.' Netanyahu sought to stave off the criticism by making a rousing speech to a gathering of 2,000 Likud party activists in Tel Aviv. In an attempt to reassure the sceptics, Netanyahu made Jerusalem the focal point of the most hawkish speech he had made since taking office.

'Jerusalem is ours. It was never the capital of a Muslim state. For 3,000 years it was the capital of the Jewish people. Whoever asks Israel to give up the unity of Jerusalem doesn't understand how this chord plays in our hearts. We are going to build on Har Homa and we will build in any other part of the city where we decide to build. No one will prevent us.' Netanyahu received a standing ovation.

Unlike so many previous Israeli land grabs, however, the Har Homa affair attracted considerable international criticism. Apart from the predictable outcry from Arafat's Palestinian Authority, King Hussein of Jordan, President Mubarak of Egypt, King Fahd of Saudi Arabia and President Rafsanjani of Iran, to name but a few Middle Eastern potentates, all condemned the decision. In Washington President Clinton expressed his 'disappointment', even though he admitted he was powerless to intervene. The European Union said it 'deeply deplored' Israel's approval of the construction project. Britain,

France, Portugal and Sweden sponsored a UN Security Council resolution which called on Israel to 'refrain from all actions or measures' that 'alter the facts on the ground' or prejudice future talks on the status of Jerusalem. The resolution also urged Israel to 'abide scrupulously' by its obligations under international law. The resolution failed only because of an American veto, after the US argued the Security Council was not the appropriate forum to resolve land disputes between the Israelis and Palestinians.

Despite this setback, the Palestinians were greatly encouraged by such an impressive show of international support. Through clever and sustained lobbying of the West – particularly the Europeans – Yasser Arafat had succeeded in making sure that, whatever else might happen in the peace process, the future of Jerusalem would be an international issue. Suddenly, all thanks to the Oslo peace process, the Palestinians discovered that they were not alone in resisting Israel's expansionist policies for Jerusalem.

Whether this international awareness can be translated into practical measures is another matter entirely. The Israelis have spent the first fifty years of their national existence cocking a snook at international indignation, especially with regard to their policy on Jerusalem. They are unlikely to mend their ways simply because their foreign foes and allies condemn them for the construction of a small housing estate. Even when Faisal Husseini, the PLO's Jerusalem representative, claims that 90 per cent of the land in East Jerusalem is Arab-owned, the Israelis merely shrug it off as Palestinian posturing. The most telling response to this particular Husseini declaration – which was actually well-founded – was made by a retired Israeli diplomat acquaintance, someone who is genuinely interested in the peace process and has been involved in several Arab–Israeli think-tanks set up to study the city's future administrative arrangements. While he was interested in making peace with the Palestinians, he was not interested in giving them back their land. 'What Faisal says,' he remarked, 'is rather like the Germans turning up at Brest Litovsk or somewhere today and claiming the return of their homes.'

# 7

# CURSES

*'Cursed shalt thou be in the city, and cursed shalt thou be in the field'*

Deuteronomy 28: 15–16

Take a group of rabbis and place them in a secluded room with a dozen black candles. Add a stretcher, some small lead balls, a few shards of earthenware and retire a safe distance. The potency of a rabbinical curse is not to be underestimated. Jews accused of less serious felonies, such as displaying posters of bikini-clad lovelies at Jerusalem bus-stops or running non-kosher restaurants on the sabbath, get off relatively lightly. The rabbis are satisfied merely to condemn the transgressors to forfeit their wordly goods or to suffer perennial bad health. It is those accused of more heinous crimes – excavation of ancient Jewish burial sites or negotiating peace deals with Palestinians – who have most to fear. In these instances the rabbis will not hesitate to invoke the ultimate sanction, what might best be described as a third-degree curse.

Yehudah Meshi-Zahav is a serial curser. 'Meshi' is a Jew who regards the creation of the modern state of Israel as the greatest act of blasphemy in the history of mankind. A slight, wiry man with a wispy beard, earnest bright eyes and a sober demeanour, he bears a striking resemblance to those New World Puritans who, in another age, devoted – and even sacrificed – their lives to making the world a more devout and God-fearing place. In between running his prosperous import-export business which caters exclusively for the burgeoning market of Jerusalem's ultra-Orthodox Jews, Meshi is in the vanguard of the conflict between the city's religious and non-religious Jewish communities. When not supervising his imports of bug-free lettuce (an insect in the salad is a Jewish housewife's nightmare), Meshi is to be found leading the demonstrations to close the city's major road intersections on the sabbath or against the lone Russian-owned sex shop that made a brief appearance on Agrippa Street in the summer of 1995 before tamely surrendering to the overwhelming moral pressure for its closure. Despite his slight appearance, Meshi enjoys a reputation as an indefatigable and ingenious adversary. Were it not for the restrictions imposed by his commitment to the Jewish faith, Meshi would probably make an enterprising officer in an Israeli commando unit. Deprived of channelling his considerable energies in this fashion, Meshi has mastered the art of civil disobedience, not to mention disturbance, to the extent that, more often than not, he and his cohorts succeed in getting their way. It is only when all else fails that Meshi reverts to the most potent weapon of them all – placing a curse on his enemies.

Meshi is quite unapologetic about his curses and quite self-assured as to their effectiveness when he invites me to visit his home in the city's Sanhedria neighbourhood, a northern suburb that is inhabited almost exclusively by *haredim*, ultra-Orthodox Jews, whose lives are regimented by Torah observance. I could almost be taking afternoon tea with the vicar, such is the politeness and courtesy with which I am received. It being summer and very hot, Diet Coke, rather than Earl Grey, is served, together with some home-baked cookies. As we are settling into our chairs for a chat, one of Meshi's daughters, a girl of beguiling beauty, comes skipping out and coyly helps herself to a glass of orange squash from a bottle on the coffee table. In a kindly but firm way her father tells her to join her mother in the kitchen while we are left alone to discuss the rudiments of the rabbinical curse.

There are three kinds of curse, but only the third kind is life-threatening, Meshi explains in a matter-of-fact way. The first kind is hardly a curse at all, more a kind of excommunication from the Jewish faith, which is usually applied to someone who has failed to abide by a rabbinical court order or those rare cases where a *haredi* man or woman decides to renounce the life of religious observance. A curse, of the ill-fortune variety, only becomes active if they continue to pass themselves off as Jews or seek to exact some advantage – financial, personal or otherwise – by virtue of their Jewishness. The second kind is altogether more serious and is only issued after serious deliberations between various rabbis: financial ruin and permanent ill-health are the most likely effects of such a judgement being passed. But this is relatively humane when compared with the third and most serious kind of curse, the *pulsa denura*, the curse of death.

For the *pulsa denura* to achieve maximum effect, and to protect those responsible for administering the curse from unwelcome side-effects, it is necessary to follow a clearly specified procedure. A stretcher, representing the soul of the accused, is placed on the ground, with candles laid out around it. A group of rabbis – ten is usually sufficient for a *minyan*, or quorum – then circle the arrangement seven times, summoning the angels of the Lord to punish the sinner with lashes of fire. This is followed by the lead pellets and earthenware being thrown on the candles; the lead represents the ammunition used in the war against the accursed, the earthenware symbolises death. The event is concluded by a blast of the *shofar*, summoning the skies to open for the *pulsa denura* to resound throughout the heavens. Such is the potency of this curse, Meshi explains, that the rabbis and holy men need to spend much time in earnest deliberation to consider whether the object of their ire was worthy of such drastic punishment.

'It is not something we undertake lightly,' he confides. 'We have to be absolutely sure that the object of our curse is completely without virtue. If we make a mistake and the individual turns out to have virtue, then the curse is likely to rebound on us and we will all be destroyed.'

If all this seems a touch medieval, only the foolhardy should doubt the effectiveness of the rabbinical curse. It is regarded as the ultimate sanction by religious Jews for vanquishing their enemies. They used it in Jerusalem against the early Christians in their efforts to suppress the new faith. Forty rabbis bound themselves under 'a great curse' neither to eat nor drink until they had killed St Paul, and the Romans needed seventy horsemen and two hundred spearmen to spirit him out of the city at dead of night.[1] Similar action was taken at the height of the 1991 Gulf War when, in an effort to detract attention from his disastrous invasion of Kuwait, Saddam Hussein, the Iraqi dictator, launched a barrage of Scud ballistic missiles at Israel. A *minyan* of fasting kabbalist rabbis convened at the tomb of the prophet Samuel. They entered a dark cave, where one of the holy men placed a copper tray (an upmarket stretcher, in deference to Saddam's importance) on a rock and lit the candles. They then chanted the curse seven times, calling on the angels not only to visit death upon 'Saddam, the son of Sabha', but to ensure that his wife was given to another man. 'Then,' explained an Israeli journalist who was allowed to attend the ceremony, 'they blew out the black candles to symbolise that Saddam's soul had been extinguished.' Even though, several years later, Saddam was still ruling the roost in Baghdad, the rabbis were adamant there had been no technical hitch. Saddam had lost the war in humiliating fashion, his country was plagued by an international boycott and even his daughters and sons-in-law deserted him for exile in Jordan.[2] Proof positive, or so they claimed, that their curses really worked.

They had even fewer doubts about the effectiveness of the *pulsa denura* that was made against Yitzhak Rabin two weeks before he was gunned down. Rabin's peace policy, especially his willingness to return the land captured from the Arabs during the Six-Day War to Palestinian control, outraged a large number of religious Jews who do not share Meshi's view that the Israeli nation is profane. There are many religious Jews in Israel who regard the creation of the modern Israeli nation as part of the *geulah*, part of the process of redemption by which Jews make the final preparations for the coming of the Messiah to Jerusalem. It is a central feature of Judaism that Jews must return to their promised land, *Eretz Israel*, the land of Israel, before the Messiah reveals himself, and when this was accomplished

1 Acts 23: 12–14.
2 They were later tempted back after Saddam promised to pardon them. But when the party returned to Baghdad, the sons-in-law were murdered by Saddam's son Uday – the curse of Saddam.

by Zionism earlier this century, many religious Jews, as opposed to non-religious Zionists, were filled with Messianic expectation. The precise geographical definition of *Eretz Israel* is unclear; some claim that it extends from the Nile to the Euphrates (which would require Israel to conquer most of modern Egypt, Syria, Jordan, Lebanon and Iraq). More pragmatic Jews settle for the area between the Mediterranean and the Jordan River, the original Land of Canaan bequeathed to Moses some 3,500 years ago. Although the concept of *Eretz Israel* was articulated in the early days of the Zionist movement, the founding fathers took the more pragmatic approach and settled for the best offer they could get. After the capture of the West Bank and Gaza in 1967, however, the *Eretz Israel* movement gained in popularity among Israelis for political as well as religious reasons. Menachem Begin, Israel's first right-wing Prime Minister, was a committed *Eretz Israelite*, and invested heavily in building settlements throughout the West Bank (he and his followers call the area by its biblical names, Judaea and Samaria) and Gaza to ensure the land would forever remain under Jewish control. By agreeing to return this land to the Palestinians, Rabin provoked outrage among this powerful Jewish constituency, some of whom decided to avenge what they regarded as an unforgiveable act of treason.

'And on him, Yitzhak son of Rosa, known as Rabin, we have permission to demand from the angels of destruction that they take a sword to this wicked man to kill him for handing over the Land of Israel to our enemies, the sons of Ishmael.'

The text of the curse, delivered in Aramaic, was read out by a Jerusalem rabbi opposite Rabin's residence on the eve of Yom Kippur, the Jewish day of atonement, a few days before his assassination. Even though Yigal Amir, the assassin, played no part in placing the curse against Rabin, and was probably ignorant of it, the rabbis nevertheless claimed the Prime Minister's murder as a famous victory. The angels of destruction, apparently, work in mysterious ways, and even if Amir thought he was working on his own initiative, the rabbis were convinced that, somehow or other, divine intervention had played its part. Amir himself justified his murderous act on the grounds of *din rodef*, whereby, according to the Torah, a Jew is justified in killing his persecutor. Rabin's offence had been to persecute Amir by committing Israelis to live in peaceful co-existence with their Palestinian neighbours. While the overwhelming majority of the Israeli public was outraged by Rabin's murder, they were also utterly bemused to discover that, hidden away from mainstream society, there existed a sub-culture of fanatical rabbis who fervently believed in the power of the supernatural.

As someone who does not even recognise the state of Israel, it was hard for Meshi to get too excited about Rabin's murder. In his view any leader of the Israeli nation is damned for presiding over a godless country. The only aspect of the whole sorry episode that might have appealed to Meshi was that Rabin's death could be attributed to divine retribution, and the role played by the rabbinical curse in hastening his demise. Meshi's own cursing activities, however, if rather more prosaic, appear to be just as deadly. As we sit sipping our Diet Coke, Meshi reels off a long list of unfortunates who have been on the receiving end of curses issued by Meshi and his Jerusalem rabbi friends. There was the case of Gershon Agron, Jerusalem's first Israeli mayor, who, in the 1950s, had the temerity to authorise the construction of the city's first mixed swimming-pool. Agron received a 'third-degree' curse for his trouble, and was dead of cancer within a year. And, just for good measure, the businessman who financed the development went bust soon afterwards. Another developer, a fit and healthy 37-year-old Israeli, who built a hotel complex on a site in Jaffa that was said to be an ancient Jewish cemetery, received a similar curse. He, too, fell ill and died. Meshi has many more examples that he claims attest to the potency of his curses. 'It's all a matter of faith,' he explains. Pride of place, however, in this lexicon of rabbinical wrath is reserved for the one group of people who, to Meshi's way of thinking, have no redeeming qualities whatsoever – archaeologists.

This dedicated group of experts, particularly those who are Jewish, frequently find themselves caught up in the crossfire in the battle between the different interests of ultra-Orthodox and secular Jews. A city as ancient and as important as Jerusalem is naturally of immense interest to archaeologists, and even today, after large areas of the city have been subjected to exhaustive excavation, there are still many issues of scholastic dispute that would benefit from further research. But the attempts of archaeologists to reveal the mysteries entombed beneath the city's multitudinous layers of stone are frequently impeded by the violent opposition of ultra-Orthodox Jews like Meshi. The city's long and complicated past means that it is littered with graveyards, some known, others not, stretching back over centuries. As the Jews have maintained an almost continuous physical presence in the city for the better part of the past 3,000 years, many of these graves are Jewish although, with some of the older sites, it is not always easy to ascertain their precise ethnic origin. This has not prevented religious Jews from using any means at their disposal, including violence, to halt archaeological excavations when they believe that graves are being desecrated.

On one occasion in 1992, when contractors were working on construction of Jerusalem's first flyover linking the city centre to the northern suburbs, the bulldozers unearthed some ancient human remains. Under Israeli law building developers are obliged to contact the Israeli Antiquities Authority, which is responsible for the nation's archaeological heritage, if, in the course of digging foundations and the like, they come across anything that might be of archaeological significance. As this can often delay important projects for many months, there have been cases where contractors have paid handsome bribes to avoid such inconvenience, and Israeli archaeologists have turned a blind eye, particularly when the artefacts are non-Jewish. In the case of the flyover there was considerable doubt about the skeletons' origins. This, however, did not prevent ultra-Orthodox rabbis from proclaiming that the bones were Jewish and could not be disturbed. Within days of the initial discovery traffic in the city was brought to a standstill as thousands of *haredi* demonstrators fought running battles with the Israeli police to prevent the archaeologists from examining the remains. The dispute continued for several months, with ultra-Orthodox demonstrators, led by Meshi, staging impromptu protests at the site, causing massive traffic snarl-ups and seriously testing the patience of secular Israelis, not to mention the Palestinian Arabs, who could not understand what all the fuss was about. The stand-off eventually subsided only after scientists were able to prove, following exhaustive tests, that the bones were not Jewish after all, but were the remains of Persian soldiers who had died during the conquest of Jerusalem nearly 2,500 years previously. Only then did the ultra-Orthodox relent and allow work on the flyover to continue.

The high point of Meshi's career as a rabbinical curser was reached during another archaeological project, sponsored by the Israeli government, where the ultra-Orthodox community believed they had incontrovertible proof that ancient Jewish graves were being vandalised merely for the sake of scientific curiosity. Meshi, like most of his co-religionists, feels very strongly about the sanctity of Jewish graves.

'If someone had only been dead for a couple years you wouldn't bulldoze their grave and stick their bones in a jar,' he explains. 'So why should it be any different if a person has been dead for 2,000 years? We should show them the same respect as we do our own dead.'

According to Jewish law, graves are inviolable. When a person dies, the small plot of land in which they are buried is their last remaining possession, and is theirs for eternity. Disturbing the graves of the dead is no different than grave-robbing. 'The grave is the property of the dead, no one else. It is our duty to protect their property for them against people who try to steal it.'

To Meshi's way of thinking the worst 'thieves' are archaeologists who are so overwhelmed by their desire to uncover the mysteries of the past that they disregard the rights of the dead. A classic confrontation involving the beliefs of religious Jews and the enthusiasms of secular Israelis arose soon after the Six-Day War when, with the Old City now under Israel's control, Israeli archaeologists could not wait to dig into the ancient treasure trove that lay beneath its walls. Although much excavation had already been undertaken by Kathleen Kenyon, the Israelis were keen to make their own study, concentrating their focus on the Jewish remnants, presumably with the intention of reinforcing their claim to ownership of the entire city. Yigal Shiloh, an Israeli biblical scholar of some repute, was placed in charge of the project, which finally got under way in earnest in 1978. If the enterprise aroused great interest among Israel's general public, it aroused even greater fury among Jerusalem's *haredim*, who insisted that the excavations of the City of David would disturb ancient burial grounds. Shiloh rejected their claims, insisting that the area of the proposed dig was a good distance from the nearest known Jewish graves. The explanation made little impact on the religious community, and Meshi was encouraged to organise a series of massive demonstrations.

In retrospect the confrontation over the City of David excavations was the turning point in relations between two very different types of Jew. Even before the foundation of the state there were tensions between Jerusalem's traditional religious community of Jews and the early Zionist settlers. During the darkest days of the 1948 battle for Jerusalem, a group of Orthodox Jews outraged the Zionist army commanders by parading through the city centre bearing placards calling for 'food, modesty and surrender'.[3] The demonstration was quickly broken up by Jewish soldiers. After the state's creation Ben-Gurion reached an accommodation with a group of Orthodox rabbis who regarded the foundation of Israel as part of God's great plan. While secular Israelis, the majority of the population, would have preferred a state free of religious laws, Ben-Gurion compromised and agreed that all public institutions would be kosher, the Jewish sabbath would be an official day of rest and that the religious would retain the right to run their own education system. These concessions went some way to satisfying the rabbis' demands that the new state be run according to *halakha*, Jewish religious law. In return the rabbis pledged to support the new state. It is often said that both groups were willing to compromise because each believed the other would soon disappear. The secular believed that in a free Jewish state, the religious would cast off their old superstitions, while the religious believed that in a truly Jewish state, the secular would see the error of their ways and live their lives according to the dictates of the Torah. Neither, of course, happened, and this uneasy tension was exacerbated further after the reunification of Jerusalem in 1967. With a Jewish government in control of the entire city, and access to the Wailing Wall restored, the city saw a sharp influx of religious Jews who believed the time of the Messiah to be soon approaching. Ultra-Orthodox Jews believe that one of the main pre-requisites for the Messiah's return is that all Jews live virtuous lives according to *halakha*, and digging up old Jewish cemeteries does not help their cause.

Riot police used tear gas and water-cannon to disperse Meshi's

3 In the early 1920s, pre-State Haganah fighters had assassinated an extreme ultra-Orthodox activist, Jacob de Haan, after he secured an agreement from King Abdullah of Transjordan for the Jews in Jerusalem to remain under his protection.

first demonstrations, and the whole issue of whether or not to dig in the City of David became something of a *cause célèbre* not just in Jerusalem, but throughout Israel. Shiloh and his supporters argued that giving in to the rabbis' demands would set a dangerous precedent that would allow the religious community to interfere in all areas of academic research and scholarship. Shiloh took his argument to the Supreme Court where he eventually won a judgement in favour of the dig being allowed to proceed. This only incensed the *haredim* further, and within days of the Supreme Court's judgement being delivered, Meshi was busy organising more mass demonstrations. So effective were his tactics that the dig was only able to proceed under a heavy police guard. But Meshi was not content simply to disrupt the excavations. He became convinced that Shiloh, by his stubborn refusal to submit to the rabbis' will, had sinned against the Jewish faith, and deserved to be punished with a rabbinical curse.

'I don't have any pangs of conscience about what happened,' says Meshi. 'We warned him and he took no notice. He was desecrating the graves of our forefathers and deserved to be punished.'

Together with a group of like-minded rabbis, Meshi arranged for a *pulsa denura* to be made against Shiloh. The ceremony was performed, in secret, and the text of the curse read out at a rabbinical court in Jerusalem's *haredi* neighbourhood. For good measure Meshi had thousands of leaflets printed giving details of the curse, which were distributed throughout the city. The curse did not work immediately. It was issued in 1982, and it was not until 1987 that Shiloh, at the age of fifty, died of cancer. Meshi and his supporters were thrilled by their success, and printed more leaflets and posters celebrating the potency of their curse and Shiloh's demise. 'He died because of divine retribution,' says Meshi.

'That's bullshit.' Tamar Shiloh, the archaeologist's widow, a smart, middle-aged woman, does not seem the type to lapse into crude vernacular on first acquaintance, but that is the effect the mere mention of Meshi-Zahav's name provokes.

'It was not their ridiculous medieval mumbo-jumbo that killed my husband. It was all the stress they caused him with their demonstrations and intimidation. He was an academic trying to do some valuable research, but they made his life intolerable.'

Mrs Shiloh continues to live and work in Jerusalem as a school inspector, but the trauma she shared and suffered with her husband during nine years of almost uninterrupted hostility and vilification from the *haredi* community has left deep scars and raised serious questions in her mind about the future quality of life for secular Israelis in Jerusalem.

'They had no case at all. We tried to reason with them, but they would not listen.' Mrs Shiloh, like many other secular Israelis, refers to the ultra-Orthodox as 'they' and 'them' – the enemy – as though to call them by their real name is to afford them a courtesy they do not merit.

'It is impossible to deal with them,' she continues. 'It's as though sixteenth-century Puritans have taken over modern London or New York and imposed their values. My view is that I don't want to interfere in their [the ultra-Orthodox's] lives, and I don't want them to interfere in mine. But they won't accept that. They want everything their way, and they are making life intolerable in this city for ordinary people. Thanks to them it is now becoming a luxury for secular Jews to live in Jerusalem.'

Mrs Shiloh is not alone in denouncing the ultra-Orthodox's increasingly intrusive influence in the city's affairs, of assuming the self-appointed role of Jerusalem's ayatollahs. Any attempt to improve the quality of life for the city's secular Jewish community, whether it is construction of the Teddy soccer stadium (named in honour of Teddy Kollek) or the opening of a non-kosher McDonald's in the city centre, invariably culminates in conflict erupting between the two radically opposed constituencies. It is not enough for the *haredim* to protect their own way of life, which they do very effectively with organisations like the Modesty Squad, which patrols exclusively religious neighbourhoods such as Mea Shearim and, not unlike Iran's Revolutionary Guards, dispense summary justice to those deemed not to be dressed or behaving in an appropriate manner. Many's the foreign female tourist who's inadvertently wandered into a *haredi* neighbourhood wearing a T-shirt and shorts, and regretted their mistake. *Haredi* leaders regard themselves as the custodians of Jerusalem's sanctity, and believe they are duty-bound to intervene against any development, particularly those undertaken by Jews, that might be offensive to God. There was a period in the mid-1990s when hole-in-the-wall cash dispensers throughout the city were set on fire because one of the Israeli banks had invested in a hotel complex which the *haredim* claimed was being built on Jewish graves. Another summer a number of bus shelters were destroyed for displaying swimwear advertisements that showed a model wearing a skimpy bikini. Some of the more tactless *haredi* leaders even called for photographs at the Yad Vashem Holocaust memorial to be removed because they showed naked bodies, albeit the emaciated victims of the gas chambers. From disputes over cinemas opening on a Friday night to demands for more roads to be closed on the sabbath, the influence of the ultra-Orthodox throughout the city is both striking and pervasive. There are no Jewish statues displayed in public in Jerusalem – they are offensive to God; many of the advertisements shown in Tel Aviv never make it to Jerusalem because they depict the female form; more than 120 roads are closed in Jerusalem on the sabbath so that traffic does not interfere with religious observance.

It is difficult to imagine a more hazardous occupation for a Jew than to run a pork butcher's shop in the centre of Jerusalem. Avi, an Israeli of Moroccan origin, opened his delicatessen in the city centre in the mid-1980s to cater for the growing demand from secular Israelis for exotic cheeses and meats, a demand that increased dramatically in the early 1990s with the influx of a new wave of Russian immigrants. Apart from stocking a wide range of salamis, hams, patés and sausages, Avi also sells high-quality cuts of pork, his pork chops being a particular speciality. Even though many Israelis are partial to pig meat, at the religious authorities' insistence pigs must not be allowed to pollute the holy land of Israel, and so pig farms are made of elevated structures that ensure the pigs do not touch the soil. When this was first explained to me by an Israeli friend I thought he was referring to the pigs themselves, not the buildings, and for some time afterwards I was troubled by the image of Israeli pigs stumbling around their sty on stilts, like a bizarre circus act. Ignoring the religious reprobation, Avi does a thriving trade, particularly on a Friday morning when the shop is full of Israelis finishing off their shopping for the weekend. Avi's business, opposite McDonald's in Shamai Street, has not gone unnoticed by the ultra-Orthodox community, which regards it as a monstrous profanity. At first they restricted themselves to making threatening phone calls to the shop, telling Avi they were going to burn down the premises. 'Don't go to hell, you'll pollute it,' was one of their favoured insults. Then they started attacking his shop. They broke the windows and kicked in the door. They filled the door-locks with superglue so that he could not reopen for business. 'It's been going on for years,' Avi says resignedly. 'Hardly a weekend goes by when they don't do something, but I'm not going to give in to them. This is my livelihood. They have no right to tell me how to live my life.'

Secular Jews are prepared to tolerate and respect some of the demands made by the ultra-Orthodox – a Jewish state, after all, cannot deny its Jewish character – but now they feel the balance has swung too far the other way. What particularly irks them is that, even though most *haredim* are indifferent to Israel, they have nevertheless become expert at taking advantage of the state's structure and institutions for their own ends. Perhaps the most dramatic example of their mounting power in the affairs of the state was provided during the 1993 municipal elections in Jerusalem which brought Ehud Olmert to power. The various religious groups organised themselves and mobilised an effective campaign which resulted in them gaining sufficient votes to become a powerful force at City Hall. To defeat Teddy Kollek, Olmert did a deal with the ultra-Orthodox parties whereby they backed his election for mayor. Of the 86,000 votes Olmert polled, 58,000 were from the ultra-Orthodox. In return they received control of some of the most important departments at city hall. Hirsh Goodman, editor of the *Jerusalem Report* and one of the most acerbic critics of the ultra-Orthodox's activities in Jerusalem, was deeply critical of this unholy alliance between the secular Israeli right and the newly empowered rejectionist religious establishment. 'Olmert has all but abdicated control of the city to the ultra-Orthodox,' he wrote in a scathing editorial, 'who have, quietly, doubled the city budget for their school system; turned the urban planning division into an arm of the ultra-Orthodox home-loan association, and put the city beautification department to work painting the walls of yeshivas, Jewish religious institutions. They control the subcommittee that grants all municipal contracts, the subcommittee that hires all municipal employees and the budget allocations committee.'

Hirsh, one of the city's better-known and respected journalists, is an intense, tenacious man with darting brown eyes that brim with ideas and intelligence. In his youth Hirsh was a paratrooper in two of the most important Arab–Israeli wars – in 1967 and 1973. A true patriot, he regards himself as a liberal Israeli and devoted Jerusalemite who supports the peace process and wants to lead a quiet and productive life in his home city. But rather than seeing the quality of his life improve as he settles in to middle age, he perceives a decline because of the ultra-Orthodox takeover. At the time of the election there were an estimated 150,000 *haredim* living in Jerusalem out of a total Jewish population of 410,000. By the year 2015 it is estimated they will constitute 260,000 out of the 600,000 Jews residing in the city. With the Arab population projected to rise from its present 160,000 to 250,000, demographic experts predict that within twenty years the majority of the population will be non-Zionist.

'Is this why we fought all those wars?' Hirsh asks. 'Is that why so many Israelis sacrificed their lives? I don't know why right-wing politicians make such a fuss over the Palestinians having a stake in the city. In a few years' time the Zionists will no longer be in control.'

Hirsh's feelings echo a remark Teddy Kollek made shortly before his electoral defeat. 'I am mayor of the most non-Zionist city in Israel,' he said.

The saddest aspect of the ultra-Orthodox takeover for secular Israelis like Hirsh Goodman and Tami Shiloh is the loss of so many friends and colleagues who, for the sake of a quiet life, move out of the city for somewhere more convivial like Tel Aviv or Haifa. Jobs, housing, education: the main factors that a family takes into consideration when deciding where to live are increasingly falling under *haredi* control. At the start of the 1994 school year 52 per cent of all Jewish children in the city under the age of ten were from ultra-Orthodox families. Consequently many school curricula have been modified to take this demographic shift into account, with a bigger emphasis on religious education that does not appeal to secular parents. Prices of properties in secular neighbourhoods have skyrocketed in recent years because the city planners' priority is to house religious families, while jobs are harder to come by because attracting investment to the city is no longer a priority. Meanwhile, the new generation of politicians at City Hall have used their influence and power to attract thousands of new ultra-Orthodox families into the city. The result is a steady drain of secular Jewish families who are replaced by ultra-Orthodox newcomers. 'If I want to have a dinner party I find myself having to phone round Tel Aviv and persuade my friends to come here,' laments Hirsh. 'And they all think I'm mad for staying here.'[4]

Nor is it just the growing political influence of the *haredim* that bothers their fellow Jews, it is their attitude. If the ultra-Orthodox have become expert at exploiting Israel's existence, they are less enthusiastic about making any personal contribution towards its upkeep and survival. Apart from their exemption from paying a variety of taxes, a major source of resentment is the refusal of the younger generation to submit themselves for military service. Young Israelis – male and female – are required to do between two and three years' national service after leaving school, but their contemporaries in the religious community can claim exemption by proving they are dedicated Torah scholars. As a consequence the number of yeshivas in Jerusalem has ballooned during the past twenty years. No one knows for sure just how many there are because the Ministry of Religious Affairs, the government agency responsible for their supervision, is so in thrall of the rabbis that it conceals the information as if it were a state secret.

An even greater source of resentment is the disrespectful attitude the ultra-Orthodox adopt towards the emblems of the state. Their resolve to exclude themselves from mainstream Israeli society means they often take this clannish xenophobia to ridiculous lengths. In many religious neighbourhoods it is impossible to buy an Israeli newspaper. The faithful regard modern Hebrew, which was developed by the State's founding fathers from the ancient biblical language, as an insult against God's chosen tongue. At one time Jewish newsagents stocked the main Israeli daily newspapers. But they soon stopped the practice after widespread protests from *haredim* culminated in several kiosks being burnt down. Such is their distaste for modern Hebrew that, in extreme cases, they refuse to speak it, preferring to converse in other languages, especially Yiddish, which

4 A study published by the Jerusalem-based Florsheimer Institute for Policy Studies in November 1996 showed that 40 per cent of the city's secular Jews want to leave the city because of friction with the ultra-Orthodox.

is often described as German spoken with a Russian accent. During the annual Independence Day celebrations in the spring some of the more extreme members of the community take great delight in burning the Israeli flag to demonstrate their contempt for the Zionist enterprise.

Another example is on Independence Day eve, when Israelis observe a minute's silence for their war dead. It is an important moment, and Israelis stop their cars and stand silently by the roadside to pay their respects. But in ultra-Orthodox neighbourhoods like Sanhedria and Mea Shearim, the religious community goes about its affairs as normal, contemptuous of the sacrifices made by others to secure their freedom. Nor has their rapid ascent to power within the Israeli political establishment occasioned any change in their attitude. In late 1996 the Israeli attorney-general seriously considered taking action against Haim Miller, one of Jerusalem's ultra-Orthodox deputy mayors, after he referred in public to the national flag, the Star of David, as 'a rag on a stick'. The attorney-general decided not to prosecute on the grounds that the remark should be 'relegated to well-deserved obscurity'.

The tensions between secular Zionists and religious Jews clearly run deep, and make a powerful argument in favour of Israeli politicians taking care not to muddle the distinction between the different philosophies of Zionism and Judaism, particularly where Jerusalem is concerned. The term 'ultra-Orthodox' came into being after the foundation of Zionism, and is used to distinguish the traditional, Orthodox Jewish community, which either supported or ignored the Zionist objectives, from those who actively rejected them. Israeli leaders might regard making Jerusalem their capital as the crowning glory of the Zionist enterprise. This is not a view shared by ultra-Orthodox Jews, most of whom regard their presence in the city more as a privilege than a right. What makes Jerusalem so important to them is their belief in God's physical presence, and their desire to safeguard the city's sanctity. This is not always so easy to achieve when the Israeli government, to ensure the city remains 'the eternal capital of the Jewish people', rides roughshod over their sensibilities in its haste to create a thriving, modern capital.

The gulf in understanding between the two communities is

exacerbated by the complicated structure of the ultra-Orthodox world, one that most Israelis view as an impenetrable constellation of contradiction, division and rancorous rivalries. With their distinctive black coats and long, curled sideburns hanging beneath broad-brimmed hats (which is why some Israelis refer to them as 'the hard-core curlies'), the ultra-Orthodox are an indelible part of the Jerusalem landscape, but that is about as much as the average Israeli knows of their customs and habits. To the modern, muscular Israeli mentality, the ultra-Orthodox are too reminiscent of the ghetto Jew they despise. A female Israeli acquaintance of mine, an intelligent woman who was training to be a film director, would not sit next to religious Jews when she took public transport, even though her Russian grandfather had been an Orthodox rabbi. 'They are dirty and they stink,' she would say. Another myth popular among Israelis is that, due to their strict religious observance, married ultra-Orthodox couples may only copulate so long as the wife is completely covered, which is achieved with the aid of a perforated sheet. For months, when I was walking through *haredi* neighbourhoods, I would discreetly look at laundry hanging from the balconies to see if I could detect any unusual bed-linen. I searched in vain.

Apart from the differentiation between those who accept the State of Israel, and those who reject it, there are many other fundamental differences that characterise the various *haredi* sects, such as those, like the Hasidic Jews, who are susceptible to believing that the arrival of the Messiah is imminent, and those of a more scholarly bent, the *mitnagdim*, who advocate a sceptical world-view based on extensive study of ancient religious Jewish texts. The strains these groups create can be every bit as intense as those between the secular and religious communities, although, because of the closed nature of their world, their arguments surface only rarely. There was one occasion when a Talmudic scholar was invited to address a group of Hasidic students in Jerusalem. In the course of his address he made a remark which they took to be a slight against their *rebbe*, the religious leader whom they believed had mystical powers that derived directly from God. The comment provoked uproar. Tables and chairs were overturned, and groups of students traded punches as insults flew about the mystical stature of the aforementioned *rebbe*. The scholar, meanwhile, was required to effect a swift exit down a drainpipe.

One of the more colourful Hasidic groups that enjoys a substantial following in Jerusalem is Chabad, a Hebrew acronym referring to the three Talmudic qualities of man – wisdom, knowledge and understanding. The estimated 10,000 *Chabadniks* resident in the city are followers of the Lubavitcher Rebbe who, until his death at the age of ninety-two in the summer of 1994, was Menachem Mendel Schneerson, a Brooklyn-based rabbi who never actually set foot in Israel. Part of the reason Schneerson was unable to make a personal visit to the Holy Land was because, in his later years, some of his more excitable followers came to the conclusion that he was more than a mere *rebbe,* that he was in fact the Messiah himself, sent by God to redeem mankind.[5] Even though Schneerson suffered a major stroke in 1992 from which he never recovered, Jerusalem was full of *Chabadniks* who were convinced that Schneerson was about to arrive in the city at any moment and reveal himself as the Messiah. They were so convinced that the end of world was imminent that they were able to identify confirmation of mankind's impending salvation from the most bizarre aspects of everyday life. One development that caused them particular excitement was the growth of the Internet 'information super-highway'. This was interpreted by the Chabad community as fulfilling a biblical prophecy that, prior to His coming, the world would be united as one. The arrival of the global village prophesied the arrival of the Messiah. For several months yellow banners with a drawing of a rising red sun and the words: 'Prepare for the Coming of the Messiah' were distributed throughout the city. Even after Schneerson succumbed to infirmity and old age in 1994, many Chabadniks remain convinced that this is merely part of the process that will culminate in him revealing himself as the Messiah. Until then they busy themselves improving their capacity for goodness, giving more to charity, devoting more time to study of the Torah and trying to persuade secular Jews to observe religious laws. Groups of them are to be found most Friday lunchtimes in Ben Yehudah Street,

5 Religious Jews are extremely wary of those who are regarded as potential Messiahs. Apart from their experience with Jesus Christ, there was the case of Sabbatai Zevi (1626–76), who proclaimed himself the Messiah in Jerusalem in 1656. After being widely acclaimed throughout the Diaspora, Zevi profoundly disappointed his followers by converting to Islam after Mohammed IV, the Ottoman Sultan, threatened him with execution if he did not comply.

distributing *Tefellin* and trying to persuade Israelis to observe the sabbath to pave the way for the Messiah's return.

All these ultra-Orthodox sects are essentially Ashkenazi, catering for the needs of Jews originating from the *shtetls* of Eastern Europe. Shas, the *haredi* group whose spiritual leader is the scholar Ovadia Yousef, primarily appeals to the Sephardic community, Jews who trace their origins from north Africa and the wider Middle East. Supporters of Shas, a Hebrew acronym for Sephardic Guardians of the Torah, come from an entirely different cultural background to the Ashkenazi political élite that has been the dominant force in Zionism since its inception. Ovadia Yousef, an Iraqi-born Jew and a former Sephardic Chief Rabbi of Israel, has managed, during the past twenty years, to turn his movement into a significant political force in Israel. In the 1996 election they won ten of the massive twenty-three seats the religious parties acquired in the 120-seat Knesset (nearly 20 per cent of the vote).[6] Shas began life helping the poor Sephardic immigrants who felt disenfranchised and discriminated against by the Ashkenazi establishment. By providing practical help, such as building all-day schools for working mothers, and maintaining a close relationship with their supporters, Shas has evolved a grass-roots religious and political movement which is the envy of many larger and longer-established Israeli political parties. One of the more effective devices employed by Shas to keep its supporters in touch with the leadership is to broadcast, live by satellite throughout Israel, Ovadia Yousef's weekly prayer meeting, which is held in Jerusalem's Bucharian Quarter. The event resembles an American presidential candidate's rally. Yousef arrives at the synagogue in a white limousine with its back windows covered by black curtains. The car is protected by armed bodyguards who run ahead of it, forcibly clearing well-wishers from its path. Yousef emerges, wearing a long, flowing robe embroidered with gold and sporting dark sunglasses. He makes his way inside where he seats himself on a throne of inlaid gold and jewels. For the next forty minutes he reads his sermon from a prepared text, either his latest interpretation of some obscure aspect of

6 One of the first demands made by the Haredi parties following their election success was to amend the Antiquities Law, which would effectively end archaeological research in the Holy Land.

sabbath observance or an opinion he has formed about one of the major political issues of the day.

Unlike the Ashkenazi ultra-Orthodox, Shas has no inhibitions about participating fully in the Israeli political process. Ashkenazi politicians are extremely reticent about their involvement in Israeli politics, even when elected to serve in the Knesset. To ensure they do not compromise their religious beliefs, politicians representing Degel Atorah and Agudat Israel, the two main *haredi* parties,[7] refuse to serve as Cabinet ministers. Until the 1996 election, they agreed to serve as chairmen on important committees, such as housing, transport and religious affairs, to enable them to ensure their religious constituencies received a handsome budget allocation. After the surprise success of the religious parties in the 1996 election, they attempted to improve their position. When Meir Porush, leader of Agudat Israel, who had previously served as one of Ehud Olmert's deputy mayors in Jerusalem, was offered a Cabinet position as housing minister, he declined. Instead he agreed to serve as a deputy minister, and Netanyahu agreed not to appoint a proper minister. This clumsy compromise meant that Porush was effectively in control of the lucrative housing budget, but was not obliged to sully his religious convictions by attending Israeli Cabinet meetings. Shas has no such inhibitions, and its politicians strive to achieve as much political influence as they can. Aryeh Deri, one of the party's most accomplished politicians, has held several ministerial portfolios, including the powerful Interior Ministry. Indeed, Shas can often be as staunchly nationalistic as right-wing parties such as Likud, especially over the Jerusalem issue. On more than one occasion since the peace process began Ovadia Yousef has threatened to bring down the government if any concessions are made over the city's current status.

The other area that distinguishes Shas's political activism from the other religious sects is its willingness to use curses, blessings and charms to win over the electorate. During the 1988 general election a Shas rabbi issued a curse against any Jew who voted for a rival religious party. The only response available to the opposition was to get one of their own rabbis to issue a dispensation against the curse to

7 During the 1996 election they combined as United Torah Jewry, and won four seats.

162

enable their supporters to vote. In the 1996 general election Shas
activists distributed good-luck charms that had been blessed by Rabbi
Yitzhak Kaduri, one of the country's foremost kabbalists. A vote for
Shas meant a blessing from the rabbi. For good measure Rabbi Kaduri
visited Benjamin Netanyahu at his Jerusalem home on the eve of
polling day to give the candidate his official blessing (Shas is traditionally a Likud ally). The next day, contrary to all predictions,
Netanyahu was elected Prime Minister.

However much all these blessings, charms and curses may appeal to
Yehudah Meshi-Zahav, Jerusalem's arch-proponent of the rabbinical
curse, he is constrained from participation – on the political level at
least – because Edar Haredit, the *haredi* sect he represents, is the
most rejectionist of all the ultra-Orthodox groups, and refuses to
have anything to do with the State of Israel. The only issue at stake at
election time for the Edar Haredit rabbis was to ensure the faithful
played no part in the procedure. The thrust of their campaign in
Jerusalem's ultra-Orthodox neighbourhoods during the 1996 election had nothing to do with the peace process; their main objective
was to convince religious Jews that, just by participating, they were
committing a sin. Edar Haredit, which claims to have about 15,000
sympathisers in Jerusalem, prides itself on being entirely self-
sufficient, in contrast to other religious groups which are prepared to
take money from the state. Located on the outskirts of Mea Shearim,
the sect boasts an impressive infrastructure to cater for all the community's needs. Apart from schools, kindergartens, community
centres and, of course, yeshivas, the sect provides material support,
such as food parcels and grants, for the poor. Because many *haredi*
men spend most of their time studying the Torah and have no
income, and as they also tend to have large families – many families
have between seven and ten children – the community is prone to
poverty. Traditionally families have relied on generous overseas benefactors, but this is not always reliable. The wealthy Reichmann family
in Toronto, one of the world's biggest property developers, has given
generously for many years. But when, in the early 1990s, their prestigious Canary Wharf project in London's Docklands went bust, the
financial effects were keenly felt in Mea Shearim.

The sect has its own administrative structure and judicial system where respected rabbis adjudicate on a whole range of disputes, commercial, criminal and personal, on the basis of *halakha*. The main courthouse, located off Straus Street, is also the place, when the occasion arises, where rabbinical curses are officially proclaimed. Hearing that a new batch of curses was about to be delivered – mainly primary curses against offenders who had failed to observe previous court rulings – an Israeli acquaintance agreed to take me to see if we could gain admittance. Our first problem was to find someone who spoke Hebrew. There were Yiddish and German speakers in abundance, but no one seemed to be conversant with the local dialect. And if they did know Hebrew, they weren't letting on.

The outer offices were musty and, in terms of fixtures and fittings, antiquated. Wizened clerks sat hunched over ancient typewriters using one finger on each hand to tap out court orders, with carbon papers attached to make copies. Finally we found someone who admitted to speaking English, and I asked him to show me into the courtroom so that I could watch the judgements being delivered. The first problem was my Israeli friend, who had offered to translate. The official took exception because she was a woman. 'Only men are admitted,' he said. 'This is man's work.' Rather ungallantly I offered to abandon my friend if it would gain me entrance to the courtroom.

'Are you Jewish?' the official enquired. I replied in the negative. 'It is not possible for non-Jews to enter,' he said. 'This is a religious establishment, and only religious people are allowed to participate.' We were asked to leave. On the way out we noticed some posters in Hebrew. One of them was a tract on the perils of married Jewish women wearing immodest wigs.[8] Another advertised a lecture by a leading rabbinical food hygienist on how to make the perfect, insect-free salad. Like the other ultra-Orthodox sects, Edar Haredit has strict kosher regulations, some of which are distinctly racist. A book published in Jerusalem which explains the rudiments of keeping a kosher kitchen, for instance, says non-Jews should be excluded from the kitchen in a Jewish house 'to prevent intimate friendship between

---

8 A wig shop in the vicinity had recently been burnt down by over-zealous *haredi* students after Ovadia Yousef had ruled that a woman who wore a wig that resembled natural hair was the same as having uncovered hair, and was therefore guilty of being immodest.

Jews and non-Jews, as it might lead to intermarriage'. It also carries a warning about the problems of purchasing a truly kosher duck, for 'a certain amount of cross-breeding between kosher and non-kosher ducks is taking place in England. The resulting ducks would not be kosher.'[9]

On a more sinister note it is claimed that Edar Haredit, this state within a state, runs its own punishment squads, which dispense summary justice against those who commit serious offences against the community. One area in which the punishment squads are said to be particularly active is in coercing teenage yeshiva students who indicate a desire to renounce the religious world for the secular. It is no easy matter for a young religious person to turn their back on the ultra-Orthodox way of life. It is considered an enormous disgrace for the family, which is regarded as having somehow failed in its religious duty by the rest of the community. There have been cases where families have gone into mourning when they have 'lost' one of their children to the outside world, treating it as a bereavement. In many cases those leaving the community are looked upon as outcasts, and never talk to their families again. But the religious obligations, the strictly structured way of life, that is asked of these young Jews is often more than they can bear.

Apart from being denied access to everyday consumer items such as television sets – even video recorders were officially denounced as 'a curse that has penetrated into the houses of Israel' – young religious men and women must live by a strict behavioural code that does not even allow them to look directly at a woman, no matter how close her proximity. They must live their lives in strict accordance to their rabbis' interpretation of the Torah, which brooks no argument. Thus, when a rabbi says the world was created in the year 3761 BC (the rabbis worked this out by scrutinising the chronology of Old Testament fables), the statement must be taken as fact. One mischievous student, when told this, asked his Hasidic teacher to explain the presence of dinosaur remains that scientists claimed were millions of years old. 'They were put there by God to test our faith,' the teacher replied. When the successful American movie *Jurassic Park*, a film

9 Rabbi S. Wagschal, *The New Practical Guide to Kashrut* (Jerusalem: Feldheim, 1996).

about dinosaurs being re-created from their DNA, opened in Jerusalem, it provoked protests from the ultra-Orthodox community which claimed it was 'offensive to our beliefs'.

A rare insight of how warped the thinking of some ultra-Orthodox rabbis can be was provided by an Israeli newspaper which managed to record a session of the mandatory 'bridegroom instruction', which is a rabbinical pre-requisite for obtaining a marriage licence. At the session, which was conducted by a leading rabbi at the Jerusalem Religious Council, the prospective grooms were warned of the dangers of having sexual intercourse during their wives' menstrual period. The rabbi warned that having sex during the woman's period, or during the following seven days, is liable to cause the deaths of both husband and wife, cause traffic accidents and could also harm the baby conceived. To stress the point the rabbi, a Likud sympathiser, claimed that Yossi Sarid, the left-wing Israeli politician, was conceived 'while his mother was having her period – that's why Yossi turned out as he did', while Shulamit Aloni, his left-wing colleague, was conceived when her parents 'thought undesirable thoughts, impure thoughts, or had intercourse at undesirable times, either during or after menstruation'.

Not surprisingly some young religious students find it difficult to cope with these rabbinical strictures and try to leave the community. In some instances they are successful, and an organisation of secular volunteers called Hillel, named after a liberal Talmudic rabbi, runs a self-help group and help-line in Jerusalem for those who seek an escape route. The number of this organisation is whispered like a code-word throughout the yeshivas, but if word gets out prematurely that a student is preparing to go over to 'the other side', they can find themselves in trouble.

'We have had cases where young students who want to leave the ultra-Orthodox world have been subjected to severe beatings by punishment squads,' says Hanan Barkai, a volunteer who has worked with Hillel since it was set up in 1990.

'In some cases the beatings have been carried out with the permission of the parents, who are terrified at the ignominy their reputation will suffer if one of their children leaves. The beatings can be so severe that the victim is hospitalised for several weeks.'

Meshi denies all knowledge of punishment beatings when I ask him, but he says nothing to suggest he disapproves of the practice. But Meshi has bigger, more ambitious goals than merely keeping a few recalcitrant yeshiva students in their place. His mission is to persuade every Jew living in the Land of Israel to abandon their heathen ways and return to the path of righteousness. As a priority he would like to see the Israeli parliament abolished.

'The Knesset is full of vermin,' says Meshi, sounding like a modern-day Isaiah. 'Anyone who participates in the Knesset is profane and therefore *vermin*. Nearly all the laws passed by the Knesset are against the Torah. That is why we ignore them.'

He says he would also like to see the whole concept of Zionism abandoned. 'The Zionist movement does not represent the Jewish people. The land of Israel is a concept, not a place. The Jewish people do not need a land or a country. Our nationhood derives from the Torah. The Jewish people without the Torah would cease to exist. In my view the State of Israel does not recognise the Jewish people.'

Meshi is assured that, with this armoury of curses, his views shall prevail. 'The wicked,' he concludes, 'are dropping like flies.'

# 8

# BELIEVERS

*'And it shall come to pass in the latter days, that the mountain of the Lord's house shall be established in the top of the mountains, and shall be exalted above the hills; and all nations shall flow unto it'*

Isaiah 2: 2–3

But now for the good news. The Messiah is coming. Not the Jewish one, but the Christian, Jesus Christ. While Jews have been waiting nearly 6,000 years for theirs to make His first appearance, Jerusalem's more excitable Christians are making ready for their Saviour's Second Coming. Everywhere they turn they find signs that tell them His arrival is imminent. With every rotation of the globe they discover the fulfilment of Old and New Testament prophecies. The dawning of a new millennium will bring about the triumphant Messianic restoration. It is, say the faithful, no longer a question of if, but when, the Saviour appears in Jerusalem. There he will establish supremacy over all the nations of the world and rule for 1,000 years. To ensure everything is in place and that they do not miss out on this cataclysmic event, the true believers are flocking to Jerusalem.

Christians have, of course, been down this road before. The early Christians, after witnessing the miracles of the resurrection and ascension, were so convinced that Jesus would return to rule the world within their lifetimes that they considered it unnecessary to preach the new faith. Nearly 1,000 years later, when the second Christian millennium commenced without the saviour's reappearance, Pope Urban II thought it an appropriate moment for the Christian world to put its house in order, and began the Crusades. One of the most bloodthirsty adventures in history was launched with a speech the Pope delivered at Clermont in November 1095, in which he warned: 'From the confines of Jerusalem a horrible tale has gone forth.' This 'horrible tale' concerned the destruction of the Byzantine Church of the Holy Sepulchre in 1009 by the mad Fatimid Caliph al-Hakim, who took exception to the Greek Orthodox rite of the Holy Fire, which is still practised every year at Easter when the miracle of the descent of the Fire occurs, and is then distributed from Christ's tomb throughout the church.[1] Al-Hakim, who regarded the 'miracle' as an act of sorcery designed to lure waverers to the Christian faith, reduced the church to rubble. To add insult to injury, he renamed the holiest shrine in Christendom the *Kanisat al-Qumama*, 'the Church of the Dungheap'. This impetuous act of sacrilege was avenged in the summer of 1099 when the gallant Christian knights of northern Europe captured the city after a short siege and conducted a wholesale and indiscriminate massacre of the Muslim and Jewish inhabitants. 'Piles of heads, hands and feet were to be seen in the streets of the city . . . In the Temple and porch of Solomon men rode in blood up to their knees and bridle reins,' boasted one contemporary Crusader apologist. For good measure the victorious Europeans placed a cross on the roof of the Dome of the Rock, thereby insulting the Islamic faith. The removal of the cross was the first priority of the Muslim liberators in 1187, when the Kurdish commander Saladin routed the Frankish forces and brought the Crusader Kingdom of Jerusalem to an ignominious end.

The immediate purpose of today's faithful is not to commit wholesale bloodshed, although that possibility cannot be ruled out if, as some of them forecast, the Messiah's return is to be preceded by the

---

1 In the nineteenth century, the Fire was borne by devoted hands to the furthest corners of Russia. The supreme ceremony of the Eastern Churches, it represents the triumph of the Christian faith. It was abolished for Catholics by Pope Gregory IX in 1238.

battle of Armageddon, the final struggle between the forces of good and evil.[2] Much of the present enthusiasm for the Messiah's return is predicated by the fact that, for the first time since the Roman holocaust of 2,000 years ago, the Jews have sovereignty over Jerusalem and most of the Holy Land, thereby fulfilling a multitude of Old Testament prophecies. While some Orthodox religious Jews regard the creation of the State of Israel in 1948 as part of God's preparations for the proclamation of their Messiah, many Christians who live their lives according to a literal interpretation of the Bible see it as a crucial development in preparing the world for Christ's return.

> For I will take you from among the nations, and gather you from all the countries and will bring you into your own land. And I will sprinkle clean water upon you, and ye shall be clean . . . I will take away the stony heart out of your flesh, and I will give you an heart of flesh. And I will put my Spirit within you, and cause you to walk in my statutes, and ye shall keep my judgements, and do them. And ye shall dwell in the land that I gave to your fathers; and ye shall be my people, and I will be your God.[3]

Once this 'ingathering' of Jews is accomplished there are various options as to what happens next, depending on one's biblical point of view. One suggestion, which draws on Zechariah,[4] is that two-thirds of the Jews will be struck down and die, and the remaining third will see the light and convert to Christianity. As this would mean more than ten million Jews being killed by an act of God – a holocaust far worse than Hitler's – Jerusalem's flourishing community of Christian Zionists, as they call themselves, tend to keep quiet about this aspect of their belief. Instead they concentrate their energies on the psychedelic prescription for the world's end contained in the Revelation of St John the Divine which says that Jesus will appear on the Mount of

2 In 1996 Israel's Parks Authority decided to develop Armageddon as a major tourist attraction in preparation for the millennium.

3 Ezekiel 36: 24–8.

4 'And it shall come to pass, that in all the land, saith the Lord, two parts therein shall be cut off and die; but the third shall be left therein': Zechariah 13: 8.

Olives and enter Jerusalem in triumph to rule for 1,000 years after the forces of good (i.e. Christianity) have triumphed over the forces of evil (i.e. everything else).

And so it came to pass that the Lord spoke to Brother David one day in upstate New York and told him to buy a one-way ticket to Jerusalem. At the time, in 1980, Brother David (the Lord also told him to forget his family name) spent his days running a mobile homes business and his nights working in soup kitchens for down-and-outs.

'I used to hang out at a black Pentecostal church in Syracuse,' he recalls, 'until the Lord took me out of denominational churches and put me into charismatic churches.'

With his thick black beard and ruddy complexion, Brother David resembles a cross between an ultra-Orthodox Jew and a fishmonger. In Syracuse he spent, by his own admission, a lively few years in a church where most of the congregation was in the habit of speaking in tongues, and the building was 'bursting' with noise.

'Then the Lord took me down to New York City' and it was while he was working one night in a soup kitchen that the Lord provided the ultimate challenge.

'The Lord spoke to me and told me to sell the business and go to the Holy Land,' explains Brother David. 'I must confess I was surprised. I was praying a lot at the time, and what people forget is that prayer is not a one-way dialogue. It is a two-way form of communication. In my prayers I asked many questions and the Lord provided some of the answers. Which is why I came to Jerusalem.'

He gave the money he received from the sale of his home and business to the church, caught a flight to Tel Aviv and hitch-hiked to Jerusalem. Brother David says he arrived in the city penniless, trusting in the Lord to provide him with comfort and succour.

'The Lord had summoned me to Jerusalem, and I believed the Lord would provide for me.'

And then the Lord spoke to Sister Sharon. In fact Sharon can do without the honorific, even though, as Brother David's constant companion, few people in Jerusalem know her simply by her Christian name.

'I don't go in for this sister thing,' Sharon explains. 'We are all human beings to me, male and female. God doesn't expect us to distinguish between the two.'

Spoken like a true Californian, which is where Sharon was living with her five children and eight grandchildren when the Lord called her and told her to travel to Jerusalem. An attractive, well-preserved middle-aged blonde, Sharon looks as though she would be more at home hanging out at the local tennis club, or keeping in trim with a Jane Fonda work-out video-tape. Instead she spends her days helping out at Brother David's House of Prayer, a ministry for the poor and destitute situated on the Mount of Olives – the anticipated location of the Messiah's return – which he founded shortly after arriving in the Holy City. Although she confesses to missing her offspring, Sharon insists she has no alternative but to serve the Lord.

'God has called me here. So if they [the children and grandchildren] want to see me, they will have to come here to Jerusalem. Unfortunately the air fare's expensive, so I don't get to see them that much.'

Sharon and Brother David are committed Christian Zionists. To advertise the fact they both wear a gold Star of David intersected with a Christian cross around their necks, a symbol they say has evolved during their residence in Jerusalem. When he first lived in the city, Brother David wore only a cross, but soon found this offended his Jewish acquaintances. Then he wore a Star of David, but found that it did not assist his mission to persuade Jewish people to accept the teachings of Jesus. For the Lord's primary purpose in calling both Brother David and Sharon to Jerusalem is to prepare the way for the Messiah's return by familiarising Jews with the Gospels.

'With the return of the Jews to the Promised Land it will not be long before the Messiah returns,' explains Brother David. 'The Lord has brought us here to prepare the way physically and spiritually for His return. It is our duty to teach the Jews that there is only salvation through Jesus.'

As part of their endeavour to put across their message, Sharon and Brother David distribute food and clothing to the city's needy, setting a practical example of the teachings of Christ. They are familiar faces to most of Jerusalem's down-and-outs.

'We are not trying to convert the Jews,' Brother David insists. 'We want to show them the love of Christ.'

That was not how some of the city's more zealous Jewish guardians regarded his mission. Much to the surprise of Brother David and, presumably, the Lord, one day he found himself, like the apostles, staring at the walls of a Jerusalem prison cell. By any standard Brother David and Sharon are fairly harmless, rather touching individuals who seem as deserving of assistance as those they seek to help. Brother David, in particular, appears to believe the most mundane functions of everyday life are predestined by the Lord. When I first met the couple, Brother David immediately gave thanks to the Lord for bringing us together. The foyer of the Hyatt Hotel where we'd met (their suggestion – it's near the Mount of Olives), was praised as 'a blessed place', especially when we entered the coffee-shop and the waitress brought us a menu. To judge by the way the two of them hungrily beheld the bill of fare, food provisions were in fairly short supply up at the House of Prayer. When our meeting ended, Brother David asked the waitress to put his left-over chips in a doggy-bag.

'Trust in the Lord and you will never be disappointed,' he said before taking Sharon by the arm and escorting her out of the hotel, the soggy doggy-bag clasped firmly in his free hand.

'And then the Lord made a way for me to be in prison.' Brother David can even find something positive to say about the period he spent locked up in the Russian Compound, Jerusalem's main remand centre. Thanks to the stranglehold the ultra-Orthodox have over the state's affairs, it is an offence to proselytise in Israel. When the Mormons built their Brigham Young University annex on the Mount of Olives in the 1980s, the elders were obliged to provide a written undertaking to the city authorities that the complex would be used solely for study. (That they were allowed to build the campus at all on such a prime location was due to the payment of a substantial cash donation to Jerusalem City Council.) Given the extreme sensitivities that characterise the city's inter-religious relations, even those Christian evangelicals who seek to spread the teachings of Christ must tread carefully. In 1982 Baptist House, the most visible Christian establishment in Jewish West Jerusalem (and a favourite haunt of former American President Jimmy Carter on his jaunts to the city), was burnt to the ground by Jewish extremists following months of intimidation which also saw the building subjected to attack by nail and fire bombs, and covered with anti-Christian graffiti. Prior to his arrest, Brother David, who was then working mainly in the city's west side, had his own home set alight three times, even though he insists he was not proselytising. He was detained in 1991 and then spent an uncomfortable nine months incarcerated with child molesters, terrorists and murderers.

'The Lord wanted me to minister in the prison, and so he created the circumstances,' is how Brother David explains his imprisonment. The Jerusalem Police department, however, has a somewhat different perspective on the case.

'Brother David was arrested for vagrancy,' says a spokesman. 'He was held on remand for nine months because he refused to co-operate with the authorities. He refused to provide his real name, and he had no passport. We wanted to deport him, but because he refused to tell us where he came from we could not even do that. In the end we had to let him go.'

Brother David and Sister Sharon might not be the most conventional of Jerusalemites, but they represent a tradition that goes back at least as far as the Protestant Reformation. As early as 1585 Thomas Brightman, an English clergyman, called for the restoration of the Jews to the Holy Land as the fulfilment of Biblical prophecy. In 1649, when Puritan influence was at its peak, Joanna and Ebenezer Cartwright, two English Puritans then resident in Amsterdam, petitioned the government of Oliver Cromwell 'That this Nation of England, with the inhabitants of the Netherlands, shall be the first and the readiest to transport Izraell's sons and daughters in their ships to the Land promised to their forefathers, Abraham, Isaac and Jacob for an everlasting inheritance.'[5] The Reformation sparked an intensive reappraisal of the Bible throughout Europe and the Puritans, through their earnest devotion to the Scriptures, came to regard themselves as the Christian heirs to Abraham. Their demand for the restoration of Israel was made not so much for the sake of the Jews as to fulfil their own Christian destiny. According to their interpretation of the Bible, man's salvation, through the Messiah's return, would only be achieved when the people of Israel were restored to Zion. Cromwell's revolution did not survive long enough for any tangible steps to be made towards this utopian goal, but the concept was

5 Quoted in Barbara Tuchman, *Bible and Sword* (New York: New York University Press, 1956), p. 121.

not forgotten, and was revived at several epoch-making junctures in later years. Similar calls for the restoration of the Jews were made during both the French and American revolutions. Even the avowedly secular Napoleon Bonaparte issued a proclamation promising to re-establish the Jews in the ancient kingdom of Jerusalem during his abortive Palestine campaign in 1799.

The efforts of these early Christian Zionists had to wait until the mid-nineteenth century before they achieved their first significant breakthrough with the consecration, on 21 January 1849, of Christ Church, the seat of the new Anglican Bishop in Jerusalem.[6] Construction of Christ Church was the culmination of years of painstaking lobbying by the London Society for Promoting Christianity Among the Jews, or the LJS, an organisation that was the theological heir to the Puritans. Founded in 1809, the Society popularised Christian Zionist doctrines, including the restoration of the Jews in Palestine, and built up a substantial following among British Members of Parliament, clergy and writers such as Samuel Taylor Coleridge, who was, no doubt, inspired by the notion of bringing ancient history back to life. Although the founders of the movement worked hard to promote their case, it was not until they secured the support of some of the leading parliamentarians of the day that they began to make headway. Some, like Lord Shaftesbury, the prominent social reformer, was an ardent pre-millennialist, someone who believed that Jesus Christ will personally return to earth to reign for 1,000 years. He was also anti-Semitic, preferring to see Jews settle in the Holy Land rather than his beloved England. Another key ally was Lord Palmerston, the British Foreign Secretary, who was attracted by considerations of *realpolitik*. He thought the Jews, once re-established in their native land, would make a useful ally against the intrigues of other European powers over the fate of the Ottoman dominions; in the words of Edmund Burke, 'this wasteful and disgusting empire'. Consequently, Dr Michael Salomon Alexander, a convert from Judaism, was dispatched to Jerusalem as the city's first Anglican bishop, accompanied by a British gunboat to ensure the Turks did nothing to impede his arrival. Dr Alexander was the first man of

---

6 As opposed to Bishop *of* Jerusalem. The unusual title was taken to avoid offending Jerusalem's other, established Christian Churches.

Jewish birth to serve as a Bishop in Jerusalem since the city was destroyed by the Romans in AD 135. While Palmerston and other imperialists regarded the primary objective of the venture as enlisting the support of world Jewry for Britain, Dr Alexander saw it as his mission to persuade the Jewish residents of Jerusalem to follow the same path as himself, and accept the teachings of Christ. Even in the 1840s, when the lot of the Jews under Ottoman rule was particularly abject (they came lowest in the Sublime Porte's religious rankings), Dr Alexander's efforts were largely in vain. A visitor to Jerusalem in the mid-nineteenth century found that Dr Alexander's congregation consisted of eight Jewish converts and one or two tourists. 'The Hill of Zion is not a likely place for a Jew to forsake the faith of his fathers,' commented a representative of the local Jewish community.[7]

Christ Church maintains the legacy of Dr Alexander and, so far as converting Jews is concerned, with about the same degree of success. Tucked away in a corner of the Old City's Jaffa Gate, the complex, with its tidy cloisters and neatly laid-out quad, resembles a typical European medieval cathedral, albeit on a more modest scale. It is the Star of David, centrally positioned in the church's stained glass nave, which suggests something unusual. Inside there are biblical inscriptions in Hebrew, and the altar is engraved with a Star of David. Every Saturday evening – on the Jewish sabbath – mass is said in Hebrew. These days the church is run by the Church's Ministry Among the Jewish People, the successor to the LJS. Ray Lockhart, a former Scotland Yard solicitor, has the daunting task of converting four million Israelis to Christianity. As with Brother David and Sister Sharon, Ray Lockhart and his wife Jill believe their presence in the Holy City has been ordained by Higher Authority.

'This is where the Lord intended us to be,' he explains.

In view of the extreme religious and political sensitivities that abound in the city, Mr Lockhart seeks to undertake his mission with the utmost tact.

'We do not indulge in proselytising,' he insists. 'That's a pejorative term. If God's purpose was that the coming of Jesus was the climax of all the Old Testament scriptures, then it is clearly His desire that the Jewish people should come to learn that Jesus is the Messiah.'

7 Tuchman, p. 207.

At present there are said to be 4,000 Israelis who accept Jesus as the Messiah, although they hesitate to call themselves Christian, with all the centuries of institutionalised anti-Semitism that term conjures up. Instead they call themselves 'Messianic Believers', Jews who have come to accept that Jesus is the Messiah referred to by the Old Testament prophets. There are an estimated ten congregations of 'Believers' in Jerusalem, and Christ Church is the focal point of their activities.

'This is how my miracle happened,' says Micki, a short, stocky Russian Jew in his early twenties who emigrated to Israel in 1990. 'I went to the Hebrew service at Christ Church one Saturday afternoon. I did not understand it, but I saw lots of happy, smiling people. There were two hundred happy people in the church, and I thought there must be something going on.'

Micki, dressed like a student in jeans and T-shirt, with neatly-cropped blond hair, is now a 'Believer', much to the chagrin of the Jewish Agency officials who went to all the trouble of bringing his family out of the old Soviet Union. Micki says his discovery of Jesus Christ was his 'personal miracle'. The 'miracle' took place when he was introduced to Christ Church by a visiting American pastor. He returned on several occasions, and befriended a Russian priest who was then working at the church. Over the course of several months he 'came to believe' in Jesus. Believers don't like the word convert; they are not abandoning their Jewish roots. In fact Micki's discovery of Jesus has only made him feel more Jewish, not less.

'The problem of Jesus Christ for most Jews is a question of identity. Either they reject their heritage of thousands of years and join the enemy camp, the anti-Semitic Christians, or they stay with their own faith. Here in Jerusalem everyone sticks to their own community – it gives them a sense of well-being. I gave up my national identity for Jesus because I believe that Jesus is more important. I believe in the kingdom of God. And now I want to bring the kingdom of God into this world by revealing the Jewishness of Jesus to Israelis.'

Micki works closely with other congregations of Messianic Believers in Jerusalem to this end, and says he is not aware that his activities are resented by ordinary Israelis. Israeli officialdom also appears to take a benign attitude towards the activities of Micki and the Believers.

'Once you are a citizen of Israel, there's not much they can do,' he explains. 'It only becomes a problem if you come to believe while you are still living in Russia.' Fortunately, most of Micki's Russian Believer friends only came to believe once they had acquired their Israeli citizenship. Now that they are firmly established in their adopted country, like most of the other Soviet immigrants, they are determined to make a new, and better, life for themselves. Micki wants to be a tour guide, and has been offered a job at the Jewish Agency.

The Israeli authorities indulge the activities at Christ Church and Jerusalem's other 'Messianic' congregations, even though they hardly seem compatible with the Zionist objective of fostering a national home exclusively for the Jewish people. Perhaps this attitude derives from some lingering, institutional affection Israelis feel for the assistance Christ Church's founding fathers provided in helping to get the Zionist bandwagon rolling in the nineteenth century. Certainly the church remains a popular tourist attraction with Israelis who are more interested in the role it played in the restoration of the Jews to the Holy Land – and the fact its first bishop was a Jew – than its ultimate goal of converting Jews to Christianity.

Ultra-Orthodox Jews, many of whom pass by the church daily on their way to pray at the Wailing Wall, take the utmost exception to this aspect of Christ Church's mission. Were it not for the fact the church is located directly opposite the Old City's main police station, it is more than likely the church would have suffered the same fate as Baptist House, and been vandalised. Even so, some of the more extreme elements among the ultra-Orthodox community wage a continual campaign of harassment and intimidation against the Christ Church staff.

'We often have people spit at us, and one day one of our staff in the bookshop was punched in the face by an irate Orthodox Jew,' recalls Ray Lockhart.

Relations between the two communities, the Messianic Believers and those who believe the Messiah has still to appear, are not helped by unnecessary acts of provocation by some of the more fanatical believers who actively seek to make Jews see the error of their ways. The walls at Jaffa Gate are frequently covered with fly-posters advising Orthodox Jews to repent and accept Christ; no sooner do they appear than the Jews tear them down. By way of revenge the Orthodox Jews stick their own posters on the main gate at Christ Church. On one occasion they put a poster claiming that a newly arrived Russian immigrant had disappeared within the Christ Church precincts, the victim, so they inferred, of some dark, satanic rite. The police were uninterested and, despite Ray Lockhart's assurances that a thorough search had been made and no Russian immigrant located, the Orthodox persisted with their whispering campaign for several months. For all this, Ray Lockhart and his staff maintain a sense of optimism about their mission and the future.[8]

'God's purpose will be worked out in due course,' he says. 'We have already seen the return of the Jews to the land. The next step will come when the Jews discover that Jesus is the Messiah. When this happens they will appreciate the central doctrine of Christianity, to love thy neighbour. The Israelis will learn to love and respect the Palestinians, and this will be the catalyst for true peace in the Middle East.'

Christ Church might be one of the more impressive buildings Jerusalem's Christian community has to offer, but its mission is at best ignored, if not reviled, by many of the other, more traditional, denominations such as the Greek Orthodox, Latins and Armenians. What offends them is not so much the mission to convert the Jews to Christianity – Christians have been trying to do that for two millennia – but the missionaries' undisguised joy at the creation of the State of Israel. It is 800 years since Jerusalem was last under Christian control, and Christians have become accustomed to living under the direction of other faiths. For centuries these ancient congregations have proved masterful at manipulating the various powers that have possessed or controlled the Holy City. But Israel's conquest of the Old City in 1967, including the Church of the Holy Sepulchre, meant that, for the first time since the Apostles first established the Christian creed in Jerusalem, Church leaders found themselves under the suzerainty of Jews. After so many centuries of direct and indirect persecution of the Jews, it was clear the relationship between the traditional Churches and their new Israeli overlords would be fraught with difficulties, even though the victorious Israelis gave a solemn

8 In May 1997 a group of ultra-Orthodox Israeli politicians sponsored a bill in the Knesset which would make it an offence – punishable by a one-year jail sentence – to propagate Christian literature, including the New Testament.

undertaking to preserve the Christians' *status quo ante*. The congregations of the major Churches are predominantly Palestinian Arabs, so their leaders are constrained from developing too close a relationship with the Israelis, even if, in their desire to get the upper hand over their long-standing Christian rivals, they have, on occasion, been sorely tempted. Thus the unfettered enthusiasm for Israel and Israelis displayed by missions such as Christ Church is not only a persistent source of irritation, it is something the Churches most solemnly seek to discourage.

Heresy is not a word the Churches use lightly, but it is the one they have chosen to describe the activities of Jerusalem's most pro-active, pro-Zionist Christian establishment, the Christian Embassy. Located in a quiet, residential neighbourhood in West Jerusalem at No. 10, Brenner Street, the modest Arab-style detached house does not on first acquaintance seem worthy of the most severe act of proscription in the ecclesiastical canon. The house itself is not without interest. The family home of Edward Said, the distinguished (Christian) Palestinian academic, whose family were made refugees by the 1948 war, it served for many years as the Chilean embassy. Then in 1980, in protest at the Begin government's decision to pass the Jerusalem Annexation Law, the Chilean government, together with most of the other foreign states which had their main diplomatic missions located in the city, ordered the embassy to relocate to Tel Aviv. The controversy acted as a catalyst for a group of committed Christian Zionists to respond by establishing the International Christian Embassy Jerusalem, to call it by its full title. The main purpose of the embassy is to represent all those Christians who support Israel and the policies of the Israeli government, but who feel that their interests are not properly defended by their own elected representatives. The embassy was inaugurated in September that year during the Jewish feast of Succoth, or Tabernacles, so that the words of the prophet Zechariah might be fulfilled: 'And so it shall come to pass, that every nation that is left of all the nations which came against Jerusalem shall go up from year to year to worship the King, the Lord of Hosts, and to keep the feast of tabernacles.'[9] The presence of so many Christians in Jerusalem who actually had something good to say about Israel

9 Zechariah 14: 16.

moved Teddy Kollek to remark: 'This has been one of the most moving ceremonies I have ever attended in my life.' Outside the new embassy grateful Israelis bore banners which stated: 'We welcome the embassy in Jerusalem of honest Christians.'

Celebrating the Feast of Tabernacles is now the highlight of the Christian Embassy's annual calendar. While Israeli families busy themselves constructing makeshift Succoth shelters out of wood and palm leaves, the embassy's volunteers devote an enormous amount of time and energy to putting on a spectacular stage show of dancing and singing in celebration of the creation of modern Israel at Binyanei Ha'uma, Jerusalem's largest convention centre. The event is billed as the world's finest model of 'Davidic worship' and is designed to allow Christians from throughout the world to worship in Jerusalem, 'and to bless Israelis in very tangible ways'. Christian sympathisers travel from all over the world for the event; in an average year there are devotees from seventy different countries. They are mainly Christians of the Born Again persuasion who regard their presence in the city as essential to the fulfilment of Zechariah's prophecy. The artists, all of whom are Christian Zionists, perform for free. One year a lead dancer who portrayed David was a former Israeli policeman who had 'discovered' Christ. Another important feature of the celebrations is a carnival-like procession through the centre of Jerusalem, which could almost pass for an Olympic opening ceremony. The participants dress in their national costumes and enthuse to bemused Israeli onlookers about how happy they are that Israel is reborn.

All this is deeply appreciated by the Israeli political establishment which is unaccustomed to foreign, non-Jews, openly praising and embracing the Zionist enterprise. Just weeks before his assassination Yitzhak Rabin was the embassy's guest speaker at the event's concluding ceremony. The normally taciturn Rabin was moved to lyricism by the occasion. 'Jerusalem,' he said to loud applause, 'is not a place, it is a spirit, it is a value.' A year later both right-wing politicians Mayor Olmert and Benjamin Netanyahu, Rabin's successor, addressed the assembly. 'I love you so much,' Olmert told the audience, 'because I can feel the warmth of your love, and your dedication to Jerusalem.' Netanyahu was equally enthusiastic. 'I have to tell you that it's good to be among true friends and dedicated Zionists. I don't always get that luxury, as you know.'

The rest of the year embassy officials are active in a variety of areas as part of their mission to encourage Christians world-wide to support Israel. Perhaps one of the embassy's finest hours was in the early 1990s, following the collapse of the Soviet Union, when hundreds of thousands of Soviet Jews, like Micki and his Believer friends, were finally allowed to make their way to Israel to start a new life. The Christian Zionists were ecstatic. They had already acclaimed the massive airlift of Ethiopian Jews to Israel during the 1980s, codenamed Operation Moses, as proof that God's Will was coming to fruition. The exodus of 400,000 Soviet Jews was hailed by the embassy as 'one of the most startling prophetic fulfilments of our time', a reference to Jeremiah. 'As the Lord liveth, that brought up the children of Israel from the land of the north . . . and I will bring them again into their land that I gave unto their fathers.'[10] The north, in this instance, was the former Soviet Union, and the embassy leapt into action to facilitate the emigration of Soviet Jewry. The first Christian-sponsored flight of Soviet Jews arrived at Tel Aviv's Ben-Gurion airport at dawn one morning in May 1990. The weary travellers were greeted by a crowd of joyful, singing Christians from the embassy, who pressed leaflets into the hands of the new arrivals telling them to accept the teachings of Christ. Altogether the embassy brought fifty plane-loads of Soviet Jews to Israel. The embassy also initiated its own bus and train service through the Good News Travels Bus Company and organised its own ships to bring Soviet Jews from the Black Sea port of Odessa to Haifa.

Jan-Willem van der Hoeven, the Christian Embassy's spokesman, regards the 'exodus from the north' as the 'key to the final exodus' of all the Jews living in countries in other parts of the world. Van der Hoeven, a smart, well-dressed and articulate man, hails from the Netherlands, where his father for many years served as private secretary to Queen Juliana. After receiving his divinity degree at the London Bible College, he travelled extensively in the Middle East, during which time he married Widad, a Sudanese Christian Arab. He finally settled in Israel after the Six-Day War. His interest in eschatology, preparing the world for its end, developed during the 1970s when he was Warden at the Garden Tomb, the site identified in 1883

10 Jeremiah 16: 14, 15.

by General Charles Gordon, of Khartoum fame, as the tomb of Christ, a claim which appears to have little archaeological or historical merit.[11] From there Van der Hoeven progressed to being one of the founder members of the Christian Embassy. A fervent Christian Zionist, he has devoted his life to preparing the way for Christ's return, and is committed to persuading the world's remaining Diaspora Jews to return to Israel so that this might happen. With most of the Ethiopians and Russians safely 'ingathered', all that remains is for the Christian Embassy, for example, to persuade the 600,000 Jews resident in Britain, the 800,000 in France and the millions in the United States to follow suit. Van der Hoeven is not very particular about how this final 'ingathering' of the Jews will occur, and refers again to the prophet Jeremiah to illustrate how this might be accomplished. 'Behold, I will send for many fishers, saith the Lord, and they shall fish them; and afterward I will send for many hunters, and they shall hunt them from every mountain, and from every hill, and out of the holes of the rocks.'[12] Indeed, Van der Hoeven believes any tactic is justified, so long as it achieves the right result. During a speech he made to a group of Swedish Christian Zionists, Van der Hoeven once said: 'I pray that . . . even if it takes anti-Semitism in America, God may use it to get his millions back to Israel. So we must have enough room there. So if we have six million American Jews coming we cannot give up the West Bank. Can we?'

It is not so much the Christian Embassy's eschatological infatuation that distresses the more mainstream church leaders; all this talk of Armageddon and the Messiah returning to reign in Jerusalem is, after all, regarded as more of an embarrassment than anything else. What really upsets them is the embassy's politics. Jan-Willem van der Hoeven and his colleagues espouse an uncompromising right-wing political agenda which is not only aggressively pro-Zionist, it is rigorously anti-Arab. It was no coincidence that the embassy was opened while Menachem Begin, one of Israel's most nationalist leaders, was Prime Minister. Begin had a network of evangelical advisers, and was more than aware that Christian Fundamentalists constituted the most powerful Christian element in the United States, with their

11 See Jerome Murphy O'Connor, *The Holy Land* (Oxford: OUP, 1980).
12 Jeremiah 16: 16.

own television stations and carefully targeted marketing techniques. Begin and successive Israeli governments have enthusiastically supported the Christian Embassy because they see it as a valuable propaganda instrument. It is a role the Christian Embassy performs with relish, drawing on a whole range of biblical quotations to justify Israel's continued occupation of the West Bank and Gaza, and in favour of Jerusalem remaining exclusively Israel's capital.[13] Indeed, the embassy is so committed to the concept of *Eretz Israel* that it actively opposed the Rabin government's decision to withdraw the Israeli army from major Palestinian population areas in late 1995. When the Israelis withdrew from Bethlehem, for example, shortly before Christmas that year, the embassy organised a protest demonstration, and urged Christian pilgrims to stage a boycott of Christ's birthplace.

Van der Hoeven is unapologetic about the embassy's politics.

'I'm sick and tired of people coming here, particularly Americans, and criticising us for not doing enough for the Arabs. They should get their own house in order before they start criticising us. What have the Americans done for the Indians or the Mexicans? Have they given one of their states to the Indians? Is there a Mexican state? Israel was given this land by the United Nations and is entitled to do with it what it pleases. It does not need to ask anyone for permission to make Jerusalem its capital. Did the Americans ask the Indians if they could make Washington their capital? Did the British ask anyone if they could have London?'

Van der Hoeven is an accomplished public-speaker: during his time at the Garden Tomb he preached before such luminaries as evangelist Billy Graham, former British Prime Minister Harold Wilson and South African heart specialist Dr Christian Barnard. He travels the world raising funds for the embassy and lecturing in support of Israel. His commitment to the Zionist cause is indisputable: both his son and daughter served in the Israeli army, even though their mother was an Arab. He says he did not have much choice about devoting his life to the Lord; the Lord made it for him. As a young child he was

13 Genesis (e.g. 12: 7, 13: 15, 15: 18, 17: 18, etc.) is used to justify Israeli occupation of the West Bank and Gaza; the Prophetical Books, especially Isaiah (27: 13, 37: 25, 52: 1, 60: 14) and Daniel (9: 24), substantiate the Zionist claim to Jerusalem.

taken seriously ill, and the doctors thought he might die. His father, a Mennonite, prayed through the night asking the Lord to save his son. Eventually the Lord responded.

'God told my father that He would save me, but that in return I would devote my life to His service,' says Van der Hoeven. When he finally came to Jerusalem he turned his back on the established Churches because he found them too provincial.

'Look at the Churches in Jerusalem. They are more concerned with fighting over their little plots and their silly privileges. It is a far cry from the teachings of Jesus. I am only concerned with the dignity of Jesus. Jesus is not interested in whether people are Latin, or Greek Orthodox or Armenian. That is why we set up the embassy. The work of the embassy is not about being pro-Israel. It's about believing in the word of the Lord.'

The Churches beg to differ. The Middle East Council of Churches, representing the interests of the thirteen 'international' Churches based in Jerusalem, were so concerned about the Christian Embassy that it established a working group to investigate not only the embassy, but the very nature of Christian Zionism. The Council's findings were unequivocal. The embassy was accused of allowing the

> Christian faith and biblical interpretation to become sub-
> servient to the policies of the modern state of Israel and
> revisionist Zionist political ideology . . . there is no room for
> ill-informed and biased 'Christian Zionist' ideologies that are
> dangerous distortions of the Christian faith. Christians every-
> where must reject all concepts of superiority of particular
> people (Israelis) over other people (Arabs) within God's
> creation . . . We urge all concerned Christians to join us in a
> categorical rejection of the Christian Zionist phenomenon, as
> representing a heretical interpretation of the Holy Scripture
> which is, in fact, hostile to the presence and witness of the
> Christian Churches in the Middle East.[14]

As for the Christian Zionists' enthusiasm for restoring the children

14 See *What is Western Fundamentalist Christian Zionism?* (Cyprus: Middle East Council of Churches, 1986).

of Israel, the Churches refer to the opening passage in the Acts of the Apostles, the final words of Our Lord before he ascended to heaven. 'They therefore, when they were come together, asked him, saying, Lord, dost thou at this time restore the kingdom to Israel? And he said unto them, It is not for you to know times or seasons, which the Father hath set within his own authority.'[15]

15 Acts 1: 6–7.

# 9

# LOSERS

*'With but little persuasion thou wouldst fain make me a Christian'*

Acts 26: 28

Their Beatitudes the Patriarchs are feeling rather pleased with themselves today. It has only taken them some seventy years, but, finally, they are going to unveil a newly decorated roof for the Holy Sepulchre. This is not just a big day for Jerusalem's Christians; the occasion is unique. Invitations have been sent to all the city's religious and political leaders, and the select gathering is now seated around Christ's tomb. Church representatives have travelled from as far as Ethiopia and Greece for the inauguration ceremony. The British and French Consul-Generals, their wives attired in dramatic millinery, have pride of place by the altar, as befits the traditional defenders of Christian privilege in the Holy Land. The Americans, relative newcomers to this world of Byzantine intrigue, have been squeezed in at the back. After lots of last-minute wrangling, even Mayor Olmert has agreed to make an appearance. He was going to boycott the event – as is his habit when he cannot dictate the agenda – because he has been invited simply as a representative of the local Jewish community, not as mayor, the city's paramount leader. He has agreed to come because the organisers have promised him a front-row seat, next to the Patriarchs themselves. Olmert arrives, bristling with self-importance, and takes his place, though he seems rather rattled to discover he has four prominent Palestinians – including Faisal Husseini and Hanan Ashrawi – seated on either side. To add insult to injury, the service is to be conducted in Arabic and English, the communal languages of Jerusalem's Christians. Not one word of Hebrew is to be uttered.

But this is not what distinguishes the occasion for the Patriarchs, even if they appreciate the *schadenfreude* of Olmert's discomfort. What makes this event so unique is that, for the first time in the long and tempestuous history of this poor church, the leaders of the different Christian communities have agreed to participate in the same service. The ceremony will be short and simple. The choirs of the three pre-eminent Churches will sing hymns in order of seniority – Greek Orthodox, Latin and Armenian – which will then be followed by prayers. At the end of the service the awning that has obscured the roof for seventy years will be removed, and daylight will stream through the windows at the top of the massive rotunda, to illuminate the Tomb of Christ.

Many of those who have been involved in the protracted debate over how to redecorate the church roof thought they would never see this day. Indeed, many of them never did, as they died long before a final agreement was reached. The origins of this particular dispute date back to the earthquake which hit Jerusalem in 1927, and severely damaged the church. Engineers employed by the British Mandate to examine the damage concluded that the roof, a massive iron structure that was originally commissioned and paid for by Napoleon III of France (to replace the roof damaged by the fire of 1808) required extensive renovation. The level of distrust that exists between the three Churches responsible for maintaining the Holy Sepulchre is so great that it took the sects until 1959 to agree that work could begin on more vital repairs, such as preventing the old Crusader structure from collapsing on to Christ's tomb. Work on the rotunda, the chamber surrounding the tomb, was started a few years later and completed in 1985. But the scaffolding remained in place for another ten years while the denominations argued over how to decorate the roof of the renovated rotunda.

The Greek Orthodox, who are responsible for the monument that covers the tomb,[1] wanted something similar to it, like a Byzantine mosaic depicting the resurrection of Christ. But the Latins and Armenians objected, pointing out that, while the original church was built by the Byzantine Emperor Constantine, the present structure was Crusader, and a Byzantine mosaic was therefore inappropriate. The wrangling continued for several more years, and at one stage the idea was seriously mooted of covering the ceiling with cherubs, a symbol familiar within both the Western and the Eastern Churches. The proposal had to be dropped, however, when a world-wide search failed to produce a cherub acceptable to all. Finally, in the spring of 1995, agreement was reached. The design was to represent 'the glory of God enveloping the Risen Christ'. Twelve golden rays, depicting the apostles, were to be painted against a background of mother-of-pearl clouds, representing heaven.

The service passes without incident. The Greek Orthodox choir sounds slightly discordant, the Franciscans – representing the Catholics – also sound slightly out of tune, despite the advantage of having an organ accompaniment. The Armenian choir, mainly comprising teenage boys, provides the best performance. It is rather undermined by the Armenian prayer of thanks, which reads like a manifesto in defence of the Armenian Orthodox faith. At the moment the Armenian Patriarch finishes the prayer, the old Crusader vault is filled with the peal of the church bells, and the awning is pulled away, to reveal the majestic, if somewhat ostentatious, new roof. Natural sunlight floods the stone chamber for the first time in living memory, and the congregation of local dignitaries emit a ripple of polite applause.

Unfortunately for Jerusalem's beleaguered Christians, demonstrations of brotherly goodwill between Church leaders such as this ceremony, which took place on 2 January 1997, are exceedingly rare. Intrigue and paranoia are the characteristics which more commonly define relations between the rival communities, especially the 'super-

1 The 'hideous kiosk', as it was described by the Marquis de Vogué in the nineteenth century, was built in 1810 to replace the monument destroyed by a fire in 1808. This in turn was one of a series of replicas which replaced the tomb destroyed by al-Hakim in 1009.

power' Churches, the Latins, Greek Orthodox and Armenians. The pre-eminent Churches, by tradition, enjoy the most prestige and, as a consequence, find themselves engaged in constant bickering.

Apart from the earliest days of the Church, when it was one and undivided, the Christian faith has been racked by conflict and intrigue, not to mention its own innumerable charges of heresy. Sir Lionel Cust, who served as Jerusalem's District Officer during the British Mandate in the 1920s, made a detailed study of the history of the Christian Churches, and its effect on the Holy Places in Jerusalem and the rest of the Holy Land. He reached the following unhappy conclusion: 'The history of the Holy Places is one long story of bitter animosities and contentions, in which outside influences take part in an increasing degree, until the scenes of Our Lord's life on earth become a political shuttlecock, and eventually the cause of international conflict.'[2]

While the status of Jerusalem during the early centuries of Christianity rose (by the fifth century the city had acquired the status of a Patriarchate), fierce doctrinal disputes resulted in a number of heresies being proclaimed, and irreconcilable divisions occurred which have a direct bearing on today's relations between the various Churches in Jerusalem. The Nestorian Controversy at the Council of Ephesus (AD 431), over the extent to which Christ assumed a human nature during his life, saw the creation of the Assyrian Church, while the Monophysite controversy that dominated the Council of Chalcedon (AD 451), resulted in the Armenian, Coptic, Syrian and Abyssinian Churches splitting from the Byzantine Orthodox. The picture is further complicated by the Crusades and the creation of the Latin Kingdom of Jerusalem. Until the arrival of the Frankish knights, Christian interests in the city were represented by the Orthodox Patriarch.[3] But the Crusaders banished the clergy of the Orthodox and other Eastern clergy from the Church of the Holy Sepulchre and installed twenty Latin canons to officiate in their stead. This slight is still frequently referred to by representatives of the Eastern Churches, even though, after the Crusaders' defeat, the

2 See L. G. A. Cust, *The Status Quo in the Holy Places*.
3 The Orthodox Patriarch Sophonius arranged the capitulation terms with the Caliph Omar during the Muslim conquest of the city in AD 638.

Orthodox regained much of their former influence, especially after the Ottoman conquest of the city in 1516.

It was not until the nineteenth century, when the rivalries between the different denominations threatened to provoke international conflict, that an attempt was made to codify the rights and privileges of the various Churches. With the French seeking to claim for themselves the mantle of protector of the Latin Patriarchate and the Russians demanding similar representation for the Orthodox Churches, the Sublime Porte in Constantinople issued a Declaration of the Status Quo in the Holy Places in 1852 to regulate the various claims. Tensions between France and Russia over which of the denominations had precedence in the Holy Places was one of the prime causes of the Crimean War. At the Treaty of Paris in 1855, the participants, including Russia, pledged themselves to uphold the Status Quo, which was further ratified in 1878 at the Treaty of Vienna following the Russo-Turkish war. One of the first undertakings made by General Allenby after Britain's capture of Jerusalem in 1917 was to uphold the Status Quo, and the Israelis made a similar commitment after they won control of the whole city in 1967.

The vicissitudes of Christian history have left their mark on Jerusalem, particularly at the Church of the Holy Sepulchre where six denominations – Latin Catholics, Greek Orthodox, Armenian, Coptic, Ethiopian and Syrian – are obliged to share the building according to the terms set out in the Status Quo. Every aspect of their religious devotion is rigidly stipulated, from the timing of the various prayer services to when they are allowed to clean their respective areas of the church. Rather than helping to ease relations between the different sects, however, the Status Quo only seems to have consolidated the centuries-old feelings of suspicion and distrust. As Jerome Murphy O'Connor, the Irish priest who has lived in Jerusalem for more than thirty years, has written, 'The frailty of humanity is nowhere more apparent than here; it epitomizes the human condition.'[4] Relations at the Holy Sepulchre are not as bad as they are at the Church of the Holy Nativity, in neighbouring Bethlehem, where, in the mid-1980s, Israeli soldiers were summoned to break up a brawl between Greek

4 O'Connor, p. 49.

Orthodox and Armenian monks that had erupted while they were doing their pre-Easter spring cleaning. But this unholy arrangement has nevertheless left its mark on the Holy Sepulchre. The tawdry aspect that greets the million or so pilgrims who visit the church each year is mainly due to the various obstacles that arise whenever the rival sects meet to discuss how the church's appearance might be improved, such as the long-running dispute over the new roof.

Of the three 'superpower' Churches, the Armenians are the least likely to stir up trouble if only because, unlike the Latins and Orthodox, they have no international backers to call upon if they get themselves into trouble. There are only about 1,000 Armenians left in Jerusalem, and to survive they have become professional fence-sitters, playing both sides, Israelis and Arabs, against the other. Even before 1967, when the Old City was under Jordanian rule, the Armenians had taken great care to establish good contacts with Israel, prudent insurance against the day the Israelis might take control of the whole city. Certainly the Armenians were less troubled about Israel's conquest of Jerusalem than many of the other Churches, as they did not much enjoy the experience of Jordanian rule after one of their patriarchs was accused of being a communist and unceremoniously dumped out of the country in the early 1960s. The Jordanians had little time for the niceties of the Status Quo. In spite of their size, the Armenians are fiercely proud of their identity and heritage. The Armenian Quarter of the Old City is a veritable shrine to what the community emotively refers to as 'the Armenian holocaust', the wholesale slaughter of hundreds of thousands of Armenians by the Turks during the First World War. The cellars of the Armenian Convent are also reputed to be filled with priceless treasures which reflect the Church's long and colourful past, although, such is the Armenian obsession with security, they are rarely displayed in public. Except, that is, for the occasion in the 1980s when some of the treasures made an unscheduled appearance at Sotheby's auction rooms in London. A vigilant Armenian visitor from the US, who happened to be browsing through the catalogue, recognised the pieces and their origin, and they were discreetly withdrawn. A Church inquiry later established that one of its members had put up the items for sale to clear gambling debts acquired while holidaying in the south of France.

The main struggle for power and influence, a contest which pre-dates the Crusades, is contested by the Latin Catholics and the Greek Orthodox, Jerusalem's two predominant Churches, which can also be the most troublesome. The Greek Orthodox, who trace their presence in the city back to Emperor Constantine, claim to be the 'authentic Church' of Jerusalem. (I once repeated this claim, told to me by a senior member of the Greek Orthodox Patriarchate, to an Armenian acquaintance, who was outraged. 'The cheek of it! Authentic church, my foot! And what of the Armenians? Do they think we don't exist?')

The arrogance of the Orthodox is due in part to their belief that they are heirs to a superior, Hellenic culture, and the fact that, during four centuries of Ottoman rule over the Holy City, they generally enjoyed a primacy over the other faiths. Initially this was because, sharing similar indigenous roots, they better understood the Ottoman Turks while the Ottoman Turks, who were invariably engaged in con-flict with Western powers in their desire to extend their influence beyond the gates of Vienna, preferred to deal with the Eastern Churches. Even as the power of the Ottomans waned, and the Turks came to rely on the patronage of European powers such as Britain, the Orthodox were able to call upon the support of 'Mother Russia' which, from Peter the Great onwards, regarded herself as protector of the Orthodox communion, a presumption which contributed to the causes of the Crimean War.[5] With the Ottomans' collapse, the Greek Orthodox establishment has found it difficult to adjust to its strait-ened circumstances, a failure which explains much of the Church's behaviour in the twentieth century.

It was bad luck on the Greek Orthodox that the Russian Revolution should coincide with the dissolution of the Ottoman Empire, for not only did the Church find itself deprived of its main guarantor, it was without its traditional source of income – Russian pilgrims. One has only to look at modern central Jerusalem to see the importance of Russian pilgrims, pre-Revolution, not just to the Church's economy, but the city's. The Russian Compound complex, surrounding the main Orthodox cathedral, today houses the police

---

5 Barbara Tuchman regarded the quarrel over the Holy Place that brought on the Crimean War as 'one of the most ridiculous causes of a major war in all history', and quotes a remark attributed to Princess Lieven: 'Tout pour un few Grik priests.'

headquarters, the main remand prison and a number of office build-ings associated with City Hall; all this was built in the nineteenth century to house the annual influx of pilgrims from Russia and its satellite states. This lucrative source of income dried up after 1917, and the Greek Orthodox were compelled to look for alternative sources of revenue. Thanks to the Church's pre-eminence over many years, it had acquired substantial property interests in the city, making it the wealthiest of all the Churches. To make ends meet the Church decided, in the 1920s, to sell substantial tracts of land on the open market. The land was eagerly snapped up by the Zionists with the result that the modern Jewish neighbourhood of Rehavia and the Ben Yehudah shopping mall are built on land formerly owned by the Greek Orthodox Church. Having done business once with the Zionists to their satisfaction, the Greek Orthodox appear to have few qualms about doing the same again, despite the protests of local Arabs always keen to curtail Zionist expansion in the city. Even after 1967, when the land issue in Jerusalem became significantly more sensitive, the Greek Orthodox Church continued to conduct secretive land deals with the Israeli authorities, so that many of the city's modern developments – the new hotels off King David Street, Liberty Bell Park – are built on Greek Church land.

The Church's willingness to deal with the Israelis, however, has become a perennial source of friction with the Palestinian political leadership, particularly after the formation of Yasser Arafat's Pale-stinian Authority in 1995, when it was made quite clear to various, senior members of the Greek Orthodox Patriarchate in Jerusalem that their safety could no longer be guaranteed if they travelled in areas of the West Bank and Gaza under Palestinian control. Nor have all the Church's attempts to raise funds met with the approval of the Israelis, even though Diodoros I, the Greek Orthodox Patriarch, in a blatant act of sycophancy, awarded Yitzhak Rabin and Shimon Peres the Church's Medal of Honour in 1995. The award was supposedly made because of the Israeli leaders' contribution to negotiating the Oslo Accords. But there were suggestions within the confines of Jerusalem's Christian Quarter that the Church was merely expressing its gratitude for the Israelis' tact in handling the potentially embar-rassing discovery of a cache of gold and heroin in the boot of Diodoros's limousine as it entered Israel from Jordan. The Israelis accepted the Patriarch's insistence that he had no knowledge of the contraband, and the affair was hushed up. 'The interest of the Israeli government was to build goodwill with the Greek Orthodox,' an official familiar with the case later explained, 'because they are our allies, as opposed to the Catholics, who are not.'

If the Greek Orthodox Church has got rich on the back of its lucrative land deals, the same cannot be said for its Arab congregations. To ensure Hellenic exclusivity is preserved in the higher echelons, the Church insists that all its Arab clergy marry. This precludes them from promotion because only single priests may aspire to the higher ranks. Various efforts have been made to persuade the Church to abandon this racist policy, including a Jordanian initiative in 1965 to have Arab priests raised to the Greek Orthodox Synod. But before the Jordanians could implement the rule, their influence in Jerusalem was ended by the Six-Day War. 'We saved the supremacy of the Greeks in the Church,' boasted an Israeli official responsible for Christian affairs. 'In return they became our friends and defended our position throughout the world.'[6]

The Church's long-standing insistence on preserving its Greek exclusivity, however, has taken its toll. Many Palestinian Christians are so disillusioned with the insensitivity of the Greek Orthodox Church to Arab needs that they have defected and joined the Greek Catholic Church, although, in one infamous case, the clergy has been somewhat over-enthusiastic in its efforts to help the needs of the local community. In 1974 Hilarion Capucci, the Greek Catholic Archbishop, was jailed for twelve years by the Israelis after being caught with a consignment of weapons and explosives in his car, as he returned from a trip to Beirut, which were destined for the PLO.

The iniquities of the Greeks fall far beneath the dignity of the Latin Catholics who, for the majority of the period since Israel's inception, have tried to maintain a haughty indifference to the brash, new Jewish state constructed on the land of the Apostles. The structure of the Catholic Church in Jerusalem is complex. After the collapse of the Crusader kingdom, and the banishment of the Latin Patriarch, responsibility for Church affairs was given, in 1342, to the

6 Interview with author.

Franciscans following a visit to the Holy Land by their founder, St Francis of Assisi. They still serve as the custodians of the Holy Land. In 1847 Pope Pius IX, to counter the proselytising activities of Protestant Churches – such as Christ Church – among Christians in the Holy Land, re-installed the Latin Patriarchate. Then in February 1948, to insure the Vatican's interests were fully represented at a crucial juncture in Holy Land history, Pope Pius XII created an Apostolic Delegation in Jerusalem. Despite this complicated arrangement, the Catholics have generally remained united in their dislike, bordering on contempt, for Israel, an attitude that has inevitably increased tensions with those denominations, such as the Greek Orthodox, which have developed good relations with their hosts. Having tolerated centuries of institutionalised anti-Semitism, the Vatican was decidedly underwhelmed by the Zionists' success in establishing their own state in 1948. Until 1967, when the main Christian sites in Jerusalem and Bethlehem were outside Israel's jurisdiction, the Catholics regarded Israel as an aberration which, given time, would fade away. After 1967 the Vatican was even less inclined to accommodate the idea that Jews were now in charge of the Holy Places, especially as the view that millions of Jews had died in the Holocaust because they did not believe in Jesus still held credence within the higher reaches of the Catholic establishment.

Unlike the Greeks, the Latins for many years refused to entertain the notion of doing any land deals with the Israelis. The Israelis could not understand why the Catholics, who had considerable land and property interests in the city which were under-utilised, would not do business. Teddy Kollek went to see the Apostolic Delegate to explore ways in which the city authorities might be able to help local Christians, but the Catholics refused to compromise. Only after the Arab–Israeli peace process began in earnest, following the 1991 Madrid Conference, did the Vatican realise that if the Palestinians were going to recognise Israel's right to exist, the Catholics should follow suit. The Vatican's decision to commence negotiations on establishing diplomatic relations with Israel was also, no doubt, prompted by a sizeable tax demand made by City Hall on the income the Church had received from its various commercial interests, such as Notre Dame Hotel, situated just outside the walls of the Old City by New Gate. Although the Church claimed the hotel was a charitable institution caring only for pilgrims, the local authorities took the view that the Notre Dame complex, with its expensive restaurant and comfortable rooms, was no different from other five-star hotels in the city, and that the Church should pay up. The issue of the Church's taxation status was one of the central questions discussed during the negotiations, which finally resulted in the signing of an agreement between Israel and Rome in 1993. The Vatican deal was not well-received by the other denominations. The Greek Orthodox, in particular, mindful of their own past behaviour, suspected that the Catholics had used the negotiations to secure an advantage for themselves over the other Churches, even though the Israelis insisted that the agreement with Rome would have no bearing on the Status Quo.

The Israelis like to portray themselves as being even-handed in their dealings with the various Christian denominations, especially with regard to the Status Quo even though, when they consider it to be expedient, they are not above bending the rules. Take the dispute between the Ethiopian Orthodox and the Egyptian Copts, two of Jerusalem's oldest Christian communities, over which of them controls a narrow stairway leading from the parvis of the Holy Sepulchre to the roof. Visitors to the church are always astounded to discover a small group of Ethiopian monks living in what are little better than mud-huts on the church roof. This is the Ethiopian monastery of Deir el-Sultan, which the Ethiopians constructed in the early nineteenth century when they were unceremoniously evicted from the main church by the Egyptian Copts, who also seized the keys to the passageway. The Egyptians retained control until Easter 1970 when the Ethiopian monks, with the help of Israeli policemen, changed the locks. The Egyptians were outraged, but there was little they could do because the Israelis, as the ultimate arbitrators of the Status Quo, sided with the Ethiopians. The reasons for this were not religious. Even though the secularist Gamal Abdel Nasser, the Egyptian dictator at the time, was no friend of the Copts, his hostility to Israel meant that the Israelis had more to gain by siding with the Ethiopians, at a time when Israel was trying to persuade Addis Ababa to allow the country's sizeable community of Ethiopian Jews to emigrate to Israel.

A more complex dispute concerns the Red and White Orthodox

Churches, a rift that dates back to the Russian Revolution. As Israel had good ties with the Soviet Union in 1948, it recognised the Red patriarchate whose churches then served for many years as KGB fronts in West Jerusalem. Jordan, meanwhile, recognised the New York-based White Church. Consequently, when Israel captured East Jerusalem in 1967, it found itself having to deal with two Russian Churches. Israel has since pledged to maintain the Status Quo even though the Whites, especially after the collapse of the Soviet Union and the revival of the indigenous Russian Orthodox Church, are petrified the Reds are after their property.

With so many disputes occupying the thoughts of Jerusalem's clergy, it is little wonder they find it so difficult to reach agreement on anything of import. There are, however, encouraging signs to suggest they are finally coming to their senses and, when practicable, attempting to present a united front to the outside world. All Christian Churches regard Jerusalem as the 'Mother Church' of Christianity. Not only is Jerusalem the location of Christ's death and resurrection, it is where both the Holy Ghost was revealed to the Apostles and where the Apostles established the Church. If the Jews regard the city as their eternal capital, the city, in religious terms, is no less important for Christians. The key difference between the two faiths is that Christians do not nurture any serious political aspirations for the city. They would prefer the sanctity of Jerusalem to be excluded from politics, and preserved as a place of worship and devotion. It was the realisation that the Churches had at least this much in common that has helped to persuade them to adopt a semblance of unity in their dealing with the wider world.

The genesis of this new spirit of co-operation, however, was not doctrinal, but the Palestinian *intifada*[7] which erupted in December 1987 and resulted in the worst Arab–Israeli violence since the Six-Day War. With scores of Palestinians being killed and injured each day, the Churches felt compelled to respond, even though the overwhelming majority of the Palestinians taking part in the demonstrations were Muslim. A statement issued on 22 January 1988 was signed by the three Patriarchs, the Custos, and representatives of the

---

7 The word in Arabic literally means to shake off, or shake out (i.e., the Israelis from Palestinian soil), but is generally taken to mean 'uprising'.

Syrian, Anglican and Lutheran Churches. It said the violence was 'a clear indication of the grievous suffering of our people on the West Bank and in the Gaza Strip. They are also a visible expression of our people's aspirations to achieve their legal rights and the realisation of their hopes.'

This was the first joint statement issued by Church leaders since 1967, and its uncompromising tone surprised the Israeli authorities, which had rather taken it for granted that the Churches were too divided and too fractious to act in unison. What was even more surprising was that, having broken new ground, the Churches did not stop at that. Throughout the course of the seven-year *intifada* they issued statements at regular intervals which were generally supportive of the Palestinian cause. It is even said that there was quiet satisfaction in some Church circles when the first Christian Palestinian was killed by Israeli gunfire in Beit Jala, a Christian village on the outskirts of Jerusalem. 'It meant Palestinian Christians could claim to support the same nationalist objectives as Palestinian Muslims,' explained one churchman.

The Churches continued to work together after the *intifada* finished and the peace process began in earnest. In late 1994 Jerusalem's Church leaders, responding to the Oslo-inspired peace process and in anticipation of any future Arab–Israeli negotiations of the city's future status, delivered by far their most important and coherent statement in centuries. Entitled 'The Significance of Jerusalem for Christians', the 'Memorandum of their Beatitudes the Patriarchs and the Heads of Christian Communities in Jerusalem' set out fourteen points that spelt out both the city's importance for Christians and how it might in future be governed to the satisfaction of all – Jew, Christian and Muslim. 'For Christianity, Jerusalem is the place of roots, ever living and nourishing,' the statement read. 'In Jerusalem is born every Christian. To be in Jerusalem is for every Christian to be at home.' The memorandum concluded by calling for the Holy City to be placed under a 'special statute' which would be administered by 'the international community'. The document was immediately condemned by the Israeli political establishment. Prime Minister Rabin, who at that time also held the Religious Affairs portfolio, dismissed it out of hand, remarking plainly: 'Jerusalem shall remain a united city under Israeli rule.' Mayor Olmert denounced the document as a 'strange combination of prejudices and distorted perceptions'. But the truth about how the Israelis really felt about the Christians' manifesto was made clear a few weeks later during a private conversation I had with an Israeli diplomat. 'Those fourteen points have been more damaging to Israel than the entire *intifada*,' he remarked.

Unfortunately, Jerusalem's Churches may have acquired this new sense of purpose too late. For the Christians are leaving. Not leaving in the way the faithful in Europe and America, disenchanted with arguments over the ordination of gay and female priests, are turning away from the established Churches. The Christians of Jerusalem and the Holy Land are leaving in search of better life, a quieter life, a life away from their homeland where they have prospects, where they can raise a family without fear for their future safety and security. Compared with the fourth century AD, when the Christian population of the Holy Land stood at around 1,400,000 souls, the modern Christian community is in a parlous state. Today there are just 45,000 Christians inhabiting the narrow, mountainous strip of land between the Mediterranean and the River Jordan, compared with 4 million Israelis and 1.7 million Palestinian Muslims. In Jerusalem, the holiest city in Christendom, there are just 12,000 Christians left. The dwindling numbers are a source of immense concern for Church leaders both inside and outside the Holy Land. How can the Churches hope to survive the next millennium if they have no congregations? Dr George Carey, the Archbishop of Canterbury, voiced the fears of many when, during a visit to the Holy Land in 1993, he said: 'In fifteen years, Jerusalem, Bethlehem – once centres of a strong Christian presence – might become a kind of Walt Disney Christian theme-park.'

Christian emigration is not a new phenomenon in the Holy Land. Since the end of the nineteenth century it is estimated that 85 per cent of the Palestinian Christian population has left. During the Mandate Christian Arabs formed the backbone of the Civil Service and held most of the other white-collar jobs. They were badly affected by the partition of Jerusalem following the 1948 war because most of the property in Arab neighbourhoods, such as Katamon, occupied by Israel after the war, was owned by Christians (which explains why Edward Said's family home is now the Christian Embassy). Schools and educational establishments run by foreign Christian missions in Jerusalem had provided Palestinian Christians with a good education and fluency in at least one European language. Most families had contacts abroad, and as it became clear they were not going to be allowed to return to their homes and jobs, many of them emigrated. The United States was and remains the most popular destination because many young Palestinian Christians are educated in American-sponsored schools, both Catholic and Protestant. If anything this trend was accelerated by Israel's success in 1967. Those Christians who had stayed on in the hope that the Palestinians might still achieve a favourable political settlement realised their situation was hopeless and left. It is estimated that since 1967 40 per cent of the Christian population of the West Bank, including Jerusalem, has emigrated. Of the remainder, one-third say they intend to leave.[8]

Some fifty years ago the Greek Orthodox Church of St James, situated at the side of the Holy Sepulchre, had 35,000 parishioners in the Old City: now there are just 3,000. Father Elias Yaghnam, an elderly Arab priest with a long, flowing white beard, lives with his wife in a cramped apartment on the roof of a nearby monastery. All his own children live in the United States, but he has chosen to remain and care for what is left of the parish's flock. A devout man who is prohibited from further promotion within his Church because he is an Arab, Father Elias represents the authentic voice of Jerusalem's native Christians, the majority of whom are Greek Orthodox.[9] Like many of his parishioners, Father Elias and his wife suffer the pain of a dispersed family. Because their four children have all lived in the US for several years, the Israeli authorities claim they are no longer resident in Jerusalem, and refuse to grant them permission to return. The Greek Orthodox Church may be wealthy as a result of its various lucrative land deals, but it is parsimonious when it comes to remunerating its clergy, particularly its Arab priests. The meagre stipend Father Elias receives from the Church – in the mid-1990s it amounted to less than $200 per month – means the couple

8 Quoted in a paper prepared by Dr Bernard Sabella, Professor of Sociology, Bethlehem University, 1995.

9 There are no precise figures, but it is estimated that 9,000 of Jerusalem's 12,000 Christians are Greek Orthodox.

cannot afford the air fares to see their children. When I met the couple they had not seen any of their children or grandchildren for five years.

'It is very painful for us,' says Father Elias, with quiet dignity. 'I could have left myself, but it would have felt like an act of betrayal.'

Losing so many parishioners has not helped matters, although the priest is philosophical about their reasons for leaving.

'It has been heart-breaking to see so many people go,' he says. 'I don't blame them, though. What can we do for them? We cannot offer them jobs and security. It is better for them if they make use of their good education and go abroad.'

Efforts by priests like Father Elias to fill their pews by encouraging Christians living beyond Jerusalem's boundaries to visit their churches have not been helped by Israel's decision, in 1993, to close off the city from the rest of the West Bank. The soldiers, on one occasion, would not even allow members of Bethlehem's Bible College Choir to pass so that they could fulfil a long-standing invitation to sing at the Holy Sepulchre. The choristers were told they did not need to travel to Jerusalem to worship, that they could pray elsewhere, and were turned away.

A more sinister element that has entered the Christian calculation whether to remain or leave is the rise of Islamic fundamentalism, a relatively new phenomenon in the Holy Land, although not in other parts of the Middle East.[10] Relations between the city's Christian and Muslim inhabitants have not always been harmonious. Under the rule of the Mamluks in the fourteenth century, for example, Christian men were required to wear a blue turban to distinguish them from Muslims, while their women had to wear a peculiar covering over their bosoms. These inconveniences do not still apply, although Jerusalem's Christian community views with alarm the insidious rise of Islamic militancy in the city, particularly in the wake of the 1996 suicide bomb attacks. Yasser Arafat has said repeatedly since returning to his Palestinian homeland that the Christians have nothing to fear, and has made several appeals for the Christian diaspora to return home to help rebuild the country. But Arafat's courtship of the radical

10 There were reports in the early 1990s, for example, that Sudan's Islamic rulers had subjected Christian rebels to mass crucifixions.

Palestinian Islamic movement, Hamas, to strengthen his own political position has not helped to allay the fears of Christians. Since Arafat's return in 1994, moreover, there have been several ugly incidents in Jerusalem where Muslims have attempted to intimidate Christians. Just before Easter 1995 a fifty-strong group of Muslim youths marched through the Old City chanting anti-Christian slogans. They then ransacked a snooker club frequented by Christian youths located close to the Holy Sepulchre. They broke chairs, tables and generally wrecked the place. They also beat up and stabbed four Christian youths. The justification for the attack was that the club served alcohol. Some young Christians tried to organise a self-help group for their future protection, but their efforts ended in farce. A young Greek Orthodox priest was injured when a home-made pistol exploded in his face. This inevitably attracted the interest of the Israeli security forces, which raided several homes, seized a variety of home-made weapons and made several arrests.

A more conventional means of airing their grievances is for Christians to seek out their political representatives. Although the Palestinian political establishment is dominated by Muslims, Jerusalem's Christians have made their own significant contribution. At one extreme there is the Greek Orthodox George Habash, the Marxist leader of the Popular Front for the Liberation of Palestine (PFLP). An uncompromising foe of Israel, he made his name masterminding various terrorist outrages during the late 1960s and 1970s. More mainstream political representatives are people like Hanan Ashrawi, the charismatic PLO spokeswoman who made an international reputation during the early days of the peace process for her measured articulation of the Palestinian cause, and Jonathan Kuttab, an energetic young Palestinian lawyer. Ashrawi and Kuttab were two of the more prominent Christian candidates who contested the Jerusalem seats during the 1996 Palestinian elections, although only Ashrawi was elected. Because of her high political profile, Ashrawi likes to play down her Christian background; she regards herself foremost as a representative of the Palestinian people, irrespective of religion. But Kuttab, who does not have the burden of high office, has more freedom, and is more forthright in defending the Christian cause. In view of the autocratic nature of the regime Arafat established after the elections, Kuttab was not too bothered about losing, because he has more freedom to represent the interests of Palestinian Christians.

'Even if I'd been elected, Arafat would have controlled everything that happened over Jerusalem,' said Kuttab. 'This way I am free to campaign for a pluralistic Jerusalem, and to stop the Israelis turning it into an exclusive, racist city. Jerusalem is too special to be the exclusive domain of one religion. Christians may be numerically small but they are very significant.'

Another increasingly popular outlet through which Jerusalem's Christians can express themselves is *Sabeel*, or 'the way', the Palestinian Liberation Theology organisation founded and run by Canon Naim Ateek of Jerusalem's St George's Episcopal Cathedral, the former official church of the British Mandate. Although it was not formally founded until 1992, *Sabeel*, and the theology Naim Ateek advocates, are children of the *intifada*. While Palestinians have suffered many injustices since the Israeli occupation began in 1967, the brutality with which the Israeli authorities sought to quell the *intifada* inspired a group of clergy and lay theologians to formulate their own brand of Liberation Theology. But it was Ateek, an intense and dedicated priest from Nazareth, who provided the movement's leadership and had the courage to lock horns with the Israeli political establishment over their treatment of the Palestinians. It is due to Ateek's diligence and hard work that *Sabeel* now has its own headquarters, a smartly renovated Arab house (rented to *Sabeel* by the Muslim Husseini clan) located in Jerusalem's Sheikh Jarrah neighbourhood. Today he is recognised as the most eloquent and thoughtful promoter of the Palestinians' own brand of Liberation Theology.

'God is not pleased with injustice,' he explains. 'The Bible has been used by the Israelis and Christian Zionists as an instrument of oppression. Our aim is to provide a more accurate interpretation of political events from the perspective of the Christian faith. This is a prophetic ministry. We try to address ourselves to the events of the day and how God is talking to us. And when we see injustice, God expects us to draw attention to it.'

The *intifada* provided a stern test for Ateek's theology, which is in essence a non-violent creed, something which did not appeal to more militant Palestinians who felt that violence was the only effective means of confronting the Israeli occupation.

'We believe that Jesus was a non-violent person,' Ateek says in his defence. 'This is one of the central lessons of the Gospels. And so we have chosen to be non-violent. But Christ also fought against injustice and deception. What the Israelis have done to the Palestinians is unjust, and we must stand against it. An unjust peace will not last, and anything that stands in the way of a sovereign Palestinian state in the West Bank and Jerusalem is unjust.'

Apart from supporting the Palestinians' campaign for political recognition, *Sabeel* also strives to promote greater unity among the Churches, and to guide them towards presenting a united front whenever Christianity is drawn into the political arena. Although *Sabeel* was not directly responsible for the Churches' controversial fourteen points, much of the material published in the document reflects Ateek's ideology. *Sabeel* has also been involved in arranging various ecumenical conferences to emphasise the continuing validity of Christian heritage in the Holy Land, and to ensure the Christian voice is heard above the more familiar clamour of Jews and Muslims for recognition.

Even the efforts of *Sabeel*, however, seem powerless to arrest the progressive decline of Jerusalem's Christians and, until the trend is reversed, the Churches must depend on the support of the million or so pilgrims who visit the city each year. Jerusalem has been the foremost centre of pilgrimage for Christians for more than 2,000 years. Some of the older churches, such as the Armenian church of St James, bear witness to the dedication of pilgrims spanning centuries. The church's stone walls are covered with small crosses, neatly carved by the generations of Christian worshippers who have fulfilled the ultimate act of homage, similar to a Muslim making the *Haj* to Mecca. This intense sense of devotion is today best represented by the planeloads of elderly Greek women who, dressed in black, fill the Old City each year at Easter. Most of them are widows, and they are one of the more familiar features of the city in spring, wandering lost around the Old City, speaking only Greek, staunchly ignoring the Arab merchants' craven inducements to purchase their grossly overpriced wares. These old ladies have come to Jerusalem to prepare for death. They bring with them their burial shrouds, some rose water, herbs and anointing oil. When they visit the Holy Sepulchre they smear some oil on the stone where it is said Jesus was annointed before burial. They then wipe the stone with their shrouds, sprinkle them with rose water and wrap them around the herbs. Greek researchers have found that an extraordinarily high proportion of these old women die within a year of their return home to Greece.

Apart from the much-needed funds they donate to the Churches, the other valid contribution made by the pilgrims who come from all over the world is the moral support they provide for Jerusalem's Christian community. So long as there are pilgrims visiting Jerusalem, the city's few remaining Christians can at least draw comfort from the knowledge that their plight is not entirely forgotten. When Jacques Chirac, the French President, made a state visit to Jerusalem in October 1996, the excitement among leaders of the Christian clergy was palpable. On the day of Monsieur le Président's visit to the Old City, the three Patriarchs were dressed in their finest robes to greet him at the door of the Holy Sepulchre. For them, especially the Latin Patriarch, it was just like the glory days of old, with the leader of one of the world's most powerful nations coming to pay homage at the heart of Christendom. The city's Christian community also took great delight at Chirac's barely concealed ill-will towards the Israeli security officials who had been deployed to protect him for his tour of the Old City.

Prior to the visit, French officials had insisted that the Israelis keep their presence to a minimum; France does not recognise Israel's sovereignty claims over East Jerusalem and the Old City, and the officials insisted it would be inappropriate for a French head of state to have an Israeli escort. The Israelis ignored this request and, on the contrary, flooded the Old City with police and soldiers. As Chirac arrived an army helicopter buzzed the rooftops of the Arab houses. The Israelis wanted no one, not even a French President, to be in any doubt about who controlled the Old City. Chirac was incensed. On several occasions Chirac's sense of *lèse-majesté* manifested itself with the French President grabbing the arms of Israeli policemen and rebuking them as they tried to control the crowds of well-wishers. At one point Chirac remonstrated with an Israeli officer: 'What's the problem now? I've had enough of this. Do you want me to go back to my plane and return to France?' Chirac's outburst paid dividends. Later that day, at an official lunch given by the Israeli government, Prime Minister Benjamin Netanyahu publicly apologised. 'We are sorry that this happened,' he said. 'It was done for a good cause, to protect a friend.' Jerusalem's Church leaders could scarcely contain their delight at seeing their Israeli overlords so humbled.

But moments of triumph such as this are, for Jerusalem's Christians, rare and illusory. For the most part Christian influence in the city is peripheral, and seldom taken seriously. It is only on those limited occasions when Church leaders can raise their parochial, often petty, disputes to an international dimension that the authorities – Israeli and Palestinian – feel obliged to listen. For the most part the Christians are seen as hopelessly divided and, compared to the muscular forces of Israeli and Palestinian nationalism, largely impotent. Rather than evoking the traditions of 2,000 years of Christianity, the Churches seem better represented by the attention-seeking pilgrims who can generally be found in the Old City each year on Good Friday, dragging their rented crucifixes along the Via Dolorosa, their heads covered in chicken blood, an embarrassing parody of the Christian heritage. In many respects, the Christians today resemble the lost tribe of Jerusalem.

# 10

# REBELS

*'Serve no other Gods besides Allah, lest you incur disgrace and ruin'*

Koran, Sura 17

For as long as anyone can remember, the signal for the daily Ramadan fast to end in Jerusalem has been provided by the firing of an old cannon situated on the edge of a Muslim cemetery overlooking the Old City by Damascus Gate. The cannon used to reside near the Dome of the Rock, but that was too close for Jews praying at the Wailing Wall below, and so it was moved outside the Old City ramparts. Local Muslims like to claim the tradition goes back more than 1,000 years, although this appears to pre-date the invention of gunpowder. The Ottoman conquest of the city is a more likely starting point, and for centuries the Turks fired the cannon which now resides, in graceful retirement, at the Islamic Museum. More recently the faithful have relied upon a First World War artillery relic, built, perversely, by an ironworks in Bethlehem.

The rigours of a Ramadan fast are not for the faint-hearted. For an entire lunar month, between the hours of sunrise and sunset, earnest Muslims are required to refrain from all food and drink; there must be no smoking, lying or cheating; sex is prohibited. Accordingly, the loud report from the Ramadan cannon that echoes across the city at the end of each day's fast is awaited with some eagerness by the faithful. As dusk falls shopkeepers close up, offices empty and roads through the city's Arab neighbourhoods are congested as Muslims head home for their evening *Iftar*, the evening meal with which the fast is broken. By sunset most of Islamic Jerusalem is primed to resume life's necessities the moment the cannon is fired. Which is why the city's Muslims were so outraged when the Israelis took away their gunpowder.

Nothing, it seems, not even a sacred religious festival like Ramadan, which commemorates the revelation of the Islamic message to the Prophet Mohammed, is above politics in modern Jerusalem. Every year the Israelis react to Ramadan as though they are preparing to repel an invasion. Checkpoints are reinforced around the city and Muslim Palestinians travelling to Jerusalem to pray at al-Aqsa are stopped and searched. Those who do not have the correct papers, and males under the age of thirty, are turned back. During the Friday prayer service, when the numbers of worshippers can exceed 300,000, the city virtually grinds to a standstill because of all the roadblocks Israeli police and army officers insist on setting up. These heavy-handed security arrangements are as vexing for Israelis as they are for Palestinians; Israelis trying to get home early for the Jewish weekend find themselves stuck in appalling traffic jams. During the prayer service itself police helicopters hover noisily overhead, seeking to identify potential troublemakers. If anything, the harassment intensified after the Oslo Accords were signed in 1993, as the Palestinians regard al-Aqsa as the paramount symbol of their nationalist aspirations. For them al-Aqsa, and the whole Haram al-Sharif compound, is incontrovertible proof that their claim for Jerusalem to become a Palestinian capital has solid foundations. The Israelis disagree, and view the Palestinian attachment to al-Aqsa, the eighth-century mosque built to commemorate the Prophet's night journey to heaven, and the Dome of the Rock as nothing more than an underhand ploy to undermine Israeli sovereignty over the whole city. Consequently the Israeli authorities, and especially Mayor Olmert, devote much energy to containing and undermining Jerusalem's Muslim tradition, which includes silencing the Ramadan cannon.

Raja Sandouka, a tall, thin Palestinian actor in his forties, holds the honorary Muslim title 'keeper of the cannon'. He inherited it from his father, observing a heritage passed down over many centuries. No one in the Sandouka family knows for sure when or how this honour was acquired, but the family can trace its origins in the city back to Saladin's conquest. For at least the past two hundred years a member of the Sandouka clan has had responsibility for firing the cannon to commence and curtail each day's Ramadan fast. Until, that is, the great Israeli gunpowder plot. Without warning, Mr Sandouka says he received a demand from Israel's Labour and Social Welfare Ministry that he must first obtain a gunpowder licence before he would be allowed to operate the weapon in future. In order to qualify for the licence, Mr Sandouka was told he would need to take an intensive, three-day explosives course in Tel Aviv. Unfortunately, Mr Sandouka was otherwise engaged with rehearsals for a Palestinian production of *Sesame Street*, and was unable to make the time available for the training course. And so the cannon remained silent for the month of Ramadan because the 'keeper of the cannon' was deprived of his normal supplies of gunpowder. As an alternative, the authorities at City Hall provided him with a box of Chinese firecrackers, enough for one controlled explosion each day.

'Look, this is all they've left me,' says Mr Sandouka, holding up his Chinese firecracker like a dead rat. 'This is just too ridiculous. It is not as though I'm firing the cannon at the Israelis. I only use gunpowder, nothing else. They do this just to persecute the Muslims.'

Certainly the gunpowder restrictions hinder the normal Ramadan observance for many Muslims. Many complain that they cannot hear the firecracker, and so tune in their radios, listening out for the Islamic equivalent of the Greenwich time signal. But even this has its drawbacks. While watching Mr Sandouka prepare his evening firework, I encounter one young Muslim in the cemetery who is perturbed that his family has broken their fast early because they have been listening to Radio Jordan. 'Our Ramadan is just not the same,' he laments.

If all this seems rather petty, it nevertheless serves to illustrate the extreme sensitivity aroused by anything remotely related to Jerusalem's Islamic heritage. Whereas the Israeli authorities are more confident when confronting purely political establishments, such as Orient House and the plethora of PLO organisations that sprang up all over the city in the wake of the Oslo Accords, they realise they must be more circumspect in their dealings with the Muslims' religious institutions. Palestinian leaders, for their part, are well aware that, in their campaign to make Jerusalem the capital of a future Palestinian state, this is the one area that they have the Israelis at a disadvantage. Why else would Yasser Arafat and his whisky-drinking, womanising PLO cohorts have discovered their Muslim roots after their return from exile abroad? Suddenly everyone in the PLO leadership wanted to travel to Jerusalem to pray at al-Aqsa. Almost every time Arafat made a breakthrough in his peace negotiations with Israel – the autonomy deal for Gaza and Jericho, Israel's military withdrawal from Hebron – he held up the prospect that he would soon travel to *Al-Quds* to pray. It was, of course, only bluster on Arafat's part. It would have been political suicide for him to enter Jerusalem for religious reasons before he had successfully negotiated a political settlement on the city's future. But it nevertheless succeeded in arousing extreme consternation among Israelis who hated the idea of Arafat setting foot in the Holy City; they realised that, as custodians of all the city's holy places, this was one privilege they could not deny. However much the Israelis resist the Palestinians' political claims to the city, they know they are on far weaker ground when it comes to the Muslim holy places.

This might explain why, since the mid-1980s, more and more Palestinians have become practising Muslims. This has little to do with the influence of Hamas, the Palestinian Islamic fundamentalist group which carried out suicide bombings in 1996 and 1997. Jerusalem's Muslims are essentially followers of mainstream Sunni Islam, and are not inclined towards extremism. Hamas makes its presence felt in insidious ways, such as persuading the Palestinian Authority to fine any Palestinian – Christian or Muslim – found eating, drinking or smoking in public during Ramadan.[1] In fact Ramadan is the time when the new-found religious fervour of the city's Muslim inhabitants is most in evidence, even in the most unlikely quarters.

A Palestinian money-changer acquaintance, whom I know, from painful experience, is partial to heavy all-night drinking sessions,

1 Such an edict was passed by the Palestinian Authority for the 1997 Ramadan fast.

suddenly announced that, for the first time in his fifty or so years, he was going to observe the Ramadan fast. This was a man who used to joke openly that only the grape was prohibited by the Prophet; the Koran made no mention of grain, and so, as a Muslim, he was perfectly entitled to consume significant quantities of his favourite tipple, Johnny Walker Black Label. What was more surprising was his declaration that, once Ramadan was over, it was his intention never again to imbibe alcohol. What, I enquired, had brought about this dramatic change of heart?

'Allah knows I am a sinner, and the time has come for me to repent,' he explained. 'Allah punishes the Palestinians because we are not good people. Perhaps if we become good people, and live virtuous lives, Allah will reward us, and give us back our land.'

Knowing the man to be a venal, if disarming, rogue, I found this attempted *mea culpa* somewhat hard to digest. And so I enquired among some mutual acquaintances what the real reason was, and discovered that it was in fact a response to a matrimonial edict of the 'it goes, or you go' variety.

Not all Born Again Muslims are quite so cynical about the rediscovery of their faith. In view of the city's all-pervasive and intoxicating religious fervour, it is hardly surprising that native Muslims should feel drawn to Islam. However much the city may have changed since it came under Israeli jurisdiction, the Islamic tradition permeates the lives of ordinary Palestinian Muslims in a multitude of ways. When doing their embroidery, for example, Palestinian women will deliberately drop a stitch to remind themselves that only Allah is perfect. Then there was the case of the middle-aged Palestinian labourer I used to know. Despite his attempts to be friendly, Ahmed was essentially a sad man. Whenever I met him he had the fatalistic air of one who believed life was irredeemably set against him. The root of Ahmed's problem was that he wanted a son. But, alas, for reasons known only to Allah, his wife produced a seemingly endless line of daughters. When I last saw Ahmed his wife had just given birth to their fifteenth baby girl, and the poor man was finding it extremely difficult to summon any enthusiasm for this latest addition to his family. 'She is very beautiful, and my wife is very happy,' he said, 'but all I want is a son. Perhaps next time Allah will provide, *inshallah* [God willing].'

\*

The annual *Haj* to Mecca is another useful barometer of the city's Islamic mood. Even though Muslims regard Jerusalem as being almost on a par with Mecca and Medina, the fifth Pillar of Islam specifies only that Muslim pilgrims visit the shrines located in Saudi Arabia. The annual arrangements are handled in Jerusalem by the Wakf, the Islamic organisation responsible for administering property, schools and other religious institutions. A combination of the strict quota system administered by the Saudis, and the various restrictions imposed by the Israelis, means that only a small percentage of Palestinians who want to make the *Haj* actually get the chance to go. Munir Osman, who runs the Office of the Haj from a building close to the Haram, has the difficult task of selecting potential *hajji*, as the successful pilgrims will be known. To qualify they must be over eighteen, sane, and have the financial means.

'God understands those who cannot make the *Haj*,' explains Munir. 'But then it is not a problem for people in Jerusalem, because God blesses Muslims here for looking after the holy al-Aqsa mosque.' Islam regards it as a holy mission for Muslims to live in Jerusalem.

Each year more than 100,000 Muslims apply to make the *Haj*, but only 10,000 are allowed to make the trip. Jerusalem itself only qualifies for six hundred permits, which makes it even more of a special privilege. Those who have successfully completed the trip usually announce the fact by adorning the entrance to their homes with a brightly painted depiction of the Kabah at Mecca, examples of which can be found in abundance throughout the Old City's Muslim Quarter. There would be many more, were it not for the Israelis' tough restrictions on Palestinian residency in the Holy City.

'Many Muslim Palestinians would like to live here for religious reasons, especially those who have completed the *Haj*,' says Munir. 'But the Israelis won't let them.'

Munir made the trip himself in 1994, and regards it as the most important experience of his life.

'It was very special, and somehow now I feel like a more complete person.'

As he enjoyed it so much, would he, then, prefer to live in Mecca?

'Mecca is very lovely, but I prefer Jerusalem,' he replies. 'I feel it is very special to live in Jerusalem. It is like living in Mecca all the time, only Jerusalem is the closest place to God.'

It is not, however, just godly inspiration that accounts for the rising trend in Islamic observance; many Palestinian Muslims regard attendance at the mosque as an assertion of their political and cultural identity. Exact figures are hard to come by, especially as the Israeli authorities continually use any number of ploys to reduce the city's Palestinian population, from unilaterally withdrawing identity cards of existing residents to refusing to register the city's new-born Palestinian babies. But a pattern appears to have formed whereby the harder the Israelis try to deny local Palestinians expression of their nationalist ambitions, the more Muslims seek to emphasise their Islamic heritage. The impressive edifice of the Haram al-Sharif, the most dominant and central architectural feature of the Jerusalem landscape, is used to refute any suggestion that the Palestinians have no claim to the city.

This is not, of course, the first time the Islamic holy places have become embroiled in unholy political wrangling over the city's future. Haj Amin al-Husseini, the malevolent Grand Mufti, exploited his position at the Haram in the 1920s and 1930s to reduce Palestine to a state of all-out civil war. King Abdullah of Transjordan was assassinated by a Palestinian gunman as he went to pray at al-Aqsa in July 1951, shortly after concluding a secret peace deal with Israel. More recently the politicisation of the Haram derives from the eruption of the Palestinian *intifada* in December 1987. The *intifada* may have been, in essence, a grass-roots revolt against twenty years of Israeli occupation, but the *shabab*, the Palestinian youths who daily risked their lives in the violent confrontations with Israeli troops, looked to the mosques for leadership and guidance. After the disturbances commenced, the weekly al-Aqsa Friday prayer service was seen as a rallying point for the Palestinian rebels. In the early days of the conflict hundreds of thousands of Palestinians would converge on the Haram each Friday lunchtime. Apart from their devotions, the faithful would listen intently to the sermons, which were overtly political in tone, for direction. Pamphlets and newsletters printed by the various Palestinian groups orchestrating the violence were passed from hand to hand. Afterwards, as they left the compound, the worshippers would become involved in running battles through the narrow streets surrounding the Haram with the Israeli police and soldiers who had been drafted in to the Old City, anticipating trouble. These weekly clashes emphasised the Islamic nature of the *intifada*; no police reinforcements were needed outside the Church of the Holy Sepulchre for worshippers leaving Sunday Mass.

During the early years of the *intifada*, these clashes became a weekly ritual, almost like the preparations for a crunch football match. Early each Friday morning police reinforcements would arrive in the city, and post look-outs on the rooftops of buildings overlooking Damascus Gate. Palestinians making their way to al-Aqsa for the prayer service were stopped and searched, often roughly, so that by the time they arrived at the Haram the mood of the crowd was restless and aggressive. On one occasion I persuaded the commander of an Israeli police post by Chain Gate to let me watch the service from the roof, which afforded an extraordinary view over both the whole Haram and the Wailing Wall. (The British turned it into a police post in the 1920s to stop Arab boys climbing on the roof and urinating on Jews at the Wailing Wall below.) It was impressive to watch a crowd of some 250,000 Muslims all praying at the same time, prostrating themselves in unison towards the *qibla*, the Kabah at Mecca. From time to time they would chant '*Allua Akbar*', 'God is Great', in response to the Imam leading the prayer service. Each time the refrain seemed to rise in volume, until it sounded almost like a battle-cry. By the time the service ended, the younger participants were wrapping their *keffiyehs* around their heads, and picking up stones, ready for the next round of confrontation with the Israeli occupiers. This was a rite of passage for young Muslims. It was as though they had not proved their manhood until they had either been beaten, arrested or shot at by the Israelis.

I came down off the roof to find the Israeli police already dressed in full riot fatigues, and no sooner had I arrived than a great stream of *shabab* came rushing towards the police station entrance, hurling rocks and stones at the Israelis inside. Overwhelmed by the sheer force of numbers, the commander ordered his men to close the large wooden doors. As they did so one of the policeman fired a tear gas canister, aiming at the rioters outside. The projectile hit the closing door and bounced back inside the police post, filling the old Ottoman building with acrid fumes. For those of us without gas masks, which included the Israeli commander, it was not exactly an experience to relish.

It is at times like this that the deep antagonism between Muslim and Jew all seems rather ironic. This intense hatred, which so often manifests itself in Jerusalem, particularly in the Old City, is only a twentieth-century phenomenon. It was the Jews, after all, who helped the Muslims capture the city nearly 1,400 years ago, and provided Omar with the idea of building his mosque on the site of the Temple. Unlike the Christians, who have never been particularly well-disposed towards Jerusalem's Jews, most Muslim regimes (with the exception of the Mamluks, who treated everyone badly) have been tolerant towards the city's Jewish community. Saladin welcomed the Jews back into the city after he defeated the Crusaders, and a Jewish presence has remained in the city, almost without interruption, ever since. It is not religion, but politics that is responsible for the deep rupture in the tolerance of the two faiths. While Palestinians find it difficult to distinguish between Zionism and Judaism, Israelis have the same difficulty with Islam and Palestinian nationalism. Consequently most Israelis regard Islam as a demonic code, and most Palestinians are congenitally anti-Semitic.

Ekrima Sabri, Grand Mufti of Jerusalem and the Holy Land, Orator of al-Aqsa Mosque and the supreme religious leader of the Palestinian Muslims, likes to lead by example. Short and rotund, with a neatly clipped beard and an engaging smile, he made no attempt to hide his scorn for the Jewish people when I first met him, shortly after his appointment in late 1994. He was particularly contemptuous of their claim that the Wailing Wall, which forms part of the outer wall of the Haram and is situated a few hundred metres away from his office, was in any way related to the Temple.

'This is nonsense,' he averred, slapping his palm upon his desk for emphasis. 'This is the wall of Al-Borak, which brought the Prophet to *Al-Quds* before his ascent to heaven. This is the place where the Prophet tethered the beast. It is a Jewish fantasy that the Temple used to exist here. There is nothing that proves it. It is all in their imagination. The Haram has nothing to do with the Jews. They have no right to be here.'

But the Temple must have been somewhere, I suggested. It seemed absurd to claim that the Jews had spent most of the last 2,000 years worshipping the wrong relic.

'I am not responsible for the Jews and it is not my job to help them find their Temple,' he retorted. 'I just don't want to think about it. They have spent most of their time digging around the Haram, and they have found nothing. They have done more damage to the Haram with their archaeology than the Crusaders did when they conquered the city. They have attacked the holiest place in Islam. They have offended our culture, our history and our beliefs.'

Mr Sabri would brook no argument. I tried to point out that, irrespective of all the historical and archaeological evidence, it is a central feature of the Islamic tradition that the Prophet ascended to heaven from the Temple, and that the Dome of the Rock was built on the site where that ascent originated. But the Mufti was not in a mood to listen.

'This is a Muslim shrine. It is a fundamental tenet of Islam that Muslims should respect other religions and their holy places. We also believe that Allah is just. It is therefore inconceivable that Allah would tell his [Muslim] people to build our Holy Mosque on a Jewish site. The Jews can pray here because we are not a vindictive people. Muslims have large hearts. If the Jews want to pray here, that is up to them. We will not stop them. So long as they leave us in peace.'

When I met the Mufti a couple of years later, he sought to be more circumspect. The issue of Jerusalem had become so sensitive that he had no doubt been told by the Palestinian political leadership to be a little more tactful in his references to his Israeli neighbours. He still insisted on calling the Wailing Wall the 'Wall of Boraq', because that was how it was known to Arabs. But his tone, at first, was more accommodating.

'It is very important that you understand this point,' he said, his plump palm again slapping against the top of his desk. 'We don't have a problem with the Jewish religion. The only problem we have is with the Jewish people who attack us and humiliate us. These are the people we cannot tolerate. If you want to be liked, you have to behave properly. But they behave very badly towards us, so it makes it hard for me to understand them and respect them. The Jews have always treated people badly, and that is why they have suffered so much misfortune.'

Mr Sabri is a man confident of his place in the world. If he has a fault it is that he appears to derive enormous satisfaction from his own importance. But he exudes none of the malice that characterised the position when it was occupied by Haj Amin al-Husseini. Mr Sabri's office, situated in the warren-like Wakf complex by one of the main entrances to the Haram, is a modest affair, filled with black leather armchairs and plastic coffee tables. When he enters the room he is attended by two burly Palestinian bodyguards who escort him from his home in Jerusalem's northern suburbs. On the back of his chair is a brightly decorated prayer mat, and his bookcase is lined with Islamic texts. Behind his desk is a large, framed photograph of Yasser Arafat, adorned by two Palestinian flags. Mr Sabri is dressed in a neatly tailored brown cloak and wears a smart white and claret, turban-style hat. His aides produce an endless supply of sweet tea, served in small china cups. As the religious leader of the Palestinian Muslims, he has many responsibilities. He is constantly being asked to issue a *fatwa* on a whole range of issues, from whether a man can marry the sister of his divorced wife to how much money a family should pay as a dowry. (The Mufti does not support the Iranian *fatwa* calling for the death of British author Salman Rushdie, although he thinks the book *The Satanic Verses* is a grave insult against Islam.) Our meetings are constantly interrupted by various petitioners. On one occasion the administrator of an old people's home wanted to discuss a problem. He had just sacked three female workers for striking for higher pay. But the old folks had started complaining that they were not being properly looked after. The Mufti listened intently, and asked a few questions. He then suggested the man should contact an Islamic institution and ask for more funds. He would then be able to rehire the women and pay them better wages. A couple of hours later an old woman, her face covered with tattoos and completely dressed in green, wandered in. She said her name was Khadra, the colour of her garments, and that she had no money and hadn't eaten for days. The Mufti put his arm around her in a comforting way, and asked one of his aides to take her to a nearby hostel where she would be fed.

Jerusalem being Jerusalem, Mr Sabri is not the only Mufti in the city. There are three Patriarchs and two Chief Rabbis; so why not two Grand Muftis? While the origin of the three Patriarchs, at least, dates back over many centuries, the two-Mufti phenomenon is a recent development, originating, to be precise, in 1994, following the death of the incumbent. Since the end of the Ottoman era, responsibility for appointing the Mufti has been shared by, first, the British and then the Hashemite Kings of Jordan. A successor was therefore duly appointed by King Hussein, who selected Abdul Khader Abdeen, a loyal Jordanian supporter. But whereas the appointment in previous years had been a mere formality once the king had made his choice, on this occasion Hussein failed to take account of the region's rapidly changing political realities. Following his return to his Palestinian homeland, Yasser Arafat regarded anything relating to the affairs of the Palestinian people as his prerogative and, even though he had nothing against Mr Abdeen personally, sought to assert his authority by appointing his own man – Ekrima Sabri.

For the first time in Jerusalem's Islamic history, the city had two Muftis. For a few months, the arrangement worked very badly indeed, with both Messrs Sabri and Abdeen vying for influence over the Muslim holy places. But eventually Mr Sabri triumphed, through Arafat's increasing influence in the city's affairs, an influence that was deeply resisted by many Israelis who objected to the PLO leader establishing what was, in effect, his personal fiefdom in the heart of Jerusalem. But because of the intense political and religious sensitivities surrounding the Haram, particularly in the wider Arab world, the Israeli political establishment accepted that there was little they could do.

The unfortunate Mr Abdeen was banished to a remote corner of the Haram, where he resided in splendid isolation, unwanted and roundly ignored. Nor was there any hint of magnanimity from Mr Sabri for his rival once his own supremacy had been established.

'There is only one Grand Mufti in Jerusalem and that is me,' he bragged, without the least hint of humility, when I asked him to explain how this unique state of affairs had arisen. 'The other man might call himself Mufti, but he is a joke. No one takes him seriously.'

Mr Abdeen was even less forthcoming when I sought him out in his little office at the side of al-Aqsa. At first he refused to see me, and when I persuaded his secretary to let me into his office, he remained obstinate. I tried to explain that I didn't want to talk about politics, I wanted to talk about Islam in Jerusalem.

'Well, go and talk about Islam with someone else,' he replied curtly, before showing me the door.

One of the more compelling aspects of the Jerusalem question is the intense passions the city can be guaranteed to arouse among the Muslim leaders of the Arab world.[2] The Arab peoples of the Middle East admire strong leaders, and the Palestinians are no exception; a strong Arab leader is expected to behave as though *Al-Quds* is engraved upon his heart. The Arab world's attachment to *Al-Quds* is so intense that a photograph, inscription or some other representation of the Holy City can be found in homes and offices throughout the region, from the most humble Bedouin shack to the palaces of kings. The loss of Jerusalem and control of the Muslim holy places to Israel in 1967 caused a profound shock not just among Arabs, but the entire Muslim world. This sense of deprivation has been heightened by the fact that, as a consequence of Israel's victory, Jerusalem is essentially out of bounds to most Muslims. But followers of Islam, whether they come from Nigeria or Pakistan, do not regard this loss as permanent, and many Muslim leaders behave as though their commitment to the recovery of Jerusalem is a test of their political virility.

In Iran, paintings of the Dome of the Rock, the most potent symbol of *Al-Quds*, adorn office blocks in Tehran, together with speeches made by the late Ayatollah Khomeini exhorting the faithful to support its liberation. The same symbol appears on the 1,000-rial Iranian bank-note, and a main square in Tehran has been named *Al-Quds*. King Hassan of Morocco, who traces his lineage directly back to the Prophet, heads the Islamic Conference Organisation's 'Jerusalem Committee', set up in 1975 to protect the Muslim holy sites and guard against the 'Judaisation' of the city, a task they have manifestly failed to fulfil. The Saudi Royal family, who regard themselves as defenders of the Islamic faith and protectors of the holy sites at Mecca and Medina, maintain a close interest in Islam's other principal shrine. On various occasions since 1967 the Israelis have allowed the House of Saud to make substantial donations to the Wakf authorities in Jerusalem for the Haram's upkeep, as much to irritate the preten-

2 Lebanon is the only predominantly Christian Arab country in the Middle East, which is one of the underlying reasons for its political turmoil.

sions of the Palestinians to control the sites as to curry favour with the Arab world's wealthiest dynasty. In the 1980s, for example, Saudi money paid for a complete new set of prayer mats at al-Aqsa.

Palestinian Muslims are constantly on the look-out for an Arab leader who will fight for them and deliver them from what they regard as the tyranny of Israeli rule. Most Palestinians have an unquenchable desire to avenge *al-Nekbi*, 'the calamity', of 1948 and *al-Neksi*, what they ironically call 'the setback' of 1967. Salah al-Din, or Saladin as he is more popularly known in the West, the liberator of Jerusalem and vanquisher of the brutal Crusaders, is almost universally hailed as the paradigm, in spite of his Kurdish roots. In Jerusalem it is almost impossible to have a serious discussion about the Muslim claim to the city without someone raising the exploits of Saladin more than 800 years ago. While Muslims regale each other with accounts of Saladin's courage and bravery, Christians are told about his chivalrous sense of honour. Saladin, for example, sent his personal physician to treat Richard, Coeur de Lion, who had fallen sick with malaria, because he admired the Crusader's courage in battle. Palestinian Muslims also admire modern Arab leaders, especially those who are prepared to confront either the 'Zionist Entity', as they refer to the State of Israel, or the West, which is held responsible for Zionism's success. The major appeal of Gamal Nasser in the 1950s and 1960s was his determination to confront Israel, while Saddam Hussein achieved heroic status in the West Bank and Gaza for firing batteries of Scud missiles at Tel Aviv during the 1990–91 Gulf War, even though they posed just as great a threat to Palestinians as they did to Israelis.

Yasser Arafat, who threw his own support behind Saddam during the Gulf War, actively seeks to claim the mantle as Jerusalem's liberator for himself, so much so that he has tailored his own, personal history to generate the impression that Jerusalem and Arafat are indivisible. Arafat's past as the founder and leader of one of the world's most infamous guerrilla movements is shrouded in myth and mystery so that it is easy for Arafat to make himself out to be something he is not. Take, for example, the issue of his birthplace. Ask Arafat where he was born and he will reply, without hesitation, '*Al-Quds*', even though what little documentation there is shows that he was in fact born in Cairo. His mother, however, was a Jerusalemite, and brought

Arafat and his brother, Fathi, to live in her home city for four years between 1933–37. This was at the height of the Arab Revolt, and Arafat's claim is probably true that, as a young boy, he can remember seeing his relatives dragged off the streets for questioning by British soldiers. The family lived in a house in the Moroccan Quarter adjoining the Wailing Wall, although this was demolished by the Israelis in 1967 to make way for the plaza which now overlooks the prayer site.

Arafat's family moved back to Cairo in the late 1930s, where Yasser completed his education at Cairo University and became actively interested in politics. Arafat says he returned to Jerusalem on several occasions, most notably during the 1948 war, when he claims he served under Abdul Khader Husseini, Haj Amin's cousin, who was killed during the 1948 battle for Jerusalem. Abdul Khader is one of the few genuine Palestinian heroes of that period and is buried on the Haram, close to the Dome of the Rock, as a tribute. Arafat also claims he was in Jerusalem in 1964 for the founding session of the Palestine National Council. Neither story, it seems, is true, and has been embroidered to emphasise Arafat's long association with Jerusalem. What is true is that, following Israel's success in 1967, Arafat was sent to Jerusalem to set up a Palestinian resistance movement to fight the newly established Israeli occupation. Arafat based himself in the Arab village of Abu Dis, on the city's outskirts, and spent several months trying to organise and co-ordinate a Palestinian response. It was during this time that Arafat was able to slip into al-Aqsa to pray, the only time he is known to have done so. But Arafat's first attempt as a military commander failed, and the Palestinian resistance achieved nothing. At the end of the year Arafat was forced to flee the country, dressed as a woman. The experience was nevertheless a salutary one for the young Palestinian leader, and persuaded him never again to rely on so-called friendly Arab governments for support.

Whatever the truth behind Arafat's various claims regarding his relationship with the city, no one can doubt his commitment to Jerusalem and his determination to make it the capital of a future independent Palestinian state. Most of the wall at his office in Gaza is taken up with a huge montage of a smiling Arafat looking out of an aircraft window at the Dome of the Rock. The picture makes it look as though the plane is landing on the Haram, but on closer inspection it emerges that Arafat's picture has been superimposed on a shot of the golden dome.[3] Another of Arafat's Jerusalem conceits is to insist that he is a member of the Husseini clan, one of the city's most important Muslim families, which can trace its lineage directly back to the Prophet. While Arafat's mother was a Husseini, she belonged to a different, and poorer, family from the aristocratic circle presided over by Faisal Husseini. Arafat's claim to be a Husseini was the subject of much derision when it was first aired at Orient House, the Palestinian leader's headquarters in the city. Soon after his return to Gaza in 1994, Arafat countered Israeli claims that Jerusalem was to remain united under Jewish sovereignty by pronouncing, at a rally: 'Jerusalem will be the capital of the coming Palestinian state, and anyone who doesn't like it can go and drink the water of Gaza', i.e. raw sewage. A couple of years later, speaking after the completion of the Israeli withdrawal from Hebron, Arafat altered the geographical reference slightly, but to make the same point. The Netanyahu government, which negotiated the drawn-out Hebron deal, had dropped several heavy hints that it was not prepared to make any further territorial concessions to the Palestinians, including Jerusalem. 'Anyone who doesn't accept *Al-Quds* as the capital of Palestine can go and drink the water of the Dead Sea,' retorted Arafat.

Arafat's principal rival for control of Jerusalem's Muslim Holy Places is King Hussein. The rivalry between Hussein and Arafat goes back over many decades, and generally has more to do with politics than religion. Over the years the two leaders have been involved in a number of exceedingly acrimonious disputes, not least the infamous Black September conflict in 1970 when the king's Jordanian troops became involved in a violent civil war with Arafat's PLO fighters over the Palestinians' refusal to accept Jordanian sovereignty. The battle, which was fought on the streets of Amman for several weeks, resulted in an overwhelming victory for the Jordanians, and the PLO relocating its operational base to Lebanon. In addition there have been various joint Jordanian–PLO peace initiatives which have failed because of the lack of trust between the two men. So it is hardly surprising that tempers should flare over Jerusalem, in which both men have a deep, and visceral, interest.

3 The 'picture' was created by a French photographer who wanted to make a good impression on the Palestinian leader.

King Hussein has been the landlord of the Holy Places since he acceded to the throne in 1953, when East Jerusalem was still under Jordanian control. The Jordanians continued to administer the Wakf and the Haram after 1967 – this was one area the Israelis admitted they could not touch – paying officials' salaries and maintaining the buildings. The king's influence in the Holy Places continued after the commencement of the Oslo peace process and was actually reaffirmed, much to Arafat's chagrin, when Israel and Jordan signed their historic peace treaty in November 1994. Article 9, paragraph 2, of the document states that 'Israel respects the present special role of the Hashemite Kingdom of Jordan in Muslim Holy Shrines in Jerusalem. When negotiations on the permanent status will take place, Israel will give high priority to the Jordanian historic role in these shrines.' While the Israelis and Jordanians might argue that what they put in their peace treaty is their affair, this innocent-looking codicil could not have been better conceived to provoke the Palestinian leader.

King Hussein had been disconcerted by his lack of involvement in the secret Oslo negotiations that resulted in Arafat's 1993 deal with Yitzhak Rabin. The Israeli–PLO treaty was primarily dealing with territory which, until 1967, was part of Jordan and, having participated in the 1991 Madrid ceremony that initiated the peace process, Hussein felt that he ought, at the very least, to have been consulted about such an important undertaking concerning the future administration of this territory. Consequently, Hussein felt it perfectly within his rights to negotiate his own, secret peace deal with Rabin, and the clause on Jerusalem was inserted as much to safeguard Hussein's interests in the Holy Places as to remind Arafat that the Jordanian royal family should not be taken for granted. What was perhaps even more irritating for Arafat was that Yitzhak Rabin, and the Israeli public, appeared immeasurably more enthusiastic about the peace treaty with Jordan than the deal with the PLO.

When the treaty with Jordan was signed in November 1994, Arafat, who only a year previously had enjoyed the international spectacle of a White House reception, did not make it on to the invitation list. And President Clinton, who had hosted Arafat and Rabin in Washington, said he was too busy to visit Arafat at his new headquarters in Gaza. As if to rub it in, Rabin spent the last year of his life seeing Hussein as often as possible, making a visit to Jordan the centrepiece of his

Independence Day itinerary in May 1995. By contrast Rabin would only see Arafat when it was deemed absolutely necessary. Hussein's special relationship with the Israeli public continued after Rabin's murder. In March 1997, when a Jordanian soldier lost his senses and murdered seven Israeli schoolgirls on a trip to the Jordan Valley, the king flew to Israel the following day to pay his condolences person-ally to the girls' parents. Afterwards the king travelled to Jerusalem to give a joint press conference with Israeli Prime Minister Benjamin Netanyahu at the King David Hotel. The king's presence in the Holy City was of far greater import than the press conference, at which both leaders muttered familiar platitudes. This was the second visit Hussein had made to Jerusalem since signing the 1994 peace treaty (the first was for Rabin's funeral), and Arafat had still not set foot in the city he claimed as his future capital.

The importance of Jerusalem for the Hashemite dynasty in Jordan was traumatically revealed to the young Prince Hussein in 1951 when he saw King Abdullah, his grandfather, murdered by a Palestinian gunman as he went to pray at al-Aqsa. Abdullah is buried in a tomb on the Haram, next to Abdul Khader Husseini, the Palestinian hero of the 1948 war, which neatly illustrates the modern rivalry between Jordanians and Palestinians over the Holy Places. The Hashemites, who also trace their lineage back to the Prophet, come from the Hejaz, in what is now Saudi Arabia. Abdullah's father, Sharif Hussein of the Hejaz, also held the title Custodian of the Holy Places of Mecca and Medina, a title his family had held for centuries and which was their *raison d'être*.[4] Although the Hejaz ruler won much respect in Britain for helping T. E. Lawrence to orchestrate the Arab revolt against Ottoman rule, the wily Sauds took advantage of Sharif Hussein's preoccupation with the Turks to conquer his country, which resulted in the ejection of the Hashemites from the Hejaz.[5] After the war Winston Churchill sought to make amends by having Hussein's sons appointed monarchs in Syria and Iraq, and Abdullah was given the new state of Transjordan. Hashemite rule did not last long in either Syria or Iraq, but Transjordan, with British support, flourished.

4 It is now held by the Saudi royal family.
5 The tomb of Sharif Hussein is also located at the Haram al-Sharif.

Throughout the British Mandate Abdullah was always keen to extend his family's role as Custodians of the Holy Places to include Jerusalem and, during the 1948 war, retaining the Holy City was one of his top priorities.

Despite the concessions contained in the Israeli–Jordanian peace treaty, the Jordanians are keen to play down the significance of their claim to Jerusalem. It is one of the curiosities of the modern peace process that it is necessary to travel to Tel Aviv's smart business district, the location of the Royal Hashemite Kingdom of Jordan's diplomatic mission to Israel, to find out what the Jordanian government has to say on the question of Jerusalem. The embassy is staffed by hand-picked, smart young Jordanians who do not seem at all out of place among the brash hustle and bustle of Israel's commercial nerve centre. They provide a remarkably well-presented, and no doubt well-rehearsed, resumé of the Jordanian position, stressing that the king only sought to include the provision relating to Jerusalem as 'a safeguard' against future events.

'It is a defensive measure. We hope that the Palestinians are successful in their quest for statehood, and that Jerusalem is their capital,' explained a young Western-educated, Western-dressed Jordanian official. 'But what if the Palestinians are not successful? What if they do not get their state? What becomes of Jerusalem then? The Jordanians merely wish to ensure that the Muslim Holy Places are protected for the future. It is ridiculous to suggest that Jordan has any interest in keeping them for herself.'

This might all appear highly plausible, but the Palestinians remain sceptical. The 'Jordan Option', whereby Israel negotiates directly with the Jordanians on a deal for the West Bank and Gaza, has been popular in Israeli circles for many years, especially right-wingers who argue that 'Jordan is Palestine'. Israelis have not forgotten that, just before 1967, King Hussein actually commenced work on building himself a palace in Jerusalem's northern suburbs – the foundations are still visible on a hilltop overlooking Beit Hanina – and many would like to see the work completed and the 'plucky little monarch', as Israelis fondly refer to him, take up residence. Indeed, the Jordan Option, which seemed to have become an anachronism once Rabin and Arafat signed their peace treaty, enjoyed a revival with the election of the Netanyahu government which was determined to hold on to the land of *Eretz Israel*. Palestinians therefore viewed with some suspicion King Hussein's claim that the Holy Places would be handed over to Palestinian control 'only when a Palestinian–Israeli agreement is reached over the final status of occupied Arab East Jerusalem, and sovereignty of those areas is transferred to the Palestinian people'. As it had taken the Netanyahu government nearly nine months to negotiate an agreement over Hebron, where there were only 250 Jews, the Palestinians had little confidence that any final status agreement could be negotiated over Jerusalem, where there are 500,000 Jews, which would result in them being granted sovereignty over the Haram and Arab East Jerusalem.

Palestinian misgivings over King Hussein's attempts to justify his real intentions mean the Jordanian monarch is not the most popular figure in Islamic circles in Jerusalem. While it would be an exaggeration to suggest that Hussein might suffer the same fate as his grandfather were he to enter the sacred sanctuary of the Haram, any attempt by the king to express his interest in, or commitment to, the Holy Places is rigorously rebuffed. The humiliating treatment meted out to Mr Abdeen, the king's choice for Mufti, is just one of many examples of the Palestinians' low regard for the Jordanian monarch. In the early 1990s King Hussein paid millions of dollars from his personal fortune for an Irish company to lay a new roof of gold leaf on the Dome of the Rock. When the work was complete, and the new roof unveiled, a small, stone inscription was carved at the Dome's entrance recording the fact that the renovation had been carried out through the king's benevolence. That night an over-zealous contingent of the *Horras al-Aqsa*, the sanctuary's Palestinian bodyguards, destroyed the inscription with chisels and hammers. And soon afterwards, when the king expressed concern about the condition of his grandfather's tomb at the Haram, PLO activists said they would be happy to put Abdullah's bones in a crate and ship them to Amman.

Feelings run extremely deep over the Haram, the Dome of the Rock and the al-Aqsa mosque, and it is hard to underestimate the importance for Muslims of their Holy Places in Jerusalem, whatever the Israelis might say. Not only is this sacred ground, revered by Muslims the world over, it is the icon of Palestinian nationalism. With so many disadvantages to overcome in their battle for statehood, Palestinians take the Haram's commanding presence to legitimise their claim to make Jerusalem the capital of a future Palestinian state. And whoever disturbs a stone of the holy Haram does so at their peril.

It was this sensitivity over the Haram that resulted in one of the worst outbreaks of violence between Israelis and Palestinians in the thirty years since Israel had captured East Jerusalem in 1967. The disturbances were sparked by the Netanyahu government's unilateral decision, in September 1996, to open an ancient archaeological tunnel, which runs along the western foundations of the Haram, as a tourist attraction. Successive Israeli governments had toyed with the idea of opening the tunnel, but had decided against it on security grounds. The tunnel, which is said to date back to the Hasmonean period and is about five hundred metres long, had been excavated, without proper archaeological supervision, by Israel's Religious Affairs Ministry. The entrance to the tunnel, which directly adjoins the Wailing Wall, had been open for some years, and was popular with Jewish tourists who could explore further the Herodian foundations of the Second Temple, and with religious Jews, who regarded it as an extension of the Wailing Wall. But the tunnel was highly unpopular with Palestinians, particularly the Wakf authorities who accused the tunnellers of damaging Muslim homes with their excavations. Any attempt to alter the religious *status quo* in the Old City, particularly when it concerns the Haram, is bitterly resisted, and the tunnel was seen by the Palestinians as a Jewish plot to lay claim to the Haram.

The tunnel's only drawback was that it had no proper exit, which meant that visitors had to double back once they had completed the tour. Various attempts were made to find an exit. In the 1980s an ancient water tunnel was discovered, said to date from the Hasmonean period, which would have provided a suitable way out, but the idea was dropped. Israeli officials approached the Sisters of Zion whose convent on the Via Dolorosa, in the Muslim Quarter, lies near the tunnel's northern end. But the sisters did not want to become involved in such a sensitive political issue. The Arab owner of a souvenir store agreed to have the tunnel exit on his property, but later backed down for fear of Arab retaliation. Finally the Religious Affairs authorities decided to go its own way, and built a staircase leading up to the side of the Omariya girls school. All that remained was for an opening to be knocked through.

Meir Ben-Dov, a respected Israeli archaeologist who was asked to oversee the tunnel project from its inception in 1968, opposed the project from the outset.

'So far as I was concerned, it had no archaeological merit and was not cost effective,' explains Ben-Dov. 'There were plenty of other sites in Jerusalem which could have done with the money. But immediately after 1967, the government of Levi Eshkol wanted to assert its authority in the Old City. Eshkol's attitude was: "We will build the tunnel because Jerusalem is ours and we don't have to ask the Muslims for anything."'

Palestinian resistance to the project was so vehement, however, that various Israeli governments refused permission for an exit to be opened. One indication of the project's extreme sensitivity had arisen in 1981 when Ariel Sharon, then Israel's Defence Secretary, helped a group of religious Jews to open part of the wall leading off the tunnel known as 'Warren's Gate', after the nineteenth-century British archaeologist. The fact that an Israeli Defence Minister was poking around ancient tunnels underneath Jerusalem illustrates how seriously these matters are taken. Sharon wanted the opening, which lay directly beneath the Haram, to be turned into a synagogue. But the Wakf authorities got wind of Sharon's plan, and the al-Aqsa 'bodyguards' flocked to the site. Fist-fights erupted, and the police were called. When order had been restored, and the Jews and Arabs evicted from the disputed area, the police commander ordered 'Warren's Gate' to be sealed with bricks and cement, which is how it has remained ever since. The Israeli authorities learned their lesson, and whenever the tunnel issue was raised, permission was refused. Even Yitzhak Shamir, one of Israel's more hard-line Prime Ministers, signed an order in 1988 forbidding the opening of a tunnel exit.

'He took the view that it would cause too much trouble just to make a few tourists happy,' recalls Ben-Dov. 'He did not want to cause unnecessary problems.'

The issue was raised again, with the peace process well into its stride, in the spring of 1996, shortly before the Israeli general election, when Shimon Peres's advisers told him he could pick up important votes from religious Israelis if he gave permission for the tunnel to be opened. Ben-Dov got wind of the plan and warned Peres that the whole peace process could be destroyed. Peres decided to defer the issue until after the election.

To the outsider, all this fuss over something as insignificant as making an exit door for an ancient tunnel might appear ridiculous. But in Jerusalem, where every stone is sacred, issues like this are treated literally as matters of life and death, which is why Palestinians and Israelis came close to full-scale war when the tunnel exit was finally opened, at dead of night, in September 1996. Ever since he came into office the previous May, Netanyahu had been waiting for the opportunity to show the Palestinians he was not a man to be trifled with. It was not sufficient for him that the peace process, which had made some impressive achievements under the previous Labour government, had shuddered to a halt. Netanyahu sought a high-profile issue which would allow him to demonstrate his political virility. Netanyahu's election had also provided Mayor Olmert with a new lease of life. Unfettered by the constraints that had been imposed upon him by the previous government, Olmert had spent the summer throwing his weight around the city, dispatching municipal bulldozers to demolish buildings in the Old City without proper building permits. In late August a bulldozer had actually been hoisted over Herod's Gate by a crane to enable workmen to demolish the Burj al-Laqlaq Centre for the Aged and Handicapped. While the Palestinians took no action to prevent the demolitions, the actions did not pass unnoticed.

Mayor Olmert took part in the short operation to unblock the tunnel exit, wielding a sledgehammer to knock a hole in the thick stone wall. The deed, which was conducted with all the secrecy of a commando raid, took place in the middle of Monday night at the end of Yom Kippur. Olmert, who had experienced no difficulty persuading Netanyahu, his close political ally, to open the tunnel, wanted it operational for the forthcoming Jewish feast of Succoth. But when, next morning, news spread that a tunnel exit had been opened in the Muslim Quarter, Palestinian protesters took to the streets demanding its immediate closure.

Police were able to contain the initial round of stone-throwing in the Old City at Tuesday lunchtime, although on Wednesday clashes between Palestinians and Israelis were erupting throughout the West Bank and Gaza. By Thursday the situation was quickly spiralling into all-out war with the Palestinian police firing on Israeli soldiers, and Israeli commanders deploying tanks at entrances to all the major Palestinian towns. On Friday the violence broke out in Jerusalem itself, following Friday prayers at al-Aqsa. Three Palestinian worshippers were shot dead and scores more wounded by Israeli security forces after it was claimed stones had been thrown from the Haram at Jews praying at the Wailing Wall. When the violence was finally brought to an end, 84 people – 15 Israelis, 68 Palestinians and 1 Egyptian – were dead, all because of a narrow, nondescript doorway on the Via Dolorosa. The doorway that caused so much suffering is located at the second Station of the Cross, where Christ was sentenced to death by Pontius Pilate and scourged, before being sent on his final journey to Calvary.

The recriminations went on for weeks. Netanyahu was accused of arrogance, of political opportunism and naïvety, and of failing to coordinate properly with the Israeli security establishment, which was deeply opposed to opening the tunnel. An Israeli newspaper accused Mayor Olmert of opening the tunnel to detract attention from his forthcoming court case on corruption charges. The Israelis accused Arafat of orchestrating the violence for his own political ends. King Hussein complained that the Israelis had not consulted with him, as they were supposed to under the terms of the Israeli–Jordanian peace agreement, while the Arab League, representing the majority of Arab states, claimed Netanyahu's precipitate action would create 'a whirlpool of violence, instability and bloodshed'. President Clinton hinted he blamed the Israeli government for instigating the violence, although with a presidential election only two months away, he took care not to be too explicit, for fear of alienating America's influential Jewish vote. In Jerusalem Naim Ateek's *Sabeel* group organised a protest march along the Via Dolorosa, in which a number of prominent Palestinian Muslims participated. The 'Patriarchs, Bishops, Clergy and People' of Jerusalem's Christian Churches issued a joint statement condemning the tunnel opening for touching 'the religious nerve of our Muslim brothers and sisters. The religious nerve in our country,' the statement warned, 'is the most sensitive nerve of all.'

# 11

# ZEALOTS

*'For wide is the gate, and broad is the way, that leadeth to destruction'*

Matthew 7: 13–14

Blowing up the Dome of the Rock is not going to be easy. Forget the fact it will probably start World War Three. The real problem will be using enough explosives to destroy the building without wrecking the rest of Jerusalem. Those great slabs of stone will certainly take some shifting. And whatever happens, there must be no damage to the sacred rock inside. That would be rather self-defeating. The whole purpose of the exercise is to get rid of the pagan Dome and build a new Temple over the holy rock. Of course it would be far simpler to bring in the cranes and bulldozers and just knock it to the ground. But that would be a bit too public. People would see what was happening and start protesting, assuming that it was possible to get the demolition gear on to the Haram in the first place. And the Muslims are bound to make a fuss. So blowing it up, preferably at dead of night, is the best tactic. That would present a *fait accompli*. People would wake up the next morning and find that the magnificent golden dome that has dominated the Jerusalem sky-line for the past

1,300 years is gone. Then work can start in earnest on building the Third Temple.

Whoever carries out the operation is going to need all the cunning and skill of an élite commando unit, especially after the last attempt to blow the Dome to pieces ended in such failure. That was back in the mid-1980s when members of the Jewish underground were arrested by the Israeli authorities before they could put their plan into action. They were going to creep up to the Haram, plant explosives around the Dome, and then blow it up after retreating a safe distance. A new Temple was to be built on the rubble. But the Israeli security forces got wind of the operation, and arrested them. The ringleaders were jailed. Who would believe it? Jews arresting Jews. Surely the whole point of having an Israeli government is to allow Jews to reclaim their heritage, especially here in Jerusalem, God's anointed capital. Put it down to politics. Yehudah Etzion, the ringleader of the botched attempt, later founded a fanatical Jewish group called Hai Vekayam, which wants to abolish democratic government in Israel and restore the Israelite monarchy to rule the land. That explains why the Israeli government is so set against it. These fanatics think the Zionists are cowards. Everyone knows all Jews want to see the Temple rebuilt. But the Israeli authorities are too terrified of the adverse international criticism to take the appropriate action.

Look at Moshe Dayan. Days after the Six-Day War he takes off his shoes, sits on a prayer mat in al-Aqsa and promises Muslim officials they can retain control of the Haram, or the Temple Mount, as religious Jews prefer to call it. By giving the Muslims exclusive rights over the sanctuary, Dayan wants to prevent the Arab–Israeli conflict from degenerating into a Muslim–Jewish holy war. What a schmuck. Thanks to Dayan, Arafat and his people have control of the sacred Temple Mount, and the Israeli government won't do anything about it. So it's all down to small, dedicated groups of individuals to do the government's dirty work for it, and rid the city of the pernicious Dome.

The main obstacle is going to be the Muslims. Ever since that last fiasco, they've been on their guard. The authorities at the Haram are on the look-out for any sign that the Jews are planning a new attack against their shrine. They treat the smallest archaeological investigation of the area surrounding the Haram with the greatest suspicion.

These misgivings are not new. Haj Amin al-Husseini incited the Arab mob against the Jews in the 1920s by claiming – at that time, wrongly – that the Zionists intended to turn al-Aqsa into a synagogue. Now the Muslims have good reason to be afraid, because the Jews are deadly serious about the removal of the entire Haram complex and rebuilding the Temple. Some of them have proposed practical solutions, such as dismantling the whole complex and shipping it, brick by brick, to somewhere like Mecca, rather as happened when the old London Bridge was shipped to the United States. Others simply want to resolve the problem by exploding the shrine into tiny little pieces.

That was certainly what Yehudah Etzion had in mind when he planned his operation in the 1980s. Etzion (whose name translates as 'Jew of Zion') is an ordnance expert whose baptism into the world of Jewish terrorism was to devise a series of car-bombs which blew up the Palestinian mayors of Nablus and Ramallah in June 1980; both men lost their legs. Etzion's plan to destroy the Dome of the Rock was extremely sophisticated. Three bombs, each containing seventy kilos of Semtex, were to be placed at the foot of three of the four solid stone columns supporting the golden dome. Smaller charges of five kilos each would be placed by the smaller pillars that prop up the rest of one of the world's finest examples of Omayyad architecture. Etzion made the larger charges in three pieces so that they were light enough for the bombers to carry them to the target area. The bombs were then to be assembled once they were inside the Dome. 'Like pieces of Lego', he explains, helpfully. While Etzion was to be in charge of the explosives, an accomplice would provide a synchronised timing device.

'The whole operation was very carefully planned because we had to be careful not to touch the rock inside,' Etzion explains, in between drawing conspiratorially on a short, dark brown cigar. 'The outside wall of the Dome is one and a half metres thick, so we knew it would require a lot of explosive. But we planned it in such a way that only three columns would be destroyed. This would cause the dome itself to fall on to the rock, and protect it from all the other masonry.'

Altogether forty people were to be involved in the operation: twenty to conduct the bombing, the other twenty to overpower the Wakf guards and prevent them from raising the alarm.

'If everything had gone according to plan, no one would have been hurt,' says Etzion. But the plan was never put into effect, even though the explosive charges and detonators were all assembled, ready for use, and hidden in bunkers throughout the country, in hide-outs from Petah Tikva to the Golan Heights.

'We did not think the moment was right to carry out the plan, but we thought it important to have a plan that we could implement at a moment's notice if the right circumstances presented themselves.'

Etzion is still vague about when that time might be. 'It is possible that even though we conceived the plan over fifteen years ago, we might still not have implemented it today.'

Apart from ensuring that no damage befell the sacred rock that is housed in the Dome, Etzion and his fellow plotters also needed to overcome the highly sensitive issue of whether they were allowed to enter the Haram complex at all. The sacred rock that lies beneath the Dome is said to be the Holy of Holies, where both Jews and Muslims believe the Ark of the Covenant stood, and the only place on earth that the Lord God has chosen to reveal himself. Many Jews and Muslims believe this is the foundation stone of the entire universe. When the Temple existed, only the High Priest was allowed to enter this inner sanctuary, and then only at Yom Kippur, the Jewish feast of atonement. Jews are therefore strictly forbidden, even today, from entering the Haram, even if it is just to blow it up.

A group of rabbis who supported Etzion's scheme, however, pro-vided him with the religious justification to boldly enter where most Jews fear to tread. It all had to do with red heifers, or rather, the absence of red heifers. According to biblical tradition,[1] the Temple can only be rebuilt once Jews have been purified with the ashes of a sacrificial red heifer. Despite much searching, no red heifers have yet been located in the Land of Israel. As the Jewish nation, therefore, is in a state of impurity, there was nothing to stop Etzion and his com-rades compounding the sins of the Jewish people by creeping into the Holy and Holies and planting their bombs.

Before that could happen, however, the whole conspiracy was exposed when one of Etzion's co-conspirators suffered the inconve-nience of being detained by the Israeli authorities in connection with the murder of three Arab students in Hebron. 'He did all this without

1 Numbers 19: 2–6.

consulting me,' Etzion complains. The police investigation not only uncovered the plot to bomb the Dome of the Rock, but Etzion's involvement in maiming the Arab mayors.

The trial of twenty-seven Jewish underground members – including three army officers – in June 1984 illustrates the difficulties the Israeli political establishment faces when trying to rein in the activities of Jewish extremists like Etzion. President Chaim Hertzog reflected the views of Israeli liberals when he described the details of the Jewish underground's activities that emerged at the trial as an 'unspeakable horror' and a 'mortal threat' to the Israeli people. But the defendants also had their apologists. Meir Cohen Avidor, a Likud Knesset member, declared: 'My heart goes out to the defendants. These boys are the pride of Israel. They are the best.' The only comment made by Yitzhak Shamir, the Likud Prime Minister, after the ring-leaders – including Etzion – were sentenced to lengthy jail terms was: 'It is too early to speak about clemency.'

Etzion, who served a total of just five years, comes from a distinguished line of Jewish troublemakers. His uncle was Shamir's secretary when he was a commander of Lech'i, the pre-State Jewish underground otherwise known as the Stern gang, which in 1944 murdered Lord Moyne, the British minister-resident in Cairo, and Count Folke Bernadotte. Shabtai Ben-Dov, the man Etzion claims as his spiritual guardian, was a member of the same organisation. Born in 1951, Etzion attended a military yeshiva, where he combined religious studies with national service, serving in the Israeli army's specialist explosives unit. From childhood Etzion was taught the Jewish State had been created without Jerusalem 'proper', the Old City with all the ancient Jewish sites. Like all Jewish fanatics, Etzion regards the Arab presence at the Haram as an illegal occupation, and that it is the obligation of every Jew to liberate it.

A tall, thin man with a straggly, greying beard, Etzion lives with his wife and seven children at Ofra, one of the first Israeli settlements to be built on the West Bank. Etzion helped found Ofra, in defiance of the Israeli government, by occupying an unused Jordanian army position in 1975. Unlike many other settlements, which are located away from Arab centres of population, Ofra directly adjoins an Arab village, although that does not bother him. 'They have learned to live with us. It's not that difficult,' he says.

Etzion drives to Jerusalem at least three times a week to pray. Sometimes he will go to the Mount of Olives, where he can look down at the Dome of the Rock. Other times he will try to force his way through the Israeli police checkpoints into the sanctuary itself. Invariably he is arrested.

'I've lost count of the number of times they've arrested me,' he says. 'They arrest me for stupid offences, like improper behaviour in a public place. It would be the same offence if I dropped my trousers. And all I want to do is pray. It all goes to show the stupidity of the Israeli government.'

As he recounts his various exploits, whether it is blowing up Arab mayors or plotting to start the next world war, Etzion allows himself a mischievous grin, rather like a schoolboy caught scrumping in an orchard who has already eaten all the best fruit. He believes he has the agenda, and there's nothing anyone can do about it. Etzion might be vilified by most of Israeli society, but he certainly has an unerring belief in the justice of his cause.

'We live in a time of paradox,' he explains. 'The Temple Mount occupies a central place in Judaism, a central place in our culture and religion. Without it the Jewish people cease to exist. And yet we have an Israeli government that will not allow its own people to pray at their most important shrine. That is why I reject the Israeli government. It does not fulfil the will of God.'

In many ways Yehudah Etzion resembles Yehudah Meshi-Zahav, Jerusalem's pre-eminent rabbinical curser. Both men reject the State of Israel and both, in their fanatically intense way, seek to create their own version of what a Jewish state should be. The central difference is that while Meshi-Zahav totally rejects the modern Israeli nation on the grounds that it can only be created by the Messiah, Etzion believes Israel's creation is God's work and that rebuilding the Temple is part of the necessary preparations that must be undertaken before the Messiah reveals himself. Etzion believes that, for this to happen, some of the fundamentals of the modern Israeli nation, like the constitution, are in need of radical adjustment.

To help this come about, Etzion has formed Hai Vekayam, which can be freely translated as 'alive and kicking', a reference to King David's immortality. Etzion likes to draw a parallel between himself and Shimon Bar Kokhba, the second-century Jewish Zealot who fought the Romans after the city's destruction in AD 70 for the right to rebuild the Temple. While Etzion is not afraid of resorting to armed force, for the moment he believes the best way to accomplish his aim is by re-educating the Israeli people. His mission is to persuade Israelis to abandon their present form of Western-style, democratic government, and institute a monarchy, based on the Temple Mount. Apart from the Temple itself, the Knesset, the Supreme Court, and all the other main branches of the government would be located in the same place to govern the new Kingdom of Israel. The Sanhedrin, the ancient Jewish council which deliberated on matters pertaining to everyday Jewish life, would be re-established. Etzion has already given the matter serious thought. The monarch, for example, would not be an autocrat, but subject to the counsels of the Sanhedrin, rather like the Roman consuls and the Senate.

'Of course we need to do a lot more research, but we can provide a rough outline of how it should be,' he says. 'We are obligated to the law of the Bible and the law of God. The present Israeli government contradicts that law. It is against the law of God to forbid a Jew from praying on the Temple Mount.'

To advertise his campaign to replace the Israeli government, in the spring of 1995 Etzion advocated that Israelis should not pay any taxes in protest at the Rabin government's decision to trade land for peace with the Palestinians as part of the peace process. He also called on Israeli soldiers not to obey orders if they were commanded to take action that would result in handing over the biblical land of Israel to the control of foreigners – namely the Palestinians.

'It is not the government's land to give,' Etzion insists. 'This land belongs to God. We are not the owners. We live here with the permission of God and we must honour that responsibility.'

When Yigal Amir, a graduate of several, radical anti-Arab yeshivas, murdered Yitzhak Rabin in the autumn of 1995 to 'save' Israel from the peace process, many Israelis attributed his action to the climate of hatred and vengeance that had been stirred up by fanatics like Etzion. Certainly his views on how the peace process should proceed are unlikely to advance it in a positive direction.

'There will only be peace when the Arabs agree that we are the owners of the land and they are the guests.'

The main focus of Etzion's activities, however, is to rebuild the

Temple. 'I have devoted my entire life to this cause,' he says. 'And yes, I am prepared to die for it.

'I pray three times a day that the Temple will be rebuilt. We are the divinely appointed guardians of the holiest place at the centre of the world, and we should take care of it not just for ourselves, but for the whole of mankind.'

Etzion says he has given up his plans to blow up the Dome, even though he believes the idea is, in principle, valid.

'But it should only be carried out when the majority of the Jewish people want it to happen,' he says.

He is, however, available for consultations on any future plot to destroy the Dome.

'The big difficulty now will be the security. Since our plan was exposed, the authorities have wised up.' He allows himself a small smile of satisfaction.

'When we planned our operation there were only about fifteen Arab guards on night-duty. Now they have about thirty. In addition the Israeli police have about twenty remote-control cameras all over the place, which are linked up to a central command post. From there they can see everything. Today they guard it like they would guard a nuclear missile bunker. But for all this there are ways to get around it. It just has to be the right time, that's all.'

Despite the failure of these modern-day Jewish zealots to destroy the Islamic shrines, preparations for rebuilding the Temple are already well advanced. In the Jewish Quarter of the Old City, a team of dedicated researchers at the Temple Institute are busily putting together a collection of authentic sacrificial vessels and priestly vestments ready for use in the Temple once it is constructed. Sympathetic architects have drawn up plans to illustrate how the new Temple will take shape, based on reconstructions of the temples of Solomon and Herod, which have been compiled by a dedicated team of archaeological, historical and biblical scholars. To give visitors an idea of how modern Jerusalem will look once the new Temple is complete, the Institute sells framed photographs with a model of the new structure, embossed with gold, superimposed on the site of the Haram. At Christmas 1996 Prime Minister Netanyahu mistakenly sent as a present to the head of the Greek Catholic Church – a Palestinian – a silver relief map with a Jewish Temple in place of the Dome of the

Rock. The present was intended for someone with a more sympathetic view of the city's destiny. Netanyahu apologised, and his spokesman said that 'if it hurt people's feelings, we will apologise for it. We
didn't notice that al-Aqsa was missing from the map.' The Mufti condemned the present as 'racist'.

The day I visit the Institute, a sign in the window of an adjoining gift
shop advertises: 'Pre-Third Temple Sale – Buy Now Before The
Temple Is Rebuilt'. Inside the Institute, which was established in
1988, is screening a video account of its activities, using sophisticated
computer imaging to provide the viewer with a guided tour of the
Temple's inner sanctum. Rabbi Chaim Richman, an American Jew
who has come to Jerusalem to devote his life to rebuilding the
Temple, helps to illustrate how the different vessels are to be used.
There is a large, cylindrical copper wash-stand, a *kior*, resembling a
Russian samovar, which will be used by the Temple priests to wash
their hands and feet before entering the sacred site. The priests will
wear light blue vestments, covered with a gold breastplate. Their
heads will be adorned with a crown of pure gold. They will use shov-
els made of solid silver to remove the ashes of each day's dawn
sacrifice. The musical accompaniment will be provided by 22-string
harps – one string for each letter of the Hebrew alphabet. The video
concludes by informing the audience that 'the Temple Mount is occupied by strangers. Jewish hearts will only regain their strength with
the rebuilding of the Holy Temple.'
    This Jewish fantasy world would be highly entertaining were it not
taken with the utmost seriousness by all those associated with the
Temple Institute, who are determined to make their dream reality.
Rabbi Richman and his friends, for example, are spearheading the
international hunt for red heifers so that the pre-Temple rebuilding
purification rituals can commence. And the exciting news for Third
Temple enthusiasts is that Rabbi Richman believes they have found
some.
    'Yes, that is true,' says the rabbi, a nervous tremor of excitement
filling his voice. 'We believe we have located red heifers and we hope
to bring them to the Land of Israel.'
    'And where are they now?'
    'I'm sorry, I cannot reveal that information.'

'Why not?'

'You have to understand, this is a very sensitive subject. There are many people who would like to find the heifers and kill them before we bring them to the Holy Land. So we have to be careful. We hope to bring red heifers to Jerusalem in preparation for rebuilding the Temple.'

The rabbi does not want to say when this might be – 'Only God can decide when the Temple should be built' – but he has no doubts that it will happen.

'It looks difficult at present because the Temple Mount has a different geo-political reality from biblical times,' he explains, referring somewhat disingenuously to the some of the holiest sites in Islam. 'The Israeli government doesn't want to start a world war. But it is important to remember that the Muslims took advantage of the Jewish exile from the city to squat on our sacred property. So we do not have to make any apologies. God has said that it is the obligation of the nation of Israel to rebuild the Temple.'

Rabbi Richman promises that rebuilding the Temple will not just be good news for Jews, but for the whole world.

'Once the Temple is rebuilt, the world will be a much better place, for all mankind. And if that should happen sooner rather than later, we will be ready to provide all the vessels for its service.'

Despite its radical agenda, the Institute receives grants from, among others, the Israeli Ministry of Tourism, the Ministry of Education, the Ministry of Religious Affairs and Jerusalem City Hall, and was given money from the municipal budget during the tenures of both Teddy Kollek and Ehud Olmert. The Institute also receives private donations, especially from the large numbers of Christian Zionists who visit the centre each year. 'These are people who truly believe the Temple will be rebuilt,' says Rabbi Richman. Nor is the Institute shy about fund-raising. It informs visitors it is looking to raise $1.75 million for a pure-gold, metre-high menorah and $450,000 for the 'uniform of the High Priest'. The Institute would probably receive more funds were it not for the antics of its founder, Rabbi Yisrael Ariel. Known as one of the most extreme figures on the religious far right, Rabbi Ariel's outrageous behaviour has resulted in various bodies suspending their donations, even though they still support the Institute's overall objectives. Apart from regularly calling for 'bulldozing those places now

standing on the Temple Mount', Rabbi Ariel has a long record of association with the most extreme Israeli groups. As head of the yeshiva at
Yamit, the Israeli settlement in the Sinai desert, he was one of the leaders of the violent resistance in 1982 against returning the territory to
Egypt after the signing of the Camp David peace treaty. The previous
year he stood for the Knesset, unsuccessfully, as a candidate for the
extreme-right Kach party, which campaigns for the complete expulsion of all Arabs from the Land of Israel. During the campaign Ariel
explicitly called for the destruction of the Islamic shrines on the
Temple Mount. Rabbi Ariel also provided theological backing for
Yehudah Etzion's Jewish terrorist underground movement in the
1980s, and he eulogised Baruch Goldstein, the American-born settler
who murdered twenty-nine Palestinian worshippers during prayers at
the Hebron mosque in February 1994.

The physical task of rebuilding the Temple is in the capable hands
of the Temple Mount and Land of Israel Faithful Movement, to give
it its full title, an organisation set up in the immediate aftermath of
the Six-Day War in protest at Moshe Dayan's decision to place the
Haram under Muslim control.

'What Dayan did was a sin and a terrible mistake,' insists Gershon
Salomon, the movement's founder and leader. 'He broke the hearts of
Jews all over the world who had dreamed for 2,000 years of returning
to the Temple Mount and rebuilding the Temple.'

Salomon, now is his early sixties, has a rugged complexion which
is graced by piercing green eyes and a head of neatly clipped white
hair, adorned by a blue-and-white kippa, representing Israel's national
colours. He was with the first group of Israeli soldiers to step on to
the Temple Mount in 1967. One of his proudest possessions is a
faded black-and-white photograph of himself and a group of fellow
soldiers standing triumphantly in front of the Dome of the Rock
shortly after the conquest of the Old City. For a few hours that day
the Star of David was actually hoisted from the roof of the Dome of
the Rock – in imitation of the Crusaders nine hundred years previously – but was quickly removed on Dayan's orders.

'This is the place that symbolises Zionist redemption,' says
Salomon. 'Without it there is no meaning to Jewish life in this land.
And Dayan gave it back to the Arabs!'

Salomon is a tenth-generation Jerusalemite and is descended from

Rabbi Avraham Solomon Zalman Zoref, who came to Jerusalem in 1811 from Lithuania to help start the redemption process for the Jewish people. He founded the Hurva Synagogue – destroyed in the 1948 war – but was eventually killed by Arabs, a point Salomon emphasises with relish.

'They told him they were going to kill him because they were afraid of what the Jews were doing in the city. And so they knifed him in the back, as they said they would.'

Salomon regards it as his personal mission to continue the work started by this ancient relative. As with so many of the city's fanatics, appearances with Salomon are deceptive. Born in Jerusalem in 1937, he lives in a smart, middle-class Israeli neighbourhood in north Jerusalem with his wife and daughter. The house, by Jerusalem standards, is spacious and comfortable, and has a strange-looking fortified turret attached to its back wall which provides a panoramic view of the city. Salomon claims to be an expert in oriental studies, although most of his time is devoted to issues relating to his Temple rebuilding programme. Before he founded the Temple Faithful Movement, Salomon subscribed to the far-right policies of the Cherut party, the ideological heirs to Jabotinsky's Revisionists. Cherut, which is the dominant partner in the Likud bloc, believes that Israel should expand to its full 'historical' borders on both sides of the Jordan River, stretching from the Nile to the Euphrates, and that Jerusalem should be an exclusively Jewish city.

Salomon enjoyed a politically active youth propagating these views through the Cherut youth movement. But the inspiration to rebuild the Temple came later, when he was badly wounded fighting the Syrians in the Golan Heights in the early 1960s. Salomon was the officer in charge of an elite Israeli commando unit sent to attack a Syrian position in the early 1960s. He was shot and badly wounded during a ferocious gun battle that lasted for seven hours. As he lay helpless, a group of Syrian soldiers approached him.

'I expected them to finish me off. But suddenly, without explanation, they turned and fled. God and the angels had saved me from certain death.'

A few weeks later, when he was convalescing in hospital, he received a visit from a UN observer who had been in Damascus and had talked to the Syrian soldiers who spared his life.

'The Syrian soldiers told him that while they were prepared to fight against Israeli soldiers, they could not fight against God. They said that when they found the Israeli soldier – me – he was surrounded by angels, and they were afraid. That's why they ran away.'

The experience made a deep impression on Salomon and, as he lay in his hospital bed, he resolved to devote his life to God's work and rebuilding the Temple.

'It was clear to me that God had saved me for a purpose, and that purpose was to ensure that His Temple rose again in Jerusalem.'

As a consequence of the horrific injuries he suffered, Salomon has a pronounced limp and walks with the aid of an antique cane. The photograph taken of him on the Temple Mount in 1967 shows a smart young officer, with a thick black moustache, dressed in full paratroopers' kit, standing next to his victorious comrades while leaning casually on a smart walking stick.

'I just had to be there. I was not fully recovered, but when I heard what was going on, I asked to be allowed to rejoin my unit. This was the experience of a lifetime, and I could not miss it. Little did I realise the terrible mistakes that would be made afterwards.'

Salomon's experience has nonetheless instilled in him the belief that Israel's armed forces are invincible because God is their commander-in-chief.

'That's the reason a tiny little country like Israel has been able to win so many wars.'

Salomon has spent the past thirty years campaigning vigorously and uncompromisingly for the Temple Mount to be returned to Jewish control, and for the Temple to be rebuilt. For ten years he aired his views as a city councillor, although he made little headway against the redoubtable Teddy Kollek. Undaunted, he has managed to build up an impressive network of political and religious contacts, both at home and abroad, who subscribe to his ideology. And whereas, when the movement was first founded, it was regarded as occupying Zionism's lunatic fringe, Salomon and his followers can now claim a fair degree of legitimacy, particularly when there is a Likud government.

The biggest obstacle to the movement's hopes of fulfilling its agenda remains the rabbinical ban on Jews entering the Temple Mount. They can visit, but the moment a word of prayer is uttered they are liable to arrest.

'This is an outrage,' Salomon fulminates. 'What other country in the world would forbid its own citizens to pray at their holiest and most important shrine.'

The official attitudes, however, are starting to soften, particularly as leading rabbis in the national religious camp believe the restrictions on Jews entering the Haram are too stringent. If, as is generally believed, the Holy of Holies is the holy rock housed beneath the Dome, then some rabbis argue that there is no reason why Jews should not be allowed to enter the rest of the Haram area, the wide expanse adjoining al-Aqsa and beyond. Yisrael Meir Lau, Israel's Ashkenazi chief rabbi, won't endorse 'going up' to the Temple Mount; at the same time he won't condemn it, implicitly acknowledging that some parts of the Mount can be accessible to Jews. With the election of the Netanyahu government in 1996, this subtle shift of emphasis meant that Jewish extremists were encouraged to intensify their efforts to gain access, especially after David Bar Ilan, one of Netanyahu's closest advisers, informed the activists that he sympathised with their position.

Zealots like Gershon Salomon are confident they will soon be able to effect a change in the *status quo* whereby Israeli police control access at the gates to the sanctuary, but the Muslims have supreme control within.

'As far as I'm concerned the Wailing Wall should be turned into a museum,' says Salomon. 'For me the Wailing Wall is a symbol of destruction [of the Temple] and foreign occupation. But the Jews are no longer exiles from their own city. Jerusalem belongs to the Jews, and we have every historical, religious and legal right to pray at the holiest site in Judaism.'

After years of being regarded as a religious freak, Salomon can claim that he is attracting genuine support from a wide section of the Israeli public. A 1996 opinion poll[2] showed that more than 30 per cent of Israelis supported Salomon's cause, and that 3.4 per cent of the electorate would vote for his movement at an election, which would give them four seats in the Knesset.

As part of the ongoing campaign to establish a permanent Jewish presence on the sanctuary, a small group of Jews, mainly students

2 'The Loyalists of the Temple Mount', Gallup Israel Ltd, February 1996.

from *hesder*, military yeshivas, enters the Mount every Tuesday morning, escorted by Israeli police and a sulky Wakf official, who watch to make sure no words of prayer escapes the participants' lips. These people have absolutely no respect for the Muslim shrines, and it would not be surprising if the next attempt to destroy the Dome and al-Aqsa comes from within their ranks. When I asked one of the worshippers why he insisted on taking this kind of provocative action, he spat at me, before being restrained by his fellow devotees.

Apart from rebuilding the Temple, Salomon shares Yehudah Etzion's design to have the area now occupied by the Haram turned into the centre of Israel's political life.

'The whole Israeli government should be moved from West Jerusalem to East Jerusalem, which is where King David first established the city.'

The only significant difference between the ideologies espoused by Etzion and Salomon is that Etzion is prepared to use violence to achieve his goal, whereas Salomon says he is committed to achieving his objectives through Israel's democratic process.

'I believe we must respect the law. The Jews cannot start fighting against each other. When we did that 2,000 years ago we lost Jerusalem and the Temple was destroyed.'

Salomon's desire to use peaceful means to rebuild the Temple does not always meet with success. With so many different groups of Jewish fanatics casting covetous eyes at the Haram al-Sharif, the city's Muslims are highly sensitive to any suggestion that their precious shrine might be endangered. Apart from Etzion's failed bomb plot, Muslims have been particularly wary of deranged Jews since Allan Goodman, an American immigrant doing his Israeli army service, went on a crazed rampage around the Haram in March 1982. Using his army-issue automatic rifle, Goodman shot dead two Arabs and wounded twelve others before Israeli troops subdued him. He was later sentenced to twenty years' imprisonment.

Eight years later, in October 1990, a full-scale riot broke out at the Haram when the rumour spread through the crowd attending the weekly Friday prayer service that Salomon and his supporters were planning to lay the foundation stone for a new Temple. Salomon had taken advantage of the Jewish feast of Succoth, when thousands of Jews come to pray at the Wailing Wall, to renew their campaign to gain access to the Haram (their request was thrown out by the Israeli High Court). As the Jews arrived to pray, officials at the Haram broadcast over the loudspeaker system that the sanctuary was in danger. According to Israeli officials who were monitoring the prayer service, the loudspeakers carried the messages *Allua Akbah*, 'God is Great', which was quickly followed by *Idbah al-Yahud*, 'Death to the Jews'.

Arab youths on the Haram responded by gathering large stones and rocks from a nearby building site. They attacked a police post by the Moghrabi gate before proceeding to hurl their missiles at Jews praying at the Wailing Wall below. The police, who were ill-prepared to deal with the crowd of an estimated 2,000 rioting Palestinian youths, initially responded by firing tear gas and rubber bullets. When this failed to quell the crowd, they opened fire with live ammunition. Eighteen Arabs were killed and scores of others wounded. The police response forced the rioters to seek refuge inside al-Aqsa, and the Arabs claimed that the police continued to fire live rounds inside the sanctuary itself, although this was rigorously denied by the police authorities. The violence continued sporadically for several days. Three Jews were stabbed to death in the Old City, and an Israeli taxi-driver was shot through the head. A Jewish woman soldier was stabbed to death in the Jewish neighbourhood of Bakaa, and an off-duty policeman was killed trying to prevent her murderer from killing an Israeli gardener. Despite the Jewish fatalities, the affair is referred to as the al-Aqsa massacre. The blood-stained, bullet-riddled clothes of the Arab victims form a macabre memorial which is on permanent display at the Haram's Islamic museum.

The affair not only severely strained relations between Jews and Arabs in Jerusalem, it had serious international repercussions. The killings on the Haram took place at a highly sensitive moment in the political destiny of the wider Middle East. Following Saddam Hussein's invasion of Kuwait the previous August, American President George Bush was that autumn in the process of putting together a highly complex coalition of Western and Arab troops for a massive military operation to liberate the Emirate. One of the key Arab demands for participation in Operation Desert Storm was that there should be no Israeli involvement. The actions of the Israeli security forces at the Haram, however, not only tempted several of the participating regimes – Syria, in particular – to withdraw their services, but enabled Iraqi dictator Saddam Hussein to claim that he was justified in confronting the US because of the Bush administration's unwavering support for an Israeli government which massacred innocent Palestinians.

Salomon is unrepentant about the dramatic fall-out his failed attempt on the Haram caused both in Jerusalem and elsewhere. His solution to prevent a future Arab outburst is to have the city's Palestinian Arab population removed. Nor does he make any attempt to conceal his racist contempt for their presence.

'The Arabs live in small ugly streets in small ugly houses. They spoil the city. The Jews are trying to make Jerusalem a beautiful city, full of life, children and trees. The Arabs try to make it look like a slum. They are stopping the holy process of redemption.

'So they must leave. They cannot live here. There are twenty-one other Arab countries where they can go. The Israeli authorities can help them to leave. We want to be humane about this. And it is the only way to ensure that there is no repetition of this appalling behaviour by the Arab occupiers of our holy Temple Mount.'

Although removal of the Islamic holy sites and rebuilding the Temple constitute the ultimate ambition of modern Jewish zealots, they also busy themselves in many other areas of the city's life, going out of their way to assert Jewish supremacy at the Palestinians' expense. It is one of Jerusalem's great misfortunes that it is regarded not only as the supreme symbol of Jewish nationalism, but the headquarters for most of the Jewish extremist movements. As a consequence the city often resembles a frontier town of the American wild west, with the streets full of gun-toting Jews taking a brief respite from the rigours of their daily battles with the Arabs. The knitted kippas most of them wear with an air of studied belligerence identify them as ideological settlers who like to live close to Arab centres of population, like Hebron and Nablus, as a rather primitive expression of their military supremacy. There can be no other city in the civilised world like Jerusalem, whose citizens are allowed to wander the streets with loaded, semi-automatic weapons slung over their shoulders, or pistols tucked under their shirts or skirts (guns are not an exclusively male preserve). There is a firing range in the centre of West Jerusalem where they practise their accuracy; the most popular targets used to be pictures of *keffiyeh*-clad Palestinians, but they have since been withdrawn after attracting protests from less ideologically committed Israelis. On Thursday nights at the local discotheques, the younger members of the settler fraternity are known to place their guns on the floor and dance round them. Young settlers are also particularly attracted to violent, action-packed movies of the Bruce Willis variety; one suspects that in their minds they substitute Arabs for the stereotypical Hollywood baddies. Any Arab, of course, found brandishing a weapon in Jerusalem would be shot on sight. The overall effect of all these guns is one of insidious menace, and undermines the sanctity of the place.

The extremists, whether settlers or religious zealots, are often at their most aggressive, and in their element, in the narrow confines of the Old City. Mostly these two groups are indistinguishable. Ideological settlers (as opposed to those who live in settlements for purely financial reasons) generally subscribe to the fanatical religious agenda advocated by people like Etzion and Salomon. The well-spring of their ideology comes from organisations such as Gush Emunim (Community of Believers), a militant settlers' group, which announced its arrival in the mid-1970s by establishing settlements, against the wishes of the Israeli government, on the outskirts of Nablus, one of the PLO's main centres of support on the West Bank, and in the centre of Hebron. The young activists who commute to Hebron to lend moral and practical support to the community of 250 Jews who insist on residing in the heart of a Palestinian city, even after its return to Palestinian control in January 1997, come mainly from Jerusalem's extremist, military yeshivas associated with Gush Emunim, many of which are based in the Old City.[3] One of Gush Emunim's more controversial forays into Jerusalem was in October 1991, when hundreds of its members took over a group of six Arab houses in the Palestinian village of Silwan, directly adjoining the southern flank of the Haram. Claiming that Silwan occupies land that comprised the original City of David, the settlers are committed to re-establishing a Jewish presence in what today is a Palestinian residential neighbourhood. They live in a heavily fortified compound bristling with guns and barbed wire. To mark Benjamin Netanyahu's

---

3 Yigal Amir, Rabin's assassin, was a regular Hebron visitor.

election victory in May 1996, they occupied another two Arab houses.

Another Jewish extremist group with a substantial following is Kach, founded by the late Rabbi Meir Kahane.[4] Kach, which means 'by force', was taken from the motto of Menachem Begin's pre-State terror group Etzel, and its main objective is to expel all Arabs from the 'Land of Israel'. Most members of the Jewish underground – including Yehudah Etzion – who perpetrated various atrocities against Arabs in the mid-1980s were Kach sympathisers. Kahane, who was ordained in a Brooklyn yeshiva, fled to Israel in 1972 to escape federal prosecution for conspiracy to commit violence. He founded Kach in Jerusalem two years later and immediately made a name for himself for his virulent, anti-Arab rhetoric. In a typical speech made during the 1981 election, Kahane said: 'The Arabs are cancer, cancer, cancer in our midst. There is only one solution, no other, no partial solution: The Arabs are out! Do not ask me how . . . Let me become defence minister for two months and you will not have a single cockroach around here!'[5] In the 1984 election Kahane actually won a seat in the Knesset, but the parliament passed a law the following year banning him from using the democratic process to lobby support for his 'solution'.

Yigal Amir, Rabin's assassin, was associated with Eyal, a Hebrew acronym for The Jewish Fighting Organisation and an offshoot of Kach, which claimed responsibility for a number of racially-motivated Arab murders. Amir denied being a member of the organisation, and said he acted out of religious conviction alone when he murdered the Prime Minister. But when police raided Amir's home following the assassination, they found a substantial stockpile of weapons and explosives that Amir said he intended to use for attacks he was planning against Arabs. Following Rabin's murder the Israeli security forces instigated an extensive clampdown against Jewish extremist groups, arresting most of the leaders of both Kach and Eyal. That did

---

4 Kahane was murdered by an Egyptian ex-patriate while addressing a rally in New York in November 1990. The Shamir government published an official statement expressing its sorrow.

5 Quoted in Howard M. Sachar, A History of Israel (New York: Alfred A. Knopf, 1996).

not prevent Kach activists lauding Amir as a hero. At a memorial service held in Jerusalem just a few days after Rabin's assassination in November 1995 to mark the fifth anniversary of Kahane's murder, Kach activists praised Amir as 'a messiah' for ridding the country of Rabin.[6]

The most controversial group of Jewish extremists active in the Old City is Ateret Cohanim, the 'Priestly Crown'. Apart from being committed to demolishing al-Aqsa and the Dome of the Rock, Ateret Cohanim's 300 activists want to colonise twenty-two 'unsecured', or Palestinian-occupied, areas of East Jerusalem to complete Jewish domination of the entire city. Although some of these designated areas are outside the Old City – in the autumn of 1996 they occupied an Arab house close to the East Jerusalem American Consulate – the main focus of their activity takes place within the old Ottoman ramparts. Most of their activities are directed towards establishing a Jewish presence in the Old City's Muslim Quarter. To that end they have set about acquiring numerous properties, building up a network of Jewish 'safe houses' along the main thoroughfares. One of their more prominent acquisitions is an old Arab apartment built on an arch over Bab al-Wad, the main passage used by Muslims for access to and from the Haram al-Sharif. The apartment, which was purchased by Ateret Cohanim, is occupied by Ariel Sharon, the right-wing former defence minister. The building is easily identified by the contingent of heavily armed Israeli Border Police who are always positioned at the entrance, harassing Arabs going about their daily business.

The poisonous atmosphere that often descends on the Muslim Quarter can be attributed to the activities of Ateret Cohanim and their followers, who swagger through the narrow confines of the Old City like ill-disciplined vigilantes. A law unto themselves, they go on regular patrols, equipped with walkie-talkies and automatic weapons. Their primary function, they claim, is to protect Jews making their way to and from the Wailing Wall. They also guard the plethora of yeshivas, synagogues and other Jewish institutions that have been

6 Avigdor Eskin, a Kach rabbi, was arrested in March 1995 for placing a rabbinical curse on Prime Minister Shimon Peres. He claimed Peres was 'endangering Jewish lives' following the suicide bomb attacks in Jerusalem and Tel Aviv.

established in the Muslim quarter. Observation and command posts have been set up on rooftops at strategic points nearby to enable the settlers to react quickly to an Arab provocation. An escort service is provided for mothers and children wishing to move from one point to another. Any attempt by local Arabs to interfere, let alone object, to their activities is dealt with robustly, and sometimes with violence. Most Arab shopkeepers in the Muslim Quarter have had their stores attacked and ransacked on more than one occasion. After the start of the Oslo peace process, shopkeepers were attacked merely for displaying the Palestinian flag. Anti-Arab graffiti is sprayed on adjoining walls, together with the Star of David.

Successive Israeli governments must take the blame for permitting this state of affairs to develop. Gush Emunim was allowed to flourish in the 1970s during a Labour government. Ateret Cohanim has been ensconced in the Old City since 1978, when Teddy Kollek ran the city. It is unlikely that Kollek had racist groups such as this in mind when he said he sought to maintain Jerusalem as a mosaic of pluralism. Although Kollek often condemned the activities of the settler groups in the Old City, little was actually done to stop them. Occasionally court injunctions would be issued, and lengthy legal proceedings would ensue. But the settlers were rarely evicted, and no effective action has been taken to prevent them from pursuing their inflammatory, and racist, programme. Under Likud governments, and especially after Mayor Olmert came to power, these groups flourish. It is a Likud article of faith to enlarge Greater Jerusalem to a population that ultimately encompasses 1 million Jews, and these groups of zealots claim they are merely helping to fulfil these objectives. Indeed, after the 1993 municipal elections, some of their most ardent supporters were elected on to the council. Among them was Samuel Meir, who became one of Olmert's deputy mayors. Meir, a tall, aggressive man with a settler's beard, was often to be found in the vanguard of the various provocative actions undertaken by these groups, whether demonstrating outside Orient House or opening a new yeshiva in the Muslim quarter. He was killed in late 1996 when his car was involved in an accidental collision with a lorry driven by an Arab.

One of Ateret Cohanim's more spectacular propaganda coups,

however, took place in the Christian Quarter, an area of the Old City which is generally trouble-free. It is rare to see the Israeli security forces deployed in Christian residential areas, whereas they have an almost permanent presence among the Muslims. The security forces were out in force, though, the day a group of 150 settlers took possession of St John's Hospice, a 68-room building less than a hundred metres from the Church of the Holy Sepulchre, during Easter Week 1990. Although owned by the Greek Orthodox Church, the property had been leased to an Armenian businessman, who illegally sold it, through a Panamanian 'front' company, to Ateret Cohanim for $3.5 million. While the settlers received a congratulatory visit from Ariel Sharon, their action sparked a worldwide protest. All the major Christian churches in Israel and the West Bank, including the Holy Sepulchre, closed on Good Friday. New York's Cardinal John O'Connor denounced the take-over as an 'obscene' plot. At a demonstration organised by the Greek Orthodox patriarchate a few days later, Israeli police had to use tear gas to disperse the rioting Greek monks. Patriarch Diodoros, who was present at the demonstration, collapsed after being overwhelmed by the tear gas fumes, and was hospitalised. Ateret Cohanim was unrepentant. The organisation renamed the building Neot David, David's Dwelling, and moved in ten families of Jewish settlers.

While groups like Ateret Cohanim revel in the publicity they generate from stunts such as these, most Israelis are not only critical of their activities, but deeply irritated that so many of the Jews who make up these fanatical groups are not native-born Israelis. It is not unusual to hear members of the more extreme settlements, whether in Jerusalem, Hebron or the West Bank, speaking with heavy American accents. Many of the worst atrocities committed by Jews – Goodman's attack on the Dome of the Rock, Goldstein's massacre in Hebron – have been carried out by Jews of American origin. Kach, the only political party to be banned in Israel because of its racism, is the creation of a Brooklyn-educated rabbi. Ateret Cohanim, which is shunned by most Israelis, receives the bulk of its funding from an American Jew who runs a multi-million dollar bingo hall business in Los Angeles. Dr Irving Moskowitz, who claims to have lost more than 100 relatives in the Holocaust, has donated millions of dollars to acquiring properties in Arab areas of Jerusalem for use by settlers. His name appears on many of the title deeds of properties the organisation has acquired in East Jerusalem, and he is thought to have financed the purchase of St John's Hospice. He also funded much of the work for the Hasmonean tunnel that provoked so much violence when it was finally opened in September 1996.[7]

It is not so much the amount of money that Moskowitz donates that concerns Israelis, it is the political agenda that goes with it. Moskowitz has made no secret of his total opposition to Israel returning land to the Palestinians as part of a peace deal, and so he uses his considerable personal fortune to pre-empt the Israeli government. Ornan Yekutieli, a left-wing member of Jerusalem's Municipal Council, is outraged that Jews who are not Israelis can exert so much influence in the city's affairs.

'These are people who live a long way away and like to play with a big box of matches,' he says. 'They sit and throw the matches, and one day one of the matches will succeed and make a big explosion.'

Israeli journalists, particularly after Yitzhak Rabin's assassination, have criticised the government's failure to take firmer action against foreign-born and foreign-based extremists, particularly those who plot or commit atrocities in the name of the Jewish people.

As one leading Israeli columnist has written: 'The raw material is American, the money is American, and the joke is on us.'

7 The timing of the tunnel opening was arranged by Mayor Olmert to coincide with Moskowitz's presence in Israel for Succoth.

# 12

# MARTYRS

*'You shall surely die hereafter, and be restored to life on the Day of Resurrection'*

Koran, Sura 23

It must take more courage to be a suicide bomber than to plant a bomb outside an ancient shrine and run away. The rewards, potential martyrs are told, are considerable. In paradise the dead bomber will be allowed to choose seventy relatives to join him. He will be able to indulge in truly celestial pleasures: there will be rivers of milk and wine (non-alcoholic, of course), lakes of honey, and the undivided attention of seventy beautiful virgins. For a young man reared in the squalor and brutality of a refugee camp, with no job, no money and no prospects, the offer is almost irresistible.

But to attain these fantastic delights, the bomber must first press the detonator button, and that cannot be easy. Either strapped to his body, or stashed away in a duffel bag, the volunteer will be required to explode a bomb of monstrous ferocity. Not only will the device obliterate its conveyor, it will be designed to kill, maim and traumatise anyone in the near vicinity. A typical bomb will contain seven kilograms of TNT, five kilograms of nails or metal balls and, if the bomb is contained in a bag, four litres of petrol. Survival is most certainly not an option. The force of the blast will devastate the surrounding area for at least 100 metres. If exploded on a bus, the vehicle will be reduced to a twisted heap of metal. The petrol will create an explosive fireball, incinerating anyone or anything in the immediate vicinity. Rescue crews given the macabre task of piecing together the remains of the victims will need to consult dental records for identification. To press that button the bomber must be certain paradise awaits. The rewards must be out of this world to commit such an atrocity. Despair at what this world has to offer must be unequivocal.

Majdi Abu Wardeh did not fit all the characteristics of the suicide bomber stereotype. One of eleven children, Abu Wardeh came from Al-Fawwar refugee camp, a ten-minute drive from the centre of Hebron. Compared with the refugee camps in places like Gaza, Al-Fawwar is tolerable.[1] Located in a long valley among impressive, open hills, it does not suffer the same degree of teeming squalor that distinguishes so many other camps. Majdi came from a warm and loving family. His father Mohammed, a geography teacher for twenty-five years at the local high school, is a pleasant, softly-spoken man who, given the family's circumstances, holds moderate political views. A Muslim, he respects his faith, but would not consider himself devout. His parents were made refugees during the 1948 war, and Al-Mansheyeh, their village, was destroyed. The land today comprises the Israeli community of Kiryat Gat. Many of the other residents of the refugee camp trace their origins back to Al-Dawaymeh, a neighbouring Arab village. This was the location of one of the worst, and least documented, massacres conducted by Zionist troops during the 1948 war, part of the Haganah's policy of ethnically cleansing Arabs living close to Jewish centres of population.

'I am a peaceful man,' says Mohammed Abu Wardeh. 'Like most ordinary people I just want to live in peace with my family. But the Israelis make life very hard for us. I do not hate the Israelis, but I wish they would treat us like human beings.'

In late February 1996, at the age of twenty-five, his son Majdi became a *shaheed*, a martyr, when he boarded a number 18 bus in

1 Literally a 'bubbly place' like a spring or brook.

Jerusalem at 7 A.M. on Sunday morning and detonated a bomb hidden in his duffel-bag as the bus reached the top of Jaffa Street. Twenty-two people travelling on the bus died instantly in the explosion. His mission was the first of two suicide bomb bus attacks that took place in Jerusalem within a week.

'It was a great surprise and a terrible shock,' his father remembers. 'And after all this time I still can't believe what happened.'

We are sitting on the top floor of a half-built house on the outskirts of Al-Fawwar. Mohammed, a thin, wiry man, sits cross-legged on the floor, a red and white *keffiyeh* wrapped around his head. Intisar, his wife, a well-built woman with a weather-beaten face, makes tea on a camping stove while an abundance of children and grandchildren cavort around the building site. A biting wind blows through the windowless walls. The original family home, in the centre of the refugee camp, was demolished by the Israeli army soon after Majdi was identified as the perpetrator of the first Jerusalem bus bomb. The Israeli policy of instituting collective punishment against Palestinian communities has not changed in fifty years. In the 1940s whole villages were destroyed for providing refuge for Palestinian fighters: now the homes of families of any Palestinian who commits a terrorist offence against Israel are summarily demolished. The policy only applies to Palestinians. The family home of Yigal Amir, Rabin's Jewish assassin, was left untouched, even though he murdered the Prime Minister.

Abu Wardeh's family learnt of his death from a video-recording he made shortly before he killed himself. One of the more macabre aspects of the appalling suicide bomb phenomenon is the way these agents of death seek to glorify their actions. Before carrying out their mission, it is usual for the bomber to make a video telling how they are sacrificing their lives for the sake of the Palestinian cause, and that their bereaved relatives should not worry, for they will soon join the deceased in paradise. Making the video is all part of an elaborate ritual that takes place in the build-up to the 'operation', rather like the preparations for a wedding. The bomber is the groom, and death will be his bride.

Majdi's video shows a smart young man, with well-groomed hair and a thin moustache, wearing an old college scarf wrapped nonchalantly around his neck. With an off-white shirt and a grey V-neck pullover, he looks like any of the thousands of other students – Israeli and Arab – who board the city's buses each day. He apologises to his parents for the pain he will cause them, and asks them not to worry, because his reward will be in heaven. He says he is carrying out the mission to avenge the injustice the Palestinian people have suffered at the hands of the Israelis. 'Victory to Palestine, Death to Israel, God is Great,' says Majdi, and the video ends abruptly.

'I remember that shirt,' says his mother. 'I bought it for him when he wanted to go to college.'

The video was delivered to a television station after the bombing by a member of Hamas, the militant Palestinian Islamic movement which has planned most of the suicide bomb attacks against Israel.[2] The Abu Wardehs only realised their son was responsible for the suicide bombing of a Jerusalem bus when a crowd of Palestinians from the camp gathered outside their home, chanting victory slogans and passing sweets around, to celebrate Majdi's triumphant entry into paradise.

Mr Abu Wardeh was not happy about the sweets, and insists they were not his idea. 'I didn't want sweets being passed around. I had just lost a son who was very dear to me,' he says. But he has mixed emotions about the nature of his son's death.

'I am proud of what he did, although I am sad that he died. He died in a way that I can feel proud of him but, as a father, if I'd known what he was planning, I would have stopped him. He has left a big hole in our lives.'

As with any family involved in a major tragedy, the Abu Wardehs have sought to rationalise their grief, in particular what led their son, who had shown no previous inclination towards violence, to act in this way. The Hamas movement is generally held to be a child of the *intifada*, and its followers, especially those who volunteer to sacrifice their lives for the cause, are assumed to be young men brutalised by the experience of engaging in almost daily, violent confrontations with Israeli soldiers. But even though there were numerous violent clashes at Al-Fawwar during the *intifada* between Palestinian rioters and Israeli soldiers, Majdi Abu Wardeh, his father says, was never directly involved.

2 'Hamas' is an Arabic acronym for The Islamic Resistance Movement. It is also the Arabic for 'zeal'.

'It is not easy to be a young Palestinian in a place like this. All the restrictions, all the harassment. But Majdi tried to keep out of trouble.'

His sister was not so lucky. As a teenager, she was shot in the mouth during a clash with Israeli soldiers in the refugee camp. She lost her top, front teeth and suffered serious injury to the back of her neck; she suffers from a speech impediment as a consequence. A first cousin of the family was shot twice by the Israelis – once in the hand, the second time in the head – and suffered brain damage.

'Perhaps this affected him more deeply than we thought,' says Mr Abu Wardeh. 'But he never said anything about it.'

The fourth of six boys, Majdi hoped to be a builder. At one time he entertained the idea of going to college, but his parents could not afford the fees.

'It was tough for him, but no tougher than it is for anyone else,' his father continues. 'He wanted to make a good life for himself and he could have succeeded if he'd lived.'

A few months after the bombing, the Abu Wardehs started work on building themselves a new home. They found some unused land on the outskirts of the refugee camp and began work on a three-storey house to accommodate the whole family. As soon as they started work, however, the camp gossips started the rumour that the house was being paid for by Hamas – a blood debt for the family's dead son. But Mr Abu Wardeh is insistent the project is being paid for entirely out of his own savings.

'Thank God, no,' he says. 'I have enough money of my own to build a new house. I don't have to rely on Hamas. I don't want anything to do with them. I don't like Hamas; they helped to kill my son. The way Hamas acts will never solve the problem between the Palestinians and Israelis. The real solution needs understanding on both sides.'

The Islamic suicide bomber is a relatively new phenomenon to Israel, appearing for the first time as recently as April 1994. Jerusalem's first suicide bombing occurred in August 1995 when a Hamas fanatic blew himself up on a bus travelling through the Ramat Eshkol neighbourhood, killing four passengers. The principle of using suicide as a means of devastating the enemy can be traced back to the twelfth century and the assassins of Alamut, who wreaked havoc among the

Persian caliphate. It was the Crusaders, who experienced these deadly tactics on their way to liberate Jerusalem, who coined the word 'assassin', believing the ferocity of their foes could only be explained by the liberal quantities of hashish they consumed. The suicide bombers who caused so much chaos in Lebanon during the 1980s can almost be described as direct descendants of these medieval warriors. Israeli troops based in southern Lebanon bore the brunt of these attacks, which were primarily conducted by the Iranian-backed Hizbollah militia, an organisation of committed Islamic fundamentalists. These attacks were so effective that it was only a question of time before they were adopted by Palestinian Islamic militants.

It was probably no coincidence that suicide bomb attacks against Israel began after the Rabin government in late 1992 deported more than two hundred Hamas activists to southern Lebanon. The action was taken in an attempt to curb Hamas's attempt to radicalise Palestinian youth. In spite of international protests, the Hamas activists spent nearly a year living in tents on a bleak Lebanese hillside. During that period many of them formed close alliances with Hizbollah militia leaders, who took the opportunity to educate them in the more advanced form of terrorist technology that they practised with such success in Lebanon. At the end of 1993, after the signing of the Oslo Accords, the Rabin government relented, and allowed the Hamas deportees to return. Soon afterwards the suicide bomb attacks began in Israel. Whenever the Israeli security forces manage to penetrate a Hamas terrorist cell, they often find that the activists have strong connections with terrorist organisations in Lebanon.

There appears to be no shortage of young Palestinians willing to sacrifice their lives in this grisly manner. After Majdi killed himself, another thirty young men from Al-Fawwar volunteered to meet a similar fate. Most of those who have taken part in suicide operations against Israel come from similar backgrounds. They are young men, aged between nineteen and twenty-five, and tend to come from devout Muslim families. They are unmarried, usually the middle child of a large family (and so not the principal wage-earner), and live in refugee camps, usually in the Gaza Strip.[3] Many will claim to have

3 In 1997 none of the suicide bombers had been recruited from Jerusalem, where support for Hamas is not strong among the Muslim Palestinian population.

suffered arrest or physical injury at the hands of the Israelis, especially during the *intifada*. One bomber, who killed twenty-one Israelis at a bus-stop at Beit Lid in January 1995, came from a Gaza refugee camp where he worked as a nurse. In his pre-martyrdom video address, he claimed to have been wounded by Israeli gunfire on six separate occasions during the *intifada*, held without trial for three months and tortured by his Israeli interrogators. Another bomber, who killed seven Israelis by driving a car packed with one hundred kilograms of explosives into a bus at Afula in 1994, claimed he had been repeatedly tortured. He said that while being interrogated by the Israeli security forces he had endured regular beatings, sleep deprivation, being stripped and threatened with rape.

A typical Palestinian suicide bomber will come from an aspiring middle-class background, even if their parents live in a refugee camp. A survey of twenty-three bombers conducted by the Israelis in 1996 showed that nineteen had been to college or university. Candidates are hand-picked by older Hamas activists who are expert at constructing the bombing device but are less keen to immolate themselves. They excuse themselves on the grounds that they have families to provide for, or that they are too important to the organisation to sacrifice themselves. The bombers are used like cannon fodder by Hamas's military commanders. 'Hamas does not waste experienced members with proven military successes on suicide missions,' explained one Israeli intelligence officer, an expert on the organisation's operations. 'The suicide bombers are merely human fuses, replacing a chemical or electrical device.'

One of the more infamous masterminds of the Hamas suicide bombings was Yahyah Ayyash, a Gaza-based activist, who was known as 'the engineer' for his expertise in constructing particularly lethal bombs. Trained as a chemical engineer – hence the nickname – Ayyash, who was married with two children and lived in Gaza, constructed most of the early bombs used by Hamas's suicide squads. On one occasion when Ayyash was instructing two volunteers, an argument broke out between them over who was to have the honour of sacrificing their life first. Having chosen one, Ayyash reassured the other: 'Don't worry, your time will come.'

The Israelis finally got their revenge on Ayyash in January 1996 in one of their typically ruthless, 'eye-for-an-eye', counter-terrorism operations. Having tracked Ayyash to his Gazan lair, Israeli security agents managed to switch the mobile phone used by the 'engineer' for one filled with Semtex. When Ayyash dialled a specified number, it detonated the device, blowing off his head. He who lives by the bomb, dies by the bomb.

The three suicide bus bomb attacks – two in Jerusalem and one in Tel Aviv – which devastated Israel in February and March 1996 were carried out as much to avenge Ayyash's death as to cause maximum disruption to the peace process. In the poisonous world of Middle East politics, it seems a rationale can always be provided for the most senseless waste of human life. Mohammed Abu Wardeh, Majdi's cousin, who helped to recruit and train the three bombers, provided a detailed account of how the bombings were planned in a confession made after shortly after his arrest by the Palestinian security forces. Apart from the operational details, Abu Wardeh said in the confession, which was video-recorded and shown on Israeli television, that the bombings had been carried out to help the right-wing Likud party win the forthcoming Israeli elections. This comment was seized upon by Prime Minister Peres as proof that Likud was waging a dirty tricks campaign against him.[4] The text of the confession, which must have been made within days of Abu Wardeh's arrest, seemed as though it had been written by Arafat's security chiefs, who were anxious that they should not be blamed for these horrific attacks. Jibril Ragoub's security apparatus therefore ensured that Abu Wardeh was kept well away from the Israeli security forces, for fear that he might provide incriminating evidence to Israeli interrogators. The video-taped confession was only made public after Abu Wardeh had been tried by a Palestinian military tribunal and sentenced to life imprisonment.

Apart from disrupting the peace process, Izzadin Kassam, the military wing of Hamas and the group responsible for the Jerusalem bombings, conducted the attacks to avenge Ayyash's death.[5] This would explain why they went to so much trouble to conduct attacks on consecutive Sundays, on the same bus at exactly the same time. If

4 See Chapter 3, pp. 72–3.
5 Izzadin Kassam is named after a Syrian fanatic who was killed in a shoot-out with the British security forces in Haifa in the 1930s.

the Israelis felt they had been clever to kill Ayyash with his own phone, Hamas terrorist leaders felt they should respond by providing a demonstration of their own expertise. Jerusalem was chosen because it is Israel's capital, and Israeli security is said to be tighter in the city than anywhere else in the country. Israeli buses were chosen because they are the most vulnerable symbol of Israeli claims to control the whole city; Egged, the national bus company, runs a service through both West and East Jerusalem. By blowing up a bus the terrorists could be assured of causing the optimum number of casualties.[6]

Mohammed Abu Wardeh was a student at the United Nations-run Teachers' Training College in Ramallah, the Arab satellite city ten miles north of Jerusalem. He was well-known on the campus as a Hamas sympathiser when he was contacted by someone calling himself 'Abu Ahmed'. The man, who came from Gaza's Khan Younis refugee camp, said he was a member of the Hamas military wing, and that he needed people to carry out bombing operations. Mohammed agreed to work with him, and within days had recruited three volunteers, including his cousin Majdi. He recruited the bombers 'by sounding them out, then afterwards I received their agreement in principle,' he says in the confession. 'Then I worked with them directly and finally they agreed.'

Ramallah Teachers' Training College seems an unlikely starting point for one of the worst terrorist outrages ever committed on the streets of Jerusalem. Founded in 1962 when the city was under Jordanian control, the college was the West Bank's first institute of higher education, training Palestinian students from both the West Bank and Gaza Strip. Funded almost entirely by the UN, the college boasts a spacious, well-maintained campus. The students are smartly dressed and, according to the teachers, diligent.

'Many of our students come from refugee camps. They know all about suffering,' explains Samir Abu Wahad, the deputy principal. 'They know that this is their best chance of making a better life for themselves, so they work hard to succeed. We push them hard, and they respond well. They are more interested in studying than politics.'

6 The Tel Aviv bombing was carried out by Islamic Jihad, an Iranian-backed group of Islamic extremists, in revenge for the assassination of their leader in Malta the previous October by an Israeli hit-squad.

The college authorities are not at all proud that their campus helped to produce two of the bombers who killed fifty-six people in the Jerusalem bus bombings, and another eleven in Tel Aviv. The atrocities are regarded as an unfortunate aberration that will not be repeated, even though Hamas continues to enjoy strong support on campus.

'They do not cause us too much trouble,' says Mr Abu Wahad. 'They campaign for the college elections, and that is all. The rest of the time we do not hear much from them. Nor do we interfere with them. Everyone is entitled to their opinion.'

In spite of the college authorities' attempts to promote a normal, hard-working academic environment, students face abnormal difficulties in order to complete their courses. During the *intifada* the college was closed for months at a time when the Israelis accused the students of inciting violence through their political activities. Several students were killed, and scores more wounded, in clashes with the Israeli security services. During lapses in the violence, college staff would attempt to keep the students occupied by conducting classes at secret locations in Ramallah. The situation has not improved since the *intifada* ended and, though the violence has subsided, the restrictions imposed on the students are just as punitive, particularly for those coming from Gaza. Of the four hundred students the college trains each year, one hundred are supposed to have their homes in Gaza. The Israelis' strict travel restrictions, applied for 'security reasons' on young Palestinians passing through the West Bank and Gaza, means that in most years since 1992 less than twenty Gazan students have been able to enrol. And many of those who do make it to the college do so illegally, and run the risk of being jailed if caught.

'This is the way it is,' says a philosophical Mr Abu Wahad. 'Students run the risk of going to jail so that they can get an education.'

Some students go to the most extraordinary lengths merely to travel the eighty miles between Gaza and Ramallah. One Gazan student I met had journeyed by way of Egypt and Jordan to avoid Israeli checkpoints. The journey had taken three days and cost several hundred dollars. The taxi fare would have been no more than a few shekels. The checkpoints set up around Ramallah after it was handed back to Palestinian control in late 1995 made it seem like a besieged city for most of the students. To leave Ramallah it is necessary to pass through checkpoints manned by Israel's Border Police, who have a fearsome reputation for the way they treat Palestinians who attempt to enter without proper authority.

In early 1997 a Palestinian shopkeeper living near the main A-Ram checkpoint between Ramallah and Jerusalem made a video-recording of a group of Border Police, distinctive in their green berets and olive green uniforms, casually beating up three Palestinian workers who had been caught trying to enter Jerusalem illegally. The film, which was aired on Israeli television, showed the policemen smoking and talking among themselves. Occasionally they would break off their conversation and aim a few well-directed kicks at the defenceless Palestinians, who had their hands tied behind their backs and were sitting in a squat position. At other times they beat the Palestinians around the head. The film provoked outrage among Israelis when shown, although Israeli and Palestinian human rights activists could not understand what all the fuss was about. For years they have been documenting cases of Palestinians suffering physical abuse by the Border Police. A favourite Border Police haunt is the wasteland on the Mount of Olives, where generations of Palestinians have been sub-jected to severe beatings. The victims are then dumped at the nearby Palestinian-run Makassed Hospital for their injuries to be treated. All this has been reported by human rights organisations. But the Israeli authorities generally turn a blind eye, preferring to believe the policemen's claims that they were defending themselves rather than the Palestinian claims of assault.

None of the students at Ramallah's Teachers' Training College can visit Jerusalem; what could one day be the future capital of a Palestinian state is like a distant mirage, even though it is only a ten-mile drive away. Without the proper authorisation, they are not prepared to risk a confrontation with the Israeli security forces simply for the privilege of paying a visit to the Holy City. The situation is more claustrophibic for the Gazan students, most of whom are too afraid to stray far from the campus. Two young students I met, who came from Gaza, had not seen their families for nearly two years. Polite, well-dressed young men, they said they preferred to stay at the campus and concentrate on their studies rather than risk getting into trouble. Their biggest fear was how they would return home once their studies were complete.

'We are here illegally. If the Israelis catch us we will go to prison,' one of the students explained. 'But we cannot stay here when our studies are complete. We must go home. It is a big problem. For us it is like living in a big jail.'

This, then, is the type of environment which produces young men willing to sacrifice their lives on the streets of Jerusalem. Mohammed Abu Wardeh, the bombers' recruiter, was nearing the completion of a four-year training course at the college to become a teacher when he agreed to help the mysterious 'Abu Ahmed' organise the bombings. Three of the volunteers he recruited came from the campus, and the fourth was his cousin Majdi. Mohammed himself briefly considered sacrificing his own life, 'but for various reasons, I refused,' he says in his confession. Majdi and one of the students carried out the Jerusalem bombings; the other two conducted suicide missions in Tel Aviv and the coastal port of Ashkelon. Preparations for the bombings took just four weeks.

At Hamas gatherings, those who have volunteered to be suicide bombers don white shrouds, and it often looks as though a blanket of white snow has fallen. Training for the mission is both physical and spiritual. Many volunteers are rejected as not being suitable for the grotesque initiation ritual. One Hamas specialist, who supervises training, says that many applicants are dismissed at an early stage. 'Some volunteers are motivated by emotion, and we do not want that,' he explained. Candidates are required to undergo gruesome trials designed to test their nerve. Two seventeen-year-olds who were captured in 1995 before they could carry out their missions said they had been taken to a graveyard at Gaza one night, and buried alive until dawn, with just one small breathing hole.

Secrecy and mutual trust are also regarded as essential require-ments, which is why the recruiters tend to target friends and family. Apart from enrolling his cousin, the bombers picked by Mohammed Abu Wardeh included his neighbour's cousin, a fellow student. Wardeh told his captors: 'There was trust between us. At the begin-ning when I spoke to them I checked their pulse. There were no problems.' To insure against the danger of informers, all the opera-tions are compartmentalised to maintain optimum secrecy. The candidates are passed from the recruiter to the bomb-maker. The bomb-maker then passes the recruit to the operational commander who explains how the mission will be carried out. The shorter the time span between recruitment and detonation, the better. The actual training for a mission, once a candidate has been thoroughly vetted and tested, can take no longer than three days.

None of these practitioners of the deadly terrorist's art know each other, so that if one is caught he cannot reveal the identity of the others. After his arrest, for example, Mohammed Abu Wardeh was unable to tell his interrogators anything more about 'Abu Ahmed', his 'controller', other than that he belonged to the military wing of Hamas, and that he came from Gaza. Despite the exhaustive search that was undertaken by both the Israeli and Palestinian security services following the Jerusalem bombings, the mysterious 'Abu Ahmed' was never caught. The Israeli authorities did, however, capture Hassan Salameh, the leader of the Hamas cell which organised this particular series of suicide bombings. Salameh was caught during a shoot-out with Israeli troops in Hebron in May 1996. Salameh, who had received extensive terrorist training in Iran and Syria, was badly wounded by Israeli soldiers, and took refuge in a Palestinian hospital. But Israeli troops tracked him down and took him away after an Israeli doctor was called to remove a bullet lodged in his back. As he was driven away, Salameh shouted: 'I want to be a martyr, not arrested by the Israelis.' In February 1997, Salameh was jailed for life by an Israeli military court for his role in the suicide bombings.

Koranic instruction is another important element in the ritual of the suicide bomber's final preparation. It can also be the most lengthy part of the process, especially if the volunteer is not fully cognisant of the subtleties of Islamic faith. The Imams, the religious authorities, will insist that the 'martyr' is fully aware of his religious obligations and rewards before he sacrifices his life. Women are not prohibited from participation – a seventeen-year-old Lebanese girl killed herself in an attack against Israeli troops in the mid-1980s. But female suicide bombers are generally frowned upon in Palestinian society where the role of women is more traditional and conservative.[7]

Apart from the promise of heavenly delights, the Imam, who will

7 After the Jerusalem suicide bombs, a group of women in the West Bank town of Tulkarm complained that they were not being allowed to volunteer.

267

be a Hamas sympathiser, promises that the suicide bomber's relatives will be provided for by various Islamic charities (which is why it was assumed the new home built by Majdi Abu Wardeh's family was financed by Hamas). Keeping the relatives happy is the easiest part of the Imams' duties. A more difficult task is attempting to resolve the disputes that arise within the different branches of Islam, such as whether it is right for a Muslim to sacrifice his life deliberately, as opposed to being killed in battle. Another significant theological objection that the Imams of Hamas have had to overcome is whether or not someone who has blown themselves to pieces can be accepted into paradise.

Palestinian families, particularly in rural areas and the refugee camps, tend to hold a rather superstitious view of Islam. They like their deceased relatives to enter paradise in the most perfect state possible, as they believe this is how the deceased will spend the rest of eternity. Muslim families therefore like to bury their relatives as soon as possible after death to ensure the deceased reaches paradise before the process of decomposition sets in. Most Muslims are opposed to disturbing the body after death. During the *intifada*, when many Muslims were killed in suspicious circumstances, their relatives were deeply resistant – sometimes violently so – to post-mortem examinations being conducted to establish cause of death. The bodies of people killed during clashes with the Israeli security forces would be spirited away and buried before the Israelis could get to them. In rural areas it became part of mythology that the only reason the Israelis wanted the bodies was to steal their organs for use in transplant operations inside Israel.

The reluctance of Palestinian families to permit autopsies was a cause of great frustration to both Israeli and Palestinian human rights activists in April 1995 after Abed Harizat, a suspected Hamas activist, died while being interrogated by Israeli security agents at Jerusalem's Russian Compound lock-up, the forbidding old Ottoman prison located in the centre of Jerusalem, just behind Jaffa Street. The activist, a midget in his early twenties, who had been arrested in Hebron, suffered severe brain damage after being severely shaken during interrogation. Violent shaking had recently been adopted by the Israeli security services as a means of torturing Palestinian suspects. The interrogator seizes the suspect by the shoulders, and shakes the body so that the head rocks back and forth, causing the victim extreme pain. Israeli interrogators had found the method extremely effective, and it had the added advantage of leaving no tell-tale signs to bother judicial officials, except, perhaps, for some deep bruises on the shoulders. In the case of Harizat, however, the torture routine proved fatal because his under-developed body could not cope with the same level of violence that can be inflicted on a fully developed male. He was taken unconscious from the lock-up to Hadassah Hospital in Ein Karem, where he never regained consciousness.

The Israeli security services make no secret of the fact that they torture suspects, particularly Hamas militants, to extract crucial information that can save innocent Israeli lives. Officials in charge of the General Security Service (GSS), responsible for Israel's internal security, claim that numerous terrorist attacks have been foiled – including suicide bombings – and dozens of lives saved as a result of information extracted from Palestinian militants through torture. GSS officials also stress that usual psychological and physical methods of intimidation make little impression on the suspects. After GSS officers, in August 1995, cracked a 30-strong Hamas cell that was planning a series of suicide bomb attacks in Jerusalem and elsewhere that had been ordered by 'the engineer', the head of the GSS, in a rare newspaper interview, explained why it was necessary to use special interrogation methods when dealing with Palestinian extremists.

'You must understand,' he said, 'these Hamas people are prepared for interrogation, especially those who have been in Israeli jails.'[8]

The issue that raises most concern is that the use of torture is far more commonplace than the security forces are prepared to admit. The Landau Commission, which was set up in 1987 to investigate the legal and moral issues raised by torture in Israel, recommended that 'moderate physical pressure' could be applied against suspected terrorists in a 'ticking bomb situation' – the only occasion a Western-style democracy has sought to legitimise the use of torture. The definition of a 'ticking bomb situation' is when interrogators believe they have knowledge of an imminent attack, and are satisfied that the individual they are holding can provide vital information that can

8 Quoted in the *Jerusalem Post*, 24 August 1995.

prevent it. Opposition Israeli politicians and international human rights organisations like Amnesty International, however, claim the Israeli security services routinely torture Palestinian suspects, in breach of the Landau guidelines.

The GSS has had a special interrogation unit for many years at the Russian Compound, and many of the worst abuses are said to take place here, in the heart of Jerusalem. Severe sleep deprivation, severe beatings, forcing suspects to stand or sit in excruciatingly painful positions for long periods of time, stripping them naked and exposing them to the cold, are among some of the more familiar torture techniques that have been practised at the Russian Compound over the years. Most of the victims do not fit the 'ticking bomb' syndrome. They will be guilty of nothing more serious than throwing stones at Israeli policemen, or being members of the PLO. One of the more perverse aspects of this abuse is that it is carried out within ear-shot of the lively bistros and bars that surround the compound. While young Israelis are out savouring the delights of Jerusalem's night-life, less than one hundred metres away their Palestinian counterparts are being routinely assaulted and humiliated. Every day long queues of Palestinian families form outside the Russian Orthodox Holy Trinity Cathedral, opposite the main police station entrance, while they wait to discover the fate of relatives detained within the Compound.

The problem for civil rights activists has always been to accumulate sufficient evidence to force the Israeli authorities to react. While there is no shortage of Palestinians to provide graphic detail of their maltreatment, the evidence is rarely strong enough to disrupt 'a system protected by a conspiracy of silence', as one Israeli human rights activist has described it.[9] Even when Palestinians provide convincing testimony of their ordeals, the security services are able to hide behind the kind of lame excuses that might inspire Dario Fo to pen a sequel to his hit play *The Accidental Death of an Anarchist*. In Harizat's case, for example, one of the explanations advanced by

---

9 'We're not taling about a handful of sadists in the lower echelons. We're talking about a system protected by a conspiracy of silence': Tamar Gozansky, of the Democratic Front for Peace and Equality, speaking during a Knesset debate on torture, 16 June 1993.

security officials for his death was that he had suffered from an epileptic fit, and hit his head on the cell floor. While these interrogation methods are commonplace at Israeli military institutions in the West Bank and Gaza Strip, which is under military law, campaigners believe they have a better chance of challenging their application in Jerusalem, a city that is under the jurisdiction of Israeli sovereign law.

With Harizat's death, it seemed the campaigners at last had an irrefutable case that exposed the Israeli security forces' abuse of the Landau Commission's torture 'guidelines'. Their only problem was Harizat's family. While they fully supported attempts by both Israeli and Palestinian human rights activists to prove Harizat had been tortured to death, they raised strong objections when the Israeli attorney acting on the case insisted that an independent post-mortem be conducted. The family objected on the grounds that, if Harizat's organs were removed, this might jeopardise his chances of being accepted into paradise as a 'martyr'. They were finally persuaded to allow the autopsy to proceed by Bassem Eid, a Palestinian human rights activist. The examination was finally conducted by a Scottish pathologist, an expert in child abuse, who confirmed that Harizat's death had been caused by violent shaking. As a result of submissions made by the Association for Civil Rights in Israel to the attorney-general's office, new orders were issued to the GSS which stipulated that 'shaking' as a form of torture could only be used after permission has been granted by a government committee. As one Israeli commentator pointed out after the inquiry into the Hamas activist's death was complete, 'after Harizat's killing, no Israeli citizen can claim ignorance of what goes on in the GSS cells'.[10] Significantly, no disciplinary action was taken against the officers responsible for his death.

The argument used to persuade Harizat's relatives to allow the autopsy to be performed is similiar to the one concocted by radical Imams to reassure their suicidal candidates that blowing themselves up will not obstruct their ascent to heaven. The concept of *Jihad* is more complex than its customary Western definition of 'holy war'. A *Jihad* is essentially an act that is pleasing to God, whether it is maintaining the structure of al-Aqsa or liberating Jerusalem from the

10 Jon Simons, lecturer in political science at the Hebrew University, writing in the *Jerusalem Post*, 5 May 1995.

infidel Crusaders. A martyr, a *shaheed*, is someone who dies in the act of committing *Jihad*. Not all Islamic scholars agree that committing suicide, even for the cause of Palestinian liberation, is a *Jihad*. Ekrima Sabri, Jerusalem's Grand Mufti, for example, opposes the tactic of suicide bombs because it is against God's will. 'God created man to do his Will. A man cannot do things that are pleasing to God if he kills himself.' The radical Imams of Hamas disagree, and argue that it is a holy mission to rid the land of those, such as Jews, who do not observe the teachings of Islam.

When ordinary Muslim mortals die, relatives wash their bodies and wrap them in a white shroud before burial to prepare them for entry to heaven. But when a *shaheed* is killed, either on the field of battle or in an Israeli interrogation cell, the body is not touched before burial because the martyr is deemed to have been purified by death. Whether this means, as a result, that Muslim Heaven is filled with grisly ghouls wandering around covered in blood with various body parts missing is a matter of serious Islamic conjecture. Some Muslims argue it is not the body, but the soul, that enters paradise, while others disagree.

Islamic fundamentalist Imams argued that as Harizat was a martyr, his relatives did not need to worry about the state of his body. Whatever wounds he incurred as a consequence of his martyrdom, including the removal of his organs for forensic examination, they would be treated the same as if they had been incurred on the field of battle. The same arguments have been advanced by Hamas Imams to reassure potential suicide bombers that, even though they will be physically obliterated by the force of the blast, they will enter paradise in the same way as a soldier who has been badly mutilated on the field of battle. Some Israeli academics also appear to concur with Hamas's interpretation of the Koran. After the 1996 Jerusalem bus bombings, one Israeli scholar suggested wrapping the suicide bombers' remains in pig skins before burial to prevent them from being admitted into paradise.

A few days before he carried out his suicide mission, Majdi Abu Wardeh was smuggled into Jerusalem from an Arab village on the outskirts of the city, where the final preparations for the 'operation' were made. Other Hamas activists, using Israeli identity cards and driving cars with Israeli licence plates, helped Majdi negotiate the Israeli army check-points. One of those who helped Majdi plan the operation had worked as an Egged bus driver, and was able to provide valuable advice on how to conduct the bombing. The explosives had already been smuggled into the city from Gaza, and were stored in safe houses and mosques throughout the city. Majdi spent the final days of his life at a Hamas 'safe house' in the city, waiting for the final order to carry out the attack.

On the morning of the operation Majdi would have awoken early and shaved and bathed with meticulous care, like any groom preparing for his wedding day. Majdi would have visited a mosque to offer a *shahadeh* (I devote myself to God) prayer. After all the military and Koranic training had been completed, the final stage in the preparation ritual was to dress in as inconspicuous a manner as possible. In a city like Jerusalem, where Jews and Arabs are required to co-exist on a daily basis, it is relatively simple for a young Palestinian to dress, and behave, like an Israeli. Sometimes they will dye their hair with a fashionable tint, or wear an earring. In one celebrated case in October 1994, a group of Hamas terrorists dressed as ultra-Orthodox Jews, complete with wide-brimmed black hats and long black robes, to abduct Nahshon Wachsman, a young soldier from the north Jerusalem suburb of Ramot.[11] Living in such close proximity to Israelis, Hamas terrorists have no difficulty appearing like their intended victims.

At the appointed time Majdi was driven by another Hamas activist to the centre of Jerusalem, and dropped off at the bus stop outside City Hall, at the southern end of Jaffa Street, and close to the old Green Line that divided the city pre-1967. At shortly before 7 A.M. Majdi, wearing an Israeli army uniform and carrying the bomb in a duffel-bag slung across his shoulders, boarded the number 18 bus. In his hand he carried the detonator, which was connected to the bomb by a wire running up the sleeve of his jacket. According to the few survivors who saw Majdi in the minutes before the bomb went off, he

11 Wachsman's kidnappers demanded the release of hundreds of Palestinian prisoners and Sheikh Ahmed Yassin, Hamas's spiritual leader. Wachsman, an Israeli soldier and three Hamas terrorists died when Israeli soldiers stormed the kidnappers' hide-out on the outskirts of Jerusalem.

looked like any off-duty soldier making his way back to base after weekend leave. There was nothing about him that made anyone suspicous. Displaying remarkable calm for someone whose life was about to end, Majdi travelled on the bus for more than five minutes as it made its way along the length of Jaffa Street, a distance of just under a mile. Then, as the vehicle approached the central bus station at the northern end of the street, Majdi pressed the detonator button and committed his soul to Allah.

# 13

# COLLABORATORS

*'And beside all this, between us and you there is a great gulf fixed'*

Luke 16: 26

It seems unlikely, but it happens. It happens on a number of levels and in a bewildering variety of ways. Arabs and Jews working together, co-existing with each other. Forget the hatred, the violence, the perennial clash of culture and identity. The mundane business of everyday life compels Israelis and Palestinians to co-operate civilly, sometimes to their mutual advantage. Whether or not they like each other is immaterial although, inevitably, personal relationships – good and bad – develop with familiarity. It might be Palestinian construction workers building new Jewish neighbourhoods, or Arab and Jewish peace negotiators seeking to resolve their century-old conflict. Whatever the reason, irrespective of the activity, any act which brings Arabs and Israelis together serves to demonstrate the extent to which Jerusalem is an unfathomable mass of contradictions. Here, in a city where divisions are set in stone, and bitter passions collide with tiresome regularity, these polarised communities, in spite of everything, somehow find a way to collaborate.

One of the more visible manifestations of this unlikely arrangement can be found each working day morning on Route One, the main road artery connecting the city with the northern suburbs and Ramallah. From dawn onwards scores of Palestinian labourers, *keffiyehs* wrapped around their heads, wait patiently by the roadside, close to Damascus Gate, offering themselves for employment by Israeli contractors. Only about one half of them will find work; the others will be left standing forlornly by the roadside, wondering how they are going to feed their families. For Jews the Palestinians represent a ready pool of cheap labour; for the Arabs, most of whom come from poor rural areas, it is their only chance of work.

This dismal daily ritual defines a characteristic that permeates Jerusalem's entire social fabric; the Arab labourers soliciting for work merely occupy the bottom rung of the employment chain. Drive into any garage in the city, either east or west, and an Arab will tend to the car. Call out an electrician, a plumber, a telephone engineer, and the manual work will be done by Arabs while an Israeli supervises the operation. Eat at any Israeli restaurant and, while the service is provided by pretty young female students from the Hebrew University (Arabs, as well as Jews), the cooking and washing up will be carried out by Arab men. One Jewish restaurateur, who runs an Italian establishment, says he actually prefers to have Arabs rather than Jews working in the kitchen because they are better cooks.

'Palestinians come from large families and everyone is taught from an early age how to cook,' he explains. 'So an Arab man knows his way around the kitchen better than a Jew. My main problem is to try to persuade them not to mess with the menus. Italian cooking is very simple, but Arabs like to think they can improve on it all the time.'

A restaurant relationship that I have never fully understood, although it has been one of compelling interest over the years, concerns Katy, an Israeli of Moroccan extraction, and Umran, her (generally speaking) loyal Palestinian chef. Katy's, her restaurant, was one of the first places I visited when I first came to Jerusalem in the mid-1980s, mainly because it opened on Friday night when everything else was closed. Katy, a warm-hearted if over-emotional woman, behaves as though each day is either the happiest of her life, or the most miserable. An attractive personality nonetheless, who fiercely resists the advance of middle-age, she provides her customers with the most intimate details of her private life. Over the years, while tucking into the pepper steaks or duck *à l'orange*, I have heard about various aspects of her love life, her husbands, her lovers and other details too intimate to recount.

If her customers sometimes find her behaviour rather eccentric, they should spare a thought for Umran. A thin, diminutive man who lives on the Mount of Olives with his large family, Umran can be found leaning on the wall outside the kitchen, smoking a cigarette with the philosophical air of a man who is determined to remain calm, no matter how great the provocation. Depending on Katy's mood, she will summon Umran over to a table to introduce the diners to her 'star chef'. On other occasions when she spies Umran taking one of his 'cigarette breaks', she will bawl him out in public for being the worst cook in the Middle East, and accuse him of seeking to destroy her business by preparing uninspiring food. There have been many occasions when Katy and Umran have retired to the kitchen where, despite Umran's efforts to maintain a calm exterior, angry voices have been raised, accompanied by the unmistakable sounds of crockery being broken and pots being thrown. On other occasions there has been no sign of Umran. Inquiries as to his where-abouts are met with expletive-coloured abuse.

'Don't ask me about that lazy, good-for-nothing Arab,' Katy will reply. 'I don't care if he rots in hell. The bastard. I give him everything and then he leaves me.'

The nature of the particular dispute that has caused the break in relations is never explained. On the less serious occasions Umran simply decamps to the Mount of Olives and stays with his family until tempers cool; Katy makes do by getting friends to help out in the kitchen. When the break is of more terminal nature, Umran will find himself a job elsewhere and Katy will hire a new cook. There have been times when the split has lasted months, with neither of them prepared to talk to each other.

'Katy, she's just too impossible, she's too much,' I remember Umran telling me on one of these occasions. 'I do not need to work in that madhouse. I am a good cook. I can work anywhere.'

Katy was equally intransigent. She would make an enormous pro-duction of introducing her new chef – another Palestinian – and telling everyone how much better the food was now that Umran was gone.

Eventually there would be a reconciliation. The new chef would find Katy impossible to work with, and walk out. Umran would find that, even though he might have found himself a better job at one of the big hotels, life was not quite the same without the more familiar, and personal, atmosphere at Katy's. Umran would reappear, working in the kitchen as though nothing had happened, and Katy would be back to her effusive self. Like the archetypal couple stuck in a bad relationship, they found it impossible to be with each other, and impossible to be apart.

After restaurants and hotels, the main source of employment for Arabs is construction. For the past fifty years, and especially since 1967, Jerusalem has resembled an enormous building site. Every day the roads are clogged with cement-mixers, dumper trucks and JCBs. The city reverberates from massive pile-drivers drilling through the ancient rock to lay the foundations for new developments. The days of Jewish labour, the cherished ideal of Zionist pioneers, are long gone. Israelis have a monopoly over the white-collar jobs – planners, architects, engineers, lawyers, developers – while the more menial tasks are left to the Palestinians. Given the political sensitivity that surrounds any new building project in the city – particularly in East Jerusalem – it is ironic that most of new Israeli Jerusalem has been built by Arabs. Although Palestinian leaders have, on occasion, tried to persuade their fellow countrymen not to assist the Israeli settlement of the city, most working-class Palestinians have little alternative. The Israelis pull all the economic strings, and without their patronage, many Palestinian families would be reduced to desperate straits.

This symbiosis is not all in Israel's favour. There are several Palestinian families that have made considerable fortunes through lucrative sub-contracting deals with Israeli developers. Some senior members of Yasser Arafat's Palestinian Authority who, officially at least, are vehemently opposed to further Israeli expansion in Jerusalem, have made their fortunes constructing Israeli homes. At the other end of the scale it often seems as though, while Palestinians are prepared to work for Israelis, they do their job as badly as possible, almost as a way of getting their revenge on the Jewish hegemony over the city. Certainly the quality of workmanship, even at Jerusalem's more prestigious developments, falls well below acceptable standards of competence. Roofs leak, walls crack, drains block, electrical sockets fall from walls, exposing live wires. The difficulty is always trying to decide whether this incompetence is the work of Palestinian workmen deceiving their Israeli employers, or the Israeli contractors simply trying to short-change the poor old customer. Jerusalem being the way it is, the possibility cannot be ruled out that it is a combination of the two.

On a more personal level the working relationships between Jews and Arabs can result in some unlikely building ventures. It is traditional for religious families during the Jewish festival of Succoth to build a succa, a home-made shelter. The walls are made from old pieces of timber, and the roof consists of palm branches. The succa is built to represent the makeshift dwellings the Jews built for themselves in the desert during their return from Egypt, and Jewish families commemorate this important aspect of their religious heritage by spending the night in a succa. As the festival falls in early autumn, when the nights in Jerusalem are still balmy, the ritual is popular, particularly among children. One year a Jewish acquaintance, an accountant by profession, who, by his own admission, is no handyman, wanted to build a succa for his family, but was unsure how to complete the task. So he contacted a local Palestinian handyman, whom he usually employed for odd-jobs around the house, and asked him to build the family a succa. The Palestinian was happy to oblige and, thanks to his efforts, the family spent a pleasant night sleeping beneath Jerusalem's star-covered sky.

There is a level of economic interdependence between Israelis and Palestinians which both groups are reluctant to acknowledge. The extent to which Israelis and Palestinians rely on each other in the workplace is best illustrated when the Israeli government imposes one of its punitive closures: when the army sets up roadblocks around the city to restrict Palestinian access, preventing Palestinians entering Israel to work. The measures are usually applied in the wake of a terrorist incident, such as a suicide bomb attack. The closure is imposed both for reasons of security and to punish the Palestinian population for the attack, on the grounds that the terrorists must have been provided with shelter and support by the Palestinian community. These closures can last for months, as did the one imposed after the 1996 Jerusalem bus bombings. The measures are aimed primarily at Palestinians, although they can also severely affect Israeli businesses, particularly in Jerusalem where co-employment is a fact of life. Hotels and restaurants were particularly badly hit by the closure imposed after the 1996 suicide bomb attacks; in one large hotel two-thirds of the entire staff – all Palestinians – were unable to report to work for weeks, and the managers had to help out making the beds and cleaning the bathrooms.

On occasions like this foreign workers have been encouraged to come to Israel to replenish the depleted stocks of menial labourers created by the closures. Many of Jerusalem's cheaper hotels are filled with Romanians who have been brought in to work on the building sites; Filipinos are hired to carry out domestic chores, such as cleaning and cooking. Some Israeli politicians have suggested that the way forward might be to enforce a complete separation of the Jewish and Arab communities and, for a period in the mid-1990s, Israelis were enthusiastic about their new foreign imports. But the novelty soon wore thin. While the replacements for the Palestinians proved adequate in the workplace, Israeli bosses found that they could not develop the same personal relationships that they enjoyed with the Arabs. As one Israeli contractor, who normally employs a dozen Arab labourers, explained: 'I feel more at home working with Palestinians. I speak their language and I understand their culture. I like the Romanians, but they do not come from here. I don't feel they understand the way we live.' The Israeli military, which is responsible for enforcing the closures, also accepts that the measures can be counterproductive.

'We don't need foreign workers,' is the view held by Major-General Oren Shahor, one of Israel's main negotiators with the Palestinians and who, for many years, has been the government's 'co-ordinator of activities in the territories'.

'We have to allow more and more Palestinians to become involved in the [Israeli] economy. This also protects our security by giving them something to lose. There is a balance. When we make decisions to ease the closure we are taking security risks.'

When the closures are not in force, it is estimated there are thousands of Palestinians working illegally in Jerusalem, without proper permits. It would be impossible for them to escape the attention of the Jerusalem Police Department, which is responsible for dealing with illegal workers, without the assistance of their Jewish employers. So long as the employers and employees stick together, it is difficult for the police to find Palestinians working in the city illegally. It is only when the relationship breaks down, or when something untoward occurs, that the police can intervene.

The difficulty police encounter in their attempts to unravel these perplexing working relationships was illustrated by the case of a young Palestinian who, in February 1997, drove a car into a crowd of pedestrians on King George Street in West Jerusalem, killing one Israeli and injuring six others. The immediate reaction of the crowd of Israeli passers-by was that the Palestinian was carrying out a suicide attack and, though injured himself in the crash, he was lucky that the enraged crowd were unable to vent their anger on him. The police arrived and began to investigate the incident. They discovered the car belonged to a Jewish tradesman who worked in the nearby market. They duly interviewed the tradesman, who told them the Arab had stolen his car. The Israeli policemen might have been forgiven for accepting this explanation at face value, and attributing the crime to the city's more familiar excuse of inter-communal rivalry. But the police were not satisfied with the tradesman's explanation, and pursued their inquiries for another week, eventually exposing an entirely different explanation.

The Palestinian had been employed by the tradesman – illegally – as a labourer. The tradesman's car was illegally parked, and seeing a traffic warden approach, he gave the young Arab his car keys, asking him to move it. The Arab was willing to oblige, but omitted to mention he could not drive. He managed to start the car and drove it away, but when he reached the King George intersection, he mistook the accelerator for the brake, and crashed, with fatal consequences. The Jewish tradesman had lied about his involvement to conceal the fact he was employing the Arab illegally. The Arab was charged with illegal driving, and the Jew was charged with illegal employment.

The lot of a policeman in Jerusalem is not one to envy. When they are not dealing with rampaging ultra-Orthodox protesters trying to close one of the city's main thoroughfares, they are required to control rioting Palestinians in the Old City. Left-wingers, right-wingers, ethnic minorities, nationalists and religious fanatics. Jerusalem is a riot of different interest groups each competing, sometimes violently, for their voices to be heard, and it is the duty of the police to maintain some semblance of law and order. Security, rather than crime, is the main police preoccupation in Jerusalem. Bomb alerts, terror attacks, security clampdowns and protecting visiting dignitaries takes up far more police time than investigating criminal activities such as burglaries, thefts and traffic violations.[1] For the funeral of Yitzhak Rabin, when most of the world's leading statesmen flew to Jerusalem, nearly half the nation's 22,000-strong police force was on duty on the city streets. Fortunately those of a criminal disposition did not think it appropriate to take advantage of this opportunity to cash in on the absence of available law enforcement officers.

Crime, surprisingly, is not a major issue in modern Jerusalem. While it might be expected that the world's holiest city should be a place of peace, its average of five criminal murders a year seems rather modest considering that the city bristles with the ever-present threat of violent conflict. Murders, however, should not be confused with the violent deaths arising from confrontations between Jews and Arabs. In an average year there are about sixty people killed as a result of inter-communal violence, although this fluctuates depending on the general security situation.[2] For a city of Jerusalem's modest size, the level of violent deaths is as high as parts of New York, and they take place in a smaller geographical area. After offences relating to the 'conflict' are removed from the equation, Jerusalem is a relatively crime-free city. Unlike a large metropolis like Tel Aviv, the crime in Jerusalem is of a relatively minor nature. There are no Russian mafia gangs, no massive white-collar fraud, and street violence is rare, not the norm. The most serious type of crime committed in Jerusalem is car theft, and the police claim to have a high clear-up rate. In the fight against crime, the difficulty facing the Jerusalem police force is to determine, when an offence is committed, whether

1 There are on average two official visits by VIPs each week to Jerusalem.
2 Estimates provided by Jerusalem District Police, March 1997.

the motives are purely criminal, or due to what the detectives describe as 'nationalist'.

Take the case of the Jewish contractor who was stabbed to death in his apartment at Bayit Vegan, an Israeli neighbourhood in West Jerusalem, in early 1997. That morning the contractor had driven to Route One to hire a Palestinian labourer for the day because the Palestinian who normally worked for him was off sick. Shortly after the stabbing the contractor's neighbours said they saw a 'Palestinian-looking' man run from the apartment. He jumped into a taxi and sped off. While most Israelis immediately assumed the Palestinian had killed the Israeli for nationalist reasons, the police insisted on keeping an open mind. Their investigations concentrated on questions such as whether the two men knew each other previously, and whether the man seen running from the apartment was in fact a Palestinian, or was merely *dressed* as an Arab. The suspect was never caught and the files on the murder remain open.

In the early 1990s there was a spate of incidents in East Jerusalem where several Arab women, on separate occasions, attempted to stab Israeli Border Guards on duty in Saladin Street. The Border Police are well-protected, and wear protective vests when on patrol in Arab neighbourhoods. None of the policemen suffered serious injury, and the investigating officers were naturally inclined to attribute the attacks to nationalist motives. But, as with the case of the Arab driving the run-away car, the police opted to ignore the obvious assumptions, and to conduct a proper investigation. They later discovered that in all the cases the motive was not primarily that the women wanted to stab an Israeli policeman, but that they wanted to escape from their families. In one case the family of one of the women was refusing to allow her to marry her intended; the only way she could think to escape the pressure was to get locked up in an Israeli jail where they would not be able to touch her. So far as crime in Jerusalem is concerned, nothing should be taken for granted.

The *intifada*, although it mainly concerned the West Bank and Gaza, was undoubtedly a watershed in the intricate relationship between the city's Arab and Jewish communities. Before the *intifada*, Israeli politicians like Teddy Kollek were still able to talk in terms of Arab and Jewish co-existence within the city boundaries, even if the Israeli attitude towards the Palestinians bordered on the negligent. Indeed, even after the *intifada* erupted in Gaza in early December 1987, liberal Israelis continued to believe that Jerusalem would remain immune from the violence by virtue of the different and special relations that had developed since the city was placed entirely under Israeli control in 1967. That optimism was rudely shattered in late December when rioting erupted in Arab neighbourhoods throughout the city.

At the time I was living in Abu Tor, in the Israeli part of a mixed residential neighbourhood on the old Green Line. There was an Arab community only a few hundred metres away and, until the *intifada*, relations between the two communities were cordial; Jews would use the local Arab stores to shop, and the Arabs would work for the Jews as cleaners and general help. This pattern was repeated in many areas of the city, enabling one to grasp a sense of how Jerusalem must have worked in the 1930s when there was a degree of tolerance between Jews and Arabs that has rarely manifested itself since. In Abu Tor this modest attempt at co-existence vanished overnight when the Jewish residents awoke to find several of their cars had been torched during the night. Barricades of old oil drums and burning tyres had been set up at the dividing line between the two communities, and even though some of my neighbours, those of a more forgiving disposition, attempted to persuade the Palestinians that it was still possible to live in peace, the damage had been done, and the communities' polarisation confirmed. The same communal breakdown occurred throughout the city, and has remained so ever since. Israelis no longer shop in East Jerusalem or the Old City, and contact between Jews and Arabs is kept to a minimum. Trying to persuade an Israeli taxi-driver, even one who lives in Jerusalem, to go to the 'east side' is like asking them to put their hand in a burning furnace. The *intifada* succeeded in making Jerusalem as divided as when the Israelis conquered the city in 1967.

If the *intifada* destroyed the aspirations of liberal Israelis to make the city a model of Arab–Israeli co-existence, it does not seem to have affected the sturdier roots or Arab–Israeli criminal collaboration. On one level the violence of the *intifada* provided a cloak for both Palestinians and Israelis to conceal criminal intent. In particular it was used as a cover for a number or car insurance scams. Israelis whose cars needed repairing would report to the police that the damage had been caused by Palestinians. Cracked windshields, damage to the body-work and anything that looked as though it might remotely have been caused by stone-throwing Palestinians was claimed against the insurance policy. Palestinians were no different. If their cars needed repairing, they would claim the damage had been caused by a rival Palestinian faction that wanted to teach them a lesson.

Apart from blaming each other for their misfortunes, Jewish and Palestinian criminals have proved more than adept at joining forces to commit crime. Cars have proved a particular speciality, particularly since the Palestinian Authority took control of the autonomous areas of the West Bank. Gangs of Israeli thieves steal the cars in Jerusalem and then pass them over to Palestinian criminals who either dismantle them, to sell the spare parts, or relicense them for sale among the Palestinian community. Many of the top-of-the-range models driven by members of the Palestinian Authority once had Israeli owners, and Israelis have come to assume that Gaza is the final resting place for their stolen vehicles.

The thieves can also display remarkable imagination when choosing their contraband. When a television studio camera, the size of a large sofa, disappeared from the Jerusalem headquarters of Israel Television, it was widely rumoured that it had reappeared in the studios of the Palestinian Broadcasting Station in Gaza. Illegal drugs are another lucrative area of Arab–Israeli co-operation. While drug-taking is mostly alien to Palestinian culture, it is endemic within Israel. Most of the drugs – soft and hard – are smuggled into the country from neighbouring Arab states by the Palestinians who then sell them to the Israelis. It is a neat arrangement; the Palestinians supply, the Israelis deal and consume.

One of the more unlikely criminal conspiracies was uncovered in the spring of 1995, when a team of Jerusalem detectives found wealthy ultra-Orthodox Jews collaborating with Palestinian money-changers on a million-dollar gold-smuggling scam. The two groups in the city which most resent paying taxes to the Israeli authorities are the *haredim* and Palestinians, neither of whom have much regard for Israeli claims to sovereignty. While most *haredi* families are impoverished, there are nevertheless a number of wealthy individuals, with a wide-ranging network of international contacts, who need to move large sums of money in and out of the country. To avoid the attentions of Israeli tax officials, *haredi* businessmen hit on the idea of channelling their funds through a family of Palestinian money-changers in Saladin Street. With their wide-ranging connections throughout the wider Arab world, Palestinian businessmen are expert at smuggling large quantities of gold and foreign currency in and out of the country. In return for a handsome commission, they were more than happy to make their services available to their ultra-Orthodox neighbours.

After a lengthy surveillance operation the police swooped. In a series of well co-ordinated dawn raids in Mea Shearim, the main ultra-Orthodox neighbourhood, and the suburbs of Shuafat and Beit Hanina, wealthy, middle-class Palestinian neighbourhoods, nearly thirty ultra-Orthodox businessmen and Palestinian money-changers found themselves detained at the Russian Compound 'helping the police with their inquiries'. At times like this it might be expected that Jews and Arabs would attempt to blame each other. Not so. Despite the efforts of the investigating officers to extract confessions, none of those arrested said a word, except to ask to see their lawyers. After being held for ten days, both Jews and Arabs were released and the charges against them quietly dropped for lack of evidence. The police had hoped that one or other of the group of suspects would provide incriminating evidence against their erstwhile accomplices, enabling the authorities to mount a successful prosecution. But neither Jews nor Arabs would oblige.

Prostitution is another area where Palestinians and ultra-Orthodox Jews share a similar interest. The world's oldest profession has changed considerably since the time when prostitution in Jerusalem was considered a religious ritual, preferably performed within the confines of a pagan temple. Of necessity prostitutes need to be discreet as they go about their business in the Holy City, although the large influx of Russian Jews in the early 1990s appears to have coincided with the ladies of the night taking a more brazen approach, with street-walkers becoming a familiar sight in areas like Jaffa Street and Agron Street. When the police conduct one of their periodic crack-downs (most of the women arrested turn out to be illegal immigrants, and are deported), the women relocate to the wasteland off the Bethlehem Road, and return to the city centre when the heat is off.

As two of Jerusalem's most sexually repressed communities, ultra-Orthodox Jews and Palestinians ensure the whores of Jerusalem are never short of work. Sex before marriage is deeply frowned upon among the cultures of both religious Jews and Palestinians, and some of them seek to relieve their frustrations elsewhere. Religious Jews, however, are hesitant about availing themselves of street-walkers in Jerusalem because they fear it is doubly offensive to God to commit the sin of fornication in such close proximity to His divine presence at the Holy of Holies. Those who have the time and money therefore prefer to travel to Tel Aviv, where the Lord is likely to be less censorious, and where there is less chance of being caught. The Palestinians are also said to have their own peccadilloes. One of the more popular requests Arab men ask of the prostitutes is that they first dress in Israeli army or police uniforms. Afterwards the Palestinians can boast, in the crudest manner imaginable, that they have got their revenge on the Jews. It has become one of the city's modern legends that the *intifada* was caused by Israeli pimps bringing prostitutes infected with venereal disease to East Jerusalem, who deliberately infected their Palestinian clients.

Different Arab–Israeli physical needs are catered for by the city's medical staff. The casualty ward at Hadassah Hospital, the main Israeli emergency facility which is located on the outskirts of the old Arab village of Ein Karem, reflects the ebb and flow of the city's political, religious and social confusion. Many Palestinian medical students choose to do their training at Hadassah because of the breadth of experience it offers, although wounded Israeli soldiers often request that they are treated by Israeli doctors, not Palestinians. After a major terrorist incident the perpetrators, if they survive, can end up being cared for in adjoining beds to the victims. In one incident when a Palestinian went berserk on a bus in Jerusalem and stabbed a number of Israelis, the knifeman, who was shot and overpowered, and his victims were taken to the same emergency ward for treatment. Palestinians who have suffered severe injuries while being 'interrogated' by Israeli officers are sent to Hadassah to be examined. If the doctors do not consider the injuries life-threatening, the suspects are returned to the Russian Compound for further questioning.

Israeli doctors at Hadassah saved the life of Hassan Salame, the Hamas terrorist who masterminded the 1996 Jerusalem bus bombings, after he was badly wounded during a shoot-out with Israeli soldiers in Hebron. Once he recovered he was handed back to the Israeli security services for interrogation.

Jews are rarely, if ever, treated at Arab hospitals such as Makassed, on the Mount of Olives, while Palestinians freely make use of the best medical services the Israelis can provide. One of the benefits of being under Israeli 'occupation' is that Palestinian residents of Jerusalem are treated as Israeli citizens, and qualify for the state's medical care. Nor are Palestinians shy about making use of the facility. The out-patients' department at most Israeli hospitals in Jerusalem will have as many Arabs as Jews waiting in line, and the staff will treat all of them on merit, not race. A Palestinian acquaintance who needed a heart-bypass operation insisted that the operation was conducted at a Jewish hospital in the centre of the city that had a heart specialist unit. 'The Israelis have brought us some of the world's finest heart doctors,' he said. 'It would be foolish not to make use of them.'

The Israeli authorities insist that their medical staff tend all patients according to the standards of the Hippocratic oath, in particular that everyone be treated irrespective of race or creed. Even so, Israeli doctors and nurses are entitled to their own, personal opinions, which suggests that, while the system is admirable in principle, in practice it cannot overcome the deep inter-communal bitterness and mistrust that more commonly defines the city's relations. An Israeli ward sister who has worked at Hadassah's emergency unit for many years, dealing with everything from the worst car accidents to terror attacks, once explained to me how she made sure that Jews and Arabs received the same treatment, but that this had not changed her own attitude towards Palestinians. She told how her car had been stoned by Palestinian youths while she was driving to a Bar Mitzva at an Israeli settlement in the West Bank. (This was during the *intifada*, and it was what any Israeli might have expected as Palestinians do not take kindly to Jews conducting social events on occupied territory.) When she returned to Hadassah later that day she had to treat three Palestinian protesters who had been injured during clashes with the Israeli army.

'Of course I didn't feel like treating them,' she says. 'They stone my car and then I have to give them treatment. And here they get the best treatment possible, make no mistake. They wouldn't be treated like this anywhere else in the Arab world. But to me the Palestinians are scum. It is Israel's tragedy that we have to live with people like this. You just can't trust them. One minute they are all smiles, the next they are sticking a knife in your back.'

Nor does there seem much hope that future generations of Arabs and Jews can be persuaded to hold each other in higher esteem. At the city's schools and universities, where the people who will guide Jerusalem's destiny for the next century are being educated, contact between Israelis and Palestinians is kept to a bare minimum. There are various projects outside the city that try to educate the respective communities in the art of peaceful co-existence, but in Jerusalem itself contacts are mainly confined to the workplace and officialdom. In education Israeli officials have overall control of the city's curricula; Israeli schools follow the national curriculum while most Arab schools are still run according to the Jordanian system.[3] Young Palestinians are taught Hebrew, and Israelis Arabic, but that is about as far as the cultural interaction goes. Arab students have little contact with Israeli schools, and vice versa. The situation is slightly better at university level where a small proportion of Palestinians – mainly those with Israeli passports – take courses at the Hebrew University, although it is unknown for Israelis to attend exclusively Arab universities such as Bir Zeit, near Ramallah. But even when the two groups are obliged to share the same campus, there is little genuine inter-reaction. Palestinian students have separate living quarters to the Israelis, and while the students observe conversational pleasantries, few, if any, genuine friendships develop.

Love affairs between Jews and Arabs in Jerusalem are also extremely rare and, when they do occur, they are highly problematic. There are few Israeli or Palestinian families that would look favourably on their sons and daughters dating non-Jews or non-Arabs, and so any relationship is considered illicit and must remain secret. Though not impossible, it would also be extremely difficult for an Arab and Jew to share the same social activities. Few Israelis

3 Private schools, which are mainly run by religious institutions, are not controlled by the Education Ministry, and choose their own curricula.

would feel happy socialising with Palestinians, the majority of whose conversation is dedicated to expounding on the continuing horrors of Israeli occupation, and Palestinians would find it equally difficult to socialise with Israelis who are mainly indifferent to the native Arab culture. At the discotheque at the Hyatt Hotel, which is popular with young Israelis and Palestinians, Arabs and Jews dance in their own little enclaves, as though an invisible line of segregation separates them. There are occasions, however, when genuine romance is able to overcome these formidable social and cultural obstacles, and sometimes it can lead to wedlock. But few mixed couples survive the tension and torment of modern Jerusalem. Either the relationship breaks under the strain, or the couple move out of the city – many go abroad – to enable them to live something approaching a normal life.

And yet, however much Israelis and Palestinians try to maintain their separate identities, a level of inter-dependence exists in Jerusalem which, though both would find it hard to admit, binds them, often subconsciously, together. In Jaffa Street Jewish restaurants compete with each other to sell the 'best falafel in the Middle East', a dish that is Palestinian in origin. But houmous – another dish that derives from the humble chick pea – bought from an Arab shop in East Jerusalem is more than likely to bear a 'made in Israel' label. Palestinian traders rely heavily on Israeli manufacturers. During the Jewish festival of Passover when, by rabbinical decree, anything containing yeast – bread and beer, for example – is banned from sale at Israeli shops and supermarkets, it is difficult to buy an ordinary loaf of bread from an Arab shop because all the Israeli bakeries are closed. When a Palestinian entrepreneur, in 1995, first started selling Taybeh, the first beer manufactured by Palestinians, he sought and received a kosher certificate so that it could be sold in West as well as East Jerusalem.[4]

Israeli night-clubs advertise traditional 'folklore' dances which are more Arabic than Jewish. Israelis swear in Arabic because Eliezer Ben-Yehudah, the Russian-born founder of modern Hebrew, omitted

4 The kosher certificate was provided by a rabbi living at the same Israeli settlement as Yehudah Etzion, the Jewish zealot who plans to blow up the Dome of the Rock.

to taint his new language with earthy vulgarisms. An Israeli company manufactures a condom called 'Sheikh' which is marketed, one assumes, on the basis that Jewish purchasers will instantly acquire the virility of an Arab potentate. During the Jewish spring festival of Purim, which celebrates the death of a wicked Persian vizier who, 1,500 years ago, planned to kill his Jewish subjects, Israeli school-children like to dress up as Arabs. The practice has been discouraged since a real-life Arab one year ran amok and stabbed several Israelis who at first mistook the attack for a Purim prank. Younger Pale-stinians also draw on various aspects of Israeli youth culture. Certain Israeli pop music radio stations have as many Arab listeners as Jews, and many Israeli fashions are also eagerly adopted by Arab youth, even though they would be loath to admit it.

The political arena, surprisingly, is one of the few areas where Palestinians and Israelis, in certain circumstances, have a more devel-oped, and even sympathetic, attitude towards each other's point of view. In the immediate aftermath of the Oslo Accords a number of joint Israeli–Palestinian projects were initiated in an attempt to find common ground which might facilitate an agreement over Jerusalem's future. On a more official level this meant that Palestinian negotiators like Saeb Erekat became familiar figures around the lobbies of some of the city's more prestigious hotels, while the nuts-and-bolts negoti-ations were carried out at more low-key venues. All kinds of models for Jerusalem's political future were explored, and teams of researchers visited cities like Belfast and Brussels, which have their own religious and racial problems, to see if they might have any rel-evance to Jerusalem's future political set-up. Friendships, of a sort, developed between some Israelis and Palestinians, although few of them would care to acknowledge it openly. The election of the Netanyahu government, however, ended any immediate hope that genuine progress might be made.

Political issues can provide some unlikely bedfellows. After the McDonald's chain opened its restaurant in Jerusalem without a kosher certificate, Nawaf Massalha, a Muslim member of Israel's Labour party, joined forces with a number of Israeli politicians to support a Knesset initiative calling for the branch to be made kosher. Like many religious Jews, Massalha was offended that McDonald's was selling products containing pork. Other Israeli–Arab political initiatives tend to concern left-wing Israelis who support the peace process working alongside moderate Palestinians. One of the more high-profile initiatives was to organise a joint protest against the Rabin government's decision to close off Jerusalem from the rest of the West Bank by establishing a network of army checkpoints around the city. The protest was scheduled for one morning in March during the period when the clocks change to summer time. Because of the Palestinians' insistence on conducting their affairs differently to Israel, the Palestinian Authority had decided that Palestinian clocks should change a week later than those in Israel. This fact was overlooked by organisers of the peace march, however, so that when, at the pre-arranged time, the group of well-meaning Israelis arrived at the designated checkpoint, their Palestinian counterparts were still in bed asleep.

Journalists working for the Hebrew and Arabic press often join forces to get stories published. Bassem Eid, who claims to be the first West Bank Palestinian to work for an Israeli newspaper, recalls how, during the *intifada*, he used his Israeli contacts to get stories published on human rights that Israel's military censor had banned from publication in the Arabic press. Eid had worked for *Kol Ha'ir* (City Voice), a left-wing weekly newspaper published in Jerusalem. Even though he had left the newspaper, and was working for an Israeli human rights organisation, Eid used his contacts at *Kol Ha'ir* to have a story published that the Israeli censor would not allow to be published in Jerusalem's Arabic daily, *An Nahar* (The Day). The Israeli military authorities find it more difficult to withstand pressure from the Israeli media than they do Palestinians, and the objections put to *An Nahar* were not accepted by *Kol Ha'ir*. Eid's story ran in full on how Israeli troops were abusing international human rights conventions in their treatment of Palestinian demonstrators. The next day *An Nahar* reported what had appeared in *Kol Ha'ir*. There was nothing the Israeli censor could do to stop publication, and Eid succeeded in getting his story published for Palestinian readers. The same kind of co-operation exists in the televisual media. The Palestinian who shot the video showing a group of Border Police beating up a group of Palestinian workers at the A-Ram checkpoint on the outskirts of Jerusalem in early 1997 initially sold the film to an Israeli television company, because he felt it would have greater impact.

In the field of human rights, co-operation between Palestinians and Israelis is essential, but not always easy to achieve. After working for several years as a journalist covering the Arab–Israeli conflict in the Occupied Territories, Bassem Eid in 1989 became a field worker for B'Tselem,[5] a Jerusalem-based human rights organisation set up by left-wing Israeli politicians to monitor human rights abuses by the Israeli security services during the *intifada*. A neat, energetic man with close-cropped dark hair and gold-rimmed glasses, Eid was born in Jerusalem in 1958, where his parents lived in the Old City after being made refugees during the 1948 war. Fluent in both Hebrew and Arabic, Eid was personally invited by Israeli politicians such as Yossi Sarid to be the organisation's main field worker in the West Bank. That the Israelis held him in high esteem, and trusted him to carry out such a sensitive task, inevitably raised questions among the Palestinian victims the organisation sought to help.

'People were very suspicious,' he recalls. 'We were working in a very difficult political situation, not a humanitarian situation. The families of Palestinians who were killed in the *intifada* could not understand what I was trying to do. They would say, "The Israelis have killed our child and now they want to protect us?" It didn't make any sense to them. But eventually we were able to establish trust.'

Ironically the biggest difficulty Eid has faced in his human rights activities has come from the Palestinian security forces, not the Israelis. Throughout the *intifada* B'Tselem published numerous reports detailing Israeli human rights abuses, with Eid doing most of the field-work. The Israeli authorities did not attempt, nor dare, to curtail Eid's activities. The trouble began for Eid after the organisation, in the autumn of 1995, published a report detailing the human rights abuses committed by Palestinian leader Yasser Arafat's Preventive Security Force, which had been given responsibility for controlling the Palestinian areas granted autonomy as part of the Oslo Accords. Arafat proved to be far more sensitive to criticism than the Israelis, and in early January 1996, shortly before the Palestinian elections were held, Eid was detained by members of Arafat's security apparatus, and taken to Ramallah for questioning. Jibril Ragoub,

5 B'Tselem's name comes from a biblical quote which means that God's people should live without fear of discrimination.

Arafat's security chief, accused Eid of being 'a cheap Israeli police agent', the equivalent of calling him a collaborator – in the less attractive sense of the word – and a deeply serious allegation. During the *intifada* an estimated 1,500 Palestinians were killed by fellow Palestinians for collaborating with the Israelis.

'Ragoub thought he was signing my death certificate,' says Eid. 'Fortunately I had enough friends and supporters to ensure these accusations did not stick against me.'[6]

Intense diplomatic pressure was brought to bear on Arafat's Palestinian Authority, and Eid was released after being held for only twenty-four hours. He was never given a reason for his detention, although one of Arafat's officials told him that he had been arrested 'because your tongue is too long'. Shortly after his release Eid decided to leave B'Tselem and establish his own organisation, The Palestinian Human Rights Monitoring Group, based in East Jerusalem. The main purpose of the organisation is to investigate human rights abuses committed by Arafat's security chiefs, which includes detaining suspects without trial and the widespread use of torture, sometimes with fatal consequences.[7]

'They told me my tongue was too long,' says Eid. 'Now it is much longer, and it will not remain silent.'

While much of this social, cultural, professional and political interplay is to be expected when two peoples are obliged to live in close proximity, there is another, altogether more sinister, level of Arab–Israeli collaboration. Most Palestinians who trade information about their fellow countrymen to the Israelis might better be described as traitors or spies, although they are more familiarly known as collaborators, like those French citizens who assisted with the Nazi occupation of France during the Second World War. In this sense collaboration is a dirty word, and collaborators are dirty people. Israelis are the first to admit that they owe an enormous debt to Palestinian collaborators, many of whom suffer brutal deaths as a

---

6 In certain months during the *intifada*, more Palestinians were killed by Palestinians than by Israelis.

7 In April 1997, twelve Palestinians had died from wounds received during interrogation by Palestinian security officers.

consequence of their actions. Most Israelis believe they are involved in a desperate battle for survival, and that any action undertaken by their security forces which helps to ensure their protection is justified. The most nauseous aspect of the arrangement is the cynicism which seems to define most of the clandestine relationships between Jews and Arabs.

The tradition of collaboration in the region goes back at least as far as the British Mandate, although the institutionalised sycophancy of the Ottoman court also schooled generations of native Arabs in the art of accommodating the desires of alien masters. Thousands of Jews and Arabs collaborated with the security forces during the Mandate as the British struggled to maintain order, but most of the bloodshed was caused by Arabs collaborating with Jews. During the Arab rebellion of the 1930s an estimated 5,000 Palestinians were killed by their fellow-countrymen. Some of the deaths were due to substantial differences of political opinion, but many were caused by the all-important issue of land. Had the early Zionist pioneers not been able to purchase large quantities of land from the native Arabs, their dream would not have been able to succeed. The proclivity of the Palestinians for selling land to Jews was a cause of much friction with Jordanian members of the Arab Legion during the 1948 war. The Jordanians taunted their Palestinian comrades-in-arm for selling land to the Zionists, and the Palestinians teased the Jordanians for being crude Arab mercenaries who were so unsophisticated that they asked for their salads to be warmed up.[8] Fifty years after the creation of the State of Israel, old habits die hard. Much of the land sold to Israeli property developers for the controversial Har Homa building project in East Jerusalem, which caused such a major international crisis in the spring of 1997, was originally sold to them by a local Arab sheikh who did not even own it.

Captain P has worked for many years as an agent with Israel's Shin Bet domestic intelligence service, otherwise known as the General Security Service. For more than twenty years he has worked closely with a large number of Palestinian collaborators, interrogated numerous Palestinian suspects and claims to have prevented innumerable acts of terrorism. He knows all about Palestinian traitors, what

8 Said K. Aburish, *Children of Bethany* (London: I. B. Tauris & Co., 1988), p. 113.

motivates them, how to control them, their hopes and their fears. He knows how to manipulate them, to frighten them, to make them do whatever he wants.

'The work of the Shin Bet is to prevent terrorist attacks, not to apprehend the culprits afterwards,' explains Captain P. An intense man in his early forties, Captain P has left the secret service and works in Jerusalem as a journalist for one of Israel's leading newspapers, mainly reporting on security issues. We meet at a coffee shop in the centre of town, and he chain-smokes as he tries to guide me through the murky depths of the collaborators' underworld. Even then I cannot be sure I am to believe what I am told, or if I am participating in the creation of yet another elaborate deception.

According to Captain P there is no shortage of Palestinians wishing to work for the Israelis. In fact the Israelis inherited a flourishing network of collaborators that had been established when the West Bank and Gaza were part of Jordan.

'Basically, they all started working for us the moment we took control. There was hardly a village in the West Bank that did not have at least one collaborator,' says Captain P.

Money, and making a better life for themselves, are the main reasons why Palestinians agree to sleep with the enemy. Whether it is the British, Jordanians or Israelis, there are always people who are prepared to co-operate with the authorities for their personal advancement, whether it is acquiring building permission for a new house, getting a new passport or adding to their personal wealth.

'The relationship works in many ways. Personally I always found it difficult to persuade a potential agent [Captain P hesitates to call them collaborators] to accept money. But once they had, we knew we had them. They could no longer refuse us. If they did, we could easily expose them. Put it this way. Very few of them worked for us for ideological reasons.'

The Israeli security forces' use of Palestinian collaborators has been extremely effective. According to Captain P, at one time Israel's penetration of the PLO's Fatah wing was so comprehensive that 'we had two agents for every terrorist'. For the system to operate effectively, each Israeli controller works with a handful of hand-picked Palestinian 'agents', particularly those who can provide detailed information about possible terror attacks.

'It takes about six months to train these people, and then we develop very close relationships with them,' says Captain P. 'In some cases it is like a father and son relationship. If they need something, they call me. If one of their children is sick, I will organise a doctor. Often I know more about their private lives than their wives.'

The most dangerous part of the operation is arranging a meeting between the Israelis and Palestinians. In many cases these meetings take place in Jerusalem, where the Shin Bet has a number of 'safe houses'.

'This is the weakest part of the whole operation,' says Captain P. 'This is where it can go horribly wrong. It is vital that our agents have a good excuse for leaving their village. We have to take many, elaborate precautions. It can take hours of surveillance to make sure we are clear to meet.'

During one 'meet' in 1994 that went badly wrong, a Shin Bet agent died when a shoot-out erupted between Palestinian gunmen and Israeli secret service agents in the normally tranquil Jewish residential neighbourhood of Rehavia.

'It was one of those things,' says Captain P, with a shrug of his shoulders. 'The wires got crossed and the whole thing blew up into the open. It made us feel rather stupid.'

But for the Israelis, at least, the risks are worth taking because of the number of lives that are saved by the information the collaborators provide.

'I'd hate to think how many innocent people would have died without the help these people give us,' says Captain P. 'Literally hundreds of Jewish and Arab lives have been saved. It would be fair to say that 95 per cent of the information that prevented these attacks was provided by our Palestinian agents. These people take enormous risks for us and deserve better treatment than they receive.'

This is Captain P's way of saying that Palestinian collaborators do not deserve the brutal end many of them have met at the hands of Hamas and PLO punishment squads. Captain P estimates that only between 25 to 30 per cent of the 1,500 Palestinians murdered for being collaborators during the *intifada* actually worked for the Israeli security service.

'Killing collaborators became a national sport for the Palestinians,' says Captain P. 'But most of the people who died were merely victims of local village feuds.'

To protect their genuine agents, the Israelis were obliged in the early 1990s to set up a special collaborators village near Jerusalem, where agents whose security had been compromised could seek refuge until the Israelis could help them to make a new life. A major problem for the Israelis concerned the cases where Hamas activists learnt a collaborator's identity and agreed to spare his life so long as he revealed the identity of his Israeli controller.

'This made life very dangerous for us,' says Captain P. 'We lost some very good men as a result.' With this last statement one wonders whether Captain P is referring to his Israeli colleagues or his precious Palestinian 'agents'.

Abu Fatty and Abu Sly are collaborators, and proud of it. To meet them I have been escorted by another Israeli journalist acquaintance to Shepherd's Hotel, a rather dilapidated building in Sheikh Jarrah on the road to Mount Scopus, just behind the Jerusalem police head-quarters. Shepherd's Hotel was once the family home of George Antonius, the Palestinian writer, and later became a hotel run by an English family. The hotel was sold after 1967 to what the family believed was a Swiss company. It was only after the sale had been completed that they discovered it had been sold to Irving Moskowitz, the Californian-based bingo hall entrepreneur who funds various fanatical Jewish groups in Jerusalem. The hotel, which occupies a prime piece of development land, has been loaned to the Israeli security services while Mr Moskowitz considers what to do with it.

Abu Fatty and Abu Sly are not their real names which, not surprisingly, they are unwilling to reveal. So I am obliged to make them up. Abu Fatty is a well-proportioned gentleman who, during the hour I sit with him in the hotel garden, eats large quantities of nuts and sips sweet tea. The only relief he allows his digestive system is when he draws heavily on a hubbly-bubbly pipe wedged incongruously between his corpulent thighs. Abu Sly is a thin, nervous man who hovers behind Abu Fatty. He says little, nods his head in agreement at certain points, and eyes me with deep suspicion. It soon becomes clear from what Abu Fatty tells me that neither of these men possess an iota of moral fibre. They are the lowest form of human life.

Certainly Abu Fatty appears to have a low regard for the rest of humanity. 'My father worked with the Israelis under the Jordanians, and I started working for them when the Israelis came to East Jerusalem,' he explains. 'Most of the work I do is with the settlers. I help them to buy Arab houses. They pay me a good commission. Who am I to complain?'

Whenever the settlers succeed in purchasing an Arab property, it inevitably provokes an enormous political row between the Israeli and Palestinian leadership, which sometimes results in violence. Why, then, does he do it?

'I have to make money somehow,' he says, without a hint of regret. Abu Sly nods agreement. 'It's all very well helping the Israelis, but I have to live.'

Doesn't he feel any regrets for the Palestinians he exposes to the Israelis, who are jailed for lengthy periods?

'What do I care? They are nothing to do with me. I don't care about anything except my own survival. No one in this city takes anything seriously. The Israelis say they want peace and do nothing about it. The Palestinians say they want peace, but all Arafat's intelligence agents seem to want is an endless supply of women.'

I can't help but ask the obvious question.

'Yes,' says Abu Fatty, smiling lasciviously. 'Of course I supply the women. If that's what they want, that's what they get.'

He emits a deep chuckle that makes the rolls of fat on his stomach bobble furiously, like an electrocuted jelly. Abu Sly merely grins.

'You have to understand that there is nothing else we can do,' Abu Fatty continues. 'If we stop working for the Israelis we would both be dead.' Abu Sly looks more serious.

'I am not afraid of anyone except the judgement of God,' Abu Fatty says, concluding our conversation. 'And who knows what God thinks?'

# 14

# APOCALYPSE

*'Repent therefore; or else I come to thee quickly, and I will make war against them with the sword of my mouth'*

Revelation 2: 16

With such an abundance of religion, a blind man might expect a little respect. But not here, in the world's holiest city. It is Friday lunchtime in the Old City, and the blind man is trying to make his way through the crowded streets. This is no ordinary Friday. By a rare confluence of the Jewish, Christian and Muslim calendars, this is a day pregnant with religious significance for the three monotheistic faiths. It is the start of the Jewish Passover, Good Friday for Christians and the middle of the Islamic holy month of Ramadan.

The streets leading from Damascus Gate to the religious centre of the Old City are crowded with worshippers of the different faiths. They are either making their way to, or returning from, their respective places of devotion. This human maelstrom is at its most intense outside the Austrian Hospice at the junction between al-Wad, the narrow concourse leading from Damascus Gate to the Haram and Wailing Wall, and the Via Dolorosa, which cuts diagonally across it. Along the length of al-Wad crowds of observant Jews, dressed in their best prayer shawls, are making their way to the Wall to pray. Coming in the opposite direction are crowds of Muslims leaving the Friday prayer service at al-Aqsa. To add to the confusion crowds of Christian pilgrims, some of them carrying crosses and others wearing crowns of thorns, are attempting to perform the stations of the cross.

The blind man is attempting to negotiate this teeming throng. An elderly man, he wears a large overcoat and a Russian-style woollen hat. With the aid of his white cane, normally he would find his way without difficulty. He has made the same journey from the eye hospital to his house in the Muslim Quarter on countless occasions, using his cane to tap out the contours of the ancient slabs of stone forming the pavement. But today the journey is not so easy. As the worshippers jostle to force their way through, no one takes much notice of the blind man. He is pushed one way by a Jewish family, then another by some Muslim men, and is nearly knocked to the ground by a procession of East European pilgrims. A contingent of Israeli Border Police, which has been positioned at the narrow intersection to enforce security, does nothing to assist. They carry on leaning on their riot batons, chewing gum and watching the blind man's attempts to find a way through the crowd, as though it were a spectator sport, staged for their amusement. In the five minutes it takes the blind man to travel less than fifty metres, none of the people who have come to this holy place to observe the rituals of their faith can find the time to lend the blind man any assistance.

It is hard to be holy in Jerusalem. There are moments when it is possible to catch a glimpse of the city's spiritual essence, but they are rare. Watching dawn break from the Mount of Olives, when the first rays of sun bestow new life upon the city's ancient landscape. Sitting in one of the old Crusader churches, like St Anne's, when they are empty of tourists. Walking through quiet, empty terraces in the remoter corners of the Haram, or watching the moon rise from the Jordan Valley over the Wailing Wall. These are the moments when Jerusalem reveals herself in all her glory, the holy Jerusalem, the spiritual Jerusalem, Jerusalem the sacred. The eternal inspiration of prophets, psalmists and poets, saints, sinners and lovers; the noble cause for which so many generations of kings, caliphs and ordinary soldiers have sacrificed their lives. Jerusalem can appear like a mysterious but beautiful phantom, who reveals her purity and majesty for a fleeting moment, only to disappear, abandoning the beholder to the chaos of the modern city.

The Old City is Jerusalem's soul, its very essence, but the city's ancient spirit is trampled beneath the clamour of the modern conflict. The streets are always filled with soldiers, the air punctuated by their terse commands issued over walkie-talkies. The visitor is besieged by intrusive Arab tradesmen hawking their wares, who will not accept a polite refusal. Most of the buildings in the Muslim and Christian Quarters, which comprise most of the land, look weary from years of neglect, and the walls are covered with the latest graffito. Too much of the newer construction in the Jewish Quarter appears provocatively ostentatious, an assertive statement that the Jews have returned to assert control of the city's destiny, this time for good. Special feast days – Jewish, Christian and Muslim – are marked with reinforcements of riot police, bristling with guns and tear gas, being drafted into the city's narrow confines, while military helicopters hover overhead like angry wasps.

Beyond the confines of the Old City, the intensity of Jerusalem manifests itself in a myriad of ways. The roads provide one of the more graphic illustrations of the city's raw passions. Israeli and Palestinian drivers manoeuvre their cars through the traffic as though they are waging their war on wheels. Many Mediterranean cities have dire traffic problems, but there can be few places where drivers conduct themselves with so much aggression and blatant lack of regard for their fellow motorists. Visiting drivers who stop to allow a pedestrian to cross are treated as though they have just been released from an asylum.

Jerusalem must be the most intense and impossible city on earth, the unhappy consequence of having the modern Arab–Israeli political dispute superimposed upon centuries of religious antagonism and division. The intense emotions the conflict arouses have been even more inflamed since the advent of the 1993 Oslo peace accords, which were initially conceived to act as a balm, not an irritant, upon the city's turbulent populace. The atmosphere has not been helped by the shift among Jerusalem's Israeli population towards a more nationalist, and therefore more uncompromising, standpoint, a trend best reflected by Ehud Olmert's election as mayor in late 1993. It is noticeable that most Israeli peace rallies tend to take place in Tel Aviv, while protests against the peace process, and therefore against the notion of Israelis enjoying a more harmonious relationship with their Palestinian neighbours, are held in Jerusalem. Israeli national holidays, in particular, are taken as occasions by nationalist Jews to flaunt their domination of the city. Cars and buildings, in East as well as West Jerusalem, are bedecked with Israeli flags. If the Palestinians had total control of the city, it is unlikely they would conduct themselves any better. The Palestinians nurture similar aspirations to the Israelis, although public expressions of their nationalist objectives are more modest by virtue of their limited influence in the city's affairs. While the Haram and Muslim areas of the Old City are held as the Palestinians' *raison d'être*, public demonstrations are confined to Arab boy scouts parading through East Jerusalem on special anniversaries, such as Land Day, which commemorates the confiscation of Arab land by the Israelis.

The more one side raises its voice, the more their opponents increase the stridency of their rhetoric, which plays into the hands of the extremists. If anything, proximity has made relations between Jews and Arabs worse, not better. On the Israeli side, militant settlers and religious fanatics demand, and receive, an ever greater say in the nation's affairs. Palestinian extremism, on the other hand, is not confined solely to the Islamic hardliners who mastermind the suicide bombs. The less Israel is prepared to compromise on Jerusalem's future, the more the hardline regimes of the Middle East, such as Iran and Iraq, draw encouragement. One of Tehran's better organised terrorist structures, for example, is known as the *Al-Quds*, or Jerusalem, Brigade. In South Lebanon, most of the Iranian-backed Hizbollah guerrillas, who, in spite of their inferior military equipment, consistently manage to inflict significant casualties on the Israeli armed forces, claim they are fighting for 'the liberation of Jerusalem'.

One of the primary objectives of the much-vaunted Middle East peace process was to find a lasting political settlement for Jerusalem. In recognition of the immense difficulties posed by 'the Jerusalem issue', as it became known, Israeli and Palestinian negotiators agreed to leave the issue to the last stage of the negotiations, the talks on 'final status' issues. Under the terms of the Oslo Accords, a final decision was to be reached by 1999. The two sides agreed to discuss Jerusalem in earnest only after all the other outstanding issues were resolved, such as whether or not the Palestinians should have their own state, the future of the Israeli settlements in the West Bank and Gaza, and whether the millions of Palestinian refugees from the wars of 1948 and 1967 should be allowed to return. These issues in themselves are highly problematic, and both sides recognised that it was pointless talking about Jerusalem until substantive progress was made elsewhere. If solutions could be reached on sensitive questions such as whether Jewish settlers should be allowed to reside in Palestinian population areas, or if Palestinian refugees could return to their former homes, then it might be possible that the trust and mutual respect created during the negotiating process could result in a negotiated settlement on Jerusalem.

The very mention of Jerusalem in the Declaration of Principles that Rabin and Arafat signed in Washington in 1993 was a significant breakthrough, even raising the hopes among die-hard Palestinian pessimists that a proper agreement might be reached. As Faisal Husseini, the PLO's Jerusalem representative, stated: 'In the Oslo Accords it was established that the status of Jerusalem is open to negotiations on the final arrangement, and the moment you say "yes" to negotiations, you are ready for compromise.' Nabil Sha'ath, one of the PLO's main negotiators, went even further, saying that Israel's commitment to discuss Jerusalem's future 'calls into question the legality and finality of their annexation' of the city in 1980.

In the early stages of the peace process, when Yitzhak Rabin was still alive, there was a remote possibility that a lasting solution might be agreed. A number of *ad hoc* Israeli–Palestinian committees were formed to explore various ways in which some form of power-sharing might be established. The big, and insoluble, issue of sovereignty was set to one side, and the teams (because of the highly sensitive political nature of the task, they could on no account by called negotiators) explored practical power-sharing arrangments. Although the discussions were carried out with the blessing of both the Israeli and Palestinian political establishments, neither side officially acknowledged their existence. To do so would have amounted to political suicide for both camps. After Labour was voted out of office in the May 1996 Israeli elections, and it became clear that the whole Jerusalem issue no longer figured in the peace process agenda of the new government, some details of these secret exploratory talks began to leak out. While Jerusalem was to remain united under Israeli sovereignty, new frameworks were to be established to grant Palestinian residents of the city's Arab neighbourhoods a status that would allow them to share responsibility for the administration of their lives in the city. The Muslim holy places would remain under Palestinian control, and the Palestinian Authority would be allowed to establish an administrative centre in one of the city's Arab suburbs, such as Abu Dis.

Yossi Beilin, who as Labour's deputy foreign minister played a key role in the Oslo negotiations, explained the significance of Jerusalem to the peace process during his bid to succeed Shimon Peres as leader of the Labour Party in the spring of 1997. He claimed that Peres, when negotiating the structure of the Oslo Accords, had deliberately left Jerusalem to the final stage of the process because Peres did not want Jerusalem on the agenda. 'That's the last thing we want,' Beilin reported Peres as saying. But Beilin believed Jerusalem's future should be discussed. 'If we leave Jerusalem as it is today, it means that no country will recognise it as the capital of Israel. Talking about Jerusalem doesn't mean giving up sovereignty or dividing it. That's rubbish. But a government which doesn't talk about Jerusalem is irresponsible, because it means we will remain the only country without a recognised capital.'[1]

The election of the Netanyahu government in 1996, as previously stated, effectively ended any prospect of realistic progress being made on Jerusalem. Netanyahu is heir to the *Eretz Israel*, the revisionist political heritage articulated by Vladimir Jabotinsky in the 1920s, and upheld more recently by Netanyahu's immediate Likud prime ministerial predecessors, Menachem Begin and Yitzhak Shamir. Maintaining the whole of *Eretz Israel*, which for convenience's sake is defined as the land between the Mediterranean and the Jordan River, under Jewish suzerainty is the *sine qua non* of Likud's political ideology. Likud is opposed to returning *any* of the Jewish bibilical inheritance to Palestinian control, let alone Jerusalem, the holy grail of Jewish aspirations for nearly two millennia. It was, after all, a Likud government which, in 1980, formally annexed East Jerusalem to Israel, and it remains a key party objective to

1 Interview with the *Jerusalem Post*, 3 January 1997.

settle one million Jews in the 'greater Jerusalem' area by the next century.

At the time of Netanyahu's election victory, the Israeli government was already committed, by the interim agreement negotiated by the previous Labour administration, to grant Yasser Arafat's Palestinian Authority control over most of the West Bank. During the first phase of Israel's military redeployment, control was handed over to the Authority in late 1995 – prior to the Palestinian elections in January 1996 – of the major Palestinian towns, with the exception of Hebron. Agreement was delayed on Hebron because of the sensitive issue of whether the two hundred or so Jewish settlers based in the centre of the town should be allowed to remain. The outgoing Peres government negotiated a deal with the Palestinians, whereby the settlers would be allowed to remain in Hebron with Israeli army protection, while the rest of the city was handed over to Palestinian control. Netanyahu, whose new right-wing coalition government was opposed to relinquishing Hebron, delayed implementation of this agreement until January 1997, arguing that the security arrangements for the Jewish settlers were inadequate. Another reason for the delay was that Israeli forces were supposed to withdraw from large areas of the West Bank – the second phase of the interim agreement – at the same time as pulling back from Hebron.[2] While few Israelis would shed tears over relinquishing a hornets' nest of Palestinian nationalism like Hebron, handing back large tracts of *Eretz Israel* was anathema to Likud supporters, and Netanyahu played for time while his advisers worked out how to turn the agreement to their advantage.

The collapse of the Middle East peace process in the spring of 1997 was not caused, as is commonly claimed, by the Netanyahu government's decision to authorise work to commence on the Har Homa/Abu Ghneim housing project in East Jerusalem.[3] It was caused by Israel's failure to hand back control of a significant proportion of

2 The Israeli–Palestinian Interim Agreement on the West Bank and Gaza Strip, which was signed in September 1995, set out a timetable for the transfer of the occupied territories from Israeli to Palestinian control under the terms of the 1993 Oslo Accords.

3 See Chapter 6, pp. 140–2.

the rural areas of the West Bank to the Palestinian Authority as stipulated by the Interim Agreement. Implementation of the Hebron
agreement in late January 1997, which gave the Palestinians control
of all six major West Bank towns and cities, was hailed by Arafat as a
key breakthrough in the peace process. It even inspired him to articulate his thoughts on the future of Jerusalem, which he regarded as
the last remaining Palestinian city under Israeli control. Arafat drew
a parallel between Jerusalem and Rome, where the Vatican and the
Italian state enjoy a harmonious power-sharing arrangement. Arafat's
sense of optimism, however, was short-lived. A few days after the
Hebron redeployment was completed, the Israelis undertook their
pull-back from rural areas of the West Bank. The Palestinians had
been expecting to receive about 30 per cent of the land, with the rest
being handed over at regular intervals up until 1999, the date when
all the negotiations on the Oslo process were due to be completed.
Instead they received less than 5 per cent. Netanyahu's advisers had
found that, while Israel was committed to handing back a portion of
the West Bank to Palestinian control, the precise amount had not
been specified. The Netanyahu government therefore decided to
return the bare minimum, citing security considerations as its excuse.
Even this parsimonious act caused trouble within Netanyahu's coalition, with some of the extreme members denouncing the hand-over
as a 'betrayal'. Benny Begin, son of former Prime Minister Menachem,
resigned in protest and Yitzhak Shamir accused Netanyahu, his
former protégé, of reneging on his nationalist ideals.

To shore up support within the coalition and silence his critics,
Netanyahu authorised work to begin on Har Homa, a Jewish housing
project in East Jerusalem. Coming so soon after the humiliation
Arafat had suffered over the West Bank pull-back, the Har Homa
project shattered completely whatever vestiges of trust and co-operation still survived between the two sides. During the Hebron
negotiations, when Netanyahu and Arafat were in almost daily contact, most observers concluded that, in spite of their many political
differences, the two leaders had developed a good working relationship, a crucial prerequisite for the peace process to succeed. That
relationship was seriously undermined by the events of early 1997.
Netanyahu, who had been elected on the strength of his commitment
to confront Palestinian terrorism, claimed the cause of the mistrust

was the failure of Arafat's Palestinian Authority to take effective action against radical groups, such as Hamas. Netanyahu's complaints appeared to be justified when a Palestinian suicide bomber destroyed a Tel Aviv café during the Jewish festival of Purim in March 1997, apparently in revenge for the Har Homa project. Arafat countered by claiming Netanyahu had provoked the terrorism by embarking on a course of action which had destroyed the peace process. Relations between the two leaders deteriorated further in late July, when two suicide bombers killed fourteen civilians and injured more than a hundred when they carried out simultaneous attacks at the main Jewish market in central Jerusalem.

Both the Israelis and the Palestinians were content to blame the controversy over the Har Homa project as the main reason for the collapse of the peace process. By focusing on Har Homa, both sides were emphasising their resolve to protect their respective claims to Jerusalem. But it was the suspension of a constructive negotiating dialogue on the other aspects of the peace process which effectively ended any hope of a negotiated settlement on Jerusalem's future by the initial target date of 1999. The real cause of the crisis was that, four years after the peace process had commenced amid a fanfare of optimism and good intentions, Israel still held more than 90 per cent of the land of the West Bank and, with a Likud government in power, showed little inclination to relinquish it. This state of affairs rather undermined the Palestinian attempts to make Jerusalem the focal point of the dispute. Without a state, there seemed little point in fighting over its future capital.

A telling insight into how the Netanyahu government regarded not only the future of the peace process, but the crucial issue of Jerusalem, has been provided by Dr Dore Gold, Netanyahu's key peace process adviser, shortly before Likud came to power in May 1996. In a pamphlet written on the Jerusalem issue for a prestigious Israeli think-tank, Gold, an American-born Jew, concluded that 'a solution to the Jerusalem question that is acceptable to all parties in the Middle East, including Israel and the Palestinians, is highly unlikely'.[4] Dr Gold, who served as an adviser to the Shamir government during the

4 Dore Gold, *Final Status Issues: Israel–Palestinians. Study no. 7 – Jerusalem* (Tel Aviv: Jaffee Centre for Strategic Studies, 1995).

early, pre-Oslo, stages of the peace process, concludes by quoting an observation attributed to Dr Henry Kissinger, the former American Secretary of State, on the nature of Arab–Israeli diplomacy. Conflicts like the one between the Arabs and Israelis over Jerusalem, says Kissinger, usually 'have produced a stalemate broken from time to time by a series of wars until exhaustion produced the equilibrium that wisdom had been unable to define'. Dr Gold certainly believes war is the more likely solution to the Jerusalem issue, as he believes it would be impossible for Israel to accept the hard territorial concessions demanded by both the Palestinians and the wider Arab world. 'A territorial solution in Jerusalem,' he writes, 'would likely tear the fabric of Israeli society and raise serious questions about the legitimacy of Israel as a Jewish state.'

As Israel celebrated, in June 1997, the thirtieth anniversary of its conquest of East Jerusalem and the West Bank during the Six-Day War, all the portents suggested that Dr Gold's predictions may yet materialise. In early May Martin Indyk, in his final report before standing down as US Ambassador to Israel, concluded the peace process was effectively dead. 'The Oslo package has crumbled and there are no quick fixes possible,' wrote Mr Indyk. 'The core bargain of Oslo has broken down. Israel was promised security and the Palestinians were promised self-government.' The ambassador's comments coincided with the leaking of a top secret intelligence report to the Israeli press compiled by Ami Ayalon, the head of Shin Bet, Israel's internal security service. The report, which was submitted to Netanyahu in late May, predicted that Israel would become embroiled in a 'regional war' with its Arab neighbours if the Israeli Prime Minister persisted with his policy of refusing to compromise. The report said the main causes of the crisis were Netanyahu's policy of expanding Jewish settlements (including Har Homa) and his public humiliation of Yasser Arafat by holding the PLO leader responsible for suicide attacks carried out by Islamic fundamentalists. 'Mr Arafat is angry and frustrated,' the report stated. 'He wants a respectable compromise. We emphasise again that further expansion of the settlements will lead to escalation of violence in the West Bank on a scale we have not seen so far.' An indication of how serious the situation had become was the report's revelation that, if violence erupted, the Israeli armed forces had already drawn up a plan – codenamed

'Operation Thornbush' – to reoccupy the Palestinian cities that had been returned to Arafat's control under the terms of the Oslo Accords.

May 1997 was also the anniversary of the Netanyahu government's first year in office, and the Israeli press leaked details of maps which were said to show the boundaries for Jerusalem proposed by Netanyahu for the final status negotiations. The maps, which were drawn up after consultations with the military, envisaged returning just 40 per cent of the land to the Palestinians. In return, Israel would demand a substantial extension of Jerusalem's municipal boundaries, which would remain exclusively under Israeli control. The city's boundaries would be significantly extended. To the east they would take in the massive satellite settlement of Ma'aleh Adumim (which contains 20,000 settlers, the largest on the West Bank). Gush Etzion, fifteen miles south of the city on the road to Hebron, would be included to the south (effectively bringing Bethlehem under Jerusalem's jurisdiction). Beit El, five miles north of Ramallah, would form the northern boundary. The proposed boundary changes are almost identical to those drawn up by Rehovam Ze'evi in 1967, and reluctantly turned down by Moshe Dayan.[5] Jibril Ragoub, speaking on behalf of the Palestinian Authority, said he was 'disgusted' by the maps. Right-wing Israeli settlers also registered their protests. Left-wing politicians denounced them as 'dangerous'. In the Knesset the opposition responded to the Netanyahu government's anniversary by launching a damning attack on Likud's peace process policies. Ehud Barak, the acting Labour Party leader and a former Israeli chief of staff, said the threat of an Arab–Israeli war, caused by the government's failure to proceed with the peace process, should keep the Prime Minister awake at night. 'Where's the peace? Where's the security?' Barak demanded. 'Where's the unity of the [Israeli] people? Where's the hope? It's all broken, shattered, sad and hurting.' A few days later Barak won the election to replace Shimon Peres as Labour Party leader, defeating Yossi Beilin.

The recalcitrant attitude of Yasser Arafat, it should be stressed, did not exactly help the situation. To avenge what he regarded as Netanyahu's betrayal of the peace process principles, Arafat released scores of Palestinian prisoners who were involved in the various

5 See Chapter 6, p. 134.

Islamic terror organisations. He also appeared to give his blessing in the spring of 1997 to the murder of a number of Palestinians accused of selling land to Israel. Rather than condemning the murders, Arafat's Palestinian Authority warned that selling land to Jews was a crime punishable by death. This assertion provoked outrage within the Netanyahu government, which accused the Authority of adopting racist policies, even though Israel itself has adopted numerous measures to make it impossible for Palestinians to buy land under Israel's control.

In spite of the warnings and criticism of its failure to proceed with the peace process, the Netanyahu government showed little inclination to modify its approach. In Jerusalem this manifested itself in what amounted to a systematic campaign of intimidation against the Palestinian population. The government determined to close any office or institution associated with Arafat's Palestinian Authority. International diplomatic pressure meant Likud officials were unable to act against Orient House, Arafat's main headquarters in the city. But a number of Arafat-affiliated research institutes were closed, with Netanyahu's government making it clear that it would not tolerate any Palestinian political activity in the city. The government also authorised the Interior Ministry to tighten the regulations relating to the issue of residency permits for Palestinians living in Jerusalem. Israeli and Palestinian human rights groups accused the government of implementing a 'deportation' policy, to limit the number of Palestinians resident in the city. Cases were reported of Israeli soldiers breaking into Palestinian homes to confiscate identity documents, thereby forcing Arab families to move out of the city. This policy was given even greater urgency for the Likud following a report published in late May 1997 which showed that the overall rate of growth of the city's Jewish population was falling each year.[6]

It is more of a privilege than a pleasure these days to live in Jerusalem, even for Israelis. The vacuum created by the failure of the peace process to make substantive progress on Jerusalem's future means that daily life is a non-stop series of challenges for the city's residents. Mainly because of the conflict, Jerusalemites live in a highly

6 Jerusalem Institute for Israeli Studies, *1997 Statistical Yearbook*.

militaristic and violent atmosphere. Hardly a day passes without the papers carrying reports on some gruesome, bloody event; a Palestinian suspect dies in custody; an Israeli schoolchild is murdered while on a hike; scores of young Israeli soldiers are killed in a helicopter crash in south Lebanon; Iran is developing a long-range missile that will be able to fire nuclear warheads at Jerusalem within five years. To this must be added the endless cycle of air-raid siren drills and gas-mask practice.

At schools throughout the city Israeli parents take it in turns to perform guard duty during recreation periods. Every time anyone boards a bus, even for the most mundane trip, the thought is always in the back of their minds that the bus could be blown to pieces at any moment. It is not uncommon to see an Israeli housewife with a pistol strapped to her waist while out shopping with her young children. Jerusalem is like a frontier town, always bristling with guns, whether carried by off-duty soldiers, settlers, or reinforcements of Border Police drafted in to deter terrorist attacks. Most weekdays are punctuated by loud explosions, normally caused either by Israeli Air Force fighter-jets breaking the sound barrier or construction workers blasting the city's stubborn stone-scape. But the citizens can never be certain, and the sonic booms, in particular, so resemble the noise made when the suicide bombers destroyed two commuter buses that city officials eventually complained to the Israeli Air Force that it was causing unnecessary distress to the city's residents. 'Every boom of this kind brings hundreds of telephone calls from worried citizens to the municipal emergency room and the police, asking if there has been a bomb explosion,' a city official explained. He appealed to air force commanders to avoid supersonic flights over Jerusalem 'in view of the great sensitivity among residents of the city'.

This underlying sense of menace has somehow corrupted the city's soul. Perhaps the most potent symbol of the city's rotten moral fabric is the general acceptance, among both Jews and Arabs, that the use of torture on suspects is a necessary evil. That torture is widely used by both the Israeli and Palestinian security forces is undeniable. A report issued by the United Nations Human Rights Committee in Geneva in May 1997 accused Israel of violating the UN convention by using interrogation techniques such as sleep deprivation, playing loud music, death threats and using the type of violent shaking that caused the death of Abed Harizat. Another report, produced by Bassem Eid's Palestinian Human Rights Monitoring Group, made similar allegations against the Palestinian Authority. The report detailed the case of a suspect who was interrogated by Arafat's intelligence officers in Bethlehem. The man was stripped naked, and the officers attempted to rape him. 'But my screams prevented them,' the suspect says. 'They inserted a baton in my rectum. At that moment I signed the confession.' The report accused Palestinian officers of whipping suspects with electric cables, locking them in solitary confinement and leaving them tied in painful positions for lengthy periods. The Palestinian Authority has also displayed a marked disregard for basic civil liberties. In May 1997 Daoud Khuttab, one of Jerusalem's leading Palestinian journalists, was held for one week without charge for broadcasting meetings of Arafat's Legislative Assembly without proper authorisation. A Palestinian cameraman who was sent to interview Khuttab was himself arrested and detained.

The conduct of both sides in this bitter dispute leaves much to be desired, and makes it hard for those not directly involved to feel too overwhelmed with sympathy for the protagonists. This is a conflict where the participants play by their own rules. They acknowledge values that are regarded as unacceptable and indefensible anywhere else in the civilised world. Furthermore there is a form of symbiosis between these two peoples that is beyond the comprehension of even the most well-informed outsider. It is hard to feel sympathy for Palestinians, for example, when one encounters long queues of them outside the offices of the Israeli Interior Ministry in East Jerusalem, waiting to apply for Israeli permits and passports. Jews and Arabs in Jerusalem do not enjoy a love–hate relationship; it is more one that fluctuates wildly between tolerance and repulsion. Israelis work with Arabs while regarding them as an inconvenience obstructing their grand dream of reviving the Land of Israel. Arabs work for Israelis and secretly applaud anyone or anything that causes the Jews extreme distress, from an Israeli military helicopter crash to a Hamas suicide bomb attack.

Not all the blame for the city's ills, however, can be placed solely on the 'conflict'. Indeed, even in the unlikely event of a political solution being reached on the city's future, one imagines that most of the political, religious and social dynamics that characterise the modern city would remain unchanged. Jerusalem might not be afflicted by the mass crucifixions and wholesale massacres that occurred 2,000 years ago, but most of the tensions and conflicts that provoked them remain. The city is not just divided, it is fragmented, and any attempt to escape the burden of the city's religious and political heritage seems doomed to failure.

Simply attempting to accomplish the most mundane everyday tasks requires enormous reserves of patience and ingenuity. Take, for example, the complexity of the Jerusalem weekend. The working week effectively ends at Thursday lunchtime for many Jerusalemites, which means, for example, that Thursday night is when people like to let their hair down. Friday is a holy day for Muslims, most of whom do not work, and most Jews also take the day off to prepare for their sabbath, which begins on Friday evening and lasts until sunset on Saturday. Most Jews and Muslims return to work on Sunday morning, just in time to see the city's modest Christian community making their way to church. Then there are all the holidays – Jewish, Muslim and Christian, religious and official – which, when taken together, makes one wonder how anything is ever accomplished. The holiday season can start in early autumn with the Jewish Yom Kippur festival, followed by the Jewish New Year, Christmas, the Western New Year, the Muslim month of Ramadan, the Muslim New Year, the Western Easter, the Orthodox Easter, Passover, Holocaust Day, Independence Day, Land Day, Pentecost, and so on. Then there is the endless succession of demonstrations, visits by foreign dignitaries, security alerts, all of which can bring the traffic to a standstill, making it impossible to undertake the simplest of tasks, such as driving to a movie show.

Religious holidays, in particular, are observed with the utmost seriousness, and are taken as an opportunity by followers of the respective faiths to assert their confessional loyalties, rather like a tribal gathering. Every night during the month of Ramadan, for example, the city echoes to the sound of fire-crackers being set off by Palestinian youths, aimed more, or so it appears, at reminding their Israeli neighbours of their presence than celebrating the end of each day's fast. Traditional Christians tend to concentrate their energies on the Easter parades, while those of a more evangelical disposition look forward to their annual parade, complete with bands, through the city centre during the Feast of Tabernacles. The Jewish festival of Purim, which takes place in early spring, is one of the livelier events in the annual calendar, for this occasion it is the turn of with young Israelis to set off fire-crackers, traumatising further the city's more sensitive and elderly residents.

Jewish holidays, moreover, can result in exacerbating tensions among the city's Israeli community, as well as antagonising the Palestinians. During the Jewish festival of *Lag Ba'omer* in the spring of 1997, when religious Jews build bonfires to commemorate their deliverance from a plague, a young ultra-Orthodox Jew in Jerusalem's Mea Shearim neighbourhood provoked outrage by throwing an Israeli flag on to the bonfire in front of television cameras. The Bnei Akiva Jewish youth movement announced that it would fly the Israeli flag from its branches for three weeks 'as an expression of our faith and solidarity with the Zionist enterprise'. Friction between ultra-Orthodox Jews and secular Israelis, however, remains as much a source of concern for the city authorities as the dispute with the Palestinians, and is every bit as intractable. Most Friday nights religious Jews can be found attempting to block the city's main thoroughfares, and the Israeli police act to prevent them, with neither side capable of reaching a compromise. The concern felt by the city authorities at the rising influence of the ultra-Orthodox was reflected in Mayor Olmert's presentation of the *1997 Statistical Yearbook* prepared by the Jerusalem Institute for Israel Studies. Olmert emphasised that, according to current demographic trends, the city's population would reach 817,500 by the year 2010, with 251,000 Arabs and 214,000 ultra-Orthodox, giving 'non-Zionists' an overall majority in the city for the first time since reunification in 1967. On that reckoning, it is only a matter of time before Jerusalem elects a non-Zionist mayor.

Another telling statistic provided by the *Yearbook* was confirmation that Jerusalem is a poor city, with 37 per cent of schoolchildren – Jews and Arabs – living below the national poverty line. Jerusalem might fancy itself as the world's most important city; indeed, many of its citizens still appear to believe that the world revolves around it, as though those old medieval maps were right, after all. But one only has to walk through the centre of the city to realise that, for all Jerusalem's pretensions, sophistication is not one of its more noticeable characteristics. There are none of the latest fashions from New York, Paris or

London on display here. Rather the overall impression is one of dowdiness. Clothes shops sell garments made of cheap materials and out-of-date fashions, and shops in general stock goods that are of poor quality. Part of the reason for the city's general tackiness can be explained by the Israeli government's punitive taxation system; since the mid-1980s taxes of more than 200 per cent have been imposed on foreign imports. But the real explanation is, perhaps, that Jerusalem has an inadequate economic infrastructure to support the needs of its growing population. Most of the jobs are provided by the state: government departments, the university, research establishments. But the city's industrial base is underdeveloped, which means that the city is heavily dependent on government funding for its survival. The situation is not helped by the fact that Arab and ultra-Orthodox couples tend to have larger families with fewer bread-winners.

There are many aspects of everyday life in Jerusalem that are decidedly Third World. In one apartment I lived in, for example, the electricity fused every time I had a bath. Nor is this an uncommon experience. Because people cannot afford to pay for repairs and renovations to be carried out properly, everything is done on the cheap, or is improvised. Plug sockets regurlarly come out of walls, drains block, loos overflow. The pattern is reflected in public works. There is nothing the bureaucrats at City Hall, and the numerous charitable foundations that support the city, like better than an expensive, headline grabbing development project. City Hall itself, Mayor Olmert's ostentatious fiefdom (which was, in fact, commissioned by Teddy Kollek), is a classic example. No expense was spared on providing city officials with the most luxurious office accommodation in the city. And countless millions of dollars have been spent renovating the walls of the Old City and the surrounding parks, merely to emphasise the clumsy political point that Jerusalem's heritage is safe in Israeli hands. Meanwhile large sections of the population, Jews as well as Arabs, live in conditions that are little better than slums.

Even so, one of the most striking features visitors encounter is how much everything costs. No matter how badly the tourist industry might be faring, for the visitor it is always high season, premium rate. Even when the city is suffering the after-effects of a terrorist attack, and tour companies have been hit by mass cancellations, it is still difficult to find a reasonably priced hotel, hire car or restaurant.

Nor is it ever easy to accomplish a simple task such as purchasing an air ticket. The worst mistake any purchaser can make is to be too specific about their requirements, whether dealing with an Arab or Jewish agency. By asking to travel on a certain date at a certain time, the purchaser immediately places themselves at the agent's mercy. Suddenly all flights on that day are fully booked, and a special price is required to secure a place. The same applies to hire cars. On one occasion, when I needed to travel in the West Bank, I was advised to hire a car from a Palestinian company in Jerusalem to avoid being stoned. I duly took the advice, and was therefore rather surprised to find myself the target of unprovoked abuse from some Arab youths I encountered on the Mount of Olives. When I remonstrated with them, explaining that I was not driving an Israeli car, the leader replied: 'But you've hired a collaborator's car, and that's even worse.' One needs the cunning of the Levantine to survive in Jerusalem.

With so much tension, with so much conflict, with so much confusion, it is not hard to understand why Jerusalem literally drives some people crazy. The Givat Shaul psychiatric hospital, the one that is housed amid the ruins of the old Arab village of Deir Yassin, has developed a world-famous reputation for dealing with the condition known as 'the Jerusalem Syndrome'. The phenomenon, which was only officially identified in 1987, essentially afflicts tourists who are overcome by the emotional intensity of their first contact with the Holy City. It is one of the city's more perverse ironies that, every year, between fifty and two hundred tourists are taken to the site of the worst massacre committed by Zionists to be treated for mental disorders caused by being in Jerusalem.

The syndrome's symptoms can manifest themselves in a variety of ways. Mainly they involve unsuspecting visitors suddenly assuming a biblical identity. There was the case of the man who thought he was Samson. He was convinced that a stone in the Wailing Wall was in the wrong place, and, using his superhuman strength, tried to remove it. The police were called and escorted 'Samson', a young Canadian tourist, to Kfar Shaul for treatment. The affliction mainly affects Jews and Christians, who either believe they are the Messiah or some important historical figure. King David – usually carrying a harp – and Moses are popular among Jews; Jesus and John the Baptist for Christian men, and the Virgin Mary for Christian women. One of the main features of the syndrome is that sufferers, in adopting these alter egos, keep to their own religions and their own sex. So far there have been no Napoleons spotted in Jerusalem; nor have their been any female John the Baptists. The majority of those who succumb are well-educated and well-off, in their twenties and thirties, mostly from North America and Western Europe. They are equally divided between men and women. Most are Protestant.

The early symptoms are easy to recognise. Most Christian sufferers first show signs of anxiety and nervousness, and say they want to be left alone. They leave their tour group and go back to the hotel. There they begin to go through purification acts: they cut their nails and take a series of showers. Then they turn the hotel sheets into a toga. They start singing psalms or hymns very loudly, and then make their way to a holy place, connected with either the life or death of Jesus. At Easter 1996 the hospital treated three Virgin Marys. One British woman who disappeared from her group was later found near the Wailing Wall claiming she was the reincarnation of Mary and was about to deliver the second Jesus Christ. Another 'Mary', a 36-year-old British teacher, burst into an emergency room at a local hospital, claiming that she was about to miscarry baby Jesus. A young woman, found dancing naked in front of the Wailing Wall, said she wanted to bring harmony and happiness to the world. An Englishwoman regularly arrived at the same location to make Jesus 'a nice cup of tea'.

Since David conquered Jerusalem from the Jebusites and instituted the whole concept of pilgrimage, the city has acted as a magnet for generations of devotees, the sane and the not so sane. For more than 1,000 years, the ideal of Jerusalem, in its earthly and other-worldly manifestations, has inspired artists, motivated kings and popes and provided an outlet for fringe religious movements, spiritual extremists and the deluded. Millennarianists made annual pilgrimages to the city throughout the nineteenth and twentieth centuries, establishing a 'Judgement Day watch' in anticipation of the 1926 earthquake that was expected to herald the coming of the Messiah. These same forces are still at work in the city today.

The difficulty, as ever, in Jerusalem is to distinguish between the sane and the mad. The city has, over the centuries, had more prophets *per capita* than anywhere else on earth. A Spanish journalist making his first visit to the Holy City in 1996, after reading up on

Jerusalem's complex history, concluded that the city resembled a religious Cape Canaveral, with so many prophets and messiahs using this unremarkable hilltop to launch themselves into the heavens. Personally, I have always wondered about the effect the city's geographical location and dramatic climate may have had upon divine inspiration. Situated on a ridge, 2,600 feet above sea-level, that is equidistant from the eastern shore of the Mediterranean and the west bank of the River Jordan, Jerusalem is the ideal location for prophets. To the east there is a wide expanse of desert, a ready-made wilderness, which is suitable for the rigours of self-denial which are deemed necessary to summon the divine muse. To the west there is an abundance of springs and cultivated land to ensure the survival of the local population until the moment when the prophetic visions come to pass. The climate provides a dramatic backdrop, particularly in spring and autumn. When it rains in Jerusalem, it usually rains in biblical proportions. One moment it is a bright sunny day, the next thick, dark clouds sweep in from the Mediterranean and swamp the city in a deluge. There are often days when the city can experience every known climatic condition within the space of an hour: snow, thunder, lightning, slush, rain, wind and sunshine. It would, if possible, be interesting for a study to be conducted into the effect Jerusalem's climate may have had on the work of the city's prophets. Is divine inspiration more likely, for example, to appear in springtime, when the climatic conditions are at their most turbulent, than summer, when the relentless heat inhibits serious mental activity?

The advent of modern technology has only served to complicate further the question of Jerusalem's future. On one level it has made the city more accessible, easier for the Holy City to fulfil its pivotal role at the centre of the universe. If the faithful cannot visit the city personally, religious Jews may fax or e-mail their prayers to the Wailing Wall. Assistants, who are instructed not to read the prayers, collect the messages from fax machines and the Virtual Jerusalem web-site and place them in the cracks of the Wall. Not to be outdone, the *Jerusalem Christian Review* set up a 24-hour 'prayer hot-line' to enable Christians from all over the world to 'share in prayer with brothers and sisters living in the Holy City'. For those who are not aware of these services' existence, Israel's Postal Authority has appointed one of its workers to be God's postman. Every week Jerusalem's Central Post Office receives hundreds of letters addressed to God, Moses, Jesus, Mohammed and any number of saints and prophets. They are passed to the Dead Letters Office where an Israeli postman has the daunting task of sorting through letters in ninety different languages. Some of them bear addresses such as 'To God, Sky Street, Cloud 23, the City of Eden', while others are simply inscribed 'To One God, Israel'. Apart from sorting through the holy mail, the office also deals with hate mail sent to Yasser Arafat. Before the Oslo Accords, this presented a problem for the Israeli authorities, as they had no forwarding address. Now the hate mail is sent to Gaza.

Apart from drawing people closer to God, technology is being used to resolve some of the city's more difficult disputes. One suggestion that has been advanced for resolving the highly problematic dispute over the site known to Jews as the Temple Mount, and to Muslims as the Haram al-Sharif, is for the Third Temple to be constructed over the Dome of the Rock on stilts made of laser beams. A more practical experiment concerns attempts to breed the biblical red heifer that is required to cleanse the Jewish people before they can start work on constructing a new Temple. Considerable excitement was aroused among Jewish religious fanatics in March 1997 after a group of rabbis proclaimed that a calf born at Kfar Hassidim, a religious kibbutz on the outskirts of Haifa, met the 'red heifer' criteria. Secular Israeli papers claimed the calf was 'a walking atom bomb', and called on the government to have it shot. A further inspection was conducted of the beast which, after it had been thoroughly cleaned, was found to have a few white hairs in its tail. But the matter is unlikely to rest there, for Rabbi Chaim Richman, the head of Jerusalem's Temple Institute which is helping to prepare for the new Temple, has joined forces with a Mississippi cattle rancher and Pentecostal preacher to produce an entire herd of red heifers for export to Israel.

We live in an age when NASA, the American space research agency, is monitoring the progress of exploratory space probes, all part of mankind's unstinting effort to understand the mysteries of the universe. And yet it is still conceivable that mankind's continued existence could be threatened by a 3,000-year-old dispute over a barren piece of holy rock. During the Six-Day War, there was a genuine fear that the Arab–Israeli conflict, which occurred at the height of the Cold War, could degenerate into a world war, with the Americans siding with Israel, and the Soviets with the Arabs. The possibility cannot be discounted of a future Arab–Israeli war over Jerusalem escalating into a nuclear conflagration. Israel has a formidable stockpile of nuclear weapons stored in the Negev desert, while some of Israel's more uncompromising Middle Eastern foes, such as Iraq and Iran, make no secret of their ambition to develop their own nuclear capability. The Cold War, for the moment at least, is over, and has been replaced, according to Nato's top brass, by the threat posed to modern Western values by radical Islam. If the holy warriors of Islam were to launch a nuclear *jihad* against Israel, Nato commanders might be ordered to mobilise their massive fire-power, raising the banner for the defence of Jerusalem, like modern-day Crusaders.

The whole conflict, of course, could be resolved by the appearance, or return, of the Messiah. Certainly, with the start of the new millennium, expectations are running high. So many Jews want to be buried on the Mount of Olives in anticipation of their Messiah's appearance that the Israeli authorities have had to find extra burial space. It seems that only those, like the arch-fraudster Robert Maxwell, who can afford the prices for a prime Mount of Olives plot, will be allowed to accompany the Messiah on His triumphant entry to Jerusalem.[7] There will, of course, be the usual difficulty over whether the Messiah is recognised and accepted, or denounced as a False Prophet. Certainly, it would be a terrible shame if the real Messiah were to be denounced as just another deluded victim of the 'Jerusalem syndrome'.

The Jewish Messiah would, of course, make straight for the Holy of Holies, which is now enshrined by the Muslims' Dome of the Rock. To prevent the Jews over-running their holy places, the Muslims have

---

7 After it was revealed that, before his mysterious death in 1992, Maxwell had plundered the funds of Mirror Group pensioners for his own use, a group of Mirror pensioners travelled to Jerusalem allegedly for the sole purpose of urinating on Maxwell's grave.

already taken the precaution of bricking up the Golden Gate, in the centre of the Old City's eastern wall, through which the Messiah is supposed to enter Jerusalem. For good measure they have also placed a Muslim cemetery outside the Old City, knowing that it is forbidden for religious Jews to walk in a graveyard, lest they become impure. It is also to be hoped that the arrival of the Jewish Messiah does not coincide with the return of the Christian or Muslim Saviour to the Mount of Olives. If that were to happen, Judgement Day would be hell.

Alternatively Jerusalem could be destroyed by an earthquake. The fault line in the Jordan Rift Valley, located less than twenty miles from Jerusalem, is similar to the San Andreas Fault which threatens the future existence of Los Angeles. On average Jerusalem suffers a major earthquake every one hundred years, the last one occurring in 1927. Apart from causing extensive damage to the Church of the Holy Sepulchre, Jerusalem escaped relatively lightly from the 1927 tremor. An earthquake which hit the Jerusalem area during the reign of Herod, 2,000 years ago, killed an estimated 30,000 people. A tremor of similar proportions today would destroy the modern city, leaving the protagonists to argue over the rubble.

Then again, perhaps not. Jerusalem has endured invasion, conquest, destruction, plague and famine, and still she survives. Nor does she seem to have benefited from the painful experiences of the past. At the end of the twentieth century, enemies managed to make peace in some of the world's more unlikely quarters; in Eastern Europe, for example, and in South Africa. But not in Jerusalem. The Book of Genesis says that all the nations of the earth are descended from Noah, which suggests that all the peoples of Jerusalem – Jews, Christians and Muslims – should be able to live together in harmony. But the Prophet Mohammed was probably being more realistic when, on his deathbed, he said: 'Two religions cannot exist in Arabia.' We should not be surprised, therefore, that three religions find it impossible to co-exist in Jerusalem. And so, as the city embarks upon a new millennium, its defining characteristics are not honesty, devotion, love and truth. They are falsehood, arrogance, betrayal, belligerence, hypocrisy, hatred and brutality. Indeed, so far as Jerusalem is concerned, truth, as W. H. Auden wrote of another conflict, seems increasingly to be 'a subject only bombs discuss'. There is not much that one can say is good about the modern city: rather than pray for her, we should pity Jerusalem.

# ACKNOWLEDGEMENTS

This book was written between the springs of 1995 and 1997, although the research was conducted over a longer period. Some of the material draws on observations, insights and experiences gleaned from friends, acquaintances and officials I have encountered during more than a decade of living and working in the city. Some of them, given the extremely delicate nature of the subject material, prefer to retain their anonymity. This I respect, while offering my thanks for their assistance.

Of those who may be named, I wish to express my gratitude to the following: Anba Abraham, Albert Agazorian, Ziad Abu Amr, Naim Ateek, Dan Bahat, Maya Barr, Yossi Baumel, Jonathan Ben-Ari, Jessica Berry, Christophe Boltanski, Ulf Carmesund, Amir Cheshin, David Clayman, Patrick Cockburn, Hillel Cohen, Marie Colvin, Mary Curtius, Bassem Eid, Uzi Eilam, Shahal Eylan, Menachem Friedman, Martin Fuller, Rivka Gonen, Hirsh Goodman, Keith and Mary Graves, Juan Carlos Gumucio, Mahdi Abdul Hadi, Harry Hagopian, George

Hintlian, Faisal Husseini, Ali Jeddah, Nasmi Joubert, Salwa Kanaana, Baruch Kaplan, Adnan al-Khattib, Anne Killebrew, Israel Kimche, Teddy Kollek, Martin Kramer, Kevin Kunz, Tzvi Marx, Reuven Merhav, Colin Morton, Ori Nir, Jerome Murphy O'Connor, Nabih Oweideh, Gil Perient, Naomi Ragen, Pnina Ramati, Avraham Ravitz, Danny Rubenstein, Zuhair Sabbagh, Khader Salami, Roni Shaked, Bernard Sibella, Alberto Stabile, Avishai Stockhammer, Hassan Tahboub, Rami Tahboub, Naomi Teasdale, Metropolitan Timothy, Khalil Tufakji, Shaul Tuval, Valentine Vester, Tzvi Weinman and Rivka Zipper.

I am also indebted to my colleagues at the *Sunday Telegraph* – in particular to Charles Moore, Dominic Lawson, Kim Fletcher and Ivo Dawnay – for tolerating my lengthy absences, and to Alan Samson, my editor at Little, Brown, for his enthusiasm and support.

# SELECT
# BIBLIOGRAPHY

NOTE: Biblical references are taken from the Revised Edition published by the Cambridge University Press. Koranic references are taken from the Penguin Classics edition, translation by N. J. Dawood.

Abu Amr, Ziad, *Islamic Fundamentalism in the West Bank and Gaza* (Indianapolis: Indiana University Press, 1994)

Aburish, Said K., *Children of Bethany* (London: I. B. Tauris & Co., 1988)

Ahmed, Akbar S., *Living Islam* (London, BBC Books, 1993)

Antonius, George, *The Arab Awakening* (London: Hamish Hamilton, 1938)

Begin, Menachem, *The Revolt* (Jerusalem: Steimatzky, 1952)

Ben-Arieh, Yehoshua, *Jerusalem in the Nineteenth Century* (New York: St Martin's Press, 1984)

Boardman, John (ed.), *The Oxford History of the Classical World* (Oxford: OUP, 1986)

Colbi, Saul P., *A History of the Christian Presence in the Holy Land* (University Press of America, 1988)

Collins, Larry, and Lapierre, Dominique, *O Jerusalem!* (Jerusalem: Steimatzky, 1982)

Cooper, Duff, *David* (London: Harper & Brothers, 1943)

Dayan, Moshe, *Story of My Life* (New York: William Morrow, 1976)

Donin, Hayim Halevy, *To Be A Jew* (London: HarperCollins, 1972)

——, *To Pray As A Jew* (London: HarperCollins, 1980)

Elon, Amos, *The Israelis* (Tel Aviv: Adam Publishers, 1981)

——, *Jerusalem: City of Mirrors* (Boston, MA: Little, Brown, 1989)

Friedman, Thomas, *From Beirut to Jerusalem* (New York: Farrar, Straus & Giroux, 1989)

Fromkin, David, *A Peace to End All Peace* (New York: Avon Books, 1989)

Gilbert, Martin, *Jerusalem in the Twentieth Century* (London: Chatto & Windus, 1996)

Hassassian, Manuel S., *Palestine – Factionalism in the National Movement, 1919–1939* (Jerusalem: Passia, 1990)

Horowitz, David (ed.), *Yitzhak Rabin: Soldier of Peace* (London: Peter Halban, 1996)

Hourani, Albert, *A History of the Arab Peoples* (London: Faber & Faber, 1991)

Irving, Washington, *Life of Mohammed* (Ipswich, MA: Ipswich Press, reprinted 1989)

Johnson, Paul, *A History of the Jews* (London: Weidenfeld & Nicolson, 1987)

Josephus, *The Jewish War*, translated by G. A. Williamson (London: Penguin Books, 1959)

Kinross, Lord, *The Ottoman Centuries* (New York: William Morrow, 1977)

Le Strange, Guy, *History of Jerusalem Under the Moslems* (Beirut: Khayats, reprinted 1965)

Lewis, Bernard, *The Arabs in History* (London: Hutchinson, 1950)

Mansfield, Peter, *The Arabs* (London: Allen Lane, 1976)

Margolis, Max L., and Marx, Alexander, *A History of the Jewish People* (Philadelphia, PA: The Jewish Publication Society, 1927)

Masalha, Nur, *A Land Without a People* (London: Faber & Faber, 1997)

McManners, John (ed.), *The Oxford History of Christianity* (Oxford: OUP, 1990)

Morris, Benny, *The Birth of the Palestinian Refugee Problem* (Cambridge: CUP, 1987)

——, *1948 and After* (Oxford: OUP, 1990)

Netanyahu, Benyamin, *A Place Among the Nations* (London: Bantam Press, 1993)

O'Connor, Jerome Murphy, *The Holy Land* (Oxford: OUP, 1980)

Peres, Shimon, *Battling for Peace* (London: Weidenfeld & Nicolson, 1995)

Perowne, Stewart, *The Life and Times of Herod the Great* (London: Hodder & Stoughton, 1956)

Peters, F. E., *Jerusalem* (Princeton: Princeton University Press, 1985)

Prior, Michael, and Taylor, William (eds), *Christians in the Holy Land* (London: World of Islam Festival Trust, 1994)

Rabin, Yitzhak, *Memoirs* (London: Weidenfeld & Nicolson, 1979)

Rabinovich, Abraham, *The Battle for Jerusalem* (Philadelphia, PA: The Jewish Publication Society, 1972)

Riley-Smith, Jonathan (ed.), *The Oxford History of the Crusades* (Oxford: OUP, 1995)

Rodinson, Maxime, *The Arabs* (London: Croom Helm, 1981)

Runciman, Steven, *A History of the Crusades* (Cambridge: CUP, 1951)

Sachar, Howard M., *A History of Israel* (New York: Alfred A. Knopf, 1996)

Sardar, Ziauddin, and Malik, Zafar Abbas, *Muhammed for Beginners* (London: Icon Books, 1994)

Shanks, Hershel, *Jerusalem: An Archaeological Biography* (New York: Random House, 1995)

Shiff, Ze'ev, and Ya'ari, Ehud, *Intifada* (New York: Simon & Schuster, 1989)

Storrs, Ronald, *Orientations* (London: Nicholson & Watson, 1943)

Sykes, Christopher, *Crossroads to Israel* (Indiana University Press, 1973)

Thubron, Colin, *Jerusalem* (London: Heinemann, 1969)

Tuchman, Barbara, *Bible and Sword* (New York: New York University Press, 1956)

Vester, Bertha Spafford, *Our Jerusalem* (Jerusalem: Ariel Publishing House, 1988)

Wilson, A. N., *Jesus* (London: Sinclair-Stevenson, 1992)

# INDEX

# INDEX

**Loughboy Branch** '05